The Collected Stories
of Gladys Schmitt

The Collected Stories
of Gladys Schmitt

edited by
Lois Josephs Fowler
and
Cynthia Lamb

with an introduction by
Peggy Knapp

Volume 1
in the Marianna Brown Dietrich Notable Book Series

Carnegie Mellon University Press
Pittsburgh 2014

Acknowledgments

The stories in this volume first appeared in the following magazines and anthologies:

"Little Town Autumn," *Steps*, December 1931
"The History Class," *Steps*, April 1929
"The House Divided," *The Atlantic Monthly*, 1934
"Saturday," *The Atlantic Monthly*, 1934
"The Cabinet," *The Household Magazine*, 1936
"All Souls," *Collier's*, 1943
"Consider the Giraffe," *It's a Woman's World*, McGraw-Hill, 1944
"The Mirror," *Collier's*, 1944
"The Mourners," *Harper's Bazaar*, 1944
"The Furlough," *Mademoiselle*, 1944
"Another Spring," *Harper's Bazaar*, 1945
"The Avenger," *Good Housekeeping*, 1945
"The King's Daughter," *Story*, 1945
"The Matchmaking," *Collier's*, 1945
"Distinguished," *Good Housekeeping*, 1948
"On the Other Side of the Road," *Good Housekeeping*, 1953
"The Day Before the Wedding," *Good Housekeeping*, 1953
"The Uninvited," *Seventeen*, 1954
"The Man Who Found Himself," *Collier's*, 1956
"Prometheus," *Insight: Literature of the Imagination*, Noble and Noble, 1969

Cover image: *Portrait of Gladys Schmitt (1909-1972)* by William R. Shulgold (A '19), presented by the Artist and the Kenneth H. Fagerhaugh Memorial Fund

Book design by Allison Cosby and Connie Amoroso

CONTENTS

Foreword	*Cynthia Lamb*	7
Introduction	*Peggy Knapp*	9
Little Town Autumn		15

ॐ

The History Class	19
The House Divided	25
Saturday	43
The Cabinet	55
All Souls'	69
Consider the Giraffe	85
The Mirror	99
The Mourners	113
The Furlough	131
Another Spring	143
The Avenger	159
The King's Daughter	177
The Matchmaking	193
Distinguished	209
On the Other Side of the Road	239
The Day Before the Wedding	257
The Uninvited	275
The Man Who Found Himself	293
Prometheus	309

FOREWORD

The two-page prefatory mood piece "Little Town Autumn" and the following nineteen stories comprise the short fiction Gladys Schmitt published during her lifetime. *Steps*, the University of Pittsburgh student literary magazine, published five issues between 1928 and 1931. "Little Town Autumn" and "The History Class" are, therefore, Schmitt's juvenilia. We feel the quality of this work merits inclusion here. These early writings are evidence of what she was at the very beginning of her writing career just as her eleven novels are indicative of who she became.

In compiling the published stories, we discovered a number of unpublished stories, equally well crafted (currently with a working title of *The Uncollected Stories of Gladys Schmitt*), which the Press intends to publish.

For their assistance in and contributions to our editing of *The Collected Stories of Gladys Schmitt*, we would like to thank the following:

Emily Dobler and Christa Hester, students in the Editing and Publishing course at Carnegie Mellon, formatted the stories from their original magazine versions. Also of the Carnegie

Mellon community, we gratefully recognize Heather Steffen for her extensive archival searches and Emily Houck and Stacey Hsi for further archival searches and design.

We would like to acknowledge Danny Josephs for his tireless efforts in procuring all of Gladys Schmitt's published works so that their rights are housed at Carnegie Mellon University.

Thanks as well to Peggy Knapp for personal information regarding her friendship with Gladys Schmitt and her introduction, which provides insights not otherwise readily available.

For their invaluable assistance, we express our gratitude to Mary Catharine E. Johnsen, Patrick Trembeth, and Christopher Pachter of Hunt Library, Carnegie Mellon University.

Special acknowledgment goes to the Communications, Design and Photography Group of Carnegie Mellon University for providing us with the digitized cover image of Gladys Schmitt.

David Grinnell (head archivist), Clare Withers, Robin Kear, and Marianne Kasica of the University of Pittsburgh Archives furnished us with information and copies of Schmitt's earliest published stories. Their efforts have been crucial in compiling this volume.

Without the aid of Don Wentworth of Carnegie Library of Pittsburgh, Main, who engaged in wide-ranging research to locate and retrieve the stories that proved to be the most difficult to find, this book could not have been completed.

—Cynthia Lamb
Carnegie Mellon University
August 2014

INTRODUCTION

Gladys Schmitt's stories have been with me for many years. Some I read in the magazines in my parents' house long before I came to Carnegie Mellon as her junior colleague, and I recognized them when her widower, Simon Goldfield, gave me photocopies of a fairly complete set of them after her death in 1972. Most were written between 1934 and 1956 and published in respected national magazines like *The Atlantic Monthly, Collier's, Harper's Bazaar,* and *Mademoiselle.* Gladys's stories, like her novels, address wide swaths of the reading public. Even while seeming homegrown (Pittsburghers can often recognize their city), the style of these stories reflects the experimental impulses of international literary modernism. A good many of them end in what James Joyce called epiphanies: they concern protagonists who awaken from misjudgments of the social meaning and emotional tone of the situations and events they experience. All bear Gladys's hallmark of a verbal texture of detail that presents both external realities and movements of mind. One measure of success for a storyteller is that details linger in a reader's mind, and by this measure Gladys was a master storyteller. For me, certain details were literally haunting, like the color scheme—sky blue and lush green with orange and white accents—designed by the protagonist of "The Man Who Found Himself" that actually influenced my own decorating plans.

Another feature of Gladys's technique is the way her stories suddenly move from an ordinary, recognizable world into unexpected, sometimes almost surreal territory. This is the sort of thing we see in Kafka's tales, but Gladys's mode is much more subtle, and though no one wakes up to find himself a giant roach, an aura of the unexplained clings to some of them. The narrator in "The Furlough" is a second grader whose intense reactions to her father's return from war is registered in memories and observations colored by fantasy. "In the fairy books," she thinks, "things were always turning into other things," a development she suspects and fears in her own family's life. "Saturday" begins with a richly detailed dreamscape, not fully recalled by the dreamer, but hazily present to him and a key to his behavior. In "Consider the Giraffe" a lonely fourth grade girl, often uprooted by her peripatetic, distracted parents, visits a giraffe at the zoo who responds to her need for love by walking straight toward her and licking her hand through the chain link fence. The delight in his gentle glance and touch produces in this passionate, intelligent girl, who is only beginning to perceive the varieties of loving the wider world has in store, is palpably rendered yet also a bit numinous. One key to the effectiveness of stories like these is due in large measure to a disciplined restriction of point of view.

"Distinguished" also strictly limits point of view. The actions of Mr. Beatty's two young assistants and his self-deprecation are presented only through his eyes until the last pages. Similarly, in "On the Other Side of the Road," the young protagonist's scorn for her frugal Quaker aunt and uncle as she gazes at the elegance of rich folks across the way dominates the story until its closing realization. This technique veers close to "unreliable narrator" terrain, in that the reader sees more than the protagonist, but it is so subdued that it involves us with the misguided narrators and allows us to be cheered by their epiphanies. Seeing these twenty-one stories together, makes one aware of how many flavors of felt life Gladys could summon, from the youth of the girls in "Consider the Giraffe" and "The Furlough," to the fading beauty of the woman in "The Mirror," who confronts her image as "the owner of a ruined merchantman might come down to the docks to see his ship after a night of fire." Men and women, contemporary and historically distanced (like the biblical David in "The King's Daughter"), all are presented in evocative and believable inner states. The stories, like many of her novels, demonstrate Gladys's trust in imagination to bridge what some hold an unbridgeable gap between former generations and our own interior lives.

What keeps these interior monologues in touch with the real world is the remarkable detail of both settings and action in which they occur: exactly how an action is performed, the play of light in a room, or the smell of the named flowers in a vase. In "The Day Before the Wedding," the soon-to-be-bridegroom finds his prospective in-laws so uncultivated as to live with "the brown, hexagonal holes left by missing tiles in their bathroom floor." That kind of detail speaks to Gladys's powers of observation of the ordinary, but it is the use to which she puts detail that raises clever observation to the level of art. What is described is not there for its own sake (enjoyable as it is); it ends up making a difference in the story being told; in this case the brown holes disclose the haughty style of the narrator's taste.

Much in these stories will remind the reader that they were written decades ago—the phone booths from which calls cost a dime, the china lions that sat on many hearths, the female college students known to each other as Miss Watson or Miss Albert—but Gladys's management of the English sentence is not dated at all. The sentences are sophisticated, beautifully crafted, and packed with broad-ranging allusion. Consider this sentence from "The Mourners": "For months now the young Slav had been thinking that Galileo and Copernicus had done him no special favor when they rearranged the universe and excluded the possibility of a listening, tangible God." The implications billow outward from the immediate situation in which the "Slav" Koblanski desires his senior colleague's wife (the colleague being a Renaissance specialist), to the history of Western thought, to the destruction of his native Poland in a war that is only evoked in a few brief allusions to his own memories and dreams, and back to the ethical problem he and the wife (who returns his desire) now face during her piano lesson.

Many details in these stories strike one who knew the author as in some measure autobiographical. "The Uninvited" is a particularly interesting case in point. The high school girl who tags along with her friend to interview an author she ardently admires suggests one phase of Gladys's own life; the author, who accepts and answers her awkward questions, another. Although there is much of Pittsburgh and New York in these stories, Gladys's work is not provincial. National debates that swirled around the academe of her day—the social role of art and the teaching of art, the usefulness of Freudian and Marxian modes of thought—are registered in these stories, although usually in a nuanced way. In "The Avenger," though, they appear on the surface as a successful young painter is confronted by an uncompromising Marxian grad student who refers to the artist's portfolio as a "luxury" that merely produces "private little neuroses . . . when the world is boiling under your feet." Today the issue at stake cannot be seen as dated or provincial.

Gladys was a lifelong teacher, and many stories involve schools or lessons of various kinds, sometimes from the teacher's vantage point, sometimes the student's. My favorite is "Another Spring." The campus on which Miss Bishop must find a new actress for the role of Cordelia in *King Lear* is surely Carnegie Mellon's (in 1945 Carnegie Institute of Technology, then already a great drama school). The sadness of the director over losing "her" Cordelia to a car accident, her disdain for the others who aspire to the role, and her near exhaustion with the attachments and partings that accompany a long teaching career are presented in unsparing detail. What has made this, of all the fine stories in this collection, come back to me many times across the years, though, is its brilliantly rendered grasp of what Shakespeare's play makes of the love between Lear and Cordelia. There is nothing sentimental about this story, but its emotional resonance is deeply rendered and its resolution hinges on the implications of Miss Bishop's vision of the play. Even after such a long acquaintance with "Another Spring," I wept again reading it now.

—Peggy Knapp
Carnegie Mellon University
April 2014

Little Town Autumn

I SHOULD LIKE to spend my autumns in a little town, a town in the foothills, for then I should be near the things I like. I used to go for the cows in the morning and come out of the hazel clump around the spring and see the valley below a lake of fog. Ahead, as I followed it, the path melted into the gray bank that thickened until at the lower pasture gate the sun was a white smear overhead. The pasture bars looked soft and were cold to the touch, and the black and white of the holsteins were gray. The herd filed through the gate. When I walked to the end of the line to hurry the stragglers, I could feel, even through my shoes, the warm places where the cows had been lying. There were noises: the cows snuffing, the dog running but whether he was in the berrypatch or in the woodlot I could not tell; the fog muffled everything. I hurried the cows home so that I could get to town. I liked Hillside. Then it was not a town of paved streets and cement sidewalks. Nobody could have liked for themselves alone, the rows of unpainted company houses which led to Pike Street. The little park across the street from the post office had nothing in it but a dry pump and two cannons that a Washington County company was supposed to have taken from the Spaniards. Leaves clicked down from the poplars and maples in fall, but they did that other places. I think it was something intangible that I liked about Hillside in autumn: a sense of Indian summer, the hush over the place. Asters and dahlias bloomed long in the sideyards and leaned through the palings into the street. And in the houses behind the white pales women cooked chili sauce and quinces with the windows open. Leaves burned in the backyards and the air was so still that I could hear Crawford's windmill creaking on the edge of town. The second Tuesday in October (we knew it as well as we knew election day) Mr. Greaves opened his first hogshead of sauerkraut. Everybody in Hillside bought some that first day, and so somebody from every family in town was there. The last Tuesday I was home father sent me to the store for our share. There was, for Hillside, a crowd in front of Mr. Greaves' store. Bill Crawford was there with a clean chip basket of fresh pork. And there were women whom I didn't know in dust caps and aprons and men in shirt sleeves and children with granite pans in which their money jingled. Dr. Drew stopped me and asked about my father; the Reverend Hilliard, whom I hadn't talked with since the strawberry festival, said that he was coming out Friday to see mother about the cantata. Inside the store smelled of dill and salt. For awhile I watched Mr. Greaves in a stiff white jacket and a clean apron, forking out from behind the counter pounds and pounds of sauerkraut, and then I bought my sauerkraut and went home. Since then I have been taught that sauerkraut is pretty homely stuff. Perhaps it is, but in those days it was, I am sure, part of the fog in the pasture and the autumn hush over the hills.

The History Class

EVERYTHING ABOUT OUR high school history class, from the willows outside the windows to the faded, dog-eared books with their old temples and silent Caesars, was peaceful. We called it a haven for jaded souls. In the warm summer afternoons we used to come in quietly, and take our seats without scraping the chairs on the floor, and sigh with relief. The trucks might rumble on the boulevard beyond the window and the class-cutters might chatter in the halls, but we were safe from noise and excitement, with nothing to jar our nerves or hurt our eyes. There were no blaring colors, no red vases, no glistening busts. Greece and Italy were lavender on the map (lavender fading down to a comfortable gray) and Cicero on the top of the bookcase was no longer white; his wrinkled forehead was tanned with dust far too reverend for janitors to brush away. The noises were softened too. There were no sounds but an occasional discreet whisper, the slow flapping of blinds against the window panes, the quiet recitations, and Miss Slease's voice. Nobody else ever had a voice like Miss Slease's. It flowed along softly, evenly, like honey sliding out of a jar, slowly, in one long stream. It sang out the loves of Sappho; it sighed at the death of Caesar; it slipped quietly and patiently over the injustice of the Roman Rule, the decline of Greek Art, and the Crucifixion of Christ. The voice never flowed on too long. It would break off suddenly with, "Now let us look over these pictures of Phidias' sculpture" or "Come, Mr. Maslov and Mr. Cohen want to argue this point." Then there would be a show or a debate, and then a little silence, and then the soft voice moving on and on again. "It must be boring," said the senior football hero when we told him about the class one day on the way home from school, "—damned boring!" But a baby isn't bored by being rocked to sleep; and a sick man isn't bored when a cool hand strokes his forehead over and over again. There was something good in moving willows, and old books, and dead Caesars, and slow voices. It was a cure for all our annoyances, and troubles, and wearinesses, that Ancient History Class.

The Commercial Students who took Business Law in the room next door used to laugh when we raved about History. They turned up their noses and called us "artistic souls who like to fly around in ecstatic air." Well, we weren't exactly that, but we *were* a good class. We numbered twenty-two (an ideal number for a recitation group) and there were about as many pastel silks and flowered voiles as there were trousers and collegiate sweaters. At the beginning of the semester the boys were afraid of the girls and arranged themselves on the right side of the room in true Quaker Church fashion, but Miss Slease ended that state of affairs by seating us alphabetically. When we had time to look around at each other, we discovered that the class was full of celebrities. Clure, a slight fair-haired boy with an uncanny knack at geometry and physics, sat off in a corner pushing his hair out of his eyes with a nervous little jerking of the head, and drawing designs on the margin of his notebook. Miss Watson, who starred in Drama League plays and had a head of enviable red hair, was forever bringing up Cleopatra, whose biography she had read for the summer before. Miss Abbert, noted for writing verse for the *Journal*, said almost nothing in class, and amazed us all by getting A's on the tests. Hanon, president of the Debating Club, used to talk about reincarnation. He was an ardent believer—had half convinced himself that he had been a legionary under Caesar, a bowman with Xerxes, and a squire to Charlemagne. At present there was nothing military about him. According to Miss Wassel, he was "delightfully nervous, and too beautiful to be anything but an artist with a white shirt and a flowing tie, you know." Then, of course, there was the celebrity of all celebrities, Maslov. Nobody but Miss Slease had liked Maslov in the beginning. In fact, everybody had disliked him thoroughly, and some of the girls had disliked him in very loud voices. The girls would have fallen in love with him under ordinary circumstances, since he was really quite handsome with his boyish slenderness, and his wild, curly hair tumbling down over his fine brown eyes. Some of the celebrities whispered that his father was a Hungarian Count and an ardent patriot, even though the war had driven him out of his Fatherland. Young Maslov certainly had all the ardor of a patriot's son. He was so ardent about his history that he did hours of reference, and consequently, out-recited the best of us. At first we thought that he studied with malice. But later we learned that there wasn't a bit of malice in him, that he studied for pleasure, and that he was well disposed toward all of us. He wrote a study outline for Clure who had been absent, and spent half an hour after school explaining Roman Law to Andrews who was decidedly stupid. When we discovered that he wasn't a devil, we decided that he was a god, and teased him about that, too. We hated his dignity; we tried to rumple his hair and mess his tie; and we used to poke him in the ribs, just to see him curl up and laugh. Some of the girls aped his precise English in their recitations. Everybody talked about him, and talked loudest when he was nearest. Maslov wasn't human; Maslov was a touch-me-not; Maslov thought he was Jupiter sitting on Olympus watching the poor ants recite. With that sort of talk we tortured him for half of the semester. Then one humid day he proved himself earthborn by half fainting during a recitation. There was no joy in seeing him lose his dignity that time. We were all a little sick at the sight of his white face. When the period was over we left the room more quietly than usual, realizing what cads we had been. We were thoroughly ashamed of ourselves, and blushed a little deeper when we learned that he had taken first prize in a state-wide art contest. We did what we could to make amends— elected him president of our committees and all that—and he was wonderfully decent about our little gestures of repentance. By the end of the term, we all liked him. His neatly written name and quotation from Wordsworth are among the most valued notes on the autograph pages of our *Journals*. Since, he has grown into an intellectual of some note, and is famous as an art student. People ask me over and over again, "So you really know Maslov, that clever young artist?" I always blush and turn my face away a little when I say, "Yes . . . quite well."

At the beginning of June, we began to realize that there would be no more debates, no more games, no more talk about Sappho, and Caesar, and the rest. The end of the semester was just around the corner. The last days of the class (the early June days when we began to cram for our final test) were warm, lazy, and a little sad. Cramming was killing that year, because every day the weather grew more oppressively hot. As we sat and stared at our books, our clothes clung to our bodies, and had to wet handkerchiefs and drag them across our foreheads to keep our minds clear. Most of us—since we felt that we could study best in groups—sat around the same library tables in the stifling afternoons and tormenting evenings, and bothered each other with senseless questions and asinine remarks. Altogether, we did more worrying than studying. The day of the test was the hottest day of the year—the kind of day that makes boys curse their collars and the girls pant for breath. We came into the classroom and stood staring at each other. Everybody was nervous, or stupid from the heat, or crazily gay. That is, everybody but Maslov. He sat whittling his pencil and looking clear-minded and precise, his coat off and his shirt sleeves rolled up, and little beads of sweat standing out, precisely, too, on his fine high forehead. Looking at Maslov was good for the nerves. We all looked, and sat down with comparative composure. Clure and Andrews fussed the longest. Andrews was afraid of flunking, and Clure was sure he wouldn't get his A. Miss Slease came in quietly and wrote the test on the board with a squeaking piece of chalk. When we saw the questions we raised a general chatter. The test was ridiculously easy. Some of us laughed. Maslov didn't. He set to work writing long tacts with half-page quotations, and we set to work keeping pace with him. The room grew very still. Tiny heatwaves made the windowsills quiver, and the trucks rumbled sleepily outside. Our scratching pencils moved on over pages and pages. The old peace and self-reliance flowed into us, and we wrote . . . and wrote. . . . When Miss Slease handed our papers back next day, we had no surprises at all; everything was just as we expected; Andrews didn't flunk, and Clure got his A. With the test off our minds, we had time to spare and we spent most of it thinking about the coming breakup. We began the last rites with seriousness (nobody dared say wistfulness). We erased all the notations and patted all the dog-ears in our text books. Then we handed the books in, and watched them pile up in the bare shining cupboard. Maslov and Cohen, happily reconciled, washed the boards and took down the maps. The room looked naked, and sternly clean. We made a rather sickly attempt to brighten it up for our farewell party. We hung some white and lavender crepe paper on the board where the maps had been, and put vases of flowers on Miss Slease's desk. Nobody was exactly satisfied with the effect, but the party was a fine one anyhow. Miss Abbert brought some chocolate fudge, Miss Watson made macaroon cakes, and some of the boys bought lollipops. For the first half hour we sat on the arms of the chairs, chattering, singing, getting our friends to sign our *Journals*. Then Cohen gave some comic monologues, and Miss Watson sang "Drink to Me Only With Thine Eyes," and Hanon talked about the "pleasant periods we have spent in this beloved room." Miss Slease sat behind the flowers and nodded at everything, and smiled. When we called for a speech from her, she said a few kind, simple words. I wonder if it was our conceit that made us feel that she was sorry to see us go. At last the bell rang. Most of us were glad. We dreaded being sentimental, and our voices were already a little shaky. We gathered in groups in the hall, where we stood linking our arms around each other, and saying very little, and laughing, and shaking hands. Some of the other classes stopped in the halls, too. After a while the crowds thinned, and the janitors began to go up and down with their great brushes, and we had nothing to say at all. We left each other without too many goodbyes, and went down into the locker rooms. I stood alone in mine, listening to the familiar noises: Miss Watson singing "Il etait une bergere" and Maslov calling, "Say, Cohen, I wish you would give this book to Andrews, please." When I went out the street seemed very garish and the sunlight hurt my eyes.

Last week as I was walking through the Statue Hall of Carnegie Museum, I saw Clure. I didn't know him at first. Three years had changed his pale thinness into healthy vigor. When he saw me, he stopped and tossed back his hair with a nervous jerk of the head. I had seen him do that before . . . somewhere . . . where. . . ? A drowsy peacefulness slipped over my mind. I heard blinds flapping and willows moving, and a soft voice talking on and on, very slowly, like honey sliding out of a jar. Perhaps he thought the same thoughts. At any rate, he remembered my name, and talked to me about Miss Slease and Maslov and Miss Watson and the rest. Then we both looked at the still Greek gods around us, and shook hands, and smiled.

The House Divided

THE WHOLE FAMILY was on edge, and nobody liked the supper. The day was too hot for the supper. All day the vaporous heat had poured from the streets, the water-wagons had produced nothing but steam, and the house, sixty-nine years old and built of frail timber and tin, had gathered to itself the incubator-like warmth (it was a chicken coop, the sister said; it looked like a chicken coop in the first place, and in the second place, it was fit only for hatching out eggs, especially on the third story where the gables sloped almost to the floor). The dining room was scarcely better. Through the white curtains which hung luminous before the wall of the next door chicken coop, sun shone but no wind stirred. The mother was nervous. She knew that she should not have made roast beef; the steaming tureens crowded the table and plainly made the sister sick. The father who was having trouble with his teeth and with the family debts ate nothing at all. "Don't you want anything, dear?" said the mother, looking at the creamed carrots. "Huh-uh," said the father, pinching his sun-sallowed cheeks. As for the brother, he ate steadily, almost desperately, with his nose bent low over the plate. He was young and slender. He wore his fair hair cropped, and his face was too tan for his gray eyes, too leathery for the soft contours of his nose and chin. He seldom looked up; but when he did raise his startling eyes, deep granite, he fixed them on the sister who sat opposite him with her hand around her glass of iced tea. They did not smile as people usually smile when their eyes meet. Only that earnest and beseeching look which characterized them both and which made them, in spite of their evident differences, very much alike, was momentarily intensified; when they looked at other people, they hid themselves behind a masking smile; but when they looked at each other, their faces were entirely naked.

The sister was the older of the two by four years. She was a student, and a weary one; books which she had meant to read during the summer vacation were piled high on the great desk in the corner of the dining room, but she had not touched them. She was tall. She stood up to hunt a cigarette on the buffet, and her handsome, slender body showed through her gray sweat-shirt and her smooth gray trousers. But anyone could tell that her boyishness was an affectation. Her bones were small; her hands were pathetically slight below the broad cuff of her sweat-shirt; and her hair, wandering back from the pale narrow oval of her face, was dark and silken and hung almost to her shoulders.

"Darling," said the mother, touching the thin thigh in the trousers, "aren't you going to eat anything more? Couldn't you eat just a bit more potato? A nice brown potato?" "No. No, it's too hot." She sank back into the chair and began embracing her tea glass again. "It's not the supper. It's just—" The telephone rang, and her back stiffened. Her brother looked at her over the rim of his tea glass. She answered the look, balancing on one knee, with her shoulders turned toward the door. Then she ran toward the telephone, into the dark hall. The mother looked at the father and smiled. "That'll be *him*," she said. But the sister came back too soon and sat too heavily on the chair, with her elbows on the table and her chin between her hands.

"Who was it, dear?" said the mother. "It wasn't he. It wasn't anybody. It was a wrong number. Please fill my glass and let me have some lemon."

The mother was afraid of the silence. It was useless to assure the sister that *he* would call; she had assured her a hundred times, and it never did any good. You couldn't talk to her because she never listened. She sat staring at her full plate until the sight of it made her sick. At certain moments the mother was terrified; for this daughter of hers was ill and growing more so, and would not go to a doctor, and was forever saying incomprehensible things about the mind's sickening the body and about all doctors being fools. In her own time (days of corsets, fine muslin, and French cologne) people would have said that such a girl was "going into a decline." Now the young medical students who came in and out of the house called it "melancholia." The sister herself said that she had "the furies," "the jitters," or "the long blue gaze." She made fun of it; she said, "It's contagious. You see, Frere's got a touch of it, too." So the mother disliked the silence which was filled with these thoughts, and she turned toward the brother.

"It's a nice night," she said, "for the graduation." The long and earnest glance passed again between the brother and the sister. This time it was she who began it and he who answered. "Yes," he said, "but too hot." "But better than rain," said the mother with feverish pleasantness. "Yes, better than rain." There were some small chocolate cakes filled with a thin white paste of sugar. The father looked at them and shook his head. The other three ate them silently, swallowing the iced tea. "What are you going to wear to the graduation?" said the mother. The gray eyes turned on the cake, examined the cake with scorn and fury. "The hell with the graduation," he said. "But Frere," the sister looked at him gravely, "you've got to be nice about it because of Lucy. After all, it's Lucy's graduation, and she's in love with you, and she's going to look pretty, and you'll have to be pleased. Better try to get into a good humor." He lit a cigarette and stared somberly at the plate. "It's not my graduation," he said. "It's my funeral."

The mother sighed. The sister had begun to look at the clock again in that uneasy, secretive way she had when she was expecting *him*. Half past six, said the clock. "Oh, for God's sake," said the sister, "where did I put those cigarettes?" The mother felt certain that *he* would call; after all, she had to feel certain; he would leave town tomorrow, and the sister would not see him unless he called tonight. In case he did not come, she would eat less and less, buy more clothes, surround herself with the young fellows who liked her (for she was very popular in the Bohemian crowd), get drunk, wander about the house at night, and pose in the nude for any young artist that applied for her services. And the cigarettes—dear Lord, the cigarettes! You never saw her without one. If you happened past her room at three o'clock in the morning, you saw the small round glow. But the brother was even more distressing. She could not understand how she and her husband, in love and inclined to see rosy light always, even beyond the eternal debts, could have gotten such gloomy children. There he sat, twenty and handsome, smoking and smoking and calling his girl's graduation his funeral.

Everybody at the table started because it was the telephone.

The sister was gone for a gratifyingly long time. Snatches of her voice, making a hysterical attempt at coolness, drifted into the dining room. When she came back, pushing her hair out of her eyes and away from her temples, her cheeks were really scarlet. "That was *he*," she said. "I think he'll come over tonight. I'm not sure, but I think so. Frere, will you let me have some more iced tea?"

Usually after dinner the brother and the sister went into the parlor by themselves. Usually the sister opened the loose, ancient music book on the piano and tapped the keys, E, A, D, G, while the brother tuned the fiddle. Neither of them could play very well. The sister, laughing up at him when he made a particularly bad screech, would say, "It's a pity that you and

I can't miss out on the same note. Then *some* of them would be right, anyway. This way, somebody's always wrong." Then they would both laugh. It was pleasant in the parlor; the last of the sun, diluted and consoling, fell on their oval faces, their active hands, and the dark mahogany. The old songs sobbed and stammered through the seven o'clock stillness:

> *"Oh, don't' you remember sweet Alice, Ben Bolt,*
> *Sweet Alice, whose hair was so brown,*
> *Who wept with delight when you gave her your smile*
> *And trembled with fear at your frown?"*

The words, thought the sister as she played, were really quite pure. With a touch of quaintness and a changing of the names, the words might have been accepted as an elegiacal lyric.

> *"In a corner obscure and alone,*
> *They have fitted a slab of the granite so gray,*
> *And sweet Alice lies under the stone."*

Granite, now, granite had dignity. Marble was trite and ostentatious. But granite had a solid and sorrowful eternity. The brother could play that one without any screeches. Really, he played it beautifully. His bony brown hand would slip up and down on the strings, and his gray eyes would watch the notes with a mournful gravity. But the brother preferred

> *"Maxwelton's braes are bonny*
> *Where early fa's the dew"*

His girl, his own girl was Scotch, descended from an unmixed line of McDonalds and MacAfees. Her brow, below the soft waving of her hair, was "Like the snowdrop;" her neck, unusually slender, was "like the swan." At the end of the song he believed, and his chest swelled with the belief, that, for bonnie Annie Laurie, he could lay him doon and dee. Usually they played eight or ten songs and practiced for awhile on a new one. Then they went off to dress for their ordinary dates, spent the evening apart, and met again, late at night on the porch, for silence and cigarettes together.

But tonight neither of them had any desire to play. Their

hands were uncertain; their time was brief, and their excitement demanded a direct and violent expression not to be found between the covers of the loose and ancient book on the piano. So they went together, arms linked, upstairs to the sister's room, and lay down crosswise on their stomachs on the sister's bed. The room was hot, but it looked cooler than the other rooms because of the sea-green wall paper and the draperies of white dotted Swiss. The brother slept on the third floor; of late he had not been sleeping there; it was too hot, and he lay all night, naked except for his striped shorts, on the couch in the living room.

"So he called you," he said, setting a match to the sister's cigarette. She nodded and looked at the sleeves of her sweatshirt. "I hate to change into a dress, Frere. I suppose I'll have to change into a dress, won't I? While I'm in my trousers I feel—well, I feel masculine and my own. I'd rather not be a woman and dependent on *him*. I'd rather be my own. I'd like to go away, far off, to the West, I think, where the old Indian temples are."

They lay on their stomachs and remembered the same thing. Long ago (it seemed legendary to them, it was so long ago) they had invented a certain formula of love which they had recited to each other in the mornings after pillow fights. "What would you do if I hid?" the sister had said. "Oh, I'd find you." "But what would you do if I went far away? Far away in a train." "Then I'd turn into a little calf, and crawl into a box in a box car, and I'd go on the same train with you, wherever you went, anywhere." "But what would you do if I died?" Their grandmother had died, so they knew all about it. He had always kissed her on the mouth then and said, solemnly, "I'd die, too."

He turned uneasily on the Swiss spread and looked at the unstirring curtains. "Imagine having the money to go anywhere!" he said with scorn and fury. She smiled. "I might have gone to New Mexico with one of the boys." "But you didn't." "No, I didn't because of *him*." "And she's graduating tonight, and in a month they're sending her away—miles away—to Nurse's Training, and I'm not the sort that waits for a woman for four years. I'll never see her any more in this world, and who gives a damn for the next?"

The sister sat on the edge of the bed and clasped her knee in her hands. Her face was animated and pale; one of the things which drew so many of the young Bohemians toward her was this pale, animated face turned on their loving, their music, their canvases, their poesy, and their poverty. "Listen, Frere," she said, "why don't you get married?" "Get married!" "Sure, get married." "Eighteen dollars a week, and no chances for promotion. A messenger boy! A low messenger boy!" Fury and scorn. "Well, you could marry Lucy and bring her here. She could sleep in your room and eat with us. Mother wouldn't mind." It was true that the mother would not mind. For two years, now, this slender girl with the long white neck, the sea-green eyes, and the quiet mouth had kept the brother sane and monogamous. Every evening they had walked up and down the neighborhood streets. They had held hands, and everybody had said that they were a handsome pair.

"Bring her here? Into this hole? Into that boiling room—" "It wouldn't be any worse here than it is at her house. She wouldn't have to work nearly so hard. There's always enough food. She'd need nothing but clothes, and she sews well." He burrowed his face against his arm, and creases showed in his soft brown skin, and the end of his nose was distorted. "That isn't my idea of marriage," he said.

They both sat silent, thinking about his idea of marriage. The sister saw his girl in a neat apron, among new pans, tiled kitchen walls, in-a-door beds (those damn things always had accidents anyway) and tea-towels embroidered with the initials of her maiden name. And he, the brother, a married man in gray flannels, saying to the older women who sat with lap dogs on deck chairs on the apartment lawn, "I don't believe you've met my wife." A good life, to be sure. He might hope for such a life when he was thirty and a cashier, with some other girl less quiet and less chaste, with whom he had never walked hand in hand under the shadowy buckeye trees. The sister straightened and thought of her own life. She still possessed the scorn (long ago she had lost the fury), and she turned on him a cold and side-wise smile. "Your ideas of marriage, my dear Frere, are very lyrical and lovely and everything, but you'd better blow your brains out if you think they'll materialize in this world. And who gives a damn about the next?" He looked at her over his elbow. He was afraid of her still, cold face. "You're hard," he said, "my God, how hard you are." She stretched her legs and smiled down at them. "Yes," she said, "I'm like nails. I'm tough as mother's steaks. I'm hard as a girl in a Zoology Lab. Take care of your lovely little pale blue spirit. I might kick it. I'm hard."

He hid his face behind the bent elbow. The shadows length-ened on the floor, and the sea-green walls turned gray. The sister stared down at her legs, her long capable legs, her hard, learned legs, her legs in trousers, until they blurred because of tears. Her brother, too, was weeping behind his elbow. For they were both wretched and at odds. "What will I do," said the brother without moving his head, "when she's gone?" "You'll be awful again, just the way you were before you met her. You'll go out with little bums. The last batch of little bums was dreadful. I suspected them of having lice."

"They might have had, I suppose." "And what did you get out of it, after all?" "Nothing." "Yes, just nothing." "Well, no, not just nothing." He turned on his back with his head on his arm and his slate-gray, sorrowful pools overflowing in the growing shadow. He said, "You remember that last one—that last little bum?" "Yes, I remember." "Well, one night on the porch—it was moonlight—and I was in an awful hurry—and she said, 'Wait till I take off my shoes.' Isn't that funny? I never forget that. 'Wait till I take off my shoes.'"

The sister rested her head against her knee. "Yes," she

said, "you do remember the funniest things." "What do you remember?" "Queen's lace," she said. "Fields and fields of it. Timothy and queen's lace."

The mother called from the foot of the stairs that it was half past seven and that he'd better dress for the graduation. He stood up and touched the sister's cheek. Their flesh was strangely identical; their temperatures were so like that there was neither warmth nor cold, only a soft pressure, almost disembodied. At the door he paused to ask her where he could find a washcloth. While she told him the place, he looked at her; their eyes met gravely and ardently, and neither of them smiled.

THE GRADUATION TOOK place in the Soldiers and Sailors Memorial Hall which stood somberly and squarely in the middle of a large green carefully terraced lawn on the most academic avenue in the city. The brother thought as he swung up the white asphalt path between the rows of iris gone to seed that he did not care for graduations. He had never graduated himself. A long illness had kept him out of high school in his junior year, and he had refused to go back. Being proud, he could not bear the thought of associating with his inferiors, the sophomores, and had preferred working in a bank. He was not in the least sorry about that. He had been sorry about it only once, when the sister, white and dignified in her cap and gown, had taken her bachelor's degree. But she had always been the smartest one anyhow, talking about Sophocles with the young men whom she did not love and reading aloud things called sonnets to make you feel better. His white trousers flashed among the tall green blades of the irises. He looked well, and it was a good thing to look well at your own funeral. All along the paths the mothers and fathers, the sisters and the brothers, the aunts, and the uncles and the friends of the families were coming to the graduation in high, sweaty collars and in dresses that stuck to their backs and looked wilted. People were not pretty, the brother thought. The pavements burned through the soles of his shoes. But it would be cooler inside.

It was cooler inside. The vestibule was paved in marble and supported by many pillars. The shadows were long and deep. Going into the auditorium was like going under the water. The chandeliers had not yet been lighted, and the walls breathed coolness. The great central fans went round and round and stirred the faded and dusty flags upon the walls; and the flags moved slowly and regularly, like flags on the mast of some sunken battleship moving with the tide. The voices of the people, too, were like the speaking of water. A few words bubbled up and floated transiently at the surface, but not for long. The ushers (young women in white) fluttered with duty and were very glad to show him to his seat, a good one, too, in the first row of the balcony, very glad to push the seat down, very glad to provide him with a program. He sat in the shadow, bent forward, with his elbows on the railing. He felt strangely at peace. It was as though he had been born for this: to sit in the diffused watery shadow, on some high occasion, with the indistinguishable words moving around him and the murmurous sorrow in his heart. He did not wish as he usually wished, with fury and scorn, to cease being wretched. Without understanding the most rudimentary meaning of the word "aesthetic," he felt a keen aesthetic pleasure in the harmony which existed between his mood and its setting, between himself and the time. An old woman who sat at the end of his row stared at him for a full minute, wondering what had begotten his absorbed and unchanging smile.

The dignity of the place, long sanctified by the valor of a nation which had almost forgotten the meaning of valor, long haunted by the names of those who had died in action, names graven in bronze tablets at intervals on the walls, long sequestered in shadows and long mellowed in summer days— the dignity of such a place lay over his sorrow as a flag lies over the coffin of a dead hero, obscuring and ornamenting it. He did not resent his own misery; he resented only the growing volume of voices and the growing mass of warm bodies which prevented him from contemplating it.

The hall was full. Stodgy heads hid the flags; fleshy bodies broke up the shadows. Now the auditorium was as hot as the dining room where the roast beef had been. Only the rail was cool, and he leaned his cheek against it, pretending to look for someone on the lower floor.

And now the orchestra had come, and all around him the mothers and the fathers, the aunts and the uncles, were saying that it would soon begin. He saw *her* people sitting in the third row downstairs, but they did not trouble him. So long as his cheek touched the rail, he was able to maintain the dignified peace. But at the same minute the chandeliers were lit and a fat woman in pink begged his pardon. He stood up. The heat had made him a little ill, and the stage rocked before him as though he had been drunk.

Then there was no more draping of the sorrow. He sat up straight with his program in his hand, and the grief stood bare before him. This was his funeral. All the days of walking up and down the neighborhood streets, all the evenings of lying beside her on the living room couch, all the dishwater dripping from her fingertips, all the mock-orange blossoms shedding pollen on her hair, all these things were coming to an end in this tawdry place with flags where an orchestra played a Viennese waltz.

"Oh," said the mothers and the fathers, the aunts, the uncles, and the friends of the families, "they're coming, they're going to come now." Indeed they were coming. The orchestra ended the waltz on a whirl and struck up the "Coronation March" from *The Prophet*. They came from the back of the first floor, and for a minute he could not see them. Then they issued out of the dark places below the balcony, with their heads high and with the smell of ferns and roses. The boys wore dark suits, and there were roses in their lapels. The girls wore chiffon (the sister called that chiffon) in very pale colors, and it was they who smelled of the ferns and the roses. "How beautiful," thought the brother, leaning on the railing, "how beautiful young women are." He could see only their backs, and, showing through the thin cloth, all their backs were white and luminous. *She* came at the center of the line. She came out of the dark places, like a sea-woman walking from a cave, and her dress was sea-green and floated at her ankles and foamed at the shoulders. He knew that, below the knot of her auburn hair, lay the clasp of the small crystal pendant that he had given her. She carried roses, orange roses. At the curve of her elbow he saw them drooping over a dark fan of ferns.

During her slow progress down the aisle, heroism dilated his heart. His eyes never left her. From her auburn Psyche knot and her glimmering shoulders he drew long draughts of strength, and he sighed repeatedly. "I will certainly marry her," he thought. "I will marry her and bring her home. I'll marry her in spite of her parents and mine, in spite of the depression and the attic. It's possible to be happy anywhere, even there. I'll marry her. I'll marry her."

Just as she mounted the stairs, the music softened. The martial beating of it ceased, and a slow, flowing melody rose (not too much distorted) from the unpracticed violins. It was then that she turned and stood in her place, and then that he was conscious of the narrowness of her waistline. He had known before that it was slender, but he had never thought of it as being actually frail. As she bent to lay her bouquet on her chair, he thought that it looked like the waist of a china shepherdess that had stood for a long time on his mother's dressing table. Once he had taken it too quickly out of the sister's hand, and it had broken in two, just at the waistline. He saw it even now, lying on the carpet in two neat parts, with its small hands still playing with a rose.

And it was just like that, he said to himself, looking at the program, bitter with fury. You took a china shepherdess and put her in a house of tin. You never gave her a pretty dress, or a vacation, or even a baby. You never gave her anything. All night in the heat you sulked and turned over and damned the steaming walls, and damned her, more than likely. And, very naturally, you snapped her narrow waist in two.

He looked down at her, and she saw him and returned his glance. She had a long mouth, and he could see her smile plainly, even through his tears. He met her eyes and smiled back at her. Then he shook his head. She thought he was shaking his head at all the stupid people, and the heat, and the procession, and the blatant music. She thought that he shook it a little too solemnly, but he was always doing things solemnly; only last night he had kissed her on the forehead as though he meant never to see her again.

The fat woman in pink turned to the thin school teacher who sat beside her. "That young man," she whispered behind her program, "has a pretty little sweetheart on the stage." The school teacher said, "Yes. Isn't it nice to be young?" But he did not hear them. He was trying to remember some poem that the sister had once told him. It ended with:

"No more. Oh, never more."

THE BROTHER CAME home a little past midnight. He had stayed late at his girl's house and had drunk tea with her family. Now his heart actually ached like a sore thing in his chest, like an empty gum aching in the mouth, like something deserted and raw. The stars shone above the buckeye trees, and the neighbors were asleep. He was hungry for the sister's company, he wished to sit with her on the porch, with silence and a cigarette. He could almost wish that *he* would not be there. The brother did not approve of *him* anyhow. *He* came and went in his fine car, with the smell of shaving soap and fine cigars about him; and when *he* was gone, she was no better. She stopped telling people to do things for God's sake, but that was the only difference.

Yet perhaps, thought the brother, turning on the path and

facing the "chicken coop," white in the cold looks of the moon, it would be possible to have a cigarette's worth of time in her company, even if *he* were there. Perhaps she would stand up to meet him (he saw her as she would look standing up in her trousers) and say, "How was the graduation? Well, we can always sleep, and tomorrow's another day—just like today—'tomorrow and tomorrow,' you know." The brother knew that it was polite to kick the porch steps on such occasions, so he kicked the porch steps. Then he stood on the narrow oblong of the porch, made beautiful by the leaf shadows and the shadows of the dark porch blinds moving in the light of the moon.

Both of them were there. She was not wearing her trousers. After all, trousers were inconvenient, the brother thought. She lay on the wicker settee, straight, with her hands at her sides. Her dress was white and long; it swept over her thin thighs and her long legs and ended only at her feet, stretching, sandaled and solemn, on the arm of the settee. "Wait till I take off my shoes," the brother thought. Then he looked at her face. "Good evening," *he* said. "Good evening, sir," said the brother; for the one who sat on the edge of the couch beside her merited a "sir." Forty years had grayed and chiseled him, had endowed him with fame, a car, and expensive cigars. All these things were in the brother's mind, and he stood his ground with his hands in his pockets and his eyes fixed on the sister's face. She looked like a corpse. Yes, that was what she looked like: a corpse. The white oval which he had touched in her room, before he had asked about the washcloth, did not turn either his way or any way. It lay as the faces of the dead lie, looking straight up and not seeming to breathe. The brother pretended to yawn. He meant to make her look at him, at least. In this his most meager hour she would have to look at him as she had always looked at him. The yawn was very loud, and she did turn her head. "Good-night, Frere," she said. The cold, definite division of the syllables, the words of dismissal and the voice which said them, were desolating enough. But the worst thing was the turned face. The mouth smiled, and the eyes were closed. Moonlight, terror, and grief distorted his imagination. For a moment the white oval turned his way seemed featureless, blank, like the surface of an egg. *He* looked apologetic and uncomfortable. The brother sought about in his pocket, drew out a cigarette and went whistling into the house.

On the way up the stairs, he told himself that she had done something monstrous. She had denied him. In his evil hour, her eyes, the doors of her being, had been closed against him; and the being behind those doors had said coolly, like a butler in a moving picture, "The sister is out. The sister is not here. She can see nobody at all." He had a vague sense of some other denial enacted in an evil hour. There was an awe about the remembrance and a sense of an open court where women moved with water jugs upon their shoulders. But he could not quite place it; so he dismissed it and went up the stairs slowly.

When he came into his room (the gable touched the floor, and the narrow window admitted nothing but a glimpse of sky) he sat on the edge of his bed with his face bowed on his hands. All the day's heat was stored between the sloping walls; it rose and eddied about him, and the bed was moist and warm, like dough. "God damn it!" he said, jumping up. "Oh, God damn it! I can't sleep here! I won't sleep here! Oh, God damn it, God damn it anyhow!" It was her fault that he could not sleep downstairs; she was downstairs with *him*. He began to undress, and he threw his clothes against the wall, on the floor, across the foot of the bed. Then he flung his whole naked length on the mattress, and listened.

You could hear anything in that house (frail timber and tin). You could hear the father and the mother snoring in the front bedroom, and the water dripping in the bathroom, and the noises on the porch. They were familiar noises; he knew the method in them well: laughter, and throaty words, and the creak of wicker. But apparently they were a little too good for the porch; for after awhile they came inside, closing the door softly behind them. And now his fury gave way to scorn; he utterly scorned himself. For at this high minute when he had renounced her who came out of dark places like a water-woman coming out of the caves of the sea; when he had been denied by the sister whose face was the surface of an egg; when he knew by the deep, middle-aged snoring on the second floor that even love comes to nothing but debts and sweat, even now, he thought about that little bum. She looked up at him through the leaf shadows and the blind shadows. Freely, for the joy of it, she gave him complete peace. But he was in too much of a hurry. She said, "Wait till I take off my shoes."

He thought about that for a long time. The clock in the dining room struck one, and *he* went away, and the sister came upstairs. How slowly she came upstairs! He supposed that she was clinging to the banister; she had a way of holding anything: a pillow, the end of a mattress, a book, the newel post, or the yellow cat that slept in the backyard. No doubt she was wretched now, thinking that *he* had gone, that *he* would come back God knows when, and that *he* and his kisses were not so glorious after all. She went into her room and turned on the light. He heard her slow feet moving about the room, heard the tired rustle of her tossed clothes, the sinking of her body on the springs. Then (for the house was made of tin and thin timber), he heard her sobbing. He heard her clearly. She sobbed quietly and regularly, and probably between the sobs there were sighs. He did not feel any satisfaction in her wretchedness. It was as though her sorrow, like some black river, had poured into the turbulent darkness of his own. He wept with her, flattering himself that no one could hear him because he had drawn the pillow over his face. "Suppose," he thought, "that I put on my shorts and go down to visit her. Suppose I go down to the kitchen and get her something to eat—one of those chocolate cakes and some milk. Suppose I forgave her for closing up her eyes." But the remembrance of the featureless face was too galling. He struck at the rumpled sheet and hunted for a handkerchief.

As for the sister, she lay quite still, like a corpse, in the middle of the bed. She could hear plainly the sound of his sobbing. Among the other griefs that rose in her brain, demanding a tribute of tears, she saw the closing of her eyes and heard her clipped voice telling him, in so many words, to take himself off. "Suppose," she thought, "I put on my kimono and go up to him. Suppose I kneel down beside his bed and ask him to forgive me. Suppose I take my new perfume and tell him to give it to his girl before she goes away. It's foolish, the two of us crying with a ceiling between. We might as well cry together." She sat up on the edge of the bed and clasped her knee in her hands.

But she remembered his evaluation of her in the seven o'clock shadow, how he had called her hard, how day by day he and she grew further apart, how only the long glance remained of all their childhood union, how, from the days of little calves who crawled into box cars and souls inseparable even to death, only that look remained. And, being hard, she knew that, if she had closed her eyes against him once, she would do so again. It was the nature of things in this world; and who gave a damn about the next? She reasoned with all the reason left in her sickened body that "nothing remains save mutability," that all loves, chaste and carnal, are eventually divided, and that there was no sense in trying to preserve, by an artificial and violent rally, a union that disintegrated because of organic necessity.

So the sister lay back on the pillows and bowed her head to the dissolving force, and after awhile his sobbing stopped, and only the dripping of water in the bathroom remained; then, drawing the pillow across her lonely flesh, she fell asleep.

Saturday

I

IT WAS IN the snow, at the top of those mountains which he had seen only in pictures, but whose name he knew. They were the Tyrolean Alps. At their feet the countryside spread, covered with expanses of crocus, bluebell, and hyacinth; but the top was even more beautiful—it bloomed everlastingly with iridescent snow under a sky which was burningly blue. Such blueness was possible nowhere but in the eyes of the Madonna. The heat of the sun scorched him and made his head golden. Yet in spite of the sun it was impossible to feel any dampness or languor, for the air enclosed him like the hallowing breath of a god; and only dryness and exaltation could exist in that air.

He was standing on the highest peak. Only the miraculous bird whose wings were lined with violet, and the holy antelope whose hoofs scarce skimmed the snow, had been there before him. He had come alone, but he did not mind his loneliness. He stopped to triumph, rather than to rest, leaning one elbow in a crevice, stretching against the rock, and planting his feet in the snow. He was dressed like a modern angel in white wool.

His loose jacket and his breeches were soft and only a little less luminous than the side of the mountain. They fell in smooth folds around his lithe spare body. The sun had browned his face and arms and bleached his waving hair to an alloy of silver and gold. His eyes were blue, like the sky, and that troubled him a little, for they had always been gray. But nothing troubled him much—he was so unearthly beautiful.

As he stood with one elbow leaning in the crevice, he remembered that the woman was somewhere in the chalet, on the opposite peak. He did not want her in the chalet; he wanted her in the snow and the sun. But that was simple: you merely called her imperiously, and she came out of the shadow and let down her flaming knot of hair. White flesh and brown flesh, they would be undivided on the snow. So he decided to set out toward her, and that too was a simple thing. He braced himself on both his elbows, pointed his feet downward, shoved hard against the crevice, and sailed like a wind, like a gull, like an angel over the shimmering white. It was something between skiing and flying, yet he wore neither skis nor wings. The air vibrated around him like an aura, and there was a singing in his thighs.

As the singing rose, the motion through the air hastened. Now he came to a jutting crag on the side of the cliff. It stretched against nothing but blueness. He took it easily, bent forward, joined his fingertips above his head, parted them, swinging his arms like pinions at his sides, and sailed into blue space. The exaltation merged into ecstasy. He watched himself sailing, for there were two of him in the dream: the one who acted and the one who looked on. The one who looked on was a high sense of sight capable of recording everything from the broadest sweep of sky cut by the glittering peaks to the most minute iris which the sun begot on a drop of snow. But the one who acted was the glory. He stood back and stared at himself with breathless pleasure, for he was exalted and beautiful. His arms stretched like wings against the sky, and the wind of speed rippled down the white cloth which covered them. He cried out sharply, and

44

heard himself cry out, and thought, "At last my voice is free." But the cry wakened him. He found himself in the gray morning, in the companionless room, under the low roof.

And what was he? He was a nothing, an English instructor whose pupils jiggled keys while he lectured, a man with a nagging sinus pain between his eyes, a student whose dissertation was never finished but lay forever in closely written sheets among the quaint and useless books—a nothing who had dreamed something remarkable and could not even remember his dream. He lifted his hand to stop the progress of the sinus pain which seemed to force the bones of his forehead outward. The hand which he lifted was thin, nervous, and gray. He felt a sense of hopeless loss, as though some precious thing, a ring, a piece of fine pottery, or a book, had slipped from his fingers into a dull river. Then, wishing to stave off the day a little longer, he went back to sleep.

II

ON THIS DAY, which was Saturday, a holiday when other men ate lunches at grills and met their girls in town and sat holding hands in the darkness of moving-picture houses, he went to the doctor's. He always arrived at one thirty, cold with hunger because he did not dare to eat lunch. The pain of the sinus treatment always nauseated him, and he found it safer to eat nothing at all. Afterward, at three o'clock, when the pain had begun to dull a little, he regularly went to visit Emma and Katherine, his cousins, ladies verging on the fifties, virginal, well read, and makers of small sandwiches and strong tea. He had always found their living room (a place of aqueous light fallen through scrim curtains, of more solid light on chintz chairs, and of romantic light gathered in the fine tracery of the ancient tea set) a haven for him and for his pain. Once, sinking into the deepest chair, with a cup of tea in his hands, he had told them certain lines which came into his mind every time he entered their sunlit quietness—

> *Sleepe after toyle, port after stormie seas,*
> *Ease after warre, death after life does greatly please.*

They had not answered him. It would have been obvious, even blatant to have answered him, and they were never obvious. They never made an open reference to his pain. Still they respected it, walking in their pale woolen dresses softly across the floor, remarking that tea should be served early of a Saturday afternoon, saying, "I think, Emma, that the primroses are suffering from too much sun," or, "Katherine, for heaven's sake shut the window. That radio across the street gives me a splitting headache." How kindly the afternoons went by there. How earnestly they asked him just what he could make out of Archibald MacLeish. How affectionate the cat was, how amber the tea.

Usually, when he set out for the doctor's office, he stopped at a candy shop to buy a half-pound box of apricot paste or sugared almonds (his salary would permit only half a pound, but they tied it up nicely with red raffia ribbon) for Emma and Katherine. On days like this day (March icicles in the sun held coagulate the first, the virginal essence of spring) he could honor the hour with extravagance and find enough stray nickels and dimes for six street-corner daffodils. Yet, when he passed the vendors whose baskets showed their golden fillings against the snow, an uneasiness was in him. He thought with wonder as he walked toward the office that today he wanted to buy neither apricot paste nor almonds nor daffodils. Something cold and white and gold strove for life-in-remembrance at the back of his brain. He discovered that he had no intention of visiting Emma and Katherine. He walked more quickly than usual. The coldness which had always dulled him because of the hunger and the fear of the pain was dispelled by the mood and the motion. Actual warmth, steady and manly, coursed through his veins and made vital his chest and thighs. There was a singing in his thighs—a muted singing. He stopped before the window of a haberdashery where pongee pajamas were. That dream—Lord!—in that dream he had dreamed something really indecent about Miss Dorn.

He stared at the pongee pajamas and remembered Miss Dorn. She sat in the Dean's office, behind the typewriter; and sometimes she sang to herself. She wore soft woolen stuff, plaid, clinging, gray and dark blue, out of which her neck came, looking so round and warm. She was tall; there was something of the ancient Celt about her; around her were the names of legendary queens, Deirdre and Maave. And then there was her hair—positively orange. In a braid—yes, he had looked once when she had been leaning over the files—that braid went all the way around her head. And he had dreamed something unquestionably indecent about Miss Dorn.

A far clock dropped the chime of the half hour straight down like a crystal fruit through the March air. "Damn," he thought, "damn!" Now he would be late. Now the woman-with-the-hat-with-hard-green-berries would be ahead of him, she and her sensitive throat, and he would have to wait. Yet the fruit of the clock dropping through the air had been delightful. He smiled as he walked the last block of vendors and sun-washed faces, as he entered the dignity of the Arcade, as he rose in the hushed, ominous elevators and walked down the colonnade of marble and iodoform.

III

THE DOCTOR, HE thought, taking his place in the row of brown chairs, was a very nice man. He was a nice man with good taste; he kept *Vanity Fair* and *The New Yorker* on his table and hung drawings from Holbein on his walls. The woman-with-the-hat was there already, and so was the woman-with-the-baby-who-drooled. But he did not mind them too much. He sat in his grave pressed suit with his grave pressed trouser leg crossed, the crease extending before him with mathematical precision. After he had exhausted the possibilities of the crease, he turned to the drawing by Holbein. He had looked at that drawing fifty times before, with coldness and hunger in him, and with his stomach tightened by fear of the pain and his eyes blurred by the outward pressure forever pushing against his forehead. But now the picture was suddenly peeled of all those things which the days had wrapped around it; it was naked and exalted by March sun passing through white blinds; and the young girl who stared seriously from it (drawn in red against ivory paper) had a round womanly neck like the neck of Miss Dorn who worked in the office of the Dean.

The woman-with-the-hat arose to the discreet "Next" and was gone behind the heavy door. About Miss Dorn, now. What about Miss Dorn? She worked in that place until three on Saturdays. It would be possible; it had been done before—taxi drivers and shop girls, polo players and débutantes, publishers and authors. You merely went up to the Dean's office at three. You merely said, "Miss Dorn, I wonder if you'd have tea with me this afternoon." And she (who had once turned on him a pair of hazel eyes, wide and full of eager kindness) would not refuse. The young girl drawn in red against pale ivory stared at him with serious gentleness. He rested his temple against the tips of his fingers and thought of womankind. Eve and the Madonna, and Deirdre and Miss Dorn, all with breasts to vanquish and to lean upon. For he was suddenly tired, and the woman-with-the-hat was staying long. She came out with watery eyes and went away, and the woman-with-the-baby-who-drooled took her place. Now he was alone in the sunlit office. Sun on the white cover of the February *Vanity Fair*; sun on snow; there had been something in the dream about sun on snow.

Suddenly it flashed upon him, disembodied from the images in which it had taken place, the bright heroism of that dream. What he had been then he could not say, but he knew that he had been exalted. He had been lifted out of the world of futile lectures, curious books, grave neckties, swerving probes, iodoform and silence, and he had been set in a high place. The winds of that place still moved across his brow.

He knew two things clearly: he must never be again that which he had been before, and he must take Miss Dorn to tea. These things were urgent and were concerned with the salvation of his soul. They had something to do with the chasteness of wind and snow. He heard vague sounds behind the door. Very soon she-with-the-baby would come out, and it would be his turn to be mutilated and humiliated. Well, that was his burden which his destiny had set upon him; and he would endure it (he straightened his shoulders) like—really like a man.

He measured the force of the pain and decided that he could endure it. Besides, there was no doubt about it, the doctor was a very nice man. When the one-with-the-baby was gone, he rose with a springing step and approached the inner office as Mucius approached the fire. "Good afternoon!" he said to the doctor, who looked wise and lean and exalted in his white coat. He delighted in the doctor. The doctor was a man of taste and dry beauty. If any hands were to violate the dignity of his flesh, then he thanked God who had given him over into these lean brown ones.

"How's the nose?" said the doctor. He thought as he took off his coat and loosened his collar that there was something disgusting about the word "nose." It sounded as if it had meant, most considerately and politely, to sound like "rose," and then had been seized with a whimsical devil and had stuck out its tongue and said "Nya-nya-nya!" at you. Anyway, noses themselves were nothing gracious. And his own nose, torn by the probe, swollen by the disease! "New suit?" said the doctor. "No. Only an old one cleaned and pressed." He sat down squarely in the leather-and-enamel chair whose every curve was familiar to his body.

Usually at this point he looked at the ceiling. He was sickened by the machinations, the opening of the vial and the steeping of the cotton on the probe, and he had taught himself to stare at the bare flatness above him. Now he found all that cowardly and scarcely worthy of one who had been set in a high place. He looked at the vial, and he thought of Miss Dorn, and he looked at the probe. His whole body tightened, his teeth clamped together, his hands clasped the enameled arms, and his stomach drew up within him. The doctor bent over him. Really, the doctor was a very nice man. He put his hand under the set chin and tilted it upward. "Oh, now, take it easy," he said, suspending the probe. "No sense in stiffening up like that, my lad. Relax, relax. It isn't as bad as all that, you know." The act of relaxation was impossible. The best that he could manage was a tremulous and humiliating sigh.

There was nothing noble about it. It was the same nasty, disintegrating, damning pain. The probe swerved up into his head—up, he thought, into his brain. The usual moan, which he in the exalted place wished to smother, broke from the tightened cords of his throat, louder than ever. A dissolving pinkish mist quivered before him. "What the devil—" he said, revolting against nausea and the world. "'I'm sorry," said the doctor. Really he was a remarkably kind man. "That damned membrane is swollen out of God's grace, and you *had* to jerk and rip it up again. Sit still, sit still. Wait, I'll get you a bit of water." He drank the water with the quick gulps of hysteria. The vial sat maliciously on the tray. He cursed the stuff that was in it; his throat was sick with the taste of it.

He put on his coat and readjusted his tie before the small square of mirror. The pain had made him dizzy; he could scarcely stand. "What's your hurry?" said the doctor, putting the probe into the sterilizer. "Don't go rushing off before you're thoroughly integrated. There's nobody waiting. We might have a ten minutes' chat, you and I." But he went on pulling at the knot in his necktie. "No," he said, "no, really, I have to hurry. You see, I'm having tea—with a young lady—this afternoon."

IV

HE STOOD IN the street of vendors and going faces, bewildered by the light and the pain. He did not know exactly what to do. The element of space was contracted by the pink mist, and the element of time was a confusion. What time did she leave the office on Saturdays? He wasn't sure; he thought that she might leave at about three. If he walked, he would get there too late; if he took a cab, he would be much too early. He admitted, with a sense of Mucius drawing his hand from the fire, that he could not endure the street car. The jangling wheels, the rocking motion, the pressure of many bodies around him, would intensify the nausea and the headache. He thought that he would walk about for a while, look into shop windows, think, wait until he was "thoroughly integrated," and then take a cab. Really, he could not afford a cab. The cab plus the price of the tea would entirely disrupt his budget. Anyway, he could not concern himself with his budget; it was too difficult merely navigating through the Saturday afternoon crowd. The pink mist had cleared, but the pain dissolved all images at the edges. All images seemed to him soluble things which melted off into the atmosphere. As for the pain, the more he walked, the more it tormented him. Even the name of Miss Dorn, which he actually repeated now with his lips, was no talisman against the pain.

He found himself grasping back after those things which had given him pleasure before the probe had swerved upward into his brain. "Snow," he thought, "there was the snow." But now the snow glistened in his tormented eyes as did the daffodils; it was impossible to look at either the daffodils or the snow. He recalled forcibly the young woman by Holbein, whose throat had been round against the ivory paper, but everything in that office sickened him. Only the quiet plaid of Miss Dorn's dress could reach him through this evil hour. He stopped at the florist's window and leaned against the pane.

There he stood for some ten minutes, staring at the square

space of the show window, never staring beyond it, staring only at the Persian violets on their glazed stems, and desiring Miss Dorn's breast, to be leaned upon. He allowed his forehead to rest against the glass, which had been warmed by the electric lights within. For a minute which, because of its quietness and perfection, seemed an eternity, he rested his forehead there, and the warmth rose out of the glass, out of the womanly breasts of Maave and Deirdre and Eve, and comforted him and relieved the pain. Before him the Persian violets bloomed, and his mind was at peace.

He was roused from this minute by the sense of eyes looking at him, eyes seeing him steadily through the grayed shining of the glass. He looked up. The eyes were shadowy and kind. For a minute he thought that it was a dream; for beyond himself, the glass, and the Persian violets, with her hand considering a pot of primroses, Miss Dorn stood. For of course she was not at work; she had her holiday like others; this was Saturday afternoon. Her coat was open because of the tropical warmth of these places where orchids and ferns are. Above it her throat rose just as he had remembered it. Her mouth—soft, Celtic mouth—was curved upward with a smile. She knew him and nodded to him, and kept her hand poised for a long time above the primroses. He too nodded, and put the thought of the hand held over the lacy blossoms into his mind, to be remembered: to be remembered when you waken in the morning; to be remembered when somebody whistles a funeral march behind you on the campus; to be remembered when a long look comes into the eyes of your landlady because you have asked for a hot-water bottle.

It was the more like a dream because the shining glass stretched between them, and the small rom beyond the glass was rich with flowers, spread its flowers, like those of a medieval tapestry, behind her bright head whose small hat could not cover all of the redness of her hair. He nodded again, and turned away, carrying with him the thought of the hand and the smile and the lacy flowers.

He did not stay in town much longer. At three o'clock he stood on the clean mat before the door of Emma and Katherine, with silent thighs and with an unusually large bouquet of daffodils held precisely between his gray hands.

The Cabinet

THIS IS A very old story. It belongs, really, to the Great Grandmother, who always tells it to the young women of the family on the day before their weddings. It is not my story, for I do not belong to the family, I am only a friend, and I have no very great mind to become a bride. However, the Great Grandmother told it to me the other evening; we were sitting on the porch behind the wistaria; the air was hot, and she sighed. Then she said, as old people always do, that she could not stand the heat any more; maybe she would not see another spring, and maybe it was just as well, since she certainly could not stand the heat any more. "But before I take myself off," she said, "I would like to tell you my story, the one I always tell to the brides."

I said, yes, I knew about it, but I wasn't a bride; I was an old maid, with spectacles on my nose, like this! And I looked down the bridge of my nose and made her smile. "But you're interested in stories," she said, "and the brides aren't. Every bride I tell listens a little more patiently and wearily than the last. Brides care very little for such things now. I'm afraid they scarcely hear my story, and one of these days it'll be altogether forgotten." "Not," I said, "if you tell it to me. I shan't forget it. Bride or no bride, I'll hear your story and remember it."

So she told me, and really it was a charming thing. It had something of the terrible and something of the beautiful in it. It happened a long time ago, and I saw in it lilacs growing under gas lamps in an 1890 May. Long after she told it, the strange scent of it stayed with me: it is a smell which most of us can remember from our precious things like wines and fruitcakes have lain for many years. Like the Great Grandmother, I am eager now that the story should be remembered. So I set it down for the sake of those—brides or no brides—who might care to hear it again.

It is about a young woman named Emeline Delauncey who became a bride in the year 1891. (For two decades the remembrance of her beauty has lain like a shell in the Great Grandmother's thoughts.) To look at her, the Great Grandmother said, was to look at one of those white shells which have pink at the heart of them. She was beautiful as only Irish ladies can be beautiful. Perhaps she has become more beautiful by passing into legend—one cannot be sure. Perhaps the years have made her skin more transparent, her waist slimmer, her palms more delicately pink. Perhaps two decades have added a quarter of an inch to her eyelashes and twelves inches to her straight black hair. But even before legend had touched her, Emeline Delauncey must have been very beautiful. She confined her hair in tortoise-shell combs and scented her bath with dried mignonette.

She was deeply in love with the man whom she was to marry. The Great Grandmother knew little about him: only that he was a poet and that he had a little money of his father's and a long silky beard of his own.

"What was his name?" I said.

"Indeed," the Great Grandmother told me, I'm afraid that I've forgotten that. Maybe it was Philip. It might very likely have been Philip; nobody ever asked his name before, and it's all such a long time ago."

Emeline was in love with his broad, thin shoulders, his poetry, and his silky beard. She loved him past all reason; and as much as she loved him, so much she was jealous of him.

Everybody knew about her jealousy and used to chaff her about it. Whenever she saw him standing by the mantel and talking with another lady, she would cross the room and come to his elbow, and stay there, quite silent, until he turned to smile at her. One night when they were having a party, they asked her to sing, for she had a lovely voice, and she sang:

Still as the night,
Deep as the sea,
Is, Love, my love
For thee.

They asked her afterwards, laughing, whether her jealousy was as still and as deep. Yes, she said, she thought it was; but she was going to reform; after her marriage, she was never going to be jealous any more. They did not believe her; but they found her very charming in her blue ball gown and her wreath of false forget-me-nots; when she said so, she was leaning against his shoulder and brushing her cheek on his long silky beard. They said they would see, they would see.

She began well. Two weeks before her marriage, her father gave her some silverware and some furniture. Among the furniture was a walnut cabinet, a rich carven thing meant for heirlooms or linens, with embossed fruit on the top and a Grecian lute on the door. In the center of the lute was the lock, and in the lock shone a little copper key. She put the key into her lover's hands.

"And what am I to do with that, Love?" he said.

"Why," she told him, "that is to prove to you that I am not jealous any more. The cabinet is yours, and you can do with it whatever you choose. If you have a lady-love, besides me, you can hide a lock of her hair there. Or you can put poems about her there. Or you can put your sweetheart in it, if you choose, but you had better bore little holes in the top so that she won't smother. But the cabinet is yours."

He laughed at her then and kissed her mouth. "I have only one sweetheart," he said, "and I want her in the new bed, not in the new box." For he was a poet, and he smoke more freely than the other young men of his day. However, he took the copper key and put it into his pocket, and for many years she did not see it again.

They left the new cabinet and the new bed, and went to spend a year on the Continent. The Great Grandmother was on the pier when they sailed; she saw the shell-like face recede, close to the silky beard, in the bright April morning. Then for the Great Grandmother it was a matter of letters written in Emeline's neat script and scented with dried mignonette. They told gay things gaily. Emeline and Philip were being entirely happy: Now they were in Paris, going to the opera five nights a week. Now they were in Vienna, drinking yellow wine with some musicians whom Philip knew. Now they were in Italy, and oh, the fishing villages and the blue, blue sea. Now they were in Greece, living in the house of a portrait painter, another friend of Philip's who was an exile from Germany. Now the portrait painter was making a miniature of her and taking a long time about it, because, oh, she didn't want to boast, but really he was in love with her. Now the portrait was finished, and Philip had it set in a lovely frame and carried it in his vest pocket. Now they were coming home, and she was so very happy!

Here the Great Grandmother paused and stared between the twinings of the wistaria at the sky. "But when they came home, there was the cabinet," she said. And she spoke of the cabinet again, of the lute on the door, of the copper key in Philip's pocket, of the rich, sorrowful smell of the wood, long aged and perfumed with the fruitcakes and wines which had lain in it for generations, still perfumed with them, even though the cabinet was empty now. "Or Emeline thought that it was empty, or wished that it was empty, or tried to believe, waking in the new bed, that it was empty," she said.

For it was plain to everybody but Philip that Emeline was tormented by the cabinet. On days when he went to the college, where he had been given a chair in Italian literature, she would sit in the bedroom, talking to the Great Grandmother and looking sidewise at the cabinet whenever she thought that the Great Grandmother was looking out of the window. Her eyes, which had been placid and cool when she returned from the Continent, were growing feverish and hard. She was tormented by the cabinet and grieved because, in spite of their mutual longing for children, it seemed impossible for her to have a child. These two griefs were not mentioned between them. Whe he would return from the college, she would run to the porch to meet him. In the silky beard she would try to cool her face of the fever which she had brought to it all day with thoughts of his hand on a girl student's head or of his eyes appraising a passing maid on the street.

"Do you love me?" she would say.

"Of course, dear heart."

"Really love me?"

"Why should you doubt it?"

"Love me more than anything in the world?"

"Of course."

"More than the most beautiful woman in the world?"

"But you are the most beautiful woman in the world."

"But I won't always be beautiful. I'll get old. I'll have wrinkles."

"Beautiful wrinkles."

"Are you sure that you'll love me forever?"

"Until the end of the world," he said; and then added, "and after resurrection, too, my dear. For I sometimes think you could suspect me of flirting—even with one of God's angels."

The beauty of Emeline Delauncey was such a perfect thing

that the least falling-off from it was noticeable, like a spot on white marble or a streak in spring water. She began to grow old before the other young women of her set had even thought of wrinkles. The Great Grandmother paused in the story to say a few ancient things about the strain of loving too much; how too-anxious loving will age the young heart quicker than clothes to be washed and floors to be dusted; how the eyes grow hard from it; how the longing to be very beautiful stiffens the smile and makes the cheeks and eyes too vivid; how there is a temptation to put on a little more rouge every day and to dress the hair in more and more fantastic fashions. I listened and sighed in the direction of the wistaria; for I knew that the meaning of this was Emeline's beauty gone, and in my mind she had been very beautiful.

"She used to stand before the long mirror," the Great Grandmother said, "when I came to visit her. The others thought that she was vain, but I knew better, I knew that she was afraid. She used to say in an earnest voice, 'Do you like my new gown? Do you really like it? Don't you think it's just a little too—well, just a little too?' Oh, no, I would assure her, it was very fashionable and became her perfectly, the hip line was particularly beautiful, and the low cut neck was flattering. Her husband, I said, would be pleased, 'Oh, do you think so?' I said of course I thought so; he doted on her; he thought her perfectly lovely; I had heard him call her his Psyche, and among half a dozen men, too. Oh, but, she said, that might be only for the sake of appearances. And then she would stare into the mirror long and sorrowfully, not at herself now, but at the corner of the cabinet which was reflected there."

Her husband was a student and a poet. Sometimes he begged, on that excuse, to be allowed an evening at home with his books and his thoughts. At such a time he found her a young and handsome escort to the theater, or an old and elegant and interesting one. When she came home with lines from Ibsen or tunes from Mignon still floating in her brain, she would always find him as she had left him, sitting before the fire with his wine glass, his pen, and his book.

ONE EVENING SHE thought that his pose was too perfect; he sat before the fire with his hands at his cheeks and his long silky beard pointed toward the hearth too much as if he had been there all evening. She suspected him.

"What have you been doing?" she said.

"Reading, dreaming, waiting for you to come home."

That, too, was too perfect. "I don't believe you," she said.

"Emeline!"

"Well, I don't. You've been somewhere, I'm sure."

"Yes, I have been out. I went down the street to buy myself some tobacco."

"I don't believe you."

"You'll have to believe me. I've been nowhere else all evening."

She stood beside the mantel and began to cry in hard hysterical sobs.

"Oh, my dear," he said, "what's the matter?"

"Nothing. Nothing."

He drew her to his knees and sat comforting her until very late. She hid her face in the silky beard and was consoled. But not for long.

The little scenes repeated themselves and became more frequent and more violent. She accused him when he came in ten minutes late from the college; she questioned him when he dropped, late and weary, beside her on the new bed. She read his poem with fever when he was not at home, hunting there for a mention of hair that was not black and an eye that was not blue. That she found nothing, did not quiet her. She believed now, with passionate grief, that he had a mistress, and that his poems about this blond, fresh one were locked in the cabinet. She longed to open it, morning and night. She came up to it and touched the lute with the palm of her soft, hot hand. But the cabinet was his, and she had given it to him in their earlier and happier days, and she could not bear to break the promise which she had made with a younger and cooler mouth.

Then one day, when she was leaning against his chest and burying her face in the cool silky beard which was her consolation, her body stiffened and she drew away; for she missed the hard little square which had always been within his vest pocket. Her miniature was no longer there. She began to tremble.

"My dear," he said, "are you ill?"

"Yes, I have a headache."

"Poor darling, let me carry you upstairs and put you to bed."

"No, I can walk very well by myself." And she left him and returned to her room, to be tormented more than ever by the cabinet.

After that, things became intolerable between them. They began to reproach each other because they had no child. His patience was almost gone. When she questioned him, he would say, "Oh, for the love of God!" and walk fiercely out of the house and not return until long past midnight. "He is with his mistress," she would tell herself. She could not sleep. In his absence, she lay awake in the middle of the new bed, crying bitterly, but when he returned she would pretend to be asleep.

ONE NIGHT AFTER a quarrel he came in even later than usual. She lay on her side, facing the cabinet, and saw him come into the room in the wan moonlight. Then she closed her eyes and kept them closed while he stood looking down at her. She heard him sigh deeply and walk away. When she opened her eyes again, she saw him sitting in his chair, with his head bent and the moonlight making silver of his beard. She saw then that he, too, had grown old. His cheeks were hollow; there was a sharp cleft between his brows. He had been drinking, and he breathed heavily. His shoulders were stooped, and she felt such an aching pity for his stooped shoulders that she would have come from the bed to him and drawn his head against her breast, if it had not been that he moved just then, sighed, rose, and went toward the cabinet.

She watched him through her long eyelashes. She saw him take the little copper key from his pocket and put it to the lock. For the first time in her life, she heard the lock turn and saw the perfumed darkness from which the luted door swung. Then she could not lie still any longer. The pounding of her heard struck to the base of her throat, and she turned over, not wishing to see any more. She saw him look over his shoulder, and she closed her eyes.

The door was shut and the key was fitted. The small, definite click of the lock marked for her the world's end. And he had spoken of loving her past Resurrection Day!

They were giving a dinner party on the next night, and her husband had invited from the college two young men and a young woman who were interested in the writing of poetry. Emeline had seen the young woman before. She was a quiet, plump little thing with large gray eyes and a milky throat. Her hair was something between chestnut color and red; she dressed badly, and her fingernails showed traces of ink. But she talked well, and Philip had often said, "She has so much life in her quiet little body—this Sara. You'll learn to like her, I'm sure, and maybe she'll cheer you up a bit; you've been so tight-lipped lately, Love." Now it suddenly occurred to Emeline that this little Sara who had so much life and would cheer her up a bit was her husband's mistress. No doubt there were verses about her in the tormenting cabinet. No doubt it was with her that he stayed late at the college; no doubt it was with her that he walked, exchanging kisses, on those nights when she sat at the opera and he pretended to be at home before the fire. One thing gave ghastly reality to the whole matter. She had often noticed this little Sara's hips; they were broad for child-bearing; and she had the full, close bosom which always suggests motherhood.

•

BUT EVEN IN this excess of her terror, Emeline had a certain honor of her own. She would not touch the cabinet because she had promised not to touch the cabinet, and she would not convict her husband without a final trial. She called her kitchen boy and asked him to take a note to her husband at the college. It was a silly note, about making sure to get pretty flowers at the florist's—lilacs would do well, because it was early May and she had not seen lilacs for a long time. She told the kitchen boy to make sure that he took the letter straight to the professor. Then she sat down and waited.

The boy came back soon.

"Did you see the professor?" she said.

"Oh, yes, ma'am, I saw the professor, and he said sure enough he'd bring lilacs, he'd been thinking of lilacs anyway."

"Did he say anything else?"

"No, ma'am, nothing else."

"Where did you see him, Charles?"

"Up in the classroom, ma'am."

"And was he alone?"

"No, ma'am, Miss Sara was with him."

"Very well, that's all."

Then she went upstairs to dress. She was in a fever; her cheeks and her throat burned, and her hands were so uncertain that she could not make her face up well. The Great Grandmother came in during that afternoon to bring her some silver vases for the flowers. "And I tell you," the Great Grandmother said, "I knew that she had gone absolutely mad."

I do not know whether the Great Grandmother always told the story so well. Perhaps she needs a listener who looks down the bridge of her nose and is not distracted by thoughts of boudoir slippers and corsages. Or perhaps she felt that the last telling should be a good telling—the best—and that this was the last telling. At any rate, she was lost in her subject. She stared at the wistaria with harder, brighter eyes than I had ever seen glitter below her kind old brows. She said that the dinner party was fantastic, like a madman's carnival, like one of those skeleton dances you read about in old fairy tales. Emeline sat at the head of the table and served, like a dethroned queen. She had got her rouge on crooked. Her hair was piled high on the top of her head and looked a monstrosity. Her hands shook when she passed the salt cellar or the candy dish. Her voice trembled. Her dress was black, and she wore a wreath of false yellow roses. Some of them remembered her as she had been in her blue ball gown, with the forget-me-nots in her hair; and it was a bad thing to remember; it made them shudder and sigh. Sara sat obliquely opposite her. She plied the pudgy, quiet little girl with attentions. Would she have more meat? Were the creamed carrots to her taste? The child was embarrassed. She kept glancing at her teacher who sat at the head of the table, his head bowed and his silky beard almost touching the cloth.

They rose late from the table. The candles, grouped by threes on either side of the lilacs burned almost to their ends, and the lilacs themselves had drooped in the heat. Throughout the dinner, the professor had said scarcely a word. Now he rose heavily, and those who sat nearest him sighed. They went into the parlor. Emeline was more talkative and more ghastly-gay than ever.

"What a pretty, dress, Sara," she said, touching with her small hot hands the ruffle of purple taffeta around the girl's shoulders.

It was not a pretty dress, and Sara knew as much. It was an old thing, and it fitted her badly. But under the shabby skirt were the firm, motherly hips. "Thank you," she said, looking down, "it's shabby, I know."

"Why, not at all." Emeline had a clear voice, and the others turned to hear. Philip, too, came to the mantel where Sara and Emeline were standing together.

Somebody tactful had gone to the piano and begun a waltz.

"Are we going to have dancing?" said Sara, flushing.

"Why, yes, my dear, we are. I never thought of that, but it's a splendid idea. Philip, dance with Sara." Her voice had lost its false ease now. It sounded like the voice of a major in a barracks, giving polite, but definite commands.

"Ah, Sweetheart," Philip said, touching her shoulder, "I'm scarcely in a mood for dancing."

"But Sara is," said Emeline. The waltz went on, and everybody had begun to think it terribly out of place, even the lady who played it, but she did not stop because now she did not dare.

"No, I'm not," said Sara, looking down at the uneven hem of her dress.

"Don't you want to dance with my husband, dear?"

"No, thank you, not tonight."

THE WALTZ GREW louder, but not loud enough to sound above Emeline's clear hard voice. "But why," she said, "should you refuse to dance with him? You talk with him, walk with him, eat with him, sleep—"

The girl turned scarlet and stepped back, making the andirons clang.

"Emeline!" Philip said.

She looked past him into the eyes of the girl. "Isn't that true?" she said.

"No. No, it isn't."

"Emeline!"

"But there isn't any need to lie to me. I already know."

"Emeline, beg this young woman's pardon, or I swear to God I will walk out of this house and never enter it again."

"Shall I beg her pardon because she is your—your—" The person at the piano strove to bury it all under a large crescendo, but it was useless. The girl ran, crying bitterly, out of the house, without her hat and shawl. The others stood still, their mouths open, "like ghosts," the Great Grandmother said, "who have heard the stroke of midnight."

Then the person at the piano began again, faintly. "Stop that," Philip said. They were silent. In the middle of their silence he left the room and the house, brushing Emeline as he passed her with his long silky beard.

"And then," I said, "and then?"

"And then the others went, too, even I, for it was impossible to be with her. She needed to be alone.

I learned about the rest of that evening long afterwards, in a letter which she wrote me from a far country. She went upstairs at once, to the room where they had been happy together, to the empty bed and the tormenting cabinet. All her wild grief and rage centered about that cabinet. Her pain was bound up inextricably in the carved blossoms and the lute. She found a hammer somehow and smashed the cabinet to bits. And in the perfumed darkness she found her own portrait, the one that the young painter had done in Greece."

THE GREAT GRANDMOTHER sighed, for she was very old and the heat was oppressive. She was not used, any more, to talking so earnestly for so long. "Around it," she said, "was wrapped a piece of letter paper, with a poem in his handwriting scrawled on both sides. I saw that poem once, but I can't remember it, not word for word; I knew it once, but things slip your mind, more and more things slip your mind as you grow old."

"But what did it say?"

"It said that he desired to love her utterly and faithfully, as she was. It said that this picture of her as she once had been came too often before his eyes and made him unfaithful to the dear, unhappy face before him; therefore he put it away and would not give himself the unlawful joy of looking at it any more."

The evening was growing dark. A wind shook the wistaria, and the Great Grandmother rubbed her dry hands, as old people do.

"The portrait?" I said, believing for the minute that the Great Grandmother would draw it from her bosom, and that I might see with my own eyes how beautiful Emeline Delauncey had been before the cabinet tormented her. "Ah, that. She had that buried with her. He never came back—nobody ever heard of him again—and she could not stay in the country without him. Her father was going to India, and she begged to go with him, and he took her with him, in spite of the climate and the cholera, because she begged so earnestly. She died there. She took the cholera two months after they sailed into port, and she died in India and was buried there."

I knew that the story had come to its proper end, and I rose and offered the Great Grandmother my arm. As I say, it is an old story, and not mine; yet the scent of it has been with me for a long time, and I am glad to rid myself of that rich, sorrowful smell of wood in which wines and fruitcakes have lain for decades, and of that purple glimpse of lilacs seen in an 1890 May. Besides, the Great Grandmother does not want her story to be lost. So I have put it down, for her sake and for my own, and for the sake of those—brides or no brides—who may care to read it when the Great Grandmother is not oppressed with the heat of another spring.

All Souls'

I T WAS THE gray glare of the fog that wakened him. He opened his eyes, and the room and the world beyond the third-story windows were harshly white. He had never noticed before how many windows there were, and now the thought filled the dream-dimmed minute with a strange uneasiness. So little wall, really, between him and the milky, shifting stuff, and the space beyond the glass somber and unreal. It was as if the primal deluge had washed across the world again. The straw-colored tips of autumn trees, the slate slants of roofs and steeples seemed to be thrusting upward, futile and feeble, out of a sea.

He shifted his body against the mattress, and felt the ache that had been with him these last twelve years, and cursed under his breath. In cases of arthritis, the doctor had said, there is relief but no cure; with many of us it is part of the process of growing old. Under the fine puff quilt, under the blanket and the sheet, under the pajamas he sensed the burden of his body and knew its age and was not resigned.

In the three months since she had died, he had grown thinner. There was a taste in his mouth. Taste of fog. The room was drenched with it. It had crept between the metal edges of the casements; it had dampened the quilt under his dry, long, elegant fingers; it had invaded his person, and the smell of it was on his breath. It was persistent and pervading, like something else—like what?—like the thought of dissolution to those who can count on two hands the number of years they may reasonably expect to spend upon the earth.

There had been a time when he had lain long between waking and rising, when he had given himself a half-hour in the intimate and luxurious warmth of the bed for pursuing the night's dreams or anticipating some triumph of the day to come. Like phrases from old songs, like the fragrance of the back yards of our childhood, bits of the old thoughts were evoked by the brief quiet—voluptuous imaginings, fantasies of power, rare, paled remembrances of tenderness. He pushed them aside with the covers and rose to the first necessity of the day: the business of transforming his frailty into austerity—the straight steel sheen of his hair, the sharp leanness under impeccable gray wool, the perfectly knotted tie, the hard, smooth-shaven cheek—the seasoned power, the tempered sword.

BUT WHILE HE dressed, the fog kept seeping between the windows and the sills, and he was forever brushing against the bed that had been hers. Why it remained there in the room—chaste, unwrinkled, draped like a corpse in a white spread—why it remained there, he didn't know. The cool, blond daughter-in-law had removed everything else.

The job had been exemplary for its tact and thoroughness. The never-opened powder boxes, the seldom-worn jewelry no longer cluttered the dressing table; the soft, shoddy slippers no longer turned up in unexpected places; one saw for the first time that the closet had been papered in rose and white stripes—its floor was clean and shining, its hat shelf bare.

All this had been done imperceptibly, in delicate stages, by that remote young woman who was so serene and proper that he wondered how his son had ever managed to steer her into bed. That, he thought, was their problem; they looked after their affairs, and he looked after his own. Yet it gave him a subtle pleasure, for all its inconvenience—that bed standing starkly there in spite of the young woman's thoroughness. It had not fallen to her coolness; her poise had been shattered against it; she had begun and had not dared to finish. It was too much for her, that bed.

Not that he himself was proof against it. He stood and looked down upon it. He stared it out, much as, on that thick, solemn August morning, he had stared out the grave of his wife. The cumulus clouds had piled up at the edge of the cemetery; over their massed grayness had lain the oblique rays of a watery sun. Sudden wind had sown turbulence in the dignity of the poplars. Rhetoric and fallen sods had broken the quiet. But he had not been turbulent; his quiet had been invulnerable; nothing had undone his dignity.

HE HAD TOLD himself at the end of every efflorescent paragraph that this was a show, a piece of pageantry. The sorrow on his face was a removable mask; three, four more hours, and he could lay it aside. His own replies to the other mourners were like the flowers that came after her out of the abyss of the hearse; they were the appropriate ornaments of the occasion and would have the grace to die soon and be remembered no more. No, he would not remember any of it, not here in this clinging, moving mist. He had been finished with it long before it had ended; the last twenty years of his marriage had been unreal, ghostly, posthumous. Let him say it plainly to himself, as he had said it at the cemetery gate: He had buried nothing; it had been no loss.

Now the house was utterly still. The two on the second floor rose late. They could afford to; they were the inheritors; he had never lost the stern, meager ways of those who do the getting. Everything downstairs was arranged for his convenience. Before she laid her cool head on her cool pillow, his daughter-in-law discharged her duties. His coffee was meted out in the percolator; the toaster and the bread knife were ready; his glass of fruit juice, sealed with a cold little rubber cap, was set to the front of the refrigerator; the best china and the best silver were laid at his solitary place. The light in the dining room chandelier was sickly in the glare of the fog. The dishes were damp, and the taste of fog was in the food. He chewed methodically, without savor, and saw them again, now one, now the other, the grave, the bed.

But he had done what he could for her. His acquaintances kept reminding him how much he had done, how he had no reason to reproach himself now that she was dead. Love her? Who could have loved her—the dumpy, asthmatic little woman, slovenly without her corsets, slovenly without her shoes, her false teeth more often in her apron pocket than in her mouth, a fringe of hair, always smelling a little burned from the curler, fuzzy across her brow? Nobody had expected him to love her. She had not expected it herself. He was of the world and of the times; she belonged to the house and to a gone era; it was enough that he brought home to her the sour candy that she loved to suck, the lace-edged boudoir pillows that were out of fashion now.

He had spent money on her, as much as he had ever spent on the other one, the one who could still evoke in him a kind of shadowy delight. He had done what he could, he had given her all that she could use. Long ago she had asked, without prompting, for a bed of her own. A mild woman, easily resigned to the end of love . . .

He took up his flawless hat and topcoat, put out the lights, and stood for a minute in the middle of the orderly Georgian living room, staring across the sofa at the windows and the mist. The whiteness was less solid now. Through its shifting surface, slantwise and wan, lay a band of sun. He thought of her again because the house was so quiet. She had been in the habit of coming downstairs before him and going back to her rumpled bed when he left the place. Always, at this time of the morning, there had been the shuffle of her slippers on the stairs.

Always like that—he always saw her like that, nodding at him over the banister. Not the waxy thing in the coffin. That lace-shadowed, satin-covered doll had been ridiculous, offensive, a kind of final insult to the little that she was. He had looked the required number of times, kissed the tips of the still fingers, and forgotten the whole affair.

A certain old clerk of his, poetic and a little confused in the brain, had chosen to talk to him in the presence of that trimmed-up piece of nothingness. The clerk had said something about a person's youth rising out of the grave. "Now it's strange, it's very strange, but all of a sudden you see your wife the way she was when she was twenty. You see her in places you forgot, in dresses you haven't thought about for thirty years."

Some men might be able to wrest this sort of resurrection from a grave. Certainly he could not. He had buried nothing more or less than the fat little person who sloshed upstairs. He put on his hat, opened the door, and stepped into the mist.

The street was dank and yellow-brown with maple leaves. His car stood at the curb where he had left it last night in protest against his son's persistent advice. He stepped in and banged the door. A child was walking up on of the side streets, a small, pale boy in a garish clown suit. It was the last day of the month, and Halloween. The little fellow was going to school in his frippery, dragging his pointed hat behind him so that its scarlet pom-poms trailed on the wet cement.

Something in the sight was troubling. The small, grave face above the bright red ruff? The thought of taffy apples eaten in a forgotten classroom long ago? The loneliness of a single figure moving through fog down an empty street? He did not know and sensed that he did not wish to know. His hand felt masterful upon the wheel. The ache in his arm and shoulder was less. Definitely, the fog was clearing. He watched the sanity of sun returning to the world.

YEARS AGO HE had instituted in the office a practice of closing a month's business on the thirtieth. It was a good system; it kept the bookkeepers on their toes. Besides, it righted in some measure the shifting calendar. One closed the books at reasonably regular intervals for eleven twelfths of the year, and only the flaw of February remained. Yet today he found himself regretting his commendable method. It made a shifting, unanchored ghost of the thirty-first day.

The top of his desk was empty. He could see his own face, white and triangular, swimming in the dark glass. His secretary kept to her cubicle. The telephone was still. The old clerk pared his nails under a hanging lamp in the adjoining room. There was nothing to do.

He spent most of the morning at the window, staring into the soot-black canyon of the business street. The fog which had lifted from the face of his neighborhood seemed to have accumulated in this dark and angular place. The weather and the hour were equivocal, disturbing. It was neither night nor day. Lights were turned on in his and other offices, but the glare sickened them; they showed in pale, blurred squares through the mist. Below him, humanity was drowned in wet and dark. Their white, lifted faces were seen as at the bottom of a sea. Like his own face, floating in the depths of the glass—submerged, lost.

Suddenly it came into his mind that he could not go back to his own house tonight. It was as if something—fog, death, an ancient anger—waited for him in the vestibule. He saw the dining room and the table and the three of them seated around it; he saw the cold faces and the cold orderliness of the chinaware, the thin gray slices of lamb, the diced potatoes, the perfect green of the peas. And all this—this and the hard brilliance of the prism chandelier—seemed also to be immersed in the inescapable tide. He could not eat with them, answering their polite questions about his day at work. What the day was, what words he could call up to describe the day, would be unfit for their chilly ears.

HE WOULD SPEND the evening in some other place. But where? Some closed place, padded with plush and heavy with the smell of brandy and rich food. Some place where a discreet hand drew weighty curtains between guest and the night. Clubhouse? Restaurant? Alone? He walked away from the window and sat down before the bald desk. He would telephone Cecilia. To envision, to embroider, to play with the idea of loneliness was a piece of morbidity. There was no need, absolutely no need for him to spend the evening or the night alone.

Yet he could not bring himself to phone her at once. He sat for a long time above the watery glass, fondling the bronze, fish-tailed nymph that was his paperweight, a present which she had given him in the first stages of their ardor, ten years ago. Like the nymph, she had lost only a little of the first gloss. She was no fool to stand wailing after gone youth. She made the most of mellowness. There was an autumnal opulence about her—the indolent curve of her hand setting a comb straight in the dark loops of her hair, the full breasts confined in sturdy satin, the husky voice equally appropriate for carrying a new tune, commenting on the European news, telling a tastefully bawdy jest. What a woman to find by sheer accident, to stumble into at a business dinner in a dusty, savorless year! He never knew what was more gratifying—her social adaptability or the easy, openhanded way she had of making love. They had conspired together, secretively, cleverly, to wangle their share of the world's wine and roses. Sitting behind the drawn curtains, they conspired with witty words against some nameless thing—the fog, the return to the primal nothingness.

Then why should he sit dreaming and playing with the

sea nymph? Why not lift the telephone? Simply because she had—and this was part of the gleam upon her—a life of her own. Mondays, Wednesdays, and Saturdays were their evenings. This was Friday, a day when she made herself available to the insignificant remnant of her world: the cousins, the nephews, the secretary who was to be married and needed a bit of down-to-earth advice, the smart woman friends among whom she renewed her inexhaustible collection of anecdotes.

Yet it was just possible that she had no engagement for tonight. She had said once a little wistfully that Fridays were dull, filled up with such odds and ends as writing checks and mending underwear. The routine of their lovemaking was so smooth that he seldom had occasion to call her at her office. He had to leaf long through his desk calendar to find the number. He dialed it, still holding the bronze nymph in his left hand, nourishing himself upon curve and hollow until he heard her voice.

"Why, is that you, my darling?" she said. "Is anything the matter? Are you all right?"

He stared at the blank street and the moving strands of mist. "I feel a little seedy this morning." He had meant to say that he was very well indeed.

"But I *told* you, dear, I told you on Wednesday that you should go to the doctor and get some heat rays on your shoulder."

"Oh, what's the point of it?" Seeing that there is no cure for arthritis, since it is part of the process of growing old.

"The point of it? But that's ridiculous. It always helps. You know as much."

"I'll go when I choose." He had meant to sound off-hand and masculine. He was querulous instead—cranky and old.

"Let's not quarrel. It's so nice, at this time of the morning, hearing your voice."

He could sense her waiting at the other end of the line. She had implied, tactfully and affectionately, that she wished to know what he wanted. She had done it with her usual grace and was perfectly justified, inasmuch as she had a life of her own. He reached across the cold, aqueous surface of his desk, set the sea nymph down, and touched the tip of the bronze breast. "I thought, if it was all right with you . . ." But his tone was far too timid and tentative. He cleared his throat. "Shall we have dinner together tonight?"

The phone was electric with silence. It was almost as if she had said "Good Lord!" under her breath.

"Shall we have—"

"Oh, my darling, I can't." There was real distress in the speed and breathlessness of her voice. "Of all nights, I simply can't tonight. If I had only known on Wednesday. And what I have to do tonight is such a little, foolish sort of thing—"

He withdrew his hand from the nymph and rubbed it against his own hard cheek. Try as he would, he could not say the gracious words that would deliver her from the need to explain and apologize.

"My brother's children, darling—I promised to spend the evening with my brother's children because it's Halloween. They're going to be dressed up in costumes and pull taffy. I have a bag of stuff to take, noisemakers and paper hats and confetti, and they're expecting me, and if I didn't turn up it would break their hearts. I—"

"That's quite all right," he said. But he had not been listening. He was absorbed in a recollection: that small, pale boy going solitary through the fog, dragging his clown hat on the damp street . . .

"No, it's not all right. It's not all right at all. That I should be somewhere else on the one evening when you want me—"

He felt it as an affront—her knowledge of his loneliness.

"Listen, dearest." Her voice was swifter and more breathless still. He fancied that he could see the excitement of a new thought brightening her eyes. "Listen, why don't you come over there with me, over to my brother's, I mean? It'll only last till twelve or thereabouts. It would be silly—apples and taffy and doughnuts. But it wouldn't be painful, and afterward we—"

He could not understand why the thought of children in Halloween clothes should put him into this nervous, unsteady state. The hand that held the phone was actually shaking. "That isn't at all necessary," he said.

"But—"

"I'll see you tomorrow."

"But do you forgive me?"

He winced. There was a quality he had always valued in her conversation—the utter absence of such excessive words as "love," "remembrance," "yearning," "suffer," and "forgive." He cleared his throat again. There was fog in it. "Certainly. Don't be a fool. I'll see you tomorrow," he said.

He did not go back to the door. He continued to sit at the desk, gazing at the little clerk who went on paring his nails in the faint circle of light under the lamp. He had not really looked at the fellow for weeks—months—years. And now he was amazed at the change, the withered hands, the wizened face. The clerk was old, the clerk was very old.

THAT NIGHT HE left the dinner table early, before the two of them had pushed their dessert dishes aside and reached for their cigarettes. He walked into the parlor, feeling the frigid look, the lifting of the pale eyebrows behind him. "What ails the old man?" their brief silence asked. Then the question was submerged in the chill flow of their conversation: "And I said: No, I wouldn't think of paying such a price for a pair of curtains under any circumstances . . ."

Tonight he wanted every lamp in the parlor to be lighted. The daughter-in-law didn't like too much light. Once a month she gave a lecture about the matter over the newly arrived electricity bill. She always said, smiling and turning off the lamps, that really it was too intense. He wandered around the sitting room, pushing button after button, jerking little chain after little chain. He saw her through the arched doorway. Her look transformed him into a child spoiling for a fight. "But I am an adult, I am poised," her glance said. "You're evidently on some sort of tension tonight, so I'll overlook your naughtiness." Her husband handed her a cigarette and smiled. "You're wise, my love," said his eyes, "you're very wise."

Now that every globe in the room was bright, he was not satisfied. The lamps looked small and separate; the glow was confined to the silk shades; there was a troubling mistiness between. Either the smoke of their cigarettes drifting in from the dining room or the fog rolling back with the night, had clouded the house. He was cold. He huddled in an armchair near the draped window, with a pillow behind his shoulder and the stale news spread over his knees. He was irritated by the headlines; he had read them all before. The ache in him was nagging, persistent, like a bad tooth. A tooth can be pulled, but for arthritis there is no. . . . The room was too damned polished, anyhow. Wherever he looked, he saw a shimmering surface. The reflection of his face was there, distorted, in the dark wood of the coffee table. His lean ankles rippled away from him in the gleaming floor.

Suddenly he felt an uncontrollable wish to pull the velvet drape aside, to reduce the great square of the window to blank nakedness, to see and know the night. He folded the paper carefully, without a rustle. Soundlessly he rose and turned to the window. Their cold eyes were upon him. Damn their eyes! He tweaked the drapery and saw the street—the arc lights swathed in mist, the sick, washed yellow of the lighted maple boughs, the seedy asters bled of all color on the ashen lawns, the funereal mounds of hedge and bush.

"Are you expecting somebody, Father?" the son said.

"No, not a soul. I wanted to see what kind of night it is, that's all. With your permission, of course."

They were silent behind him. They were tolerant and discreet. Before him, a car moved on, casting misted yellow beams upon the damp blackness of the cement. For the fraction of a second, some brightness sprang into being on the street—smattering of colored paper, little squares of confetti, band of paper ribbon dangling from a bush. It was Halloween, and the merrymakers were about. But what was that to him? Why should it make him press his face against the glass? What conjured up this strange commingling of fear and grief, this uneasy, feeble stirring in his heart?

"Maybe the house is too cold. Maybe he'd like a fire," the daughter-in-law said.

Let me alone! Leave me in peace to pursue this labyrinthine memory. What is this old ache, not in the shoulder only? What did I lose irrevocably among scattered confetti? What, to me, is a little pale boy in a scarlet ruff? A pumpkin face flashed into existence in a far window. Down the street, distant and wavering, sounded a horn. Not here, he thought, I will not find it here at the window. It is in some other place in this house. He turned and walked through the cross fire of their wondering stares into the hall.

There was little light in that narrow place, only what seeped in from the living room. The white spindles of the banister went up before him. The uncarpeted floor gleamed beneath him. Behind him was the door that led into the fog. He stood perfectly still, waiting, afraid to breathe lest he should block the return of remembrance. He fixed his glance on the empty stair. And then it was no longer empty. There *she* stood, fat and frumpy, her false teeth in her apron pocket, her little plump hand feeling about for them because somebody was knocking at the door.

Softly, soundlessly, she began to descend to him. They clung about her—the scents that had gone from the house with her going—the smells of sliced apples, bread puddings, nutmeg, cinnamon, tea. "Oh, but it's far too late to leave the furnace unlit," she said. "Your shoulder will get worse because of that. Besides, the damp draws the spiders in. I always like a warm house."

SHE WAS HALFWAY down the steps now. In the last years, her ankles had been swollen. She had to lean on the banister and under her weight the spindles shook. But suddenly she was not limping anymore. She was standing, light as a cloud, light as a blown milkweed, in the middle of the stairs. Not these stairs. Some other flight of steps in a house where gas jets flared. Her father's house, and she in a candy-striped, green-and-white taffeta thing, she smelling of apples and cinnamon, with a cheek like the pale, creamy slice of an apple, with the soft, winglike fall of chestnut hair over her brow.

A jack-o'-lantern stood on the flat newel post. She laid her small, soft hand upon it, and the candlelight gleamed roseate through her flesh, and he could only stare in tenderness and delight. "But open the door, my darling, open the door," she said. "The doorbell's ringing. The children are outside with their paper bags. Every Halloween night we give them apples and nuts. No, now, I'll kiss you later, dearest, go to the door—"

He started out of his dream. The doorbell *was* ringing; the door was shaking under the force of a half-dozen fists; the vestibule was filled with the clack of noisemakers and the blast of horns. "Apples and nuts!" the children shouted in the fog. He flung the door wide, and let the darkness and the mist break in. There they were in their gaudy finery, their little faces floating in the shadow, confetti in their hair. Oh, he had loved her once. For his ten best years, he had loved her. Their paper bags crackled; their feet stamped on the tiled floor. Her flesh had been known and sweet. His cheek had lain against her shoulder, and there was nothing alien in her—known, known and sweet. And she was dead. And he, himself, must follow her, must be lost like all flesh in the rising of the inexorable sea . . .

The little pale boy in the red ruff stood in front of the rest. "Have you got any nuts or apples, Mister?" he said.

The two remote ones had come out of the dining room. They stood in the hall, watching the scene with their sea-cold eyes.

He turned upon them. "Where are the apples?" he asked in an old and shaken voice.

"The apples, Father? What apples?"

"Apples to give to the children."

"But we haven't any apples in the house," said the daughter-in-law. "Nobody here eats apples."

"Good lord!"

The boy wearing the red ruff was plainly frightened. "But last year and all the years before," he protested, "the lady gave us—"

A sudden quiet came upon the little crowd. One of the older girls had whispered, "Oh, but that was the lady who is dead."

THEY WENT AWAY discreetly then, as if the crape still hung upon the door. There was a long stretch of silence before the carnival noises began again, farther up the block. He stood staring at the two who stood at the other end of the hall.

"Why are there no apples?" He was amazed at himself. He had shouted it. "Why are there no apples in the house on a Halloween night?"

"I'm terribly sorry," said the soothing female voice. "It simply didn't occur to me. Nobody here cares for apples, and I—"

"That's a lie. *I* care for apples. I'm very fond of apples. I—" There were tears in his voice, the weak tears of the wounded, slighted, old. He opened the door of the hall cupboard and stepped into the dark, grasping at hanging sleeves, stumbling on overshoes. He found his own coat and jerked into it and started for the vestibule.

"Where are you going?" the son said.

"To buy some apples."

"But don't be foolish, Father. They won't be back any more tonight."

"Suppose I want the apples for myself?"

"Let me get them then."

"No."

"Let me drive you, at least."

"I can drive perfectly well myself. Let me alone."

He knew exactly where he would go to buy them. It was a store where they had shopped together, often, almost every Friday night. He had not gone into that store since the week after her death, when a clerk had commiserated with him over his loss. And afterward? he asked himself. He had never seen the finished mound of earth under the turbulent poplars. He did not know what graves were near her, or how the grass grew, or what was written on the stone. He wished to walk in the fog, among the dead. He who loathed all excessive words wished to hear himself saying aloud in the dark and the final silence, "I loved you while I could, and I have suffered, and now before I die you must have mercy and forgive."

ON THE FIRST morning in November, the sexton got up early. Halloween was a bad night for graveyards. Something was always the matter: confetti on tombstones, wreaths hung upside down, footprints in the whiteness of the rime. But this year they had outdone themselves. To save his life, he could not tell what kind of humor was behind it, why they should be there—the six bright apples arranged in a perfect circle upon the new and frosty grave.

Consider the Giraffe

IT WAS PRECISELY the right day for going to the zoo. "Precisely," like "asinine" and "intolerable," was one of her mother's words. Her father's were thicker and harder to find in the dictionary—"antediluvian," "agrarian," "bourgeoisie." Only these words and the conversations draped around them were permanent things. Everything else—furnished apartments, jobs, cities, rage, and tenderness—shifted from one month to the next. During last year she had been in the fourth grade in three different places, and knew that it was no use growing fond of the view from any window, the voice of any schoolmate, or the leaf shadows around any bed. Tomorrow or the day after tomorrow it would be necessary to be up and going again. The beloved four-poster would be lost; the ivy plant would stay behind on the abandoned windowsill. Only the conversations, thrown with differing degrees of success at different groups of people, were the same.

Anyhow, it was precisely the right day for going to the zoo.

There was enough sun to make you really want the cream of soda, and enough wind to dry the sweat on your forehead. The path was covered with jingling bits of light. The air parted the boughs and streamed down, and if you closed your eyes imaginary fingers stroked your hair. Here and there a maple tree, eager for autumn and yellow before the rest, broke upon you like an earthly sun. The caterpillar lay sleeping, curled in his cocoon on the bark, and you walked softly, not wanting to disturb his winter sleep. The park was beautiful enough; the park was a full week's share of loveliness. And the park was only a starter, like apple juice before a company dinner. After the park came the zoo.

Keeping far behind her father and mother, keeping out of the bluish shadow that trailed behind them on the walk, she thought how this holiday was a kind of miracle. Last night the zoo or anything pleasant had been out of the question. *They* had had one of their fights, screaming at each other in the midnight quiet of the apartment, so loudly that some neighbor had opened a window and shouted, "For God's sake!" They had still been fighting, hoarse now and in hissing whispers, when she fell asleep in the living room on the couch. But she had wakened in the muffling blackness that comes to unfamiliar rooms before daylight, and they had not been fighting *then*. A change, perceptible as a change in weather, had taken place. It was disturbing to waken to it, like wakening under February blankets to the thick, moist warmth of spring. Sounds, their sounds, were being made behind the bedroom door, small squeaks and bursts of laughter, soft inside sounds, like cats gurgling after food. She knew then that they had made friends again. Not as she and her playmates made friends, taking hands in the sight of the sun, but in some dark and terrifying way not possible in daylight—a business of the night.

Even though he had said that the biscuits were antediluvian and she had found the coffee intolerable, their truce had lasted through breakfast. "A magnificent day—magnificent," he had said, turning from the window and giving his wife a smart slap on the thigh. "What do you say! Shall we take Francie to the zoo?"

All morning they had been royally kind. They let her wear her scarlet jumper streaked with rabbits' hair. That gave her some color, her mother said; a good clear red seemed to take the strawiness out of her hair. Yes, said her father, more becoming all round—absolutely; not so much like a bag of bones. And now they had forgotten her entirely, which was even better. She jumped across a mossy log and could not feel her bones at all. She was smooth and all of one piece, like the sleek chipmunk racing down the lawn. She licked the last sweetness of the cream of soda from the corners of her lips, and whistled to herself.

First they went to see the hippopotamus who lived quiet like a lump of earth in a sky-green swimming pool. She could not tell why she liked him; he was really very ugly with his muddy, patchy skin and his little eyes; he blew large bubbles and had an amazingly big backside. Still, she thought she could have stayed for hours leaning her cheek against the rail and staring at the brown blob in the green water. He looked like Theodora's uncle. There was something peaceful about him. He never went anywhere. He stayed and stayed. Maybe he liked to open his eyes down there in the watery dark and see the same rough spots on the cement every day. Maybe . . .

"The Church of England to a T," her father said. "T. S. Eliot can always be depended upon to produce the perfect simile, the simile more factual than fact, more true than truth."

"Precisely," said her mother. "But don't you think she looks a little like Emma Fitzsimmons, too?"

She sighed over her own ignorance. She had made another blunder; she had taken a she for a he. The hippopotamus became what it had been in the beginning—a sexless chunk of mud, something indefinite enough to be like an English cathedral and Emma Fitzsimmons at the same time. They walked away, and she trailed after them without looking back at the little, stupid eyes.

They went to the front of the main building where the cages were, and she followed them with an old resignation. They were like that—she had been to other zoos with them in other cities—they always wanted to spend most of the time looking at the fierce ones, the ones behind bars. Afterwards they were too tired for her animals, the gentler ones, the jittery monkeys, the shy skittish zebras, the giraffes with the seeking eyes. This particular zoo had a new pair of black leopards. At the breakfast table they had talked about that. There was thunder somewhere in the line of cages, and she could tell by their eyes that they hoped it came from one of these black leopards, that somehow it would be more precious to them if it happened to be a black leopard's roar.

The insides of all the cages had an ancient, barren, Biblical look. Each of them had the same gray stone steps and the same stone-gray shadows. Flies could come in to sit on the tiger's moist nose and the lion's thick paw, but there was no way for the sunlight to get inside. These cages were vastly disheartening, like pictures of ruins. She kept thinking of something she had heard somewhere about lions creeping restlessly over a desert place where an old, old city had once been—a city with a wild name—Tyre, Nineveh, Babylon?

In the smoky grayness of the cage the soot-black leopards paced round and round, hissing with a noise like steam and glaring at people with their pale moonstone eyes. Her mother and father stayed as close to the cage as possible. They leaned on the railing and answered the dark creatures stare for stare. But she lagged behind in the shade of a kindly boxwood hedge and tried to think of pleasant matters: how fine the cream of soda had been, how clean the sky was, how red her jumper looked in the sun.

The roar *had* come out of those sleek and sinewy necks. Now they began it again, soft and gurgling at first, then stronger, more like a monstrous whine. She shivered and retreated against branches. The Bible had certainly gotten into the cage somehow; she saw the Devil twice, black and lithe and terrible, springing up on lean haunches, clawing at the bars.

"Primitive!" her father said. "The primal evil. In the beginning was Lucifer."

And her mother nodded and said, "Precisely. Yes, indeed."

But that would not be enough for her mother to say. Before they could leave this cage, before the pale Devil's eyes could be blotted out by some softer, more sorrowful animal stare, her mother would have to find something else, something clever. Today there was no war between them, and he would wait until she had said her say.

Meanwhile some change, disturbing and disturbingly familiar, took place behind the black bars. The leopards stopped clawing at the grating, they eased their long bodies languorously down; they paced back and forth in opposite directions, passing each other, brushing briefly against each other's sides. Their heavy paws beat softly on cement. They hissed whenever they met, but, moving apart, they made remembered noises in their throats, gurgling sounds that belonged in the middle of the night.

"Yes . . ." the mother said, and stretched her shoulders and turned her head from side to side.

"Ah . . ." said the father, smiling with a cold, knowing mouth.

The child, watching from the hedge, knew that this wisdom between them was a secret and had to do with he-ness and she-ness; the black leopards were a he and a she; their quarrel was over, and the whole park was about to become thick and damp with a nameless thing; day was to be turned inside out with a business of the dark.

Some of the other mothers and father made loud conversations and began to push their children toward a low building, a delightful place where you could see Malay sun bears with crew haircuts, and raccoons hung upside down. The path looked abandoned and tawdry now, cluttered with candy wrappers and the limp ends of ice cream cones. Only the three of them stayed behind in this emptiness, watching the two black Satans, the he and the she, at their angry tryst behind the bars.

Fear drove her back into the hedge, so that the branches crackled against her face. She wished to God that she might close her eyes, but she could not close her eyes. The creatures lunged at each other, collided in midair, and fell in a wriggling heap. Their mouths were hissing and drawn back; in the undulating mass of fur, you could see the whiteness of their teeth and the redness of their gums. One of them leaped at the other, buried his teeth in a black neck, soiled the clean day, the bright park, the whole world with throaty night-sounds . . .

"Oh, no!" she said.

Her mother called casually over her shoulder, "Don't be silly, Frances, they're only playing, they're doing that for pleasure."

"Shall we go along now?" her father asked. "I believe the show's over. I conclude the female's not in the mood for that particular variety of activity this afternoon."

Her mother dawdled, thoughtful, remote, still waiting for a cleverness.

One leopard came to the edge of the cage and thrust his sticky nose between the bars, into a slant of sun. The nose was not so terrible as it had seemed in shadow; it was really more brown than black; small, darker underpatches showed through.

The mother smiled. "A bad dye-job, that nose," she said. "Doesn't it look exactly like those figured curtains that Mrs. Moss had done over?"

He laughed and said, "Absolutely. Yes, indeed." And they turned to tell her it was about time to be getting on.

BY THE TIME that they had seen the lion and the condors and had waited for twenty minutes to see whether the peacock would scream, she began to think it would be better not to visit any of the other animals; she began to wish that she could go straight home. It was true that she had wanted particularly to see the giraffe. One of her teachers in Cleveland had said that he was a very tame animal who liked people and ate nothing but green leaves. Still, he would probably not like her; she did not like herself any more; she was covered with a sick, chilly sweat, and her knees felt watery and tired.

But they were in such a good humor. They had decided to have supper in a restaurant close by, and they were not hungry as yet, and it would be utterly stupid to run home. Didn't she want to see the giraffe? Hadn't she said so this morning at the breakfast table? Well, look, there will be plenty of time to rest before supper. And here is a bench right in front of the giraffe's cage, and isn't that fortunate, and now all of us can sit down . . .

For a long time she did not look at the giraffe. He was there somewhere, behind a wire fence in a small, sandy wilderness broken only by two young trees whose leaves were still green. But she did not care to see him. She sat on the end of the bench and leaned her head against the wood and spread her handkerchief over her eyes to keep out the sun. She would often sit like this, creating a closed circle of dimness for herself, feeling the cloth move up and down against her cheeks and eyelids, gently, with her breath. She called this "making a place"; wherever you went, you could always get a handkerchief, and then you could have a place. Under the handkerchief there was a warmth and a glow, and she was far away from *them* and from everything. Their voices, talking at the other end of the bench, seemed to be coming from a separate star.

"Concerning the giraffe," he was saying, "he's one of God's most witless creatures."

She sighed under the handkerchief. She was glad to have gotten that straight from the start; this giraffe was a he.

"Absolutely witless, and so mild that he probably wouldn't swallow a fly if it walked halfway down his tongue. He's herbivorous, you know. Eats green leaves—"

"And grass?" said the mother-voice, eager to get its two cents' worth of curious learning in.

"Not grass. No, indeed. Absolutely nothing off the ground." He was masculine and lordly now. "Look at him, and your common sense will tell you why."

"That silly neck? Too much trouble to get it down?"

"Trouble, my darling? Nothing so minor as trouble, I can assure you. A giraffe with his neck down is as good as a dead giraffe. He can't get it up again with any speed at all. That's why he's thirsty most of the time. He's afraid to drink. He goes for days without water, and you can imagine, in equatorial heat . . ."

She knew that word from her fourth-grade geography book. In the still place that she had made for herself, she imagined equatorial heat. There was a long, tan stretch of sandy earth, covered with smoky, weedy plumes. Here and there were little trees with a few fine leaves. For a while it was completely empty and still, and the giraffes came down. They came softly, gently, walking through weeds on their delicate feet. The great red sun burned upon them. All the lengths of their necks were dry with thirst, dry as sand. But they did not shove each other. They waited courteously, and each one had his small green spray and sucked the moisture out of it, as she had sucked a healing bitterness from the boxwood leaf.

"After a while, of course, the thirst gets to be too much for them. They have to go down to the water hole. They go in droves, for moral support, I suppose, because, of course, they're utterly useless to each other. And then, when they've got their necks down and their tongues in the water, their backs are an invitation to whatever happens to be around. The tigers leap at them—"

And the black leopards, too, she thought.

She waited until her mouth stopped shaking and then took the handkerchief away from her face.

"Had a nice rest?" her mother said. "See, all you needed was a little quiet. And now, what are you going to do?"

"I think I'll go and look at the giraffe."

"Do, by all means."

She went slowly up to the cage, hoping that the giraffe would come close enough for her to see his eyes.

The place where the giraffe lived was more open than she had supposed. They knew he was a mild creature, and they had not closed him in too much. The room between the wire fence and the iron railing was only the length of her arm, and the diamonds of space between the crisscross wires were as big as her hand. Other children were standing close to the rail with their mothers and fathers, and nobody looked troubled or afraid. A dark Italian guard in a visored cap stood by, shaking his head at a little boy who looked as if he might throw a handful of peanuts between the wires.

It would have been better, she thought, if the guard had not been there. She recalled the time when, in a Philadelphia museum, just such a cap had borne down upon her because she had touched the toe of a kind, plump Virgin made of painted wood. She consoled herself with the thought that she had no peanuts or anything that could be mistaken for peanuts, and she leaned her elbows on the railing and stared into the giraffe's place, the quiet square of tan that had been made for him—in an alien country, to be sure, but at least away from black leopards and such. He was on the other side of the sandy stretch, beyond the fragile tree. She could not see him very well, and she amused herself with wondering whether he had to get his neck down often here. Maybe the people in charge of the zoo knew how hard it was for him to do that. Maybe they held his bucket up to him on a stick. And if they didn't, maybe they should be told in an anonymous letter, and then maybe they would.

While she was making up an anonymous letter, all the other children drew in their breaths and said "Oh!" and she knew that the giraffe was coming from the other side of his place. She lifted her face and saw him, even taller than she had expected, his neck so long, his delicate nose held so high, that a person could imagine him nibbling at the stars. He walked very slowly, with a graceful forward lurch. He made no clouds of dust with his little elegant feet. Now it seemed to her that she had never known anything about a giraffe before. She had thought he would be spotted, brown on beige. Instead, his colors were laid upon him in fine, soft squares. The closer he came, the more she delighted in this coloring. It was as if his hide had been made in two layers, one creamy and pale, the other crisp and reddish brown. Maybe the dark upper layer had been too fragile for the equatorial heat. It had cracked into blocks, like the glaze on the Chinese pottery she had seen at Mrs. Moss's house. It had cracked, and the tan under layer was foaming through. Such a soft belly too, that creamy tan; and, flashing past her, moist with a dream of plentiful springs, two great brown eyes . . .

"Oh, my darling, oh, my beautiful," she said, holding the iron rail in her fists and pulling herself back and forth for pure joy.

It was as if he had heard her voice. He did not stay on the other side. He did not stop to sniff at the small tree. He made his swaying, processional way all round the inner side of the barrier of wire. She pressed hard against the rail. The other children, the guard, the two sitting on the bench behind her, the park, the whole world fell away. Her arms went up in a gesture of utter gratefulness. The giraffe had stopped just in front of her; he was looking at her; she was drowned in his sweet, wet glance. A warm brown well of sorrow and gentleness closed over her, and she was forever safe, everlastingly beloved.

"Oh, my sweet giraffe," she said, straining her body toward him across the railing, stretching the tips of her fingers to the highest wire she could hope to touch. Then she told him, not with her voice, only with her lips, that he was all the impossible things: all the friends from whom she had been taken, all the hands she had never touched, father and mother, unborn brother and sister, dear love, dear sad love.

There was an amazed chatter among the others around the railing. It was really remarkable, now wasn't it? The giraffe wanted to make friends with the little girl in the red jumper. Just look, he was stepping backward, he was getting his head down as far as he could, he was thrusting his soft, drooping nose into one of the spaces between the wires. Even so, they could not quite meet, they could not quite touch. There were two inches of space between the tender nose and the raised hand.

"Do watch yourself, darling," a stout lady said. "You might lose a finger. You never can tell."

"Not him, not him," she chanted, swaying on her toes. "He's herbivorous, he never eats anything but leaves, and look at his eyes, he's good, he's kind."

He strove, and she strove with him, sensing the rasp of the wire against his nose. Her fingers trembled with the strain; pain ran round the socket of her shoulder like a ripple of fire.

Another breathless "Oh!" rose out of the throats of the watchers. The giraffe had found a way. He was bridging the empty space by thrusting out his tongue. It came out slowly, clean and moist and beautiful. It was a pale mauve color, and it turned silvery in the sunlight. It was warm. Its warmth and wetness advanced upon her, reached her, bestowed a long kiss on the center of her palm.

Then something shot across the wonder and the delight. She did not know at first what had come between her and her love; she knew only that the love was over, and that now she must feel what she had always felt at the end of any love—loneliness and shame. The dark hand that had shoved the giraffe's nose back was the guard's hand. The shadow of his visored cap was lying near her on the cement.

"You mustn't do that, sister," the guard said.

She did not dare to look about her; there were so many staring eyes. She put her head down so far that her chin rested against the front of her jumper. "He wouldn't have bitten me," she said through the cottony mass of ache in her throat. "He was only licking my hand. He eats leaves. He doesn't bite."

"No, that's right. You're a smart girl. You know your animals, all right. He wouldn't hurt you, but you might hurt him."

I? Oh, no, how could that be, with so much love?

"You see, he's a very sensitive fellow. One little germ, and he's a goner. Now, I'm not saying your hands aren't clean. But you can't see germs. With germs, you never know."

They had risen and were coming up behind her. Her shoulders hunched against them. Their steps were soft upon the grass. And why was it so terrible? Why did she think that they had white, moonstone eyes?

"You must excuse her. Really, I thought she had better sense than that," her mother said.

She walked in front of them, away from the giraffe's home. She kept her hand closed in a fist. The moisture was still there; she still carried his kiss. All down the long path, longer because of the looks that were being turned upon her, she felt the wet glance trying to follow her. She wanted to turn to answer it, but her head was down. She had been to the deep brown pool and had swallowed a sweet drink. But now the time of drinking was over, and she could not raise her head.

"You certainly made an ass of yourself over that animal," said her father.

"But doesn't she always?" her mother said.

For weeks after that, she went about asking people questions about germs. She looked up the word in forbidding encyclopedias in unfamiliar libraries. She spent her candy money on the morning and evening papers and looked wildly up and down the columns, expecting every moment to see that the giraffe had died. Then one day she actually found an article about the giraffe. She saw his picture first and felt the cold squeeze of fear around her heart. But it was nothing; the giraffe was not dead; only he was a little unhappy because his keepers had not been able to find him a mate.

"I am your mate and your sister and your mother," she said to the picture, cutting it out with a borrowed pair of scissors in the art room at school. The teacher gave her a piece of red cardboard to paste it on and told her that it would make a beautiful bookmark. She pretended that it was a bookmark and kept it in her room in a story book.

But then they moved again, to a far city, and in the confusion the book was lost. Nothing was left but the remembrance of the silvery tongue brushing against her palm. Her mother, coming in to see that she was well covered on the winter nights, wondered why she always fell asleep with her hand pushed hard against her lips.

The Mirror

L ONG AFTERWARD, WHEN the incident had become a matter
for quiet consideration and grave questioning, she asked
herself why she had chosen to eat her lunch in that particular
place. After the morning's cataclysm, she did not care whether
she took her butter hard from a mound of cracked ice or melting from a greasy plate; in fact, she did not want any food at all.
Yet something had drawn her, and she had a need to name it.

Now at last she did name it. It was the great mirror, the
pitiless, sun-harshened looking-glass that stretched from the
floor to the ceiling. She had come to the restaurant in search
of an image of herself—not, certainly, to preen and admire.
She had never in her life been less vain or had smaller cause
for vanity. As the owner of a ruined merchantman might come
down to the docks to see his ship after a night of fire, so she
came to look at herself. As one might say to himself by way
of consolation, "At least the hull is left," so she stared into the
mirror and thought: I am still elegant.

Elegant she was—spare, gray and light—as inoffensive as a
handful of ashes left in the glow when the wood is burned away.
Nothing about her had spoiled; everything had dried and faded.

Her ankles were thin; her figure was slight as a girl's; her hands were nimble and delicate upon the cloth. If he had chosen to put her still further away from him, if he had seen fit to marry a child half her age and less than half his own, it was because of certain inevitable lacks, and not because of any disagreeable qualities which she possessed.

She had not grown brittle in the manner of the majority of clever women. She had merely paled like a fresco that retreats from too much light, that sinks back into the peaceful grayness of the wall. She had served him less and less obtrusively through twenty years. As his need for her had increased, the degree to which she was in evidence had quietly declined.

In the days when she was his stenographer, she had merited his easy, offhanded gallantry. As his secretary, she had owned his affection. As his office manager, she had claimed his respect. And as his partner, she could be the first to know of his extraordinary good fortune—how a girl, mind you, an innocent, eager, half-awakened girl, had consented all too kindly to shut herself away in his autumnal world. She had been told as much on the same morning.

Now, with the conversation of strangers flowing around her, with the menu before her and the water glass cold under her fingertips, she wondered whether he had seen the dry collapse, the fall of burnt-out timbers, the light drift of ashes behind her eyes.

She turned her head to the right and stared shamelessly into the mirror, looking for signs. There was the same spare face with nothing to damn it save a small bend at the bridge of the nose, and nothing to commend it save a gentle expectancy, a soft attentiveness; an singularly harmonious face, kind and on good terms with itself.

But could it possibly remain so, now that he was quite beyond her reach? She doubted it. She could not see herself looking kind tomorrow and day after tomorrow while he whistled and remembered his nights. She could not see herself moving with the old serenity through the changeless days, with nothing to draw her forward except the grave. She closed her eyes and saw the predestined ravages, the tightened mouth, the restless eyes, the sharp lines running from the corners of the nose to the corners of the lips . . .

"MAY I PLEASE serve you?" the voice said.

It was a strident voice, and it belonged to a strident person. The waitress, young and dark and as overblown as a late June peony, stood in a splash of light and was more painfully blatant than the sun.

How long she had been there, it was hard to say, but she had the air of one who has been kept waiting for half an hour. She was opulent, Mediterranean. Her black hair was piled like a cluster of grapes on the top of her head. Her mouth was painted thick and wide. The flap of her white pinafore was thrust outward upon the rich curves of her breasts. There was a disturbing combination of stupidity and arrogance in her big, animal eyes. They stared insolently, and yet the woman they stared at could have sworn that they saw nothing at all.

"I'm sorry, I haven't decided yet," she said.

The waitress sighed.

For the space of several heartbeats, they stared at each other. The girl's face was blank; it was impossible to study the menu in the presence of this heavy impassivity.

"I can't decide yet. Mayn't I look a little?"

"Certainly," the waitress said in a voice that implied: What can I say but "Certainly"? She thrust her order pad into her apron pocket, plainly reminding herself that she would soon have the trouble of taking it out again. The she stepped back, jarring the table with her hip, and was gone.

The older woman turned back to the menu and read the list of salads through, without knowing what she read. A persistent image of the waitress intruded between herself and the thought

101

of food. A strange, not altogether savor tinge—a kind of vague taint—had been added to her wretchedness. "What is the matter with me?" she asked herself. "How is it that she annoys me so?"

She looked at the bold light on the ceiling, the view of the park through the great glass bay, and the two sprigs of verbena that stood stiffly in a vase on her table. She played with her gloves, admired her soft gray purse, looked at her pale and subtle manicure. But nothing could quite remove the unpleasant flavor of the past minute. She took herself in hand and decided to order a fresh fruit salad in a pleasant voice.

The girl came back, walking with a firm, catlike stride. Her hips swayed. The hips seemed particularly loathsome and evoked the same troubling distaste. It is very strange, the woman thought. She has not given me any real cause. . . . And yet it was rude, it was unquestionably rude, the tone of her voice when she said "Certainly."

"Have you decided?" It was plain that the girl expected the worst. When she saw the nod, her eyes shifted in a dim, primal indication of surprise.

"Yes, a fruit salad."

"A *fresh* fruit salad?"

"Yes, please, fresh fruit."

"That," the waitress said, "will take half an hour. You'll have to wait half an hour for them to make it. It takes that long."

"To make a fruit salad?" The woman's dislike tightened her throat; her voice had a metallic ring.

"Yes. I might as well tell you. If I didn't tell you, and you waited half an hour, that would bother you more."

The implication of the speech was, of course, that she would be more upset by waiting without knowing why than by waiting in complete possession of the facts of the case. Yet for the fraction of a second, she had put another interpretation upon the matter. It seemed to her that the girl had pointed out that she was already overwrought and that further waiting would bring her close to public collapse.

"I haven't time to wait," she said coldly. "I'll have something else."

"What else would you like to have?"

Anything, anything to get this wounding presence out of sight! "A grilled cheese sandwich, I suppose."

"Anything to drink?"

"Iced tea."

"Thank you," said the girl. She wrote upon the order pad, bending her head and thrusting out the tip of her tongue. She wrote like one who had learned the skill with difficulty and practiced it only through the lower grades of the public schools. The pencil was stubborn in her hand. An ignorant fool, to be disregarded.

Other pains, less transitory but less undignified, crowded into the silence which she left behind her. The great mirror to the left of the table reflected culture, poise, the assailed but invincible elegance. She will be flabby when she reaches forty, she thought. They'll sag—those hips, those breasts. And all at once she found herself wondering what sort of figure *she* had—the young and fortunate one, his bride.

All cultivated young women looked more or less alike these days. *She* would look very like all the others; for instance, like either of the two girls who had just sat down at the next table. They were almost indistinguishable from each other, with their long brown legs, narrow brown faces, and silky, floating light-brown hair.

THEY HAD PLAINLY come to lunch from the summer classes at the university. They were burdened with possessions—books, notebooks, pencils, babushkas, purses and odd pages of class-room scrawl. They laid their books and notebooks on the padded leather bench, so close to her that they almost grazed her thigh.

Into her hard-won quiet came their chatter: "And after we

got to the house, when we were on the porch, he caught my hand so I couldn't ring the bell, and he said, 'Don't, it's so beautiful around here. Let's walk around the block just once more before . . .'"

Good Lord, she thought, what a flat little voice, without the overtones that come with understanding, without the nuances that come with suffering. Running around the block after ecstasy—and quite unripe for ecstasy. Why were these two young women attending the summer classes, anyway? Probably to make up the failures of their lyric springtime, probably because of stupidity. Half of the content of that fresh perfume is sheer stupidity. And *she* will say to *him*, "But I can't add figures, darling." And *he* will say to *her*, "Never mind, I'll add them. Why should you trouble your exquisite little head?"

The light brown heads had come close together over the sugar bowl. "So I'm going to wash my hair before he comes tomorrow, and wear my tweed skirt, and maybe you'd lend me your canary-colored sweater, because I . . ."

Where—*where* was the cheese sandwich? How long would it be necessary to sit here listening to this light April twitter? When would they look at their menus and be still?

Then, almost as if she had shouted her thoughts into their faces, they ceased their chatter. "Sh!" one of them said softly, nodding over the other's shoulder. "Marie's coming."

They bent their heads over the yellow cards and were so strangely, disturbingly still that she had to find out who it was that evoked this quiet. It was the waitress—her waitress, the one of the succulent flesh and the clustering hair. She stood behind them, broad, menacing, with her pencil held over her order pad.

Was it possible, the woman wondered, that this vulgar girl tyrannized over the trade in general? They actually seemed afraid; their little mouths had taken on that petulant droop with which youth protects itself.

"Hello, Marie," one of them said in a hangdog voice.

"Hello. Don't ask for the deviled crabs because there aren't any more," the waitress said.

"Oh, we don't want deviled crabs." It was as if the girl fearfully disclaimed any such naughtiness. "We just want vegetable salads and biscuits and tea."

"All right."

"Can we have them in a hurry?" The request was frightened; it was tentative. "We've only got half an hour."

"All right. Right away." Marie wrote it all down slowly, moving the moist, red tip of her tongue, and went her way.

"She'll get it for us in a hurry, just like yesterday," one of the young girls said. "As I was telling you, that canary-colored sweater has a spot on the shoulder, but you could cover it up with some kind of a doodad, a pin or something, you know."

Fear of a waitress, the woman thought, might be despicable, but it certainly yielded profits in this place. Her fruit salad had been a staggering problem, a project that would consume half an hour. But their vegetable salad could be rustled up in three minutes and served right away. Before she would come again to this particular restaurant, she must, like the boy in the fairy tale, learn to shudder.

She turned her head to the mirror and assumed the young girls' disconsolate look—the half-closed eyes, the drooping lips. It was a wounding image that came back to her from the surface of the pitiless glass. Such looks can appear with impunity only upon the face of the young. She sighed and watched the expression falling away. She waited to see the old tranquility, the gentle and integrated set of features that she had borne like a fair banner, a symbol of her good intentions, into offices and living rooms, theaters and restaurants and libraries, all her days. She waited and put a chilly hand to her forehead and moistened her cold lips. There was a change; something was lost; the serenity of her face had fallen away.

•

THERE WAS A cat tread and a muttered "Excuse me." She snatched up her menu to make way for the food and saw at once that the food was not for her. The damnable vegetable salads were being set upon her neighbors' table. *Their* napkins were being slapped upon the cloth, *their* dish of lemon was being banged against *their* iced tea. An icy rage, such a rage as she had never felt before, stiffened her to her fingertips. The menu fell from her rigid hand, grazed the table, lay, like a glove thrown before a duel, upon the floor.

"I beg your pardon," she said, glaring at the waitress.

"Yes?" the waitress said.

The brazen detachment of it, the plain fact that the hateful female did not care in the least—the "Yes?" was too much.

"I have been waiting here for close to half an hour. I asked to have a fruit salad, and that was impossible. I asked for a cheese sandwich and that has not appeared. Although I hardly feel disposed to enter into controversy over this trivial business—" There was a strange, hot pleasure in using words that this vulgarian could not understand—"I should like to inquire—"

"Your cheese sandwich," said the waitress, glaring back with smoldering, animal eyes, "isn't done. It isn't done."

"When will it be done?"

"I don't know."

There was a birdlike confusion, a stirring of napkins, a hastening of breaths at the neighboring table. One of the smooth little faces turned in the woman's direction and sent her a shy, fluttering look of supplication. *Oh, don't, don't!* The words might have been spoken, they made themselves so clear in the young girl's glance. And they accomplished at least some part of their purpose. They kept her silent with surprise for a second, and in that second the waitress gained time to make a sullen apology.

"The first one got burned. I'm sorry it got burned," she said.

She left all three of them in a wretched state. The young girls, embarrassed and contrite, did penance for their undeserved food. They could not eat it; they buttered their biscuits and let them lie; they stirred their tea endlessly and could not bring themselves to lift their glasses to their lips. Their twittering, too, had fallen to a kind of mechanical, halfhearted chirp. They reserved their dearest thoughts as they reserved their salads.

Now their conversation was all of a certain assignment. They had unfolded a map on which they were to trace the movements of contending armies up the boot of Italy. They bent over this map with feigned attention; they discussed it with forced vivacity. But they glanced up from it several times each minute, watching with worried eyes for Marie's return.

THE WOMAN SHOULD have been sorry for them. She told herself that their happiness was, at best, brief and precarious. He who would come to one of them tomorrow, to be enchanted by a borrowed yellow sweater and the sheen of new-washed hair, might well come only once or twice and then be irretrievably gone. Even in the isolation of her grief, even in the discreet stillness of this restaurant, she could not escape from war. No thought could wade out for any distance in these austere days without stepping into a pool of blood. And yet, and yet . . .

There they sat, beautiful and wanted, with a thousand possibilities hovering like bright butterflies about their heads; and here she sat, in October dryness, with even the last sad moth flown.

There they were, all of them, all you and all in league with one another, all sisters in spirit, whose veins were filled with the living, golden liquid of youth. These two, and that one who had taken away her beloved. These two and the coarse, dark, Mediterranean one whom they protected. These, and her nieces, and the new stenographers in the office, and the college girls in the street. All, all of them, brushing their glossy hair at a thousand mirrors; closing their firm white arms around the necks of a legion of lovers; smiling their sweet, vague, stupid smiles among the foliage of parks all over the world; moving their lithe bodies to the tune of cheap recordings; chattering, singing, kissing, sinking down on a thousand couches, a thousand bits of leaf-sheltered turf, to know that ecstasy which she had never known . . .

"Excuse me."

She started at the voice. Her own lean knee struck against the table leg, and the water glass shook. The brown face was too close. The girl had bent to set the sandwich down. Her neck was repellent—soft, full; there were creases in it when she turned her head; the hair at the nape had escaped in coarse, glossy curls. A musky sweetness tainted the air around her. The dark finger that settled the plate wore a broad band, an obvious, boastful wedding ring. The neck—how many times the neck must have been kissed!

She turned from the waitress to the plate. The sandwich was burned. The edges were black. And the hateful girl knew as much, had turned her back, was scurrying like a scared cat across the floor.

"One minute, please!"

How loudly had she said it? The distant diners straightened above their food, became absorbed in their newspapers, stared resolutely at the view of the park beyond the glass. Both the pale brown heads turned her way. "Oh, don't, don't, please, don't," the two pairs of eyes said at once. The disconsolate droop, the silly looseness, came upon their childish lips.

THE WAITRESS, FRIGHTENED out of all arrogance, like an animal that has been shouted at and can only creep back to take its beating, returned to the table.

"The sandwich is burnt."

"I know. It got burnt while I was talking to you about the other one. It—"

"You know? What sort of answer is that—you know?"

"I can't help it if it is burnt. I can't be two places at once. I can't—I can't—I—"

And suddenly the whole hushed, respectable room was filled with the sound of passionate Latin weeping. Raw grief had broken upon them all, like a salt and icy tidal wave. They all turned and looked reproachfully at the elegant woman who had let this harsh, primeval confusion in. Above all the moving things—the fluttering menus, the turning heads, the hands going up in consternation, she saw the mirror and the face in the mirror—face of an old woman, face of a harpy, hovering above all of it, staring upon it with hungry, baleful, cold, malicious eyes.

She who was to borrow a yellow sweater found her courage and her voice. "Oh, don't! Marie's in awful trouble," she said.

"Who cares? Who cares about that? Nobody cares about that," the waitress wailed. Then she raised her apron to cover her mottled face and was gone.

The silence which followed her exit into the kitchen was not so much a silence as a general sigh. Everybody sighed and waited. They waited for the hostess, the restorer of decency, the agent of human dignity. And after a short delay—for discussion with the guilty party in the kitchen, no doubt—the hostess came, a blond and tailored peacemaker, with perfect curls on the top of her head and a neat little bunch of lace under her chin.

"Is anything the matter?" she said. The question was so evidently ridiculous that she did not wait for an answer. "I hope you'll excuse it," she said and smiled.

Suddenly the aging and elegant lady on the other side of the table found that she, herself, was on the point of tears. The wild, salty grief was pulling her along with it, like a tide. She wanted to run to the kitchen, to howl aloud as the poor brown wretch must be howling now. She wished to be gone, but she knew that she could not leave the restaurant without knowing what it was—the awful trouble that Marie was in.

The hostess moved a little closer and said in a hushed

voice, "She's very difficult, I know. She's been terribly rude to a number of our guests—these girls, here, can tell you—and yet we can scarcely let her go under the circumstances. She's been with us five years. And only last week, her husband was reported killed in Sicily."

The dark, moist curls—the poor, kissed neck—the blatant wedding ring. "Oh how terrible!" the woman said.

For a thin, attenuated moment the hostess stood waiting for some suitable phrase to come into her head—some felicitous sentence that would polish the roughness from the occasion. And in that moment, the woman thought how everything is bearable, everything is even blessed and fortunate, everything this side of death.

He is not dead, she thought. Tomorrow he will stand beside me when I crumble the bread for the pigeons that come to the office windowsill. I will hand my coat beside his on the rack, and, in the touching cloth, our arms will touch. There is still the possibility that he will be on the next bus, at the next concert, around the corner of the next street. He is not for me, but he still *is*. He moves about; he speaks; his breath comes and goes, making a precious thing of the air I breathe. When I lift the account book from his desk tomorrow, I will find upon it the living warmth of his hand. He might be dead. So many are dead in places whose names I do not know, under strange trees, in foreign ground . . .

"Will you excuse her?" the hostess said.

"There's nothing to excuse. Please ask her to excuse me. I came here in a bad humor, because of some small trouble. It was entirely my fault. I—"

The felicitous phrase had come at last. The hostess delivered it with a flourish of her piled curls. "I *knew* you'd be gracious about it," she said.

"I? Why?"

It was a bald question and demanded something more than a pretty answer. The hostess blushed a little and said, "If you don't mind my saying so, you have a kind face." That phrase, too, she had turned with a neatness that surprised herself. Rosy with embarrassment and complacency, she bowed and went back to her station at the door.

THE WOMAN ROSE and left a tip on the table. It took her a long time to pull on her gloves and find her purse, because she did not see anything that her hands touched. Her eyes stared straight into the long, harsh mirror. At first they were dimmed—dilated by the impact of what had passed; but slowly they focused and saw the image bright and plain, a pale face, aging but tender, grateful and well-meaning, at peace with itself.

A few of the diners could not keep themselves from glancing in her direction. It was part of her penance, she thought, that they should see the shine of risen tears in her eyes. She bore her face through the restaurant like a fair banner, and the girl who wanted to borrow a yellow sweater lifted her young brown head and smiled—smiled beautifully at her as she passed.

The Mourners

"**D**ARLING," SHE SAID, sitting up in bed and turning toward the big shadows of buckeye leaves that were rocking on the wall. "Look, the storm's over, and the moonlight's back, and the leaves are here again, growing all over the looking glass and the ceiling and everything. Oh, darling, isn't it beautiful in this room tonight?"

She was a slight young woman, but when she sat up like that she jiggled the mattress and jarred him out of his rest. Not that he had been sleeping. He, too, had seen the last flicker of the lightning and heard the slow, sonorous recessional of the May thunder moving to the west. He had breathed the scent of buckeye blossom, borne into the room like the curtain, on a fresh wind, and had listened to the drops falling slowly, separately, like flute notes, from the ends of the floppy leaves beyond the window. But to him this was background music, a pleasantly vague accompaniment to the dramatic action going on in his own brain. In the three years of his marriage, he had learned to take advantage of the fact that his mind was particularly keen and fertile after love. He cherished the clean privacy that comes when one moves back to one's own unwrinkled pillow. In these

113

first moments of renewal and rest, confusion fell away and ideas emerged to him in classic nakedness. The form and spirit of some of his most brilliant lectures had evolved in that shadowy, satisfied quietness. Tonight he had seen exactly how to make it plain to them in class tomorrow—the phoenix-birth of a new civilization from the ashes of what purported to be a finality, a death. The upward flight of the Renaissance, the beating of the flame-tipped wings out of the black medieval pyre. Provence, the Albigenses, and the troubadours—when, damn it, she had rocked the bed.

"Are you sleeping, darling?"

"No, not exactly."

Try as he would, he had never learned to lie to her, even in minute and insignificant matters. There was in her young, ardent face—he had seen it from the beginning when she was his student staring at hint from the front row—a certain solemnity which turned the least compromise into a piece of cruel deception. She had always been in dead earnest about everything. Without turning his head, he looked at her over the ridge of his pillow. Transitory glimpses of her emerged out of the swaying masses of shadows: a thin shoulder, the long line of her throat, a small, virginal breast, gleam of her smooth red hair, gleam of her large, grave eyes. At the moment she was in dead earnest about the moonlight and the thunder. Tomorrow she would turn the same rapt arid solemn look upon the Brahms "Intermezzi" that Koblanski was teaching her to play. Sound of the piano in an empty house through six or seven wordless, pointless hours . . .

Her hands came down through dark and glimmer and played with the blanket over her knees, "Well, go to sleep," she said.

"Really, dear, you ought to be asleep, yourself." He did not approve of his own voice. There was something high-minded and professorial in it. It made him acutely aware of himself: a long, flat man, distinguished, certainly, but somehow out of tune with the melting May night; a spar of bone and lax muscle and meager flesh lying athwart the round, shifting shadows; a scholar in bed, a lover with limitations, his nose cutting into the moist, luminous atmosphere, the moonlight on his thinning hair.

"I know. But I can't go to sleep. I can't lie still. It's so beautiful in this room tonight."

Her restlessness was a reproof to him. Under the circumstances, it was unthinkable to go on with the troubadours. He relinquished the whole russet-and-scarlet world of Provence, and reached for her hand and held it against his chest. He could feel her pulse racing under his fingertips. Yes, she was drunken on long drafts of spring weather, sweetly tipsy on rich, pollinated air. It would be a long time before she would fall asleep tonight.

"Darling," she said.

"Yes?"

"I think I'm going to have a toothache."

"Now, you are not. You only imagine it. You imagined yourself into an earache—remember, when we came home from Koblanski's last Saturday night?" A person wondered about these aches of hers. It was as if some nameless distress floated in her, seeking a home for itself—a kind of wandering, easeless pain.

"Well, my ear *does* ache, even now. The whole side of my face aches, all the way up and down."

"Perhaps I'd better close the window. Maybe you're in a draft."

"Oh, no!" There was wretchedness in her voice. That he could think of shutting them out—the swish of wind in the wet foliage, the thick, fragrance of the pyramids of buckeye blossoms, the tinkle of the rolling, sliding drops. "Please don't put the window down. Just look at that curtain. Isn't it lovely—billowy, like a sail on a sailboat. Sometimes when there's wind and the shadows go up and down like this, I feel as if we were on a boat, it makes me think of the sea."

He thought of the sea. Navigation—the cartographers—
the fragile galleons moving out into that vast, inscrutable waste
of waters lying to the west. Without them, without the golden
scorpions of Mexico and the fragrant redwoods of Peru, the
Renaissance would never have flowered to the extent—

"Darling." Her hand, under his, tugged at the matted hair
on his chest. "Are we going anywhere this summer?"

He remembered New York. The imperial avenues, the
clean angles of the buildings, the radiance of the air, tonic with
salt and sun. That air alone was invaluable. It was a solvent.
Immersed in it, all husks and encrustations melted away, and
only the essential, the hidden, the long-sought answer, remained.
Walking along Riverside Drive, with the Hudson on the left and
the city on the right, suddenly, miraculously, a man saw and
understood.

"*Are* we, darling?"

And the libraries, the serene, high-windowed rooms, the
efficient, inexhaustible flow of books, the smell of old pages
that only scholars' hands have touched . . .

"Are we going away for the whole summer?"

Her voice had changed. It had taken on some of the liquid
richness of the May weather. He detected longing in it, and
melancholy. He reminded himself that she also had her dreams;
and he wondered what panorama of lighted streets, hurrying
rivers, or impenetrable wilderness was rolling out before her
grave eyes.

"I thought we'd spend the summer in New York," he said.

She was silent. He thought that her very heartbeats had been
suspended. The hand on his chest was utterly still.

"Was there some place you wanted to visit, dear?'"

"Oh, no," she said, and all the yearning had turned to resignation, and all the softness had turned to brittleness. "Any place
at all. New York would be very nice."

And now that he was alert and wakeful now that his mind
was darting after the name of the trouble that had sounded in

her voice, just now she chose to withdraw her hand and make preparations for sleep. She beat her pillow into smoothness, lay down on her back, pushed her hair away from her face, folded her hands on the coverlet. He watched her over the edge of his pillow, and the sight of her lying so still in the flux of light and shadow begot in him an old uneasiness. It was as if she had laid her crossed hands between herself and the ominous forward-surging of her dreams; it was as if she had muffled her ears in linen and down to shut out an oncoming sound. What sound? Magical tune plucked on thin strings behind the opaque curtain that hangs between the dream and the waking mind? Sound of approaching feet? Rustle of leaves in a lost garden? A voice? A name? The wind spread the boughs of the buckeye tree apart, and for the fraction of a second her whole face showed plain. In a museum, in what city he could not remember, he had seen a face like that. Head in ancient marble, yellowed from lying too long—in the earth, wan for want of sun . . .

She sighed.

"What's the matter, love?"

"Nothing. My ear aches."

The devil it does, he thought. Out of the remnants of our little fire, some phoenix-dream went up for you tonight. Where did it fly—to what city, what house, what waiting hands? Tomorrow you will catch it again and put it in its place. Domesticated phoenix, fed on our morning toast, our evening tea. And Koblanski will help you to make a cage for it out of interlocking chords and arpeggios and such—

"Darling, do you love anybody? Anybody but me, I mean." she said.

"No, of course not." He smiled a wry smile against his pillow. "I'm not insatiable, my dear."

"Am I?"

He felt that this was an occasion for laughter. But he could not produce the appropriate sound. "I don't suppose you are," he said.

"I never in my life want to love anybody but you."

She said the sentence very softly, but it seemed to him that the whole room rang with her voice. The moment was white, revealing, like the first flash of lightning that had startled them earlier at their kissing. Oh, he had never been a man to find an idea piecemeal, to fit it together facet by facet, painfully and consciously. Much that he had learned in his scholarly years had been learned without his sensing the process of the learning. Then, in a split second, the knowledge sprang forth—mature and complete, like Athena from the forehead of Zeus. With a terrible certainty he knew what ailed her—he knew it now.

"Never anybody but you, my darling," she said.

There she lay, the poor little wretch, holding off the advancing, inexorable armies of her dreams, lying to him and to herself. She wanted the young Slav, her tooth ached after Koblanski, New York was as good as any other place since *he* was here in this moon-drenched, pollen-fragrant town and nothing but loneliness was in any other part of the earth. He wondered at nothing now except the fact that he had not seen it before. The brilliant new colleague, solitary, affectionate, with the noise of a toppling Europe, still crashing in his ears. The young man, the creator, more pianist than musicologist, conjuring out of the golden warmth of Brahms a vision of generation. And she so cloistered, she so cold . . .

He was afraid to touch her. Suddenly she was rare and cherished, and the feel of her flesh might make him know the measure of his loss.

"You must never think I don't love you, dear child," he said.

She startled him then. She came to him with urgency and vehemence, flinging herself against him, pulling the blanket awry. She invaded the privacy of his pillow. She clung to him, arm and knee and little clasping feet. And he did not know how to deal with her: he found himself wishing that she had stayed on the other side of the bed; he wanted to work in peace with the naked and significant thoughts that were racing through his mind. He thought of his spare and scholarly years, how a little had always been enough—a little food, a little companionship, a little sleep. For those to whom a little is enough, an abundance may be an embarrassment. He patted her arm with the flat of his hand, and knew that she knew him far too well since the beginning, when she had gazed at him so solemnly from the first row, he had realized that she had a mind for subtleties. She had read the tension in his voice, the timidity in his eyes, the unsolved question behind every compromise. Now she read dismissal in the dry, flat palm that patted her arm.

She returned to her own pillow. "I suppose I'll go to sleep now," she said.

The cones of the buckeye bloom had passed their zenith in the night. All day long the separate blossoms kept coming down, the little calyxes with red streaks at the base, floating through the May sunlight, drifting past the windows, covering the sills with a flowery snow. While she went about the business of the house she paused often to watch them slip past her eyes. She was awkward today, absent and uneasy, oppressed by a mood which had come with her out of her sleep. She had dreamed something and could not remember it; yet the flavor of the dream remained, troubling and incriminating, like a stain on the dress of a child who has come home from a forbidden journey into the woods.

All her motions were slow and tentative. She touched the dark antique furniture in the bedroom as if it were alive, as if her hand under the dust cloth could give it pain. She stood staring for a long time before she could bring herself to shake the pillow on which her husband's head had lain, or to pick up his pajamas from the middle of the floor. She was close to tears when she remembered that she had neglected the potted plants and saw that one of them was withering. A china poodle stood on the hearth, his hide flamboyant with gilt, a bit of yellow ribbon tied to the tip of his tail. The yellow bow had fallen askew, and this was reason for distress. She tied the bow again, meanwhile avoiding the china eyes.

While she made the bed and watered the flowers, she kept seeking for the cause of her wretchedness. Certainly it was not the quiet dismissal which she had received last night. There had been many such dismissals: she was used to them now. Nor was it that he had left a note on the dressing table, saying that he would not be home for dinner tonight because he was eating in the college grill with Dr. Rosen. He was always eating in the college grill with Dr. Rosen, and that was quite all right. It was the dream and the room and everything in the room. All the objects about her—the china dog, the military brushes, the blanket, the pajamas—were suddenly incarnate. Within each of them flowed the living blood of remembrance. Dog that you bought for me in New York, she thought, dog that you said was in execrable taste but gave to me nevertheless because I wanted it. Chair where you sit when you take off your shoes. Bed, bed . . .

She wandered about the house all morning, doing everything out of turn and doing nothing well. She was not dressed at noon simply because she was painfully undecided as to what she should put on. Since Koblanski was coming to give her a piano lesson, she thought that she might wear one of her new summer dresses. She went to the cupboard and pulled the soft, creamy silk from the hanger and stood long, holding it in her hands. Dress that you like better than all my other dresses, lace into which you stuck a rosebud when we went out to dinner last Saturday night. . . . She would not wear it. God knows why, she could not wear it now. She hung it carefully back in its place and closed the cupboard door. Then she dawdled, for another hour, eating bits of dry toast and spoonfuls of sliced orange and feeling sure that her tooth was going to ache.

Koblanski usually came at two. She spent most of the intervening hour between the kitchen window and the cupboard in the upstairs hall. Uneasiness waited for her in both places. At the window where the snow of blossoms kept floating down she recalled the savor of the dream—disturbing, sweet, a cause for shame. At the cupboard she wrestled with an even less definable sense of stress. The yellow gingham? The black suit? What jewelry? What shoes? Then suddenly she knew that she had no more time for dawdling. She pulled the creamy one from the hanger again. It was cool upon her, like water rippling down. She snipped off a pink geranium blossom and thrust it into her hair and went back into the bedroom to stand before the looking glass. All at once she heard the birds; it was as though every bird in the neighborhood had suddenly broken into song among the buckeye trees outside—robin and catbird and cardinal and sparrow. She glanced up and saw herself. And she was beautiful, with the flower lying over her forehead, close to her large eyes, with the foam of lace at her wrists, at her throat, over her breasts.

What had she dreamed last night? A stair, a flight of marble steps with a gleaming balustrade, winding around the curved side of the earth, winding between the earth and a purplish expanse of mist. She leaning against the balustrade, with her hair blown into infinity, with saffron comets raining, like the buckeye blossoms, past her eyes. Moths also, thousands of moths moving soft and furry through the dusk, and little lizards darting down golden in the golden trail of the shooting stars, and a whispering all around her, and the words strange—a mingling of poetry and obscenity. And she not alone in this mothy mist. Young nakedness beside her. Who was there?

The doorbell rang.

Koblanski was there. On the balustrade among the shooting stars. On the porch where the buckeye trees shed their snow. "Oh, my God," she said aloud, seeing the china poodle's mournful stare in the mirror, "what will become of me? What will happen to me now?" The doorbell rang again. She ran downstairs to open the door.

For months now the young Slav had been thinking that Galileo and Copernicus had done him no special favor when they rearranged the universe and excluded the possibility of a listening, tangible God. Unlike his honored colleague, he resented the Renaissance. In the clean, spare days before its advent, a man had walked down a straight avenue with the Vices behind him and the Virtues before; and if he died of chastity, it was to meet his love in an aerial and desireless shape in the bowers of heaven. But the troubadours of his respected fellow-teachers had ruined everything. They had removed all decent reasons for not sinning. Furthermore, if they had brought with them armfuls of roses, they had also carried in the dank smell of the tomb. Hasten, hasten—the urgency was in every bar, every verse; love is glorious and love is finite; today is so radiant, so efflorescent, so magical only because the inevitable conclusion is the grave.

He knew the grave. He knew it too damned well. He had scarcely left his homeland when the black wave of violence dashed across it. Mother, sister, father, niece, friend, tutor—all of them were dead. The houses of his childhood, transformed into black piles of rubble, were strewn about in his dreams. His sleeping thoughts wandered aimlessly among them, watching the dust of plaster rise above a fallen wall, seeing the broken face of a marble angel or the charred spindles of a remembered stairway. Medieval man had knelt in the midst of just such destruction, raising his hands to a fixed point in heaven and saying, "I am purified in that Thou chasteneth me." But what could the children of enlightenment say? Nothing much. Only, "Give me my roses which are my rightful inheritance together with this death."

Nor had he been too apt at this business of gathering the roses. The new country was a garden of good women; the classrooms, streets, porches, were lovely with girls, bare-armed, virginal, with long clean legs and loose hair. He wanted none of them. He wanted nobody but the wife of his honored colleague, who was not a virgin, who did not laugh very often, with whom he never laughed, whom he could pity and brood upon as he pitied and brooded upon his dead.

All the way to her house that afternoon, he had sung a certain song of Schumann's to himself. He could not get it out of his head. The melancholy, romantic, unmanly words and the nervous chords beneath them intruded upon their courteous comments and made a crisis of the meeting of their looks.

> I'll not complain, although my heart should break
> Striving with hopeless love . . .
> I saw thee in a dream . . .
> I saw the night that on thy soul was lowering.
> I saw the snake at thy poor heart devouring.
> I know, beloved, the measure of thy pain.
> I'll not complain.

This, he thought as she sat down at "the piano, was all that the enlightened man could summon up for such an occasion. Before the troubadours, one might have said, "Bear me up, lest I dash my foot against a stone."

He could not trust himself today. Strange blossoms from these foreign trees had fallen upon him on the way, lightly, like a woman's touch. Longing stirred in him like sap in a dry bush, drawn upward by the sun. He had relied on the order and solemnity of the house to put him in his proper place. But the house itself was transformed; it had not been made respectable, and he came upon things that he had never seen before. Their life had risen to the surface of the house: *his* pipe on the coffee table, her pale pink evening shawl on a chair, a wine glass on the mantel, still marked with the print of her lips. He ached with a strange mingling of jealousy and pleasure. He thought how in some upper room her nightgown might be lying on the floor, still fragrant with the scent of her body, wrinkled where she had pressed against it in her sleep.

Nor was she herself as she had always been. Her dress was new and thin; the upper curve of her breasts showed through the lace: a cluster of festal flowers nodded over her brow. Her glance was erratic. It flew to every corner of the room. It was as if she heard some light sound—whispering voice, beating of unearthly wings—among the reeling, shifting patches of light and shade. He talked, and she did not listen, and he himself scarcely knew what he said. He paced back and forth while he delivered himself of a jumble of courteous triviality, technical advice, historical anecdote. Slavic memories. He followed the same route up and down the sun-drenched room, and paused a little each time when he reached the chair where her shawl lay. Once his gesturing hand came down and brushed against the silky stuff, and then he fancied that he saw her smile.

"Well, then," he said, "we had better begin." But she simply could not play the piano today. She sat at the spinet in the alcove near the blown curtains and the springtime window. A bird made flute music in a near bough; the peonies were open in the garden beyond her; and she could not keep her eyes on the score or her hands on the keys. Her hands looked slight and anemic, coming out of the ruffle of creamy lace at wrists. Her head was a child's head, pink scalp, silky hair; and when she blundered he longed to bend down and hold it against his chest. To hold her, to comfort her, to rock her in his arms—Child, lullaby, pity—pity everlastingly. If Copernicus and Galileo had completed the styptic process, if only they had burned pity out of the world, pity out of love. Nothing but compassion is left to bind us to the weak and the dead. Compassion is the enlightened man's only morality . . .

The finest bars in the "Intermezzo" were jangled under her fingertips.

"But my dear friend—" he said.

"I won't try any more. I can't play today. I'm no good for playing, for weeks I haven't been good for anything."

I saw the night that on thy soul was lowering . . .

"I have a strange kind of pain all up and down my face, and I don't know why it comes."

. . . I saw the snake at thy poor heart devouring . . .

"Really, it's a very bad pain, but nobody believes me. Even my husband says there's nothing the matter at all."

. . . I know, beloved, the measure of thy pain . . .

"I am a poor pupil, and I give you so much trouble. I suppose you wish you had never seen my face."

. . . I'll not complain . . .

She turned from the piano then and stood before him. The stool was between them, but she was very close to him. He could see the whiteness of her breasts under the lace, the shadow of the geranium flower on her forehead, the wide pupils of her large, serious eyes. *"Liebe Freunde,"* he said, using the tender and discredited language of the song, *"liebe Freunde.* I would rather give away my right hand than lose the sight of your face."

Like a moth from the chrysalis, delight crept slowly to him from her look.

"Schoene Frau lieblieche, Frau—"

"Dear love," she said, and knelt on the stool, and leaned her head against his chest. A strange, closed fragrance, as of dry rose petals shut long in a jar rose to him from her hair—*I saw thee in a dream.* And what he possessed now was fantasy paling into reality—the slight shoulders under his hands, the cool mouth against his mouth, the anemic fingers raised tentatively, fearfully, to know and touch. And God, he was sick of it. Christ, he was sick of it. He wanted her without the taste of tears. He wanted the two of them to rise together out of the black piles of rubble, spurning the charred spindles and the broken angel faces, getting utterly free of the dust. His arms closed round her, he held her ardently, and the stool trembled under the strength of their embrace. He wanted her standing against him in the middle of the room. He wanted the glow that was there and the rocking shadow of the leaves. He wanted the length of her in light, her face in the sun.

"Come, love, come, my darling," he said, drawing her with

him out of the alcove, past the coffee table, toward the gleaming place.

Her skirt swung out behind her in their jubilant going. It brushed the coffee table, knocked something to the floor. She stopped and stared. A pipe had fallen between them. It lay on the floor with ashes all around it. "Oh, my God," she said. She was down on her knees on the carpet, touching the pipe. Never in his life, not even among the ruins of his dreams, had he seen such desolation as he saw now in her face. "This is his pipe that he smokes in the evenings. This is his pipe—" She raked up the ashes and held them in the cup of her hand. He could not touch her. She was a mourner, untouchable in her pity, grieving over the death that is in the living. She shivered and laid her lips against the ashes. She wept.

Something in the sight of her young loveliness crouching over the fallen thing roused a brief rage within him. He knew it was impotent. He felt it click dead within him like a rifle that has missed fire. What have the enlightened to do with righteous wrath? That, also, departed with the coming of the troubadours. . . . She looked at him, and her face was ugly with suffering. Compassion at least was dependable; compassion returned to cover the dead face of desire.

"Dear friend, shall I go?"

"Yes."

"Shall I go and not come back?"

Her eyes were closed. She rose like a sleepwalker, bringing her handful of ashes with her. "You mustn't come back any more, because I love you," she said.

He closed the door with a sense of finality and walked down the avenue, under the flowery snow, grieving for all of them—his honored colleague, his mother in her grave, that poor child, himself—the living with the dead.

So then it had been nothing after all, the husband thought. His admiration for Shakespeare grew with the years. He had read of it in *Othello* and had found it incredible—reasonless jealousy growing out of some triviality like a handkerchief; and now he himself had lived the drama through, had put all sorts of longings into her poor little body, all sorts of schemes into her poor little brain. The evening which he had anticipated with so much chaotic indecision had passed like all other evenings. She was as loving and as docile as ever, filling his pipe, asking about his lecture, following him round the room with her big eyes. She had remained in her corner, industriously knitting under her lamp, while he prepared his notes for tomorrow. She had asked mildly if she couldn't keep the atrocious china dog on the hearth in the living room, and had concurred just as mildly when he pointed out that it would be shockingly out of place there. She had heated the muffins for their evening tea, emptied the ash trays in the living room, and gone, as usual, a little before him to bed. He sat late at his desk because his mind, liberated from its load of foolishness, felt miraculously light and free. His thoughts left the past, hurried breathlessly through the present, brooded over the future. War now, grief now, death now? In the broad view, to the farseeing glance, it made no difference. The bright conclusion was predestined. Other generations would eat the fruit of the Copernican seed. He saw the orderly cities, the white public palaces, the multitudes lifting their arms in one harmonious gesture, the unchained Will inheriting everything. A springtime storm blew over his roof, scarcely stopping to mutter above his head. He thought of last night and smiled.

When he came into the bedroom, he found no lights and concluded that she was asleep. It was a pleasure to find her so—lying half-seen among the swaying shadows. He heard her even, quiet breath. He listened, undressing in the dark. It was a good sound, and he was grateful for it—heartbeat of their mutual life, pulse of the house in which he spent his peaceful days—

"Darling," she said.

127

He waited, thinking that she might be in that dim, half-waking state when silence might ease her and a word might draw her back from sleep.

"Are you thinking, darling?"

"No, not exactly. I thought you would have fallen asleep long ago."

"When are we going to New York?"

"In a week or so, I suppose. But isn't there some other place you'd rather—"

"Oh, no, New York will be lovely. I'm very fond of New York. That was where we bought the china dog. Do you remember? It was in a shop on Second Avenue."

He could not lie to her even in the smallest matters. He said, pulling off his underclothes, that he never could remember shops very well.

"It was a little, very dirty place with a million cuckoo clocks."

"Yes?" He could not ransack his brain for the cuckoo clocks. His mind was on the trail of another idea, vaguely unpleasant and disquieting. Something about his lecture this morning. Something about incoherence and incompleteness. To be sure, that was it, he had been definitely dissatisfied with that section of the disquisition which dealt with enlightened man's morality. He lay down on the mattress beside her. The leaves rocked, the curtains streamed inward. Through the window came the smell of new-cut grass and moist earth.

"Darling, my tooth is beginning to ache."

"Now, dear, you know—"

"But my tooth *does* ache."

"Shall I get you some brandy?"

"No. I guess I only imagine it. It doesn't ache now. I'll go to sleep."

He settled himself into the cool privacy of his own pillow. Now, about the questionable section of his lecture—But the mattress rocked. She was sitting bolt upright. He could see her large, grave eyes shining beside him in the dark. And he knew that they would shine like that forever, wild and without rest. They would shine like that in her withered face when he had stepped into nothingness before her and she lay listening to May thunder in an empty bed.

"Oh, darling," she said, shivering against him. "Just look at the shadows on that mirror. Isn't it beautiful? Isn't it beautiful in this room tonight?"

The Furlough

ALL THE OTHER children had left the schoolyard. But she remained behind, solitary on the great, empty expanse of concrete. She leaned against the rail that divided the playground from the grass, pressed her second-grade reader against her chest and stared at the lilac bushes, their outer edges breaking into sprays of blossomy foam.

Every school day for a whole year it had been like this: three o'clock came, and the ache returned, and she wanted to walk home alone. With nothing to do and the flag flapping against the afternoon sky, she had to know how it was all over again; how her father, her Frank, her darling, was a soldier in the war, and how he had been gone so long that she was not sure that, when she closed her eyes and prayed, she would be able to see his face.

Not being able to see him was dangerous in some magical way. If she ever lost all of him, even the mole on his ear, then it would be terrible, then he would be dead. If you shut your eyes and saw nothing at all, just at that minute the gun would crack, the bomb would fall, the fire would spread out in one white sheet as she had seen it spread across the movie screen; and he would be lying there stiff as the poisoned cat, and no amount of shaking could ever jerk him out of that sleep.

This particular afternoon was a lucky one. She saw him as clearly as she saw the heart-shaped leaves and the little, unopened purple flowers. He was wearing a white sweat shirt and sprawling on the wooden swing. That was the way he had looked on the evening she liked best to remember, the spring evening when he and she had had the terrible fight about the guitar. The neighborhood was quiet. You could hear the birds. With every breath you drew, you had the smell of the grass and the ground and the rain. He had floated away from her; he was lost to her in folds of dreams; he was gone into some world which she did not know. For that reason, she could not let him alone. She poked his feet and asked him foolish questions and said rhyming words.

"Will you shut up for just ten minutes?" he said.

"Bear, hair, square. The bear has square hair."

"I'll tell your mother to put you to bed."

"The bear in his hair has square hair so there."

He sat up straight in his kingly way, and turned his blond head aside and began to strum and sing to the wet stars. She knew he was singing about her mother who was inside, washing the dishes, and that made her more pesky still.

> *In thy dark eyes' splendor,*
> *Where the warm lights love to dwell,*
> *Weary looks, yet tender,*
> *Speak their fond farewell.*

She sat beside him on the swing and bounced up and down until the chains rattled.

> *'Nita, Juanita,*
> *Ask thy soul if we should part—*

"Frank, don't sing anymore."

> *'Nita, Juanita—*
> *Lean thou on—*

"Don't sing, I said."

"Who said? *You* said?" All at once he was standing above her, terrible and beautiful, with thunder in his voice. He was like the picture of Loki in the storybook, coming at her with fire in his hand. "You're getting entirely too damned fresh," he shouted. "I'll show you if I have to break every bone in your body." He threw the guitar on the porch matting, and it made a long, twangy sound. He laid her across his knee. He hit her with the flat of his hand until she yowled. The neighbors came out of their front doors and went straight back in, closing their doors behind them.

And when the paddling was over, when he sat quiet on the swing again, putting the guitar back in tune, she came and sat close to him, loving him as she had never loved him, wating to hear his voice and the interrupted song. The stars, bigger and clearer now, stared down at them through the boughs. She laid her head on his shoulder. Between the verses, he laughed and turned to kiss the top of her head.

'Nita, Juanita,
Lean thou on my heart,
he sang, drawing her head down to a place where she could actually hear his heart beat.

That had been their best evening together. Maybe she would never be as happy as that again.

From the moment when she walked into the vestibule, she knew that something out of the ordinary was about to happen. Everything was washed and polished. She could see her own face made fat in the curve of the doorknob. The straw mat had been turned clean-side-up, and the tiles under it were scrubbed as white as snow.

The hall was even more orderly and expectant. All the old sweaters, coats and overshoes had been taken from the clothes rack. The top of the hall table was quite hidden under a bowl of dogwood whose leaves smelled like wet earth, like the day of her great-grandmother's funeral. Oh, Lord, she thought, suppose the magic doesn't really work, suppose he's dead—

"Is that you, Connie?" her mother said in the kitchen.

"Yes—" She could barely find her voice. It was as if hundreds of bugs were going up and down her backbone.

"What are you doing out there, quiet as a mouse?"

Certainly her mother would not talk in that airy sort of voice if he had died. "I'm coming," she said. "I was looking at the flowers."

The spell of neatness was also upon the kitchen. The linoleum floor, the dishes in the cupboard, the pans on the stove all shone. There was a new oilcloth cover on the table. There were boxes of strawberries and bottles of beer. She sniffed the air and knew the sugar-and-almond smell of a baking angel food cake.

"Are we going to have a party?" she said.

She looked at her mother, who was sitting on a high stool at the table, shelling peas. She stared because her mother was so changed and so beautiful. She seemed wondering and joyful, like the women in the Easter picture, the ones who stood beside the open tomb. She wore white sandals and a white robe. She had just come down from her bath, and the smell of the piney soap was still upon her.

"Oh, Connie," she said.

He had not died—he had written a beautiful letter.

"I had a telegram from your father."

It was something better—it was something very good indeed.

"He's coming home tonight. He has a furlough. He's coming home."

The child sat down at the table and stared at the green pods. She took one and began to pull it slowly apart. The very thought that he could return had driven his image out of her head. Now she could not see him at all. She began to chew the end of the pod. It was raw and sweet.

"Where is he now, Mother?"

"On a train, coming home."

"The train couldn't get blown up or go off the tracks or run into anything, I don't suppose?"

"Well, now, that's not very likely, is it? And *do* take that thing out of your mouth, dear. It's dirty."

She took one of the peas and began to chew on it instead. It broke into small, unpleasant pieces on her tongue and tasted even more sickeningly sweet than the pod.

"But aren't you glad?" her mother said.

She wanted her heart to be like the sun on the oilcloth, like the shining windows, like the wondering women at the empty tomb. But he had been gone so long that she could not be happy. She could not remember most of the songs that he had taught her, and she did not play with the same toys. Not a month ago she had left the panda that he had given her in the yard in the rain all night, and in the morning he had been soggy, muddy, no good, unfixable, dead . . .

Her mother was staring at her.

"Oh, yes, I'm very glad Frank's coming home," she said.

"Do you want to wear your new yellow dress?"

"Will he know me if I have a new dress on?"

"Don't be silly. Of course he will."

She swallowed one of the peas whole. It stuck in her chest. Lying there beside her, it felt like the swelling that comes before tears.

"Mother, will we know *him*?" she said.

"Of course." But the face was less certain than the voice. Her mother did not really know; she only wished to know.

"Are you sure?"

"Well, people do change, you know, especially when they are in the Army, living with a lot of men in a faraway place. He may have changed a little. And there's just one thing, Connie. I hope you'll behave yourself. He'll be very tired, and I hope you'll—"

She started for the hall and the stairs.

"Oh, don't worry about me," she said.

•

BEFORE HE WENT away, the three of them had always eaten their dinner in daylight, in the kitchen. Tonight they ate in the dining room from the fluted company plates, and by the time they sat down the world outside the window was dark. There were red roses and four white candles in the middle of the table. A breeze made the flames bend and shiver, and the wall behind her was strange with wavering light. She poked at the angel food cake and rolled the strawberries round with her spoon and thought about the way things changed.

In the fairy books, things were always turning into other things. The bodies of beautiful damsels who ran away from people they did not love were suddenly changed into trees. The voices of old, drowned sailors spoke in sea shells, and deer shot in ancient forests looked at their murderers with the sad eyes of men. She stared at her reflection in the mirror. She had not changed much and her heart was still the same. But he was different. If he had turned into a tree or a stag, he could not have been more unlike himself. It was not his uniform, not the stripes on his sleeves nor the bright buttons across his chest. It was not his skin which had turned dark and felt hard to kiss. It was not even his hair, though she grieved over that—all the blond waves gone, and nothing left but patchy fuzz, like a worn-out teddy bear. It was that he seemed to have been put in order, like the house. There was none of the old, rumpled easiness about him. And he did everything too gently, as if he thought the whole world hurt and was afraid to move because he might hurt it more. In the old days he used to smack her mother, call her funny names and pull her hair. Now he called her only "my darling," and put her hair back very carefully, the way you take tissue paper away from roses. When he spoke, he talked of unknown things in a low voice; and most of the time he only gazed into her mother's eyes. Everything was strange and sad; and, if he went on being so quiet and solemn, she would never be able to remember him when he was gone; and then the gun would crack, the bomb would fall, the fire would fan out, and he would be dead.

"Darling," he said to her mother, "I kept every one of your letters. They were all beautiful."

"I'm glad you thought so."

They were very strange. You would never think they slept in the same bed.

"I used to read parts of them to my best friends down there."

"Oh, why? I can't really write. They weren't good letters, only loving ones."

WOULD THEY GO on like that all night, talking like people in the movies? She thrust her fork down onto the middle of her piece of angel food, so hard that both ends of the slice stood up and made the strawberries jump. If she shoved a little harder, if she really jammed her fork down, the berries would leap onto the clean tablecloth.

"My commanding officer, Captain McConkey—" he said.

"Do you like him, dearest? Is he all right?"

"He's one in a million, darling. A prince among men. None of us will ever forget that night we were out on bivouac. It was in December, and it was raining, and there was a jeep there to take him back. Do you know what he did? He absolutely refused to ride. He walked back with us—a five-mile hike in the driving rain."

The fork came down with a thwack. The plate jumped, the cake jumped, two strawberries lay on the tablecloth, and one rolled about on the floor. But her mother merely sighed and looked at her in a secret way, shaking her head, and he only smiled and bent and picked up the berry that lay on the rug. "Better be careful or you'll lose all your dessert, sweetheart," he said.

She fixed her eyes mournfully on the mole on his ear. That, at least was there—the one relic of their past. She wanted to throw herself against him, her head on the part of his chest where you could hear his heart beat.

"What does he look like, love?" her mother said.

"Tall, blond, broad across the shoulders. Every inch a man."

She would not have it. He must not go on talking like people in the movies. "McConkey is a foolish name," she said.

Her mother and father exchanged glances. Their eyes said, "She is a poor little thing. We will let her alone."

"Maybe you'd like to see him, darling. I have a snapshot here." He began to unfasten the buttons and look about in the strange pockets. He was going to drag out some piece of the world of guns and mud and cedar trees—that world in which she had no part. Her mother might look if she chose. As for her, she would never allow herself to see Captain McConkey's disgusting face. Besides, she would say it, she certainly would, and he would jump up as soon as the words came out of her mouth. He would stand above her like Loki and bang on the table, and the dishes would jump, and the strawberries would fly, and all the candles would go out. Because he loved Captain McConkey, he would roar at her in his old, dear, terrible voice.

"There, the one on the end, darling, that's Captain McConkey, see?"

She took a deep breath.

"Captain McConkey is dumb as a donkey," she said.

FOR A SECOND it was as if the whole still room crackled with lightning. Her mother's mouth fell open. The snapshot jerked in his hand, and the old blue ice-and-fire was in his eyes. For a

138

second he was sure that he was going to whack her hard. Then he shook his head and sighed.

"Constance, I'm surprised at you," he said.

"Beg your father's pardon."

"Beg pardon." She chose a particularly fat strawberry and whacked it to pieces with her fork.

"Connie," said her mother, "will you behave yourself?"

Her father turned his changed face to her and stroked her cheek with the back of his hard, different hand. "You can see, darling," he said in the movie voice, "that she's all worn out. She's overexcited. I guess she'd better go to bed.

And there was no help for it. With cake stuck in her throat, with her nose dripping and tears starting down her cheeks, she went upstairs.

She lay awake, crying and listening to the clatter of dishes, the low, uncomfortable talk, the opening and shutting of doors. Maybe, she thought, when they come into their room where their bed is, some magic will happen and he will turn back into himself. But the bed creaked beneath him, and the shoes banged down, and he went on talking in the same voice. She could not hear all of what he said, but there was a great deal of "Captain McConkey" and "my darling" and "if you please." When the talk stopped, there was nothing but a shivering, sighing silence. The wind was up, and she could not tell whether it was they or the trees that sighed.

As she closed her eyes, she saw herself writing on the wooden fence at the end of the back yard. Nobody was allowed to write there; it was a bad thing; yet she went on writing in big letters, the same sentence over and over, white chalk on the dark wood. "My heart is broken," the sentence said. She started out of her sleep. She felt for her heart in all the usual places and could not feel it beat. Her heart was certainly broken, and soon she would be dead. When they got up for breakfast tomorrow, talking about my darling and Captain McConkey, they would find her stretched out on the mattress, like the poisoned cat, and they would act like themselves and shout at each other and ask why she had died. Then, when her mother went into the yard to pick pansies for the breakfast table, she would see the writing. "My heart is broken," she would read, and that would almost break her heart. But, no, her mother would not be able to see the sentence. The sentence was not really on the fence—it was only in the dream . . .

SHE SAT UP in bed and saw that the room was white with moonlight. The house was very quiet. She got out of bed, pulled up the pants of her pajamas, went barefoot to the door between their room and hers, and opened it so slowly that the hinges kept still. There was nobody in the room. Oh, Lord, had the magic come because she had been so bad, had an angel taken them away? She ran down the stairs, praying and holding her breath. They were not in the moon-washed dining room. They were not in the kitchen where the almond-and-sugar sweetness, ghost of the uneaten cake, still floated above the stove. The clock in the parlor struck one.

"Good God," said his voice, "is it one o'clock already?"

She heard their glasses clinking. They were drinking beer together on the porch in the moonlight, just as they had done in the old days.

"Watch out, darling," he said.

There was a low twangy sound. Her mother must have kicked the guitar. She listened, but there were no more noises, and she thought they must be kissing. She snapped the elastic in her pajamas, tiptoed through the shimmering hall, and pressed her face against the screen door.

They were on the swing, rocking slowly back and forth through strips of shadow and light. The porch blinds were down, and between the slats you could see the stars. Both of them had their night clothes on. He bent over her mother, and his patchy hair caught the moonlight.

"Beautiful . . ." he said.

"But am I still beautiful? Do you like to look at me still?"

"Do I still like to drink cool water and take a look at the sky?"

He began to kiss her. The swing jerked, and the chains creaked. "Monkey," he said, "you damn white monkey, you crazy brat, you—" He was pushing her mother around, tickling her and nuzzling her neck until she laughed aloud. They ought to be ashamed; all the neighbors could hear. Anyway, she hated them both. With each other, when they thought she was asleep, they were just as they had always been. It was only with her that they talked their nicey-nicey stuff. She would spoil their beer and their moonlight and their kissing. She kicked the screen door.

"Constance, is that you?" her mother said.

"Yes, it's me."

"Well, you can go right back upstairs and get into bed."

She came and stood on the porch matting, snapping the elastic in her pajamas and glaring at them.

"I won't do it. I can't sleep. I won't go to bed."

"Why not?" He shoulted at her as if she were the whole Army.

"Oh, let her alone, Frank. She's overwrought."

"Like hell she is. She's too fresh for her own good. Answer me. Why couldn't you sleep?"

"Because you people make too much noise, that's why. You laugh too much. You kiss each other out loud. You make me sick—"

SHE DID NOT have time even to see him looking like Loki in the moonlight. He was up and across the porch. Her mother made a small squeak like a mouse. Now all of them were on the swing, and she lay across his knees. He whacked her until her teeth rattled, until the stars jumped up and down between the slats, until she yowled like a dog and real dog answered her, yowling in somebody's back yard. Windows went up across the street. White faces poked out of unseen rooms and then went back into the dark. He was going to knock the heart straight out of her mouth. He was stronger than he had ever been before.

Suddenly he stopped and covered his face with his hands. "Oh, my poor little bear," he said, "on the first day I'm home, on the first day—"

She sat up and swallowed and patted his fingers. "Oh, that's all right, Frank," she said.

"I didn't mean to beat her, darling, but ever since I walked into this house she's been asking for it, and I'm so damned tired."

She pulled his hands down and saw his face. Never, not in a hundred years, would she forget his wet eyes. He loved her more than ever before; he had never cried like that, not even the time when he used the badminton paddle; and now the magic was perfect—he would come home again, because she could never forget.

She was afraid they would send her upstairs while the sting was still in her skin, but they said nothing about that. They sat on the swing, all three of them together, rocking slowly back and forth. The world was washed clean by his crying fit. He held her against his side, and the smell of his body—unchanged and loved—came to her with the smells of the grass and the hedge and the flower beds.

"Sing a song," she said.

"Any special song?"

"Lingering falls the southern moon."

He lifted the guitar and strummed it softly, because of the neighbors and the time of night.

"'Nita Juanita," he sang.

He was still singing when she fell asleep.

Another Spring

THE STUDENTS AT the drama school said among themselves
that Miss Bishop's office had been looking like a funeral
parlor ever since the day Barbara McKinnon died. That, like
most of their statements, was not entirely accurate. They were
young and eager to impress each other; they twisted the fact
to accommodate the word; they enjoyed the flourish of the
quotable simile. Besides, they were not quite guiltless of a
posthumous malice. Certain old jealousies—certain aches and
angers that should have been buried along with the fair body
which had begotten them—refused to be put underground.
The students had been stunned and contrite enough at the
funeral. They had carried themselves with the proper hangdog
air through the first six or seven days. But they could not be
expected to go on grieving forever. They were back to their
old ways soon enough, laughing the old laughter among the
gaudy Shakespearean costumes in the wardrobe room, talking
the old bright talk in the shadowy marble corners, under the
blank plaster eyes of Thalia and Melpomene. The atmosphere
of order, the atmosphere of a new beginning which always
follows a burial, imperceptibly left the place. The ashes of their

cigarettes drifted into the plaster fountain; the marble benches were cluttered with the wrappers from their candy bars. The classrooms and offices were invaded by comfortable disorder. All except Miss Bishop's office. That refused to change. Passing its open door on the way out of the building and into the foggy February dusks, the students turned their heads aside. "She remembers too long. It is just like a funeral parlor," they said.

But a disinterested stranger would have disagreed with them, would have found nothing of the mortuary in the tall little room, would have come to the conclusion immediately that he had walked into some sort of shrine. Miss Bishop, who was spare and graying, had already renounced the living flesh and was not one to keep the remembrance of a corpse close to her tempered and chastened heart. If anything of Barbara McKinnon still tarried above the desk lamp that burned solitary in the six o'clock dimness, if any part of her still moved across the speckless carpet or against the panels of polished oak, it was a spirit and an effluence; it had nothing to do with undertakers and burials.

True, the costume which she was to have worn as Cordelia in *King Lear* still lay draped over one of the office chairs—sea-green and breaking into lacy foam at the throat and wrists. But it was harshly empty, and Miss Bishop had kept it there for its very emptiness. It reminded her of her dilemma; it caught her up short whenever she fell into a dream; it admonished her every time she raised her eyes from her desk that there was an urgent piece of casting to be done. The play would, of course, open at the scheduled time; the rest of the cast had paid their tuition and were not dead. It was obvious that the pale green satin must move into the glow of the footlights among the scarlet and the purple on the appointed night. It was equally obvious that Barbara McKinnon would not carry it forward in the old way, so that it became a floating thing, a rhythmic, shimmering piece of sea. "Well, who, then?" she asked herself twenty times a day. "Who will it be?" But eight days had passed; all the scenes in

144

which Cordelia did not appear had been rehearsed into a state of mechanical lifelessness; every young hopeful on the campus had learned Cordelia's lines by heart; and as yet she had not laid the empty dress across the arms of a successor.

For Barbara McKinnon, there was no successor. Miss Bishop had said as much, and she was one who would know. She had moved across the most celebrated stages in England and America. She had known herself for a Jessica and had never aspired to Portia. She had come away at the first inward sign of disintegration, before the mildew had settled on the roses. In the ten years which she had spent in these academic halls, she had found time to ponder the setting stars and consider the rising ones. Barbara McKinnon had been weighed against the accomplishments of the great and the untarnished promise of the young. Another Barbara McKinnon to fill the sea-green gown? Not in this war-weary generation, not in this time of crassness and blatancy. The wonder was that such a girl should have existed at all.

And now, while she put her handkerchief and her glasses into her purse, it seemed to Miss Bishop that the girl still *did* exist, that she had not been utterly blotted out in noise and fragments of flying windshield on an icy road by night. Miss Bishop closed her eyes and saw the dress borne forward upon the delicate body. The thin hands, alive to the very tips of the fingers, moved upward again in the subtle gesture of resignation. *"What shall Cordelia do?"* said the voice, as clear and many-faceted as a prism. *"Love, and be silent."* Miss Bishop stiffened against the remembered sound, opened her eyes, walked to the window, and stared at the purpling February evening. So it had been every evening. So, every evening since the event, Miss Bishop had raised up the dead. So, tracing meaningless lines upon the smoggy pane, she had asked herself, "Well, who will take her place?" But there was none to take her place.

She thought for the hundredth time of Helen Miller, who had been from the beginning a weak shadow, a faint echo of

145

the one who was dead. Let it be Helen Miller then, she thought, picking up her purse and turning out the light. And the thought that it would be Helen Miller woke a strange feverishness in her, a certain sour eagerness. If it were Helen Miller, then all of them would see what they had lost. The shadow would make them hunger after the shape; the echo would make them yearn after the voice. Hearing Helen Miller whine those unforgettable lines, they would know the measure of their loss.

"What shall Cordelia do?" she said to herself in Helen Miller's voice, locking the office door. *"Love, and be silent,"* she said, stepping into the hall. The hall was vague and dusky with the accumulated smoke of a day's cigarettes. The reddish light of sunset had invaded it. The place looked vast, unpeopled, forsaken. The marble rang beneath her feet. *"What shall Cordelia do?"* she said again, thinking herself alone. But she was not alone.

Not ten paces away from her, on a marble bench beside the plaster fountain, sat Anna Sekey, with an open book upon her knees. She also had been talking to herself, after the manner of drama students. She had stayed late to inherit the empty hall. It was plain from the shining of her large brown eyes that she had converted the place into a stage, that she had made a spotlight of the slanting ray of sun, that she had filled the shadowy places under the gallery with a crowd of wondering, uplifted faces. Her stocky little body leaned forward. Her blunt hands beat against the book. *"Love,"* she was saying to the ephemeral audience. *"Love, and be silent."*

Miss Bishop glared. For a full minute it seemed to her that she would not be able to control herself, that her rage would break upon the round brown head. That this squat and awkward Slav, this graceless thing with the squashed face of a lion cub, this square being with a dull mane—that *she* would permit herself, even in an hour of dreaming in an empty hall, to imagine that *she* might be Barbara McKinnon's successor—there were no words to encompass such effrontery.

The girl reddened and shut the book. "Good evening Miss Bishop," she said.

Somebody—perhaps it had been Mr. Schrieber who taught diction—had once pointed out that this girl had a remarkable voice. Tawny, he had called it, something between brown and gold. Now in the stillness of the deserted building, Miss Bishop heard the rich ring of it, and felt more affronted than before. Maybe it was because of this voice that she had dared.

Miss Bishop opened and closed the clasp of her pocketbook. "You know, my dear," she said, avoiding Anna's eyes and staring straight at her forehead, "you know, you shouldn't stay in this building so late. It isn't precisely wholesome to sit around dreaming. We permit ourselves all sorts of fantasies when we're alone—things we'd never allow ourselves to dwell upon if we were in company."

The girl took up the book and thrust it into the pocket of her leather jacket. "Yes," she said, "I know."

She said it with a meekness and resignation that turned honest anger into cruelty. Miss Bishop looked uneasily around her. She saw the departure of the dream. The spotlight faded into a mere sick ray of winter sun; the floor was strewed with paper and ashes; the shadow under the gallery was a vast, misted emptiness. The girl was no longer Cordelia, looking with large and ardent eyes upon a kingly father. She was a wretched little Slav, a workman's daughter sent to the city from some outlying mill town. She stood up and buttoned her jacket to her chin.

"Good night," said Miss Bishop.

Long after the big door had swung shut behind her, the tawny voice pursued her, saying, "Good night."

The campus looked strange, islanded with vague spots of melting snow, netted by black boughs of maple trees, changing in the dying light from purple to gray, from gray to rose. There was a sense of movement and transition—the mild ripple of wind, the running of water along the gutters, the tinkle of icicles falling from the neo-classical pediments. Miss Bishop felt and resented the first overtures of spring. It was the dreaming season, the season for the young. Every year in February she had come out into this first soft phase of the night, had lingered along the walk, slow and tender with remembrance, had sensed the sprouts of violets loosening the thawed earth. And each spring had borrowed its particular color and savor from one of the students—some boy with a tart wild-strawberry wit, some girl with crab-apple blossom cheeks—all the glimmer of April in one voice, a whole Maytime preserved for recollection in one windy head of hair. Last year, at this same spot, walking among the silky trunks against the changing sky, Barbara McKinnon had come, with a bunch of violets pinned to her shoulder . . .

From some far towers at the busy core of the city, into the hushed emptiness of the campus, a clock dropped chimes. Miss Bishop stopped and counted. Seven? Good God, not seven? She pushed back her glove and stared at her watch. A dissolving confusion, a sense of all order dropping away, came upon her with the knowledge that it was seven o'clock. She had meant to dine this evening, as on all other evenings, in the quiet coffee shop on the first floor of her apartment house. She had meant to attend the opening night of a new comedy at the civic play-house, to stop for a glass of brandy on the way home, to lie down with a book which she had deliberately left at an exciting page, and to read herself to sleep. Now the whole program was thrown out of joint. Before she could reach home and make herself presentable, the coffee shop would be closed. At best, she would be late for the play, and suddenly she found herself doubting that she wanted to see the play at all. She stood quite immobile staring at a trail of coral cloud. Perhaps she did not want her dinner either. She bridled at such a notion, knowing it for the very essence of confusion. Of course she would eat her dinner; she would eat it in the college grill, little as she cared for the place with its endless shuffle of feet and sizzle of eggs and banging of trays. She turned sharply, like a disciplined soldier, at the next fork in the path. The sound of the grill, a clatter and a murmur, floated to her on the moist air. Behind the yellow windows she could see the shadowy and distorted shapes coming and going, carrying trays. She thought of the possible meetings, the necessary talk, and almost turned aside. But there was no help for it, and she opened the door and walked into the smoky, bacon-scented hall.

Once inside the raftered dining room, she wondered how such a small and scattered number of people could make so much noise. The rush hour was over. Its refuse—crumpled napkins, ravaged salads, and a drift of cigarette smoke—had lingered behind it. The few diners were separated by wide reaches of strewed tables and empty chairs. Most of them were students, eating late and alone, bending over books or staring at the ceiling. She ordered an omelet and a cup of coffee at the counter and carried them to a solitary corner. She ate slowly, finding the food tasteless and hard to swallow. After a few bites she pushed the plate aside and fell to staring at the melancholy expanse, like the rest. Diagonally across from her, only two tables away, Anna Sekey sat. The girl nodded with politeness and gravity. But her face was disturbing. Her lips were shaking, and there was the raw redness of recent crying around her eyes.

If Miss Bishop had fancied that the wretched scene which had taken place under the plaster stare of the Muses could be forgotten, she saw now that she had been mistaken. The girl had not forgotten it; she had a sickening conviction that the girl would go on remembering it for the rest of her days. The book that lay beside Anna Sekey's untouched supper was plainly not a copy of *King Lear*; it was a history book with pictures of some ancient city on its page. But the unhappy child thought that it might rouse some suspicion; she closed it in jerky haste, she hid it under her leather jacket and bent long over the contents of her pocket, trying to find some inoffensive thing in which she might lose herself. She found a pencil and a crumpled envelope, and began to write with nervous diligence. And suddenly Miss Bishop felt an aching curiosity, a longing to know what the blunt hand was scrawling, a desire to read behind those symbols to their source—the rage, the grief, the penitence, the disillusionment—whatever it was that she, in her own sorrow, had begotten in the young woman's secret heart.

Maybe she is cursing me, Miss Bishop thought, turning back to her tepid food. Maybe she is writing a whole string of Slavic curses. Maybe she. . . . But the questioning was brief. Her thoughts drifted to other matters, to the grades for the semester, which must be filed in the dean's office before the week was out; to the ineffectual Lear who *would* sputter the subtlest lines; to Gloucester's costume, which still bulged at the waist; to that other costume, foamy and sea-green, which lay in her office over the chair. . . . She closed her eyes and suddenly the vision which she had avoided by crowding every hour from the hour of the funeral, the vision which she had feared was upon her now. Blond, cool, and exquisite, Barbara McKinnon moved among the empty tables and the drifting smoke. Her face, flawless and patrician, glowed as it had glowed in the footlights, took on the pale and perfect tints of flowers and shells. Her words rang like shaking prisms against the after-dinner clatter. *"What shall Cordelia do? Love, and be silent."*

And now it was impossible to hold remembrance back, to keep it behind the opaque wall of duty any more. The wall was broken. The dining room was no longer a dining room, but a stage; and Barbara McKinnon moved and spoke upon it, a living presence reclaimed from death. All the hopes that Miss Bishop had never dared hope for herself, all the skills which only the humble can teach to the great, all the native grace and all the studied art came back, sweet and incorruptible, out of the grave. That scene in the fourth act—the wild night and the wind in the yellow hair and the long fingers intertwining in anxiety over a father lost. And later, later, the scene in the tent, and the old man waking from his fever dream, waking to find Cordelia above him, under the tawdry lamp. And she making everything authentic and complete, spreading the veil of her royal loveliness over everything, extending her conviction to the foolish boy who must play at being a king, to the muslin that must be silk, to the little glow that must be incandescent, living light. . . . And later, later, in the last scene of all, trailing with the grace of falling water from the old man's arms—that limp young arm, that unbelievable length of hair . . .

Suddenly the dream was gone, and there was only the reality. She knew dimly that something within the reality, some sound or tension that had not been there before, had destroyed the dream. She looked up, blinking against tears. A presence—and no ordinary presence—had come into the smoky expanse out of the dripping, spring-breathing night. A workman, a thick and stumpy man in a frayed overcoat, stood on the threshold, rubbing his coarse hair and clasping his hat between his elbow and his side. His Slavic face looked flat and pale against a two days' growth of beard. He took a few steps forward. His shoes creaked, and the creaking was loud as the year's first thunder in the uncomfortable hush. "What on earth is *he* doing here?" somebody said.

Then all the eyes in the room withdrew their gaze from the advancing figure and turned in her direction. "Are they looking at me? Is he coming toward me?" she asked herself in confusion that was close to fright. But the stares converged upon another table, settled in cold wonder upon the place where Anna Sekey had been sitting with the crumpled envelope before her and a pencil in her hand. She was rising now, slowly and with dignity. Whatever consternation had come upon her at the sight of the newcomer was mastered and put in its place. She wanted to make plain to him and to all the others that he was welcome. She straightened until her stocky body looked tall. Her hair took on a dulled sheen, a kind of earthy goldenness under the hanging lamp. "Hello, father," she said, so loudly that her tawny voice rang the length and breadth of the room and continued to ring after she was silent, like the suspended, memorable tone of a bell.

They met before Miss Bishop's eyes. Their heads came close to each other in that vague and smoky air where the ghost of Barbara McKinnon had walked only a moment since in a frothy gown. They embraced each other briefly, and Miss Bishop wondered how they could embrace each other at all. She fancied that some heavy smell, a smell of stables or cellars, must cling to the father's worn coat and rumpled hair. There was something thick and oppressive about the place: she would be going.

Yet she could not bring herself to pick up her purse and leave the table. She had to listen, she could not go. The girl said nothing of any consequence, merely called him "dear," and asked what was the matter, what had brought him all those thirty miles, away from his work, at this time of night. But whatever she said was enriched and warmed and softened in the saying. Her voice lay upon the words like the bloom upon blue grapes. While they talked they sat down on the bench beside the leather jacket. Without taking her eyes from her father's face, Anna Sekey lifted a roll and broke it into small pieces and set the heap of rusks before him on a bread-and-butter plate. It was plain that she had been breaking his rolls for him for a long time, and Miss Bishop found herself wondering why. Then she saw by the helpless movements of his mouth that most of his teeth were gone. He is old and probably foolish, Miss Bishop thought. The thought and the words wherein it clothed itself had a strange familiarity. But she could not remember the source and dismissed the matter and sighed.

The two of them were talking more freely now. The eyes of the other diners, satisfied or contemptuous, had turned back to the ceiling and the books. The father and daughter felt more secure, more alone. With the dogged directness of ordinary people, they had waded quickly through greetings and formalities. He was sorry, he was saying. He was very sorry to come in on her like this, at her school, where he shouldn't come at all. He was sorry to go to the dormitory to ask for her, to ask for her all over the place. He didn't want to bother people, but he couldn't help it. He was in bad trouble. He had to come. The truck got smashed. The truck got smashed this afternoon.

"The truck got smashed?" She sent one wild look from the top of his head to his shoes. It was as if she needed to make certain that he was there, unbruised and unbroken. It was as if she needed to prove to herself that he was not lying on some dark country road.

"Yes. A bakery truck ran into it. It got smashed this afternoon."

"But smashed? All smashed?"

There it was again, Miss Bishop thought, the remarkable voice. Somehow it had managed to endow the smashed truck with the vast proportions of classic tragedy. So a queen, hearing of a great fleet caught upon the reefs, might have said. "Lost? All lost?" So a Roman matron, hearing the tidings of a slaughtered army, might have said, "Dead? All dead?" Her mind scurried about, trying to collect what it knew of Anna Sekey, what it had read concerning her on certain cards and pages; of letter paper in the files. Yes, the girl was the daughter of a small town hauler, she remembered now. And if the poor devil's truck was smashed, then he was smashed. It was a tragedy—a minor, daily sort of tragedy . . .

What, Miss Bishop thought, is tragedy? And suddenly it seemed to her that everything in the smoke-blurred room had taken on the massy shape and dim coloration of the tragic. The boy who sat friendless by the window, staring at the ceiling—God knows what last frail barricade stood between him and utter desolation tonight. The waitress who threw the trays on top of each other—who could tell what rage and scorn had put the devil into her water-softened fingertips? And Mr. Schrieber who teaches diction, and Miss Snively who teaches the history of the theatre, and all of us who teach anything here. . . . To be a teacher—that is a tragedy. To spend your life in a remote chapel, with only two doors. Through the one door they come—the young and the beautiful—and they stay only under duress, always thinking how fine it will be when they can escape through the other door. To be forever urging them over the threshold. To say a score of farewells at the end of every June. To love them, and then to be permitted to love them no more. That is significant tragedy, the strong twinge in the heart, the salty sting of tears. But suppose one comes to the tragedy that lies beyond that, the tragedy which has no thesis, the tragedy in which the protagonist dawdles and nobody gives a damn? Suppose I am always as I am tonight, limp and empty as the costume which hangs over my chair? Suppose I never come out of it? Suppose all my Aprils are buried in Barbara McKinnon's grave? Suppose I never know another spring?

By this time the hauler had made it plain to his daughter that their particular tragedy was neither epic nor complete. The truck was not all smashed. It could be mended, the man at the garage had told him so, but my God, Anna, the cost . . .

The girl did not ask him about the cost at once. As if she wished to fortify him with some special tenderness against the pain of naming the sum, she lifted some of the rusks and dipped them into the gravy that lay dark on her untouched plate. If she were alone with him now, Miss Bishop thought, she would carry the bread straight to his lips; she would feed him as if he were a bird. Then, for no reason that she could fathom, one of Lear's lines slipped into her mind. *"We two alone will sing like birds i' the cage. . . ."* It was the strange, half-fey, half-holy speech in the last act. The old king, comforting his daughter for defeat and imprisonment and a lost crown, made broken, moonlit music in praise of the life that they would have together safe from the world, behind prison bars:

> " . . . *so we'll live,*
> *And pray, and sing, and tell old tales, and laugh . . .*
> *And take upon's the mystery of things,*
> *As if we were God's spies: and we'll wear out,*
> *In a wall'd prison, packs and sets of great ones*
> *That, ebb and flow by the moon."*

Barbara McKinnon, she thought. Barbara McKinnon listening to those lines with cool pity, remote and exquisite consideration . . .

Meanwhile the old man in the threadbare overcoat had brought himself to do it; he had said miserably that he needed two hundred dollars. The mass of the tragedy dwindled; the rock-bound fleets and ghostly armies faded; she saw nothing now but Barbara McKinnon's listening face. This business at the other table was nothing; it was a matter of two hundred dollars and a couple of poor Polish wretches. She was tired; she had dawdled again; the play at the civic playhouse had begun long ago. Well, she could still go home and read herself to sleep.

And yet, and yet. . . . The tawny voice had taken up the question of the two hundred dollars, with ardor, with dignity, as a Roman matron might speak of her husband's honor. He mustn't worry, really, he mustn't worry, even though it looked like a terrible amount of money. There would be some way, darling, there'll have to be some way. It was mid-term now, and she'd paid four hundred dollars in tuition. She'd leave the school and ask them to give her back half of what she'd paid. That's what she'd do. That was the only way. Her blunt brown hands left the rusks and moved toward him. They clasped his wrist, touched his shoulder, patted his check. They were thick hands, hut they were eloquent. Love flowed in them. Love made them warm and pliable. Love filled and quickened them to the fingertips. And the face, Miss Bishop thought, the flat little squashed-in face. It was translucent. It glowed. His love had breathed upon her face and nourished an inward light, and she was beautiful.

He leaned against the table, pulling his coarse hair in despondency and shaking his head at the offered rusk. God, it was terrible, he said. Mother Mary, it was terrible. All her hopes—everything she'd wanted and planned—all gone because a God damned bakery truck had—He could not finish. He thrust his hard, hairy fists into his eyes and wept. Old and foolish, Miss

155

Bishop thought, hearing the familiar words again. *"Pray you now, forget and forgive: I am old and foolish,"* King Lear had said.

The room was utterly quiet and almost empty now. His sob sounded against the stillness and brought the glances of the last diners back upon their heads. The girl saw and did not care. She embraced him, laid her glowing cheek against his two days' growth of beard, patted and soothed him as if he were a crying child. She told him how it would not be terrible at all. They'd be together again—she'd make the coffee the way he liked it, the way her sisters never could make it, the old way in the agate coffee pot . . .

"But are you sure you can get it back?" he said.

Suppose she couldn't. The earthy terror, the wretch's fear of authority, put out the light behind her face. She turned aside so that he might not see the fear, and her eyes met Miss Bishop's eyes. "Excuse me, father," she said. "There's my teacher over there. I'll ask her whether I can get it back. She'll know."

She rose then and came slowly toward the table through the air which had been inhabited by the exquisite ghost. Fright had bled all the glory from her. She walked with hunched shoulders and a bent head. But that is all right, Miss Bishop thought. Tomorrow I'll teach her not to walk like that. Tomorrow I'll be saying to her, "For heaven's sake, child, walk like the youngest daughter of the King of England. Walk like the Queen of France."

"Pardon me, Miss Bishop," she said, "but I want to know, can a person get back his tuition if he goes away from school in the middle of the year?"

"But you mustn't think of going away from school, Anna."

"But I've got to go, I've got to get the money back."

"But I can't let you go. Really, I can't, because—

Because I love you, she thought. Because I want to hold you in my practiced hands and sift you until there is no earth left in the gold. Because you are the one to fill the empty costume and the empty heart and the empty year. Because, before I

156

die and am buried in a little, forgotten grave, I want to hear your voice ring the length and breadth of this country, rich and unforgettable, sounding everlastingly in a thousand men's ears, memorable as the sweet, strong stroke of a bell.

"Because it would be ridiculous, perfectly ridiculous," she said. "If you need the money, there are scholarships, there are funds, I have a little money on hand myself. Tomorrow I can give you a check, so please put it out of your mind, don't give it another thought tonight. Go back and tell your father that you will have a check for him tomorrow morning—"

She wanted to apologize for eavesdropping, but she did not trust herself to say another word. She gathered up her purse and her coat in shaking hands, and turned her back upon the wondering, glowing face, and fled up the long room and through the door.

Outside, the thaw had begun in earnest. Only a few small islands of snow were left. The black earth yielded under her feet. The rivulets ran down the gutters, the icicles fell and tinkled, the street lamps, seen through the mist, were as mellow as the gold peaches of summer. She whispered to herself on the way to the trolley line; her breath went up in little moist clouds; the taste of the spring was on her tongue, on her lips. "Another spring, another child," she said. "Always another child, another spring."

The Avenger

FOR THE FIRST time in his life he could afford the luxury of traveling in a parlor car. He stepped shyly into the long, cool car with its expanse of gray carpet and its green chairs, wondering whether the passengers who had already settled themselves could tell that he never had been in such a place before. He felt that he could see the end of his poverty and the beginning of a happier, freer state. His chair in this car was a tangible symbol of his new well-being. It was a fine chair, plump and resilient, accommodating itself to the slight weight of his body, holding out its arms to support his own arms, and presenting a little towel, as clean as one of his grandmother's Sunday napkins, for his head. He sank into the chair and sighed and stared through the window at the dark, subterranean platform crossed here and there by wan strips of sun.

On top of his baggage—a briefcase and a scratched traveling bag, for hardly any of the paraphernalia of his life had had time, as yet, to catch up with his fortunes—lay the catalog. It was a slender pamphlet bound in rough paper. The cover was a soft, pale green, the green of new spring leaves or of moss on a log. He knew that whenever he saw that color again, in nature or in the folds of a woman's dress or on a book, his heart would fall open like a flower under the warmth of remembered happiness. For this was the catalog of his first one-man show. It had presented him and his paintings to hundreds of visitors in the metropolitan gallery. The critics, writing such enthusiastic reviews as he hadn't dared hope for, had drawn from these pages the titles of his pictures and the spelling of his unknown name.

The train went rocking through the tunnel that lies under the river. It was a gloomy sort of exit, and in the underground grayness he began to wonder whether he was leaving the city too soon. There were many reasons to hold him there: the telegrams of congratulation, the cocktail parties and the supper parties, the business of at last buying decent furniture for his New York apartment.

But he looked on these pleasures as a part of his future; he could not savor them completely while the taste of an old bitterness was still with him. So, while a few latecomers still straggled in to stare at his canvases, he had taken the train that would carry him back ten years in time to his college town.

The train was still moving through the tunnel. He caught a glimpse of his face on the darkened windowpane. It was gentle, and unimpressive, spare, and topped by somewhat unruly hay-colored hair. He found the sight neither too pleasing nor painful; he had grown used to it. Soon the whole countryside would be spread out for him in September opulence: dark orchards hung with pale or russet fruit, big rivers yellow with mud and tamed by willow roots and rushes, mountain land where the gray rock broke through the soil to remind humanity of the glacial days, plain land dusky with stubble or bright with purple ironweed and goldenrod. In the meantime he must amuse himself, and there lay the catalog. He picked it up and opened it across his knees. He took a whimsical, mischievous delight in the thought that the other travelers would see him studying it and never would know that it was *his*. Nobody would know that it was he who was described on the first page as being "thirty-two, a painstaking craftsman, but concerned above all else with giving form in paint to the innermost recesses of the human mind, as indicated by *Remembrance of a Lost Staircase*, Plate III."

FOR THE FIRST hour of the trip there was no landscape worth watching. The environs of New York were anticlimactic, and the flat, unblessed plains of New Jersey stretched out into one long depression. He gave himself up to the pleasures of the catalog, seeing one of his own works leap up at him in black and white. It was strangely gratifying, too, to read the little biography over and over, adding to its bare outlines all the unmentioned things, the unrecorded struggles, the room where such-and-such had taken place, the gentle, living face of the patron who appeared only as a name, the studios where he had painted, the houses where he had lived, the streets where he had walked, brooding over half-forgotten problems and sorrows. After awhile he ceased to turn the pages. He let the pamphlet lie open at page five, Plate II, *Face of a Foreknown Woman*. Somnolent, like a bee that has had too much honey and too much sun, he was nourished by outer warmth and inner glow. He closed his eyes, and, if the car had remained quiet, he could have slept.

But the car did not remain quiet. A young man, followed by an unhappy conductor and holding forth in a cutting voice, came and settled himself in a chair directly across the aisle from the dreamer's seat. The young man—he made it plain to everybody around him—did not like to travel in parlor cars. A coach was quite good enough for him, but there were no seats in the coaches. Soldiers and soldiers' wives with babies were standing back there in the packed poor man's cars. Yes, yes, he knew all about the end of the war and the need to get the soldiers back to their homes. But if the railroad company had not seen fit to build these luxury cars to accommodate the well-to-do, there might be seats for everybody. Since the company was so damned patriotic, let them make room for four times as many passengers by taking the chairs out of this particular car. Apparently their patriotism did not prompt them to let some of the army people come in here and sit down without paying an extra fee.

UNPLEASANT AS THE young man was, the artist felt a strange inclination to take his part. Perhaps the money he just had paid for the chair had been saved for books or phonograph records: he held a book in his grubby hand and seemed to be waiting to open it until his anger subsided. Plainly he was a student, a somber fellow shadowed by the thundercloud of dissatisfaction that hangs over the sensitive in their early twenties. His cheeks were sallow; his profile was clean and austere; there was a troubling animal look, half-ashamed and half-defiant, in his eyes.

When the incident was over, the painter wished to forget it. He wanted to sink back into the drowsy state of well-being from which the angry voice had roused him. But he found himself transformed. Some of the aggressiveness in the young man's bearing, some of the wrath in his voice, some of the cold scorn in the stares of the other travelers apparently had gotten into him. He felt precisely as he had felt when he had bought his ticket. The rage he had kept at the back of his mind for ten years, the rage that had sprung up to the surface of his mind at the moment of his triumph, the rage that had driven him to the station to find the earliest train to his old college town—the ancient anger was with him again. For the first time since he had entered the peaceful car, he knew his errand was one of revenge.

He turned back to the catalog and stared at Plate II, *Face of a Foreknown Woman*. But that also led him backward into the years; the turn of the neck, the soft fall of the drapery from the rounded shoulder reminded him of a drawing he had done long ago. A nursing mother, drawn in charcoal, drawn in the studio at college ten years ago. He had drawn it with so much tenderness that one of the other students, a plain and philosophic girl who worked beside him, had been moved to lyric eloquence: "It is as if you could see the milk flowing through the veins. And not just milk, either. Something else, maybe the kindness of one generation flowing into the next."

But Mr. Henry Hockland, the Head of the Fine Arts Department, had not seen it in that light. He had glimpsed it out of the corner of his eye as he stood before another student's easel. His hard, thin body in its iron-gray suit positively had quivered to annihilate it. He had advanced upon it, the sun of that lost winter morning shining in his rimless glasses and on his sparse, iron-gray hair. He had suspected it of being obscene; the cold sneer of self-righteousness had twitched the corners of his purplish lips. He was a man of few words, Mr. Henry Hockland, but he always had known how to use them with deadly skill. Whatever he said he emphasized by driving his stick of charcoal in long, forceful slashes across the work that stood before him. "Wrong here," he had said, marring the soft curve of the cheek, "and here," cutting all lushness, and all loving kindness, from the breast. "Furthermore, the whole drawing is out of perspective, a fault that naturally would arise from too much preoccupation with high significance and too little attention to draftsmanship." Then, dropping his charcoal as though it had been contaminated by so gross a thing, he had moved on.

Other bits of Mr. Hockland's malice, sharp and hard as slivers of metal shooting from a lathe, darted at him out of his past. "This piece of work here—how shall I say it?—this *thing* here," said the remembered voice, speaking above the sound of the clattering wheels, "what does it *mean?*" And the successful artist in the parlor car became the shabby boy beside the easel, flushing and stammering and trying to make the living, elusive meaning plain. How wretchedly he must have spoken in those days! The merciful processes of forgetfulness had blotted out his own humiliating reply, had left nothing but the bowed and helpless head, the hand that shook as it gestured, the eyes that had not dared to raise to the tyrant's face, because they were weak and vague with tears.

During the four most vulnerable years of his life, that frosty voice, chiller than his poverty, chiller even than his loneliness, had blown upon every sketch, every painting, until it seemed to him that no season but winter had existed while he was at college, until he remembered himself always as working with stiffened fingers in an icy studio where every breath he breathed went up in a cloud of cold. All those qualities he had considered artistic virtues had congealed into vices under the wintry witchcraft of that voice: his warm and tender rendering of human flesh became obscenity; his ardor became sentimentality; his innovations became arrogance. So he began to doubt, not his paintings only, but the state of his soul. And meanwhile *he*, the frosty wizard, sat comfortably in his little studio, serving to the elect tea in cups as thin as egg shells, spreading his dry hands before a pile of burning logs, looking up now and then to approve of his own canvases—the cherubic children, the summer porches, the moored fishing boats, and the green hillsides, all painted with the same superficial realism. How many times the discredited outcast, sent to the upper floors to find a quire of paper or a bundle of brushes, had glanced through the doorway and seen those shallow, comfortable pictures on the wall. How many times he had thought, "Wait, wait, you icy devil, the world will find you out, my day will come."

WELL HE HAD waited. Old now—he seldom exhibited his paintings anymore—Henry Hockland sat in the same studio, no doubt still holding the annihilating piece of charcoal in his hand. And now at last the student whom he had loathed and envied and persecuted might climb the narrow stairs, not as an errand boy but as a distinguished visitor, might enter the holy tabernacle and see it in its decay, might lay the pale-green catalog on the desk and say the last word in the ancient argument. Perhaps there would not even be a need for a word; perhaps the matter could be settled with one chill, superior smile.

Suddenly his dream of vengeance was broken by a sharp, painful sensation around his heart, a conviction of loss. He glanced at the window to learn what transitory spectacle had floated past him while he dreamed; but even as his glance focused on the fat September fields, he knew that the ache he felt was too private, too personal to have been begotten by any unseen landscape. He stared down then at his empty lap and knew that what he missed was the catalog. It was not in the chair, it was not at his feet, it was nowhere about.

"Pardon me, I think you dropped this." It was the young man across the aisle who spoke. His voice had the same quality the painter had noticed earlier in his face and his person—the bluish, leaden solemnity that hangs in a summer sky before the breaking of a storm, a tone of brooding gravity entirely unsuitable to so simple a statement.

"Thank you very much. I would have been sorry to lose it." As soon as the words were out, it seemed to him that he had said them with too much eagerness. "It would be hard to find another copy," he added lamely, looking at the catalog, open to Plate III, *Remembrance of a Lost Staircase*, held toward him in the lean, somewhat grubby hand.

The somber stranger glanced at the reproduction and pursed his lips. He said nothing, but it was as if he said aloud, "Why should a sane man worry over the loss of such a thing as that?"

"Don't you care for the picture?" The question was entirely unwarranted; he was afraid it had endangered his anonymity, and he wished he had held his tongue.

His neighbor looked at it again. "Oh," he said. "I suppose it's all right. It has a certain sleekness and originality."

•

HE WOULD HAVE been affronted by the cockiness of the answer if his mind had not been drawn from the young man's words to the young man's face. There was in that face something familiar. He felt convinced that he had seen it a hundred times before. Perhaps it was this familiarity that had moved him in the beginning, when he had felt, despite the young man's aggressiveness, a need to take his part. It was not the features themselves, the sallow cheeks and the sharp nose, that seemed to float upward to him out of the obscure and watery depths of his memory; it was the expression upon the face—the pained contraction of the eyebrows, the fugitive movements of the eyes, the sour smile that stirred the lips.

"This picture here, for instance," the young man continued, taking the stare of awakened remembrance for the attentive look of interest. "How can anybody allow himself the luxury of painting this sort of stuff? Imagine producing private little neuroses like these when the world is boiling under your feet."

Secure in the knowledge that "this picture here" had received the unmitigated praise of critics and had been bought for fifteen hundred dollars by a discriminating collector, he did not answer.

"The soldiers out there in the coach—what do you think they would make of a picture like this? How could they use it, what could they do with it? What value would it have for a fellow who was on his way to stand duty in Japan?"

The artist raised his chin and smiled a cold smile. "Strange as it may seem," he said, "there are still a few people left in the world who believe that the human mind has some slight significance."

"A few, a very few. A little brotherhood of neurotics who get together and console themselves with the notion of their own exclusiveness. But can art be exclusive? Doesn't an artist have to speak directly to the masses?"

Ah, thought the artist, I have clashed head on with a Marxian fanatic. With a man who speaks of "the masses" it is useless to discuss art.

"There was a day," said the young man, closing the catalog, "when people thought—as this artist seems to think—that a rehashing of Freud was the means of saving the world. But that was a long time ago. That day is past."

Indignation was quenched again by the upward surge of remembrance. The voice also was familiar, not the tone and pitch of it, but the fury behind it, the gusts of anger that drove the words forth. Somewhere in the past just such a voice had spoken just such prophecies: Make way for the unborn. Bury the dead.

The stranger handed the catalog across the aisle. He has done his Revolutionary Deed for the Day, the artist thought, and now he can take his well-earned rest. His sallow cheek was lost behind the wing of his chair. His hand hung limp against the blue upholstery. Now that he was silent, it would be possible for the artist to turn again to the window, to see the white towns of Pennsylvania floating by, to imbibe the amber well-being of the sunlight on the maples and the chestnuts, to consider cows and sheep, and to gather up again some of the scattered somnolence, some of the early peace.

But the serenity he had known at the beginning of the journey somehow had eluded him. The windows of the parlor car had lost their pristine clarity. Nor, when he turned back to the catalog, did he feel the old satisfaction. It was as if the soft cover had been sullied; it was as if dust had sifted down on the fresh greenness; and he wondered mournfully whether it ever again would seem so rich to look on, so gratifying to touch. I was up very late last night, he told himself. Maybe it's only that I'm tired. And to convince himself that his malady was weariness, he turned his cheek against the little towel and slept.

AT HALF-PAST ten that evening he rose from the long table in the Faculty Club, shook hands with the professors and graduate students who had assembled to honor him, spoke vaguely of an appointment he did not have, and went out into the hot September night. Now that he walked alone among the poplars and beeches, whose leaves showed prematurely yellow in the whiteness of the arc lights, he regretted his abrupt departure from the cordial company. They had been unable to hide their surprise at his sudden going, and some of the younger guests had actually looked sad. But the face he had sought—wintry visage with flashing spectacles—had not been among them; and the whole occasion—the roast beef, the coffee, the discussion, and the wine—had been nothing but a troublesome interlude between his arrival in the city and the moment when he would set eyes on that face.

He was afraid that he had been dull at the dinner. Like a sick man who hears only those words connected with his disease, he had waited for some phrase that would touch on his obsession. Such phrases had been conspicuously absent; it was almost as if the assembly had entered into a conspiracy of silence against him. Finally, when it was plain that the last round of wine had been served, he had asked blatantly, "Where is the Head of the Department tonight?" The silence, the flutter of napkins, the long stares into the goblets had accused him of indiscretion.

"Mr. Hockland?" somebody had said at last. "He doesn't go out much. He seldom comes to faculty affairs anymore."

And then, as if to ease this blow to his hopes, somebody had added that the professor might drop in later, he sometimes did, you never could tell. The guest of honor had not permitted himself to be misled by any such well-meaning conjecture. He knew the old man too well. In the dry, autumnal reaches of the empty campus, he saw again what he had seen in the faculty dining room: a vision of a spare, cold hand dropping a printed card into the wastebasket, a card announcing "a dinner in honor of our distinguished graduate."

•

HE MADE UP his mind to leave this place tomorrow. It stifled him; it seemed to have shrunk to half its remembered size. The rolling lawns of the campus, which had spread out so amply in his thoughts, were only a couple of blocks of drying grass; the buildings looked small and squat against the sparse patches of trees; the magical, glimmering net of glow he remembered from the nights of his youth had been reduced to a few erratic, flickering fireflies. Here and there in one of the bare, academic windows a light still burned, showing the pale blankness of the walls within. He stared up at the windows of the School of Fine Arts. A dead leaf floated slowly down, almost grazing his uplifted face; and he thought how autumn comes too soon, how the summer equinox is barely past before the lawns and gardens are tainted with the first brown markings of decay.

Suddenly he realized that, while these mournful considerations had been floating on one level of his thoughts, some other part of his mind had been occupied with counting windows. That wan, bluish square three floors up and two windows from the left—he knew that room. That was the room where the Head of the Department sat, serving tea in cups as thin as egg shells to those exalted ones who, like their master, were above attending a dinner in his honor.

It occurred to him then that he was no longer an outcast, obliged to stand in darkness and look in at the light. There was nothing to keep him from crossing that threshold and claiming his cup of the supernal tea. Tomorrow, he thought, tomorrow I will do it. Then his pulse hastened with the knowledge that he would go up now, tonight. He stood a moment longer in the darkness, adjusting his tie and staring at the halting glimmer of the fireflies. Then he walked over the mournful, crackling leaves and into the inverted shell of blackness that was the entrance to the place.

The door creaked as he opened it, but more faintly than in the past. The square hall before him, peopled with statues, shrank from the vastness of memory to the limited proportions of reality. It was too small for the plaster shapes that inhabited it. He seemed to be crowded and threatened by the twisted beard of Moses, the hanging hand of David, the stiff skirts of the Caryatids, the great foot of Venus thrust from beneath chipped drapery.

The building was thick with the stored heat of the day, somber with shadows, and alive with suddenly released remembrances. He saw his own young body leaning against the pedestal that upheld the Moses; he heard his own young voice holding forth to a knot of other students, his righteous anger driving the words forth like leaves in a gust. Then, for no reason that he could fathom, the fellow whom he had met in the chair car came into his thoughts again, making wide gestures, staring angrily at the catalog, rolling his eyes. He stopped at the foot of the stairs and saw a reflection of himself, dark and indefinite, on the surface of the library door. I have changed, he thought, I have dried and faded, it is very likely that I have begun to grow old.

On the first landing of the winding staircase, he paused again and felt the pounding of his heart through all his body. The cold, immortal face of Giotto's Dante, staring at him from the wall, suggested nothing but his own mortality. Perhaps, he told himself, it would be better to go up tomorrow. It might be best not to go up at all. Yet here, under this same picture, the old man once had taken him to task. The chill voice still sounded above the resounding voices of cleaning women calling to one another. Hurry then, avenge the insult, settle the account, the years go quickly, there is never enough time.

ON THE LAST landing he paused once more and drew a long, shaking breath. The scent of the place, the smell of his bitter years assailed him—dust, disinfectant, oil, and turpentine. In the hall, lighted only by the square of glow that fell from Mr. Henry Hockland's doorway, the past and the present merged so completely that he could not tell whether the murmurous voices he heard were sounding in actuality or in remembrance, whether the tea party in progress beyond the threshold was an assembly of the living or a convocation of ghosts.

He assumed an air of self-possession and knocked three times on the open door. The real sound dispelled the voices of remembrance. He knew that the room was utterly still. It seemed to him also that it was utterly empty, peopled only by the forgotten race that looked on him from the paintings on the wall—the cherubic children, the women whose hair and dresses had been fashionable in his mother's heyday, the ruddy old gentlemen who long since must have lost their ruddiness in the grave. The world against which these beings stood was also legendary, also lost—world of paper lanterns, translucent tea cups, cut-glass water cruets, and heavy Morris chairs. Someone moved at the other end of the room. An old man, very gaunt, very white, very neat, with his pale skin hanging loose on his bones, rose slowly from a chair. Rose so slowly it was evident that the movement was a great effort and a cause for pain.

"Good evening, Mr. Hockland," the young man said.

The Head of the Department advanced slowly, without a word, past the fireless hearth and the empty tea table, under the forgotten paintings, the roseate faces that still bestowed on him their static stares and smiles. Fear, a ghost of the old fear, stiffened the young man's body. He stood on the threshold, erect and arrogant, waiting to see the icy glance, to watch these changed, loose lips curl in the remembered sneer. Suddenly he started and stepped back a pace. The old man did not know him, could not recall him—no, the old man could not see him, was almost blind. The keen and wintry look was melted now on the surface of thick lenses. The eyes seemed large, childish, moist; the ice had been broken up by illness or worn away by tears.

Then the vague glance focused on him. A blank look of wonder passed across the professor's face, and he stepped forward, holding out his hand, and said the young man's name.

But I had not meant to shake hands with you, he thought, touching the dry fingers. This is the hand that drove the charcoal across my living work.

"I *am* right? You *are* our famous alumnus? Well, it was very good of you to climb all these stairs to visit me, very good indeed."

But I came in anger and not to visit, he thought. Let me explain that, let me drive any such notion out of your head.

"You do have a minute, don't you? You'll come in and sit down, at least until you've caught your breath. Over here by the window there's a breath of air."

But I had not meant to sit down by this window, overlooking a dry lawn in a dying season. I had meant to stand above you as you stood over me in the old days, remote and cold. What am I doing here, sitting in the seat you once denied me, staring at the fireflies? Why should I waver on pity when you keep your pride secure, when you would not walk fifty steps to sit at a table spread for my sake?

The old man eased himself into his chair. "I have to take it slowly," he said. "My back aches. I've been sick. I've had a lot of trouble with my gallbladder."

So you have come to admit that you have a gallbladder. The flesh you rejected has finally forced itself on you. Now you have a gallbladder—you who refused to admit that a nursing mother has breasts. The stillness demanded some sort of answer. He made the usual clucking sound of polite regret and stared stubbornly at the night beyond the window. A slight wind was moving among the trees. Now and then a leaf fell past the arclight and lost itself in the darkness below.

"WAS IT A good party?" Mr. Hockland said.

His mouth fell open at the effrontery of the question. Somewhere in this tall skeleton, draped in loose skin and shaken with sickness, a trace of the old malice remained. To speak of the dinner at all was to remind the guest of honor that one man at least had preserved his pride by refusing to go.

"Yes," he said in a hard voice, "it was a good party. I thought perhaps I might find you there."

"I?" The dry hand gestured at the windowsill. A piece of notepaper, half covered with a cramped and painful script, lay on it. "It's strange, just before you came in I was writing a little note to you. I was going to ask one of the students to take it down in the morning to your hotel. I thought—it occurred to me that you might possibly notice my absence, and I wanted to explain. I was going to tell you it was because of the food. That would have been the truth, in a way, because there's hardly any ordinary food that I can digest anymore." He rose and wandered about the room as he talked, perhaps because he found sitting painful, perhaps because he was embarrassed by the words he found it necessary to say. "I'm looking around for a couple of cups," he explained. "I thought if you had a minute, you might like some tea. About the dinner, that matter of the food, that would have been part of the truth. The fact is I don't go to faculty parties anymore. I. . . . Here are those cups, two of them, too, but they're terribly dusty. I'd hate to count how long it is since I've had anybody up here for tea." He struck a match and set it to the hot plate. His hands were translucent, his face was cadaverous in the blue burst of light. "Since the last time I was in the hospital—that's about three years ago—I somehow can't find the strength for anything. John Ferraro—*he* does the work—they think I don't notice it, but of course I do—he's the real head. I've got nothing really but the name. And at these parties, I cramp Ferraro's style. I cramp everybody's style in a way. Skeleton at the feast. You know what I mean."

The young man wished earnestly that he had not come to this place. He looked about him for some antidote against pity. But everything—the sorrowful night beyond the window, the fireless hearth, the dusty cups, the withered hand that tilted the kettle, the fragments of a lost world preserved on the wall— everything was a reason for tears.

"PROBABLY NOBODY MISSED me."

"Of course I missed you, Mr. Hockland," he said, "I noticed at once that you weren't there. I thought that—" But he could not say what it was he had thought. The smile of gratefulness on the sick face struck him dumb.

The professor returned to the window, bearing the two cups of tea precariously in his shaking hands. He put them on the sill and sat down again, with the air of one who finds all positions, all situations eventually intolerable, and settles only temporarily in any spot, knowing that pain soon will drive him forth again.

"You know, I never cared for your work," he said, and the glance behind the thick lenses glinted with a flash of the old malice, the old pride.

I should answer that, the visitor thought, and I cannot answer it because there is a crack at the bottom of this eggshell cup, because the roses in that still life are long since dead, and the tea that you swallow now will be a torment to you all night long. The silence was burdensome. In the hush he remembered a phrase that he had heard in church on the Sunday mornings of his childhood: "Have mercy upon all of us," There was more to that phrase, but he could not recall it. He stirred his tea with a tarnished spoon and said, "I know."

"Not that my opinion should make the slightest difference, because, I assure you, it hasn't a bit of weight anymore. The canons by which I judged you are no longer considered valid."

The younger man turned from the cadaverous face to the night beyond the window. For the moment he could neither drink nor speak; he was sick with the completeness of his own victory. He wanted now only to find some phrase that might lessen the darkness and ease the pain. "There are some canons," he said at last, "that are above such changes. I was thinking as I came upstairs how that figure of Moses you admired—"

"That figure of Moses," the professor said dreamily. "I always remember you lolling against that statue of Moses."

"It's very good of you to remember me at all."

"Lolling against that statue of Moses and looking through the catalog of one of my shows. I don't think you saw me. I was on the first landing, looking over the banister. You flipped your way through the pages, and there was an angry, dissatisfied look on your face, and when you were finished—and you were finished quickly—you left the catalog lying on the pedestal, and you went off shrugging and smiling to yourself."

He remembered the incident. He could feel the cool, plaster foot of the Moses against his arm, could sense the soft cover of the catalog under his fingertips. The catalog was blue—no, green—the color of new spring leaves. The black-and-white reproductions were called *Fishing Boats at Provincetown*, *Face of a Foreknown Woman*, *Main Street on Sunday*, *Remembrance of a Lost Staircase*. The memory was caught in a current of rushing sound. Voices of students hurrying from class to class? Clatter of turning wheels? Breaking of waves against sand?

For suddenly he saw not the room nor the night, but a stretch of coast toward which three waves hastened—one only beginning to rise out of the uneasy surface of the ocean, one crowned with a magnificent crest, and one sinking in sickly foam against the shore. And even as he stared, a new wave rose behind the last, and that which had leaped, highest was driven downward, and he heard the voice in the parlor car saying, "That day is past." Then the moving sea withdrew and gave place to another vision. He saw himself on an autumnal evening, making tea in just such a room as this; only there were other canvases upon the wall—subtly distorted figures moving in dreamlike landscapes—and the cup of tea passed from his own hand to the hand of the enigmatic traveler, who was no longer young.

•

"FORGIVE ME," HE said. "I knew very little, I was arrogant. It never would have occurred to me that a man of your prestige could have given even a passing thought to the opinions of a student."

The professor, unable to endure the pressure of the chair against his body, had begun again to wander around the room. The young man swallowed the last of the tea in his cup, and then rose also, and looked along the line of canvases for one on which he might bestow a little honest praise. "That still life there," he said, laying his hand upon the withered arm, "I remember that. It's pleasant to see it again after all these years. You had a way all your own of making objects seem to float on light."

He talked long and eloquently, moving from picture to picture, until the last square of yellow had disappeared from the other windows, until the moon was setting behind the dying trees. And long afterwards, when he walked alone across the campus, he said aloud the fragment he had remembered from the Sunday mornings of his childhood. Now he had recaptured it in its entirety. "Have mercy upon all of us," he said, crossing the withering grass, "and upon me also, O God."

The King's Daughter

THE TENDING OF the king's goats was not the tedious business that David had expected it to be. The sun had scarcely passed its zenith when the whole task was done. While the princess Michal gathered up the scraps of their noonday meal, he lay on his back in the shadow of a mulberry tree. He was pleasantly tired with so much running, and a little dizzy with the heat of the high summer sun. His mouth was moist and fresh after the milk, and his sweat had turned into a cool film in the shade. He watched her as she put the leavings of the food away, nibbling a bit here and there—now a raisin, now a curd—and he thought how it had been a blithe enough morning after all; nor was he altogether glad to see it at an end.

On the way to the meadows he had been taciturn and sullen. At the morning meal, Michal had called attention to his mean origin; she had commanded him forth for the day like any hired shepherd; she had put the ache of his dreams upon his waking hours; and because of her he was to be parted from Jonathan. Once or twice on the road she had attempted to draw him into talk. Her father, Saul, would soon be with them in Gibeah, she had said; listen to the toads croaking in the marsh; did he, like herself, delight in the feel of dew upon his feet? He had vouchsafed her scarcely a word. She had walked too close to him, so that her warm, thick curls often brushed his shoulder and her swinging hand often knocked against his thigh. And, God of hosts, he had asked himself, what does she want of me? Does she touch me out of desire, or simply because I am so insignificant that she barely knows I am nearby?

But as soon as the flock closed around him, as soon as he smelled the familiar odor of wool and felt the silky goats' hair rippling past his shins, as soon as he found himself in the middle of that flowing, leaping, mincing mass of nimbleness and lechery, all his sulkiness was gone. It had been long since he walked in the midst of a herd; the rank and pungent smell was to him as the air on a mountain is to a mountaineer who has come home from a journey upon some fetid plain. A wild and merry mood possessed him. He shouted and whistled far more than was needful. He moved among the goats as a temple dancer moves before a god—graceful, intoxicated, catching the curven horns, vaulting over the bony backs, slapping the soft white sides. It was as if the spirit of the herd had leapt from the hairy, incontinent bodies of the goats and fastened upon him. "David," Michal had said a dozen times that morning, "is the Baal in your flesh? Are you possessed?" But if there was censure in her voice, her face was the face of one in league with the spirit. Her mouth was parted, and the moist white edges of her teeth shone. Her tongue kept passing, swift as a serpent's, over her lower lip. Nor could he imagine any longer that her freedom with him was a matter of sheer indifference. She was forever wading toward him through the waves of skipping beasts; whenever she could manage it she brushed against him and the tension of his mood kept heightening under her touch. What manner of girl is it, he asked himself, who kneels and leans forward so that her tunic falls away from her breasts? Who has taught her to leap over goats so that her thighs are plain and also the down upon her thighs? Why must she forever be raising her arms to fasten her hair, showing the dark hollows of her armpits with their small clusters of curls? It had been a wild and chaotic morning. He had been hard put to keep the Baal of the goats at bay.

King's daughter, he had kept saying to himself all through the herding. Child of a royal family who can afford to let their hands wander as they please. She may catch me by the wrist, she may sidle like a cat against my shins, she may breathe her warm breath straight into my face. But if my Judahite hand should reach out and touch her breast, if my Judahite mouth should fall upon her asking mouth—what then—what wounded innocence, what affronted pride and royal rage?

Try as he would, he could not understand her. She should have despised the shepherd in him; instead she never ceased to show her wonder at his skills. "How is it, son of Jesse," she would say—and her voice would lay a veil of honor and consequence upon his father's name—"how is it that you know without question that this kid will not thrive, but will surely die?" And he would assume the role that she had put upon him; he would become the wise male instructing the childish female in obvious things. "Behold his hooves. How old is he? Then under what moon was he born? And who would expect a kid dropped under a summer moon to last longer than seventy days?" As the morning waned, she began to contend with him over certain matters: the poisonous qualities of a kind of weed, the best way to rid a goat of fleas, the comparative merits of the comb and the fingers in taking the snarls out of the silky hair. But it was plain to him that she argued for the joy of submitting. In the end she would lean back, breathless and happy to surrender. "The star of Judah," she would say, "it is with him in herding as in singing. His word is the last word and the best."

All through the meal he had been silent. His body remained quiet in the shade of the mulberry; but his thoughts, driven by the Baal of the goats, leaped and swerved and darted on. To whom was she betrothed? What lovers had spoken for her?

Had she ever been possessed? Or was she, like himself, a virgin wishing to seem wise? Had he fancied it or had he really seen a little garland of hair around her nipples? What scent was on her flesh, under the perfume? Did she fear Saul? Did she wage an everlasting war against her brother Jonathan? What cities had she visited? Were the dark curls in her armpits softer than his own? What would she do if he reached across the spread cloth, even now, and held her across his knees and kissed her full on the lips? Would she cry out at once? Or would she melt first and lie quiet long enough for his hands to know. . . . How would he kiss her? More in hate than in love, he thought, in hate until her mouth was flattened out of shape, until. . . . What thoughts to think concerning a king's daughter! Who in Israel had thought such thoughts before? Oh, but he knew that many thought them. The whole army thought them and spoke them not whenever she came forth in a tunic that flipped above her knees. It was this that they thought, all of them, when they said discreetly, "Michal is the moon of Israel, fair among the fair." Thinking of such matters, he had remained quiet over the curds and bread.

She, too, had kept her peace. And when she had risen to clear the food away, she had the air of one who has wrestled long with a bodiless and tormenting spirit. Her shoulders had sagged and her face had looked tired.

It was no great wonder that both of them were exhausted. In the wildness of their mood they had done a full day's work in half a day. On a far hillock behind them, golden under the sun, its outline shimmering and changing in the heat, Saul's favorite herd grazed, their clean, soft noses pushing through the withering grass, their flowing coats as white as milk. David lay perfectly still, staring up through the leaves of the mulberry. They looked solid and almost black against the burning blue of the sky. As he stared, a strange unhappiness came upon him. The day was crass, brazen, striding like a prostitute across the earth, with legs apart. He thought with longing of the subtle, tremulous, mothy night.

She came and sat down beside him under the mulberry tree. He lay looking up at her. She sat with her arms clasped round her knees. The weariness had apparently left her, and she looked firm and slim and fair. Her flesh glowed softly from so much running about in the sun; it was as if a lamp had been lighted within her; her cheeks, her shoulders, her throat, and the tips of her fingers were roseate. The scent of spice that had been upon her in the morning was almost gone. Now her body had the odor of sun-dried sweat, a smell as wholesome and pleasing as the smell of baking bread.

"How tall is the armor bearer of my father," she said, letting her glance move slowly over the length of him. "Being the daughter of Saul, I am of a good height. And yet were I to lie down beside David, the top of my head would reach his shoulder only. David is tall indeed."

He felt curiously remote. His desire had ebbed from him. It is strange, he thought, how much likeness there is between any wench and a king's daughter. Thrice in his life women had sat down beside him after the herding and made the same observation: "How tall. . . . Were I to lie down. . . ." In Bethlehem he had answered the children of herdsmen and farmers with a comment that always served him well; it vaunted his own manliness and drove them away at the same time. "Well, then, lie down," he had said in the hills of Judah, "lie down and see." Now the old taunt formed in his thoughts, but it did not pass his lips. He kept his peace, perhaps because even in her dallying she had reminded him that Saul's blood ran precious and sanctified in her veins, perhaps because her level look told him that she would not run giggling and squealing out of his reach. She might accept the challenge. She who had come into his room unattended that morning, she who had seen a vision of him lying upon his bed, she who had come to him through the lecherous goats, watching his body through his tunic, blowing her warm, sweet breath upon him—she might very well lie down and see.

And then? That desire which he had ceased to guard against, believing it weakened, sprang upon him again. If he had longed for her before, it had been a sickly shadow of longing compared to this. He stared at the fierce blue sky that glared between the black leaves of the mulberry, he stared until his eyes ached, trying to stare down the thought of what might happen then. His body throbbed and changed in the heat of his yearning as the outline of the distant hill quivered under the sun. The old images, the dreams that he had dreamed of women whom he had met on the road or at the shearing, were unacceptable, were not enough. It seemed to him that the daily shape of love could never serve the fervor which she had roused in him. Love must be cruelly twisted and changed, love must be tortured out of shape, love must take unto itself some of her brown, sweet, stinging violence. Desire must be wreaked upon her as a kind of vengeance—vengeance upon the king's daughter who kept her shy virginal airs for some lordly bed and turned wench among the goats with a Judahite . . .

In the midst of these thoughts, he felt her glance upon him. He raised his eyes to her face, expecting to see a coy glance glinting through lowered lashes. He encountered instead a pair of grave, wide-open eyes. There was something admirably unwomanish, something of clean, boyish honor in the frankness with which she saw and accepted his desire. A strange familiar smile, at once mocking and tender, indented the corners of her lips. Where had he seen that smile before? On Saul's face, and it was Saul's daughter whom his thoughts had ravaged and put to shame. The remembrance of her somber father stood suddenly there behind her, gazing down upon him with that strange commingling of mockery and affection that at once chastised and comforted the heart. Simply because she is a king's daughter, the eyes of Saul said, there is no need to deal with her as if she were a prostitute. And David was reproved and ashamed of the violence and crassness of his own longing. He turned upon his face. She leaned against the trunk of the mulberry tree and sighed.

In the complete quiet of the summer afternoon he could hear his heart beating more and more slowly against the earth. It was almost as if he had actually possessed her. In his imaginings, he had mastered her; in her look she had come forth to him, surrendering herself with a knowing smile. Now his longing subsided; the Baal of the goats, chastened and peaceable, re-entered the hairy bodies and grazed calmly upon the hill. He raised his head and saw her above the curve of his arm. She also had grown quieter. Her breasts rose and fell regularly against the harsh blueness; a look of dreaming had come upon her face. For the first time he asked himself what thoughts passed through the mind of the King's daughter—what she dreamed here in this sun-drenched meadow and in the darkness of her room by night when she stood at the window, pulling the golden pins from her hair. It is possible, he thought, that she thinks of me . . .

After a long silence she spoke as one speaks in a dream, letting a detached thought float serenely into the hush. "I was betrothed to Agag," she said.

For a moment he was bitter for his own sake. He was slighted, shoved without ceremony out of her thoughts to make way for the mincing heathen from the south. Then he let his own pique be eaten up by a larger and more high-minded anger. He was wroth for Jahveh and for Israel. The man of Judah, the stern man of God in him was affronted to hear it. Heathen in the King's house—uncleanness in a royal bed—"To an *Amalekite?*"

"Nay, now," she said, stretching against the trunk and smiling. "Had Samuel not given him up to God, he would have become as one of us. He had consented to be circumcised."

Another woman's tongue would have traveled around the

word or stumbled upon it. She said it as smoothly and casually as his mother or sister might have said "bread." He knew with amazement that she needed neither womanly terror nor womanly wonderment in her dealings with men. Honor—a boy's honor—would dictate her ways in love. For her, what was so, was so—good and to be used and loved. She would know the worth of what she received and pay for it in full, caress for caress. Had he known her forthright passion then, the dead Amalekite? Before he went down into Sheol, had he also walked with her to tend her father's goats among these far and empty hills? The question drew him away from her into some remote vantage place beyond the scent of her body, beyond the world. He felt no anger, only an aching heaviness . . .

"The star of Judah never looked upon Agag," she said in the same dreamer's voice.

"No."

"He was a sorrowful man . . ."

And did you comfort his sorrows? Did you rest his sorrowing face between your small, brown breasts?

"He had seen much and known much and suffered much before my father brought him home . . ."

Yes, more than I have seen and known and suffered—far more than I. For what is longing for Jesse and homesickness for the dust-brown rooms of Bethlehem beside the vision of a fallen city and a torn scarlet cloak and every brother, every good companion slain? Would I had seen the Amalekite and played before him in the evenings. Would I had sat at his knee, hearing the tales of his grievous journeys far into the night. What he knew of the world is buried in Gilgal. I cannot learn it now. He was a subtler man, a wiser man than I . . .

"We were betrothed in Gilgal. Three moons passed after his death before I took the ring that he gave me from my finger, and my hand was lonely without it. When I awoke, my finger felt empty in the night."

"Do you still mourn for him then?" he said.

"How long is it that the living can mourn for the dead? Furthermore, I never knew him. Between him and me, it was nothing but words and looks, and they are slighter and easier to lose than the other. Saul, my father, knew him well, and Saul has mourned longer than I."

He turned on his side and saw her lean brown hand lying open beside him on the withered grass. It was there for the taking; to leave it trailing loose and empty would be a piece of coldness and unfriendliness. And she had been friendly to him, frank and companionable, opening her thoughts to him as directly and decently as she had offered contact with her body. He took her hand and drew it toward him and turned his cheek against it. It was like the hand of a boy—warm, spare, redolent of earth and heat.

"I saw you in Ephes-Dammim," she said.

"When I sang in the tent of the king my lord?"

"No, earlier. Much earlier than that."

"When?"

She smiled. "I will not tell. Only tell me this, what Baal was it that you worshipped in Ephes-Dammim by the cistern in the grove of willows? It was said by the maidservant of Rizpah that you worshipped some Baal—"

"I?" He started up in consternation. A confusion of images descended upon him. The little stone Astarte slipping from Joab's fingers into his own palm; his cheek resting against the vessel by the cistern—the vessel which Jonathan's hand had touched; his body leaning over the dark water—his eyes seeking their own reflection there. He felt an unreasonable sense of guilt. It was as if he had truly worshipped some unclean god among the mustard flower and the pearly mists, and he was afraid.

"Do not fear to tell me," she said. "I am no carrier of tales. It is only that I would leave a gift by night and in secret for the Baal that is the Baal of David."

He withdrew his hand from hers and spread it southward,

asking the Lord to bear witness. "But I have no God save Jahveh who is the only God in Israel," he said.

She smiled and looked at him with pert, unbelieving eyes. "Think of it no more. I will find him for myself. I already know his nature and his dwelling. He lives in a cistern, and he is a god of pain."

"You speak a mystery, and I cannot understand it."

"No, then," she said softly, "do not tell me. A time will come when you will tell me, and meanwhile I can wait. Only, I wish from my heart that I might have communication with this spirit, because for many moons I have had need of a Baal of pain."

He stared at her in wonder. What was it in Saul's household that made them carry the wounds of their spirits like banners, so that all men might see and know? Saul's wife, Ahinoam, leaving her cheeks unrouged, walking through the garden with the tread of the weary and rejected, making it plain to all Israel that she was an old woman, despised and outworn. Saul, saying, as casually as another might speak of a stubbed finger, "Such-and-such came to pass in Gilgal, or in Gibeah, or at Ephes-Dammim on a day when Jahveh sent an evil sprit upon me." Jonathan talked freely of the hour when his heart had failed him and the blood in his veins had gone to water. And now she, the royal, the golden, the fortunate, saying to him that she stood in need of a god of pain. . . . And again he was reproved by this honorable nakedness. He who had exhibited his hurts only when there was profit to be pulled out of pity, he who had always kept silence about his own shortcomings and had hoped that the world would lock all his flaws behind closed lips—he wished now that he could find the gallantry to say, "I also have need of such a god. In Ephes-Dammim I was despised, and in the grove by the cistern I sought your brother and found him not and wept."

She moved a little closer to him and drew his hair away from his face. "Why is the rose of Bethlehem so grave?" she said.

He laughed uneasily. "I was thinking how all of us must

sometimes feel the need of such a god as the maidservant of Rizpah fancied that I worshipped by the cistern—"

"You also?" she asked.

"I? How am I different from the rest?"

"What could trouble you, and what would be denied you? All that you yearn after is at your hand even before the yearning, seeing that you are so fair."

"Then Michal my lady also would need no such god. She is as the sun."

"Truly?" She looked him square in the face.

"Yes, truly."

"Then," she said without lowering her eyelids, "let the son of Jesse kiss me upon the lips."

He was surprised that he had not the slightest desire to kiss her. In fact, there was something distasteful in the thought of laying his mouth against hers, of breathing her breath. From his babyhood he had always struggled against the requested kiss; a procession of sisters-in-laws, aunts, and aging neighbor women sprang up in his thoughts, all demanding a familiarity that he could not freely give. He bent and surrendered his mouth with hidden unwillingness. He could not find any cause for the faint tinge of disgust; her lips were moist and tender, her breath was steady and sweet. He kissed long out of courtesy and kindliness, and put her from him with a gallant sigh. "I have kissed the mouth of the daughter of the king," he thought, smiling and resting his head against the bark. But the glory of it was far less than he had dreamed. The day with all its works was a heaviness upon him. He wanted the still room in the tower, and the moonlight, and the stirring, breathing walls. She smelled of the sun. He wanted the dark.

"Are you thirsty?" she said.

"No. Wherefore?"

"Because your mouth is dry as sand."

He remembered an old wives' saying that a dry mouth never holds the wine of love. He put his hand uneasily to his lips.

She rose and smoothed the skirt of her tunic. Her eyes were no longer frank and wide. It was as if she had been tainted by the duplicity, the equivocation of his kiss. "I am thirsty," she said, "and the milk must be soured with lying so long in the sun. Let us shake down some of these mulberries."

He did not move. He continued to sit with his back against the trunk. She drew very near and closed her arms around the mulberry. Her thigh brushed his shoulder and grazed against his face. She still wishes to stir me, he thought. She gives me the scent of her body, and it is sweet; she gives me the firmness of her flesh through the moving cloth. Perhaps, if I remembered my morning longing, these dry twigs of desire might take fire again. Perhaps if I . . .

She shook the little tree with all her might. Her body knocked softly against him. Suddenly, by handfuls, loosened all at once, the ripe black fruits came tumbling down.

They fell upon his head, upon his shoulders, upon his upturned palms. They fell gently, as cool and moist as great drops of water. He closed his eyes and relinquished himself to the night. There was no sun-scorched meadow now, no burning sky; there was Saul's garden after rain, aromatic with the smell of herbs and crushed grass, lyric with a voice that spoke of fallen Shiloh and the ark of God. The hand that lay upon his shoulder was no brown hand; it was the pale, veined hand of the beloved. The mulberries continued to fall, more slowly now; and the transparent drops rolled down very slowly through the tremulous, breathing night, upon his head and upon the cloudy hair of Jonathan. Friend, cousin, beloved of my spirit, he thought, behold, I have been whoring in the fields among the lecherous goats when I might have been seeking after a sight of your face. What is she to me? A woman and a stranger. My mouth that touched your fingers is tainted by her wanton mouth. How shall I come to you again with this mark upon me? He turned his head slowly against the bark. His eyes burned. He could have wept.

"Your lap is full. Will you eat?" she said.

He started up, rolling the berries upon the earth.

"No, now, see what you have done. Do not rise. You will trample them, and they are so big and fair."

He gathered a handful and stuffed them into his mouth, but he could not taste them. His palate was salt with tears.

She picked the berries from the ground, dusted them against her brown arm, and ate them one by one. A small purple stain showed at the corners of her lips. Her eyes no longer sought his. Perhaps they knew there was that in his face which would be bitter to see. She knelt apart from him, very straight, so that the fold of her tunic no longer fell forward from her breasts.

"Let us return now to your father's house," he said.

"Now? In the heat of the sun?" It was not a protest, it was a complaint; her little tawny face was puckered like the face of a disappointed child.

"But if we have to wait for the sunset, the evening meal will be over before we have returned. It is best that we arise and go without delay. There are trees along the road. We can walk in the shade."

"Let it be as the son of Jesse wishes," she said. "Only, I had thought that it might be pleasant to the lutist to walk back to Gibeah in the wind of God, and to eat the evening bread as we ate the morning bread, in the common room, without the whole world standing by."

He saw that she regretted her speech before it was finished. Saul's anger burned in her cheeks. All her movements became angular and hard. She rose and stamped upon the mulberries. Some of the juice spattered upon his tunic, and she looked at the stain with a malicious smile.

He felt at that moment a shadow of the fear which he felt in her father's presence. She knows more than the surface of things, he thought. She is subtle and strong, and she would make a relentless enemy. He remembered with uneasiness the raisin eyes in the face of Doeg the Edomite. A man must walk

189

warily, walking on the edge of power. . . . He leaned toward her and encircled her legs with his arm, and laid his head against her side. "To speak truly," he murmured into the folds of her tunic, "I am very weary."

"With brushing the hides of a few goats?"

"With struggling all day against the longing after the king's daughter, whose lips are the first I have ever touched in love. It is with me as though I had drunk all day of a powerful wine, and my heart turns faint within me, and I have a great need for sleep."

He could feel her body grow vital and resilient as the joy tore through it. He was ashamed and could not look into her eyes. "Truly?" she said. But she wanted no answer. She believed out of her need for belief. And he knew with mingled fright and triumph that the king's daughter loved him, not for an afternoon of ardor in a distant meadow, but everlastingly. And before the world? Before Saul? Before Ahinoam? Before all the proud Benjamites who looked coldly upon Judah? Before the host where he had lain despised and unknown? Before all Israel? He could not leave such questions unanswered. He must know his value and his destiny.

"No, now," he said in a sorrowful voice, pressing his forehead against her thigh, "what profit is there in it? He who betrothed you to Amalek may take it into his mind to give you to Moab, or to Philistia, or to some Syrian, or to one in Phoenicia who owns forest land in Lebanon."

Her body stiffened again, this time with pride. "My father loves me," she said. "He will not sell me for the price of a forest, nor for any distant city, nor even for ten years of peace in Israel. Agag had charred bones and ashes for his marriage portion, but Saul loved him. Saul will give me to him whom Saul loves."

He knew that this was so. Such knowledge should have been to him as the clashing of many cymbals and the voices of many lutes. But the delight of it was muted; his heart was sorrowful; it was only his lips which smiled. Fair she was, and a king's daughter, and half-wild with longing for him. Even so, a man might turn his back upon a day of passion with her. But who could walk away from all the glories that lie in a royal bed? Son-in-law of Saul, captain over a thousand, lord of such-and-such an estate with arbors and fields and orchards, owner of such-and-such flocks and herds. . . . Dear son of Ahinoam, friend of Abner, brother to Jonathan. . . . And yet an ache stirred within him; and yet a few mulberries kept falling, moist and cool into the magical night . . .

"Come, then, beloved. We will go that you may sleep," she said.

He rose slowly. Hand in hand, like lovers, they walked toward the roofs and towers of Gibeah. No words passed between them, and to those who passed them along the way, they had the air of sleepwalkers, each intent upon some vision within his own heart.

The Matchmaking

IT MUST HAVE been the change in weather that put the idea into her head. All afternoon, thick heat had gathered under the roof of the bungalow, filling the little rooms until the polished furniture felt as hot as a feverish forehead under the touch. Heat waves had rippled along the white, glaring windowsills. Out in the garden, the crimson ramblers had sagged in the heavy afternoon, and not a leaf on the poplars had stirred.

The piano stood in the coolest part of the house, in a windowless, shadowy alcove. But the heat had invaded even this dim corner, giving an oppressive reality to the bamboo shoots and the palm leaves that wandered up the wallpaper.

All day it had seemed to her that she was teaching her piano students in a jungle. It was the heat of the Congo that had wilted their blouses and pasted their hair to their cheeks. It was into the steaming atmosphere along the banks of the Amazon that they had poured their scales and sonatas. The talk of her own two children, lolling in the shuttered bedroom, had been transformed into the chatter of monkeys, and the screeching brakes and humming tires on the avenue had become the whirring and screaming of tropical birds.

Then all at once, while the last student was wearily scattering the notes of the Chopin *Ballade* against the heat, all at once, when the voices in the bedroom had taken on that whining, urgent note that foretold a quarrel, a distant peal of thunder reduced them all to silence—sudden and mystifying, since the sun continued to shine and the sky had not lost any of its pitiless blue.

Somewhere in the far, unpeopled hills, the storm had broken. None of its violence had fallen upon the city, but its blessings came quickly, lavishly after that first thunderclap. She laid her hand upon the shoulder of the young woman who sat at the piano, and lifted her face to breathe an air light, swift, sweet with the smell of new-cut grass and roses.

The whole house was thrown into a delightful agitation. The evening newspaper blew open on the sofa, the roses in the blue bowl shed their creamy petals onto the coffee table, and the white curtains, streaming in pairs into the room, twisted with the lightness and grace of girls leaping in a ballet.

"Oh, Lord!" she said, flinging up her arms so that the wind might ripple up and down the whole length of her body. "Sally, don't play another note. Stand up and feel this. It'll never last." And the two of them had gone to the window to be present at the miracle, to see the sunlight change from molten gold to cool yellow upon the lawn, to watch the wind pluck the strings onto which her husband had trained the cinnamon vines—great, cool fingers of some wind god playing unheard music on a leafy lyre.

It was then that she looked with new eyes at the young woman beside her. Until this moment, the girl had been, for her, nothing but a gifted pianist, a crystal, meaningless and clear, through which the music of Beethoven, Mozart, and Chopin might pass.

Now, through the blowing curtain that billowed between them, she saw for the first time a living young woman—shy, awkward, and undiscovered, but startlingly beautiful nevertheless. The long body beneath the white sharkskin dress had the large perfection of classical statues. The apricot cheeks were sprinkled with golden freckles. The eyes were grayish blue under the brown, level brows. Flapping like a spaniel's ears on either side of the face, sleek and brown and silky, hung two bright lengths of hair.

Something—perhaps the wind and perhaps the sight of so much unexpected beauty—made it impossible for her to hold her tongue. "Sally," she said, "it's going to last after all. I bet it'll drop to sixty this evening. What a night to be in love!"

The grave face on the other side of the floating marquisette did not answer, could manage nothing more than a strained smile.

"Sally, do you have a lover?"

"I, Mrs. Schoen? No, I don't have a lover. I never had a lover in all my life. Not that I have anything against love."

Every leaf on the poplar was in motion. A silvery, multitudinous trembling pervaded the whole tree. The pigeons on the roof, gratified by the change in weather, made a series of deep, throaty sounds.

But, Lord, Sally, she thought, *a person has to have a lover!* And suddenly it seemed to her that fifteen years had been drawn from her own body, were streaming behind her on the wind, that her own flesh had been given back the sweet resilience of twenty, that she had never borne the two children in the bedroom, that her uplifted mouth was waiting for its first kiss.

"Sally," she said, "if you don't have a lover, you're probably free as a bird. Stay to dinner tonight."

"All right," said Sally, "I'd love to stay."

The room behind them was a restless sea on which sheets of newspaper, lengths of curtain, and petals of white roses shifted about. The moment she felt an urge to put the room in order, she knew why she had asked Sally to stay. She had a lover for Sally.

Somewhere on the other side of the city he was taking the canvas from his easel, dipping his paint brushes in turpentine, and scraping his palette. He would eat his evening meal in some cheap little restaurant, would wander along the ramp to watch the sunset change the reflections in the river, would take a trolley and arrive at eight—he always came on Saturday night. Somehow, between now and supper, she must give this bungalow an atmosphere suitable to a high and romantic occasion. She must get the children into good tempers, the toys into the playroom, the books into the bookcases, the roses into the vases—somehow she must transform this house into a hushed, windy, aerial temple of love.

"Sally," she said, "you'll stay here all evening, of course?"

"But won't I be a bother if I stay all evening?"

"A bother? I should say not. You'll be a delight."

The fresh streams of air that poured through the house seemed to be lifting her arms for her, carrying her feet across the carpet, sustaining her while she stood on the sofa to put new candles into the gilt brackets on the wall.

"Darling," she said, leaping to the floor again, "darling, just run into the back yard—there's a pair of scissors on the kitchen cabinet—and whack off armfuls of roses."

Sally stood in the middle of the room—a solemn Diana in white sharkskin—and looked at her with questioning eyes. "Are you going to have company, Mrs. Schoen?" "Just one company—an old friend of ours," she replied.

"But if you're going to have company, honestly, I'd better go home, because. . . ." She did not finish the sentence, but the rest of it sounded nevertheless in the windy room: Because I'm terribly shy and awkward and I'll be wretched, and you'll be sorry.

"Nonsense," said the lady. "You'll like him. He's a sweet poor devil with a good heart. Go get the roses."

While Sally struggled with the crimson ramblers, she cleansed the house of all the accumulations of a lazy day of heat—petals, ashes, candy wrappers, the long butts of wasted cigarettes, the half-empty glasses of iced tea. She opened the bedroom door and dressed the children in sun suits and sent them to play until supper in the front yard. And all the while she worked, she saw not the task under her hands, but the lyrical evening that was to come, the evening when Sally would fall in love.

She saw exactly how the house would look—chaste, orderly, radiant—the light filling the white silk shades of the lamps, the candles shining in the gilt brackets, the crimson ramblers filling the house with that fresh, candid scent in which the tang of currants is blended with the sweetness of roses.

Her husband, finished with his week's rehearsals, would bless the occasion with his new white suit and his distinguished beard. He would leave his violin case unopened for the week end, and give them the latest gossip about the symphony orchestra. The children, worn to meekness by the torpid day, would stand for a moment like dreamy Botticelli angels at the threshold of the living room and then go cheerfully, rosily to bed.

"Sally," she would say, nodding at the piano, "won't you play us a little Chopin?" Then the liquid notes would be sprinkled like drops of water from the cool, capable hands, and the candlelight would fall on the thick brown hair, and the apricot cheeks would shine.

And the young man, who loved white lamps and Chopin and garden flowers, who ate his dinner in miserable restaurants and slept in a narrow and lonely bed, would leave the sofa and wander to the alcove, would breathe the smell of warmth and sun that rose from the silky hair, would—long before the end of the *Ballade*—be deeply and everlastingly in love . . .

"Mrs. Schoen," said Sally, "is this enough roses? I can get more . . ."

"Oh, no, that'll be enough. Put them all around, in all the vases, and be sure to keep a big bunch for the bowl on the piano, they always look so pretty there. Now I suppose I'd better see about supper—" She stopped suddenly, like a bird held static in the midst of flight.

The thought of supper filled her with consternation, threatened to destroy the fair fabric of her dream. Last night her husband had stopped at the market and brought home some fine swordfish steaks to be broiled tonight.

"Oh Lord," she said, "what'll I ever have for supper? We have swordfish steaks in the house, but I simply refuse to cook them. It'll make the whole place smell to high heaven. Anyway, it's too hot for fish, don't you think? A cold supper—shrimp salad and biscuits and iced tea and a cheese soufflé. Would that be all right?"

Sally plainly regretted the swordfish steaks. "That'll be lovely," she said, and smiled.

"Come out to the kitchen and talk to me while I make the biscuits, darling." Her heart was floating on the wind again. The threat of the odor of fish had been withdrawn from her temple. Her dream, drenched with lamplight, dotted with crimson ramblers, was again secure.

MR. SCHOEN GOT out of the first oboist's automobile at the rear gate of the bungalow. Before driving off, the first oboist came round to help him take his belongings from the back of the car—a violin in its case, a new novel from the circulating library, a record album containing a Shostakovich quartet that he meant to play that evening and two crates of strawberries.

Partly because nobody could carry all that into the house at once and partly because he felt that some introduction would be necessary for two of these items, he left the Shostakovich and the strawberries on a bench in the back yard. Then he dawdled a little under the crimson ramblers, looking for any Japanese beetles that might have turned up in the neighborhood and thinking what a fine time he was going to have doing absolutely nothing tonight.

Of all the hours in the week, this hour between six and seven on a Saturday evening was the most blessed. Rehearsal was over, and all the best hours of Saturday hung before him like untouched fruit. Now, with the wind drying his sweaty shirt and taking the sting of long strain from his eyes, he felt a capacity for enjoyment such as he had seldom known since the days of his youth. The fact that he could take a bath in warm, water with a certain cake of pine soap, that he could sit in the parlor all evening in a pair of pajamas that still smelled of the sun and wind they had dried in—all this filled him with such keen pleasure as he used to sense in his conservatory days at the thought that he was bound to be the greatest concert violinist in the world.

Home, he thought, with the ardor of a man who sees the coastline of his own land after a year of equatorial heat. Home! He saw his wife go past the kitchen window; there was something out of the ordinary in the brief image; she had stuck a few of the ramblers in her hair. He loved her with a love profound and sturdy—she, the good companion, the provider of intelligent musical comment, the mother of his children, the source of supplementary income, the broiler of swordfish, the maker of some thirty jars of strawberry jam.

"Oh, Lord, he's here already," she said.

There was something out of the ordinary, too, in the tone of her voice. It was more merry and resonant than usual. Besides, the words themselves were not the usual ones. "Look, your dad's home," was what she always said to the children. Since she was plainly not addressing them, he concluded that she was talking to herself. Then, he thought, she is in one of her pixy moods; she's drunk on the wind, and that'll be nice. She'll take to the idea of the strawberries; and later, when she's spattered all over with strawberry juice, she'll be wonderful to kiss.

TWO FACES APPEARED in the shadow of the screen, his wife's face topped with roses and transformed by an elfish smile, and another face, shy, with two flopping dog ears of brown hair.

"Damn it!" he said in a whisper. "Damn it to hell! She's got company."

Before his dream of a happy Saturday could be shattered, hoping still to find in the kitchen something to preserve his dream intact, he hurried up the path and through the screen door. The kitchen seemed tawdry and flat. He sniffed in vain for the smell of swordfish broiling in lemon butter. The dining room table, seen through the doorway, was set for five. And here, standing before him, solid and impossible to wish away, was a big young woman, such a young woman as would make it necessary to be chatty and considerate and kind—an uneasy, attractive girl with shy eyes and a sad, self-deprecating smile.

"Sally," said his wife, "this is Mr. Schoen. Sally's having dinner with us and staying the evening. Albert's coming in later."

"Hello, Sally. What's happened to the swordfish?" he said.

"Oh, the swordfish!" His feelings were hurt because she had dismissed his swordfish—his swordfish that he had brought to her for their dinner—with a shrug and a smile. "It was too terribly hot for swordfish, so I just didn't make it for tonight."

"But it's cool now."

"Well, it wasn't cool when I started to make the meal, I can tell you that. Darling, what've you got out there on the bench in the back yard?"

"Shostakovich," he said sadly, "and strawberries."

"Strawberries?"

"Yes, I brought you two crates of strawberries, to make jam."

"Well, that's just lovely," she said, and it was impossible to say whether it was sarcasm or flightiness that gave the lilt to her voice. "You can help me hull them tomorrow. Two crates—I'll never be able to do two crates alone."

He walked to the sinkboard and ate a radish and considered the depths of his own Machiavellian perfidy. He had bought those strawberries this morning from the second cellist, partly because he liked strawberry jam but chiefly because he had seen in them a means of ridding himself of the company of the young painter who sat mournfully around the house every

Saturday night. He had hoped that his wife and the artist would spend a good half of the evening in the kitchen making the jam.

"Of course you can't do them alone," he said. "I thought maybe we could make a kind of party of it, a berrying or something, while Albert's here. I'm sure he'd be crazy about making jam. Anyhow, they're soft, those berries. If you leave them until tomorrow, they might go bad and be a total loss. You'd better finish them off tonight."

"Tonight!" His wife's face stared desolately at him over a dish of shrimp salad which she was carrying into the dining room. It was a face so amazed, so sad, so filled with childish consternation and regret that one would have thought it was *she* who saw the dream of a lyrical Saturday evening going out like a snuffed candle, "Oh, darling," she said, fixing on him a pair of dark, beseeching eyes, "not tonight."

Sally, following on the heels of the lady of the house with a plate of hot biscuits, bowed her brown and humble head. "Honestly," she said, "I knew I'd make trouble. It's because I'm here that Mrs. Schoen doesn't want to hull the strawberries, and I—"

"Not at all, my dear girl," he said, laying his hand on Sally's arm, "not at all. Fact is, you might be able to save the situation. The more hands, the better. And really, once you get started, it's fun."

"I'd love to help with the strawberries," Sally said.

He cast a conspirator's glance at his wife, a merry look that said, "There, now, I've put something over for you, my girl." But she was unresponsive; she only stared at the shrimp salad, which she set on the table with the resigned and sorrowful hands of one who lays a wreath upon a monument.

He was annoyed. It was aggravating to find himself in such a funereal atmosphere, and disheartening to realize that these lost islands of food, small on the vast cloth, made up all the dinner that was to be eaten tonight.

"What else is there to eat?" he said.

"What else do you want?"

It was a reproach, but he accepted it as a challenge. "My swordfish steaks that I went all the way downtown to get for us, that's what I want," he said.

She signaled him with one despondent flap of her hand. "But we're ready to sit down at the table—"

"It doesn't take that long to broil a bit of fish. In five or ten minutes, it'll be done to a turn."

"Mrs. Schoen, couldn't I help you fix the fish?" Sally said.

Well, at least Sally is co-operative, he thought, and left the kitchen. It occurred to him that he might use this interval for getting out of his damp clothing. He went into the bedroom, but stayed there only long enough to find his pajamas; it was a westerly room and hotter than the parlor, where he could stand in his shorts for several minutes, growing dry and cool in the delightful currents of air.

BUT HE WAS a little disappointed in the appearance of the parlor. For all its coolness and in spite of the savory smell of swordfish broiling in lemon butter, it did not measure up to his expectations. It was a little stiff, a little too orderly. It lacked the haphazard, confused air that usually graced it on Saturday night. He looked at the newspaper while he unfastened his tie and shirt. There was nothing in it that he had not already read in the morning paper, and he let it float gently to the floor, where it fluttered in the gust.

He laid his tie neatly on the piano. His shirt, billowing like a parachute, came down near the coffee table. His jersey was soaking wet and might possibly do harm to the furniture, so he thoughtfully consigned it to the middle of the floor. He left his shoes beside the jersey, his socks and trousers on the sofa, his cufflinks and change and keys in an ash tray under an ostentatious bouquet of roses. And now, feeling more relaxed and expansive, he felt a sudden desire for company. He climbed quickly into his pajamas and hailed the children in from the front yard.

He had apparently been mistaken about the length of time required for broiling swordfish. For half an hour he romped about the parlor with the children, improvising houses for them with books, newspapers and candy boxes, and going often into the bedroom to bring out a stuffed bear, a dilapidated rabbit, or a rag doll to inhabit these ingenious dwellings.

His wife, coming in to say that dinner was ready, looked first at the pajamas and then at the room. Her face was mournful. The crimson ramblers looked out of place, nodding over her creased and perspiring brow.

"Oh, well, what's the use?" she said.

After he had eaten his bacon and eggs in the little downtown restaurant, the young painter stood a long time looking down from the ramp at the river. The limestone cliffs, the smokestacks and the tawdry houses, reflected upon its surface, were all made vague and mysterious by the greenish brown of the water. The trees on the opposite bank became voluminous as a forest now that they were spread out upon the shimmering flatness below him.

Behind the reflection of the trees, the reflection of the sky kept changing. First it was rosy, then yellow, then a pale, cool blue.

How sad it is, he thought, the way everything is always changing. And it seemed to him that he saw his own life changing with the colors on the river, proceeding always to something less golden, more gray, without anything singular happening, without anything significant being done.

The spells of despondency had been coming upon him frequently of late. He had begun to think that he was sad because he had an empty heart—it was all of a year since he had been in love. He was solitary in this city; he had very little money; he worked at his painting from morning until night, and he visited nobody but the Schoens.

Suddenly, like the faces of those Watteau girls who gaze from between the boughs of elms and beeches, the image of

Mrs. Schoen's face appeared among the green, clusters reflected upon the river. It was witching, it was beautiful, it was only a little faded. It had bestowed upon him the only womanly smiles that he had known in his months of exile. Perhaps, he thought, my life would have some meaning, perhaps I could shake off this feeling of futility if I allowed myself to fall in love with Mrs. Schoen.

Not that he would ever permit himself to reveal the state of his feelings, he told himself, as he left the ramp and took the trolley. The lady was plainly satisfied with her husband; but the fact that such a love would be without recompense would not mean that it would be without a certain shadowy, sad delight. He could nourish himself on her gestures, her dresses, the way she had of curling up in a chair or asking for a cigarette.

As the trolley, singing through the fresh summer dusk, brought him closer and closer to her house, he sank deeper and deeper into the brown-green melancholy, which is suitable to unrequited love. It seemed to him that he, too, was a part of the sad reflection on the river—a thin young lutist in a satin smock, staring up at a green bower through which, sweet and tender and unattainable, gleamed the face of Mrs. Schoen.

By the time he left the trolley, the Watteau picture had become unreal to him. Walking past the schoolyard, the flagpole and the monotonous lines of boxwood, he tried to change it into something less static and more contemporary. He saw her as he would see her in a few minutes, sitting at the piano in the familiar living room where the vases would be filled with flowers and the lampshades would be filled with light. Mrs. Schoen knew that he loved Chopin and now he wished ardently that the delicate figurations of Chopin would greet him before he entered; he felt an intense anxiety lest the details of this picture which he had painted in his thoughts should not be there to meet his eyes. It was as if he needed a picture to come to life, a fantasy to become a reality, in order to set a final seal upon his desire to fall in love . . .

•

AND YET, HE thought, opening the gate and walking up the path to the bungalow, even our most modest dreams are seldom fulfilled in this chaotic world. The living room windows, which he had expected to see flooded with light, were dark and blind. Beyond the screen door, left unlocked for his arrival, the room was shadowy, empty, still. He stood in the middle of it and looked about him.

The wind had thrown his surroundings into agitation. The curtains undulated around him. Some white, ghostly thing, billowing like a parachute, swelled and subsided upon the floor. The newspapers at his feet filled the stillness with an eerie shifting and whispering. The air streamed past his face, touched his hair, stirred a sense of strangeness, of high adventure in his heart. Voices, strange and musical, sounded briefly in the kitchen. A fragrance that he could not place at first pervaded the house.

"Strawberries," he thought. And again he was back in a canvas by Watteau, seeking to taste the juice of strawberries on the mouth of some eighteenth-century lady whose face he could not see in the gathering dark.

"Albert, is that you?"

It was her voice calling to him from the kitchen. Something more like regret than love rose in him at the sound of it. It was a tired, fretful voice, lacking the buoyancy of which he had dreamed. "Yes," he said.

"Come out in the kitchen, won't you? We're having the *loveliest* evening making strawberry jam." The voice had a sharp edge to it now. It was plain that she was annoyed by the evening and the strawberries. He walked slowly to the kitchen, hoping to find the fainting magic revived in her face.

He did not see that face at once. She stood at the stove with her back toward him. Her head was bent. Her lean arm went round and round, stirring the bubbling stuff in the big kettle. She wore, not one of those graceful dresses which he had expected to see, but a ragged yellow pinafore. Mr. Schoen sat at the kitchen table, hulling strawberries in a desultory way. Over the little mound of fruit, he was reading a book propped against a bowl on the table before him.

"Oh, Lord," she said to her husband without turning her head, *"won't* you go out and help Sally bring in the second crate? She can't possibly bring it herself."

"In a minute."

She turned then and faced the young man who was trying to love her. He had never seen her so plain, so utterly unlovable before. Her face, moist and reddened by the steam, was puckered into a mask of exasperation. Wet wisps of hair clung to her cheeks. A spray of withered ramblers, like the remnants of some forgotten carnival, nodded over her brow. He felt empty, betrayed, and a little sick. Under the fragrance of the strawberries, the fried smell of the supper continued to assert itself. He wanted air, quietness, and a moment of solitude in which to readjust himself to an unsatisfactory world.

"Won't you, for heaven's sake," she began again, "go out and get the—"

"In a minute. As soon as I finish this paragraph," her husband said.

"Mrs. Schoen," the young man said sadly, "maybe I could do it, whatever it is."

"Yes," she said, "you could. There's a poor child named Sally out there in the back yard. She went out there ten minutes ago at least, because my husband felt that he needed some help to carry in a crate of strawberries—"

"I'll do it," he said, and opened the screen door, and stepped out into that strange, charged moment that comes between the end of evening and the beginning of night.

•

THE GARDEN WAS a Watteau garden. Tremulous, vaguely green against a sky still streaked with bands of gold, the poplars fluttered and swayed. The ramblers, paled by the withdrawal of the light, were no longer crimson. They nodded among their shaken leaves—great clusters of dim, rose-gray mythical flowers. A single bird dropped flute notes of song from some high and shadowy bough.

And there, at the end of the garden—so is it, he thought, that all our dreams crumble only to make way for the perfect reality—there, at the end of the garden, stood an ancient statue come to life, a young woman whose white dress flowed backward to reveal the long, sweeping lines of her body, whose face shone against the moving foliage and whose eyes had a shy, unharvested, waiting look.

"Hello, Sally," he said, coming toward her, finding with every step new bits of magic—delicate cheeks sprinkled with freckles, a throat as round as a classic pillar, a witching mouth, a mass of soft brown hair.

"I guess you're Albert," she said.

They stood for a long time in the stirring, whispering garden, saying nothing and looking at each other. The smell of the strawberries rose from the crate which stood between them, and he thought that the taste of strawberries must certainly be on her parted lips.

"What are you staring at?" she said at last.

"Nothing—you—I was thinking I'd like to have you sit for a portrait."

"All right, I'd love to sit for a portrait," Sally said.

Distinguished

H E HAD BEEN sitting in Doctor Fleming's waiting room more than twenty minutes before he realized that all the others were in pairs. Everyone had somebody to talk to. Daughters had come with their mothers, husbands with their wives, sisters with their little brothers. He was the only one who had come alone.

Not that he saw any point in dragging along a companion. It was ridiculous to think that anybody could get between you and the thrust of bad news, that anybody could mitigate apprehension or lessen pain. He had no pain for the moment. The spot under his right ribs was just a little tender to the touch. He felt it secretively, and knew that at least three of the other patients had caught him in the act. He saw himself as he must look to them: tall, a little stooped, graying. And now he wanted somebody beside him merely to show them that he needed nobody, that he was not in the least concerned about the X-ray report.

Even if his private life was so solitary there was no one he could bring with him to a place like this, he was a man of consequence. It was he who had stuck by the amateurs in the days when the symphony was raw and small; it was he who had brought the glamorous guest conductors, who could fill the auditorium, and less popular disciplinarians, who could whip the men into shape. By aggressiveness tempered with elegance, by demanding and scrimping and daring, he had given the city a symphony orchestra. How long he would remain manager, he refused to ask himself. In any case, it was not a matter for consideration at this particular time, certainly not in this place.

On the table were some lilacs, which made him think of Tibby. Somebody had brought lilacs for Tibby's desk yesterday—possibly that damned, jiggling fool. He cleared the damned, jiggling fool out his mind and concentrated on Tibby. Five years of Tibby at the office, and still he had not outworn her—a charm so quiet that he had let himself think of her too much, with the mistaken assurance that nobody else would take her much to heart. He had seen her in all the guises except the ultimate and not-quite-wanted one; he had seen her in winter sweaters and summer blouses, fuzzy minded and swollen lidded in the morning, tense and haggard in the late, harassed hours of the afternoon. And yet that charm had not lessened in the least. And while he had weighed and waited, somebody else had very much taken her to heart—his new assistant, the crazy young man who had been sent by the Chairman of the Board of Trustees. Fifty times a day he was on her side of the office, sitting on her desk, cutting strings of paper men out of the correspondence bond, pinching her ear. Between his goings-on and the ridiculous plans he had cooked up for the summer fund-raising campaign, he had made an utter idiot of himself— the damned, jiggling fool.

Somebody came out of the doctor's inner sanctum; somebody else, beckoned by the nurse, went in. Suddenly his stomach quivered, not at the thought of what would pass between him and the doctor, but at the realization that he must walk some ten paces before all these eyes, from this chair to that door. Only last week it had been brought to his attention that he had a walk worth commenting on, a special walk, the gait of a stuffed shirt. The new refugee conductor, Max Hauser, had mentioned the fact to the new assistant manager, and the new assistant manager had mentioned it to everybody, including Tibby, no doubt.

The new conductor was, by common consent, screamingly funny—such a quaint turner of phrases, so capable of exquisite pantomime with his delicate hands. The new conductor and the new assistant manager had been standing at one end of the corridor, watching the old manager—oh, yes, he supposed they called him that these days—walking toward the drinking fountain. And the new conductor had said, "Mr. Eggers, will you look just a minute, please. What a distinguished man! Such a distinguished walk! Every step distinguished!" No doubt it was vastly amusing, as everyone who heard it was convulsed by it. It was probably not malicious, either. And yet he wished he had not thought of it: it filled him with bitterness; he did not wanted to think about his distinguished walk while he was on the way to find out whether he had a distinguished case of cancer or only a couple of undistinguished gallstones.

Whatever devilish and secret things were going on inside his body, they would not interfere with his customary dignity or with the summer fund-raising campaign. He meant to stay in his office until the last letter was out and the first fat checks were in. Max Hauser and the Board of Trustees would never be able to say he had left the worst burden of the year in the hands of an untried young man. And they would never be able to say of the young man that he had done very well, maybe even better than the old dodo would have done.

The door to the doctor's office opened again, and a girl came out. "You're next, Mr. Beatty," the nurse said.

So I am, so I am, he thought, and walked with distinguished steps to the door.

Doctor Fleming sat behind his desk. Three or four X-ray films were fanned out in front of him. "Sit down, sit down,

Mr. Beatty," he said, squinting through rimless glasses at the gruesome revelations, the faint envelope of flesh, the shadowy bones. "Have a good night? Able to digest your lunch?"

"Bad news?" he asked.

"Well, now, Mr. Beatty, that depends on what you call bad news. I'd say that an assortment of large gallstones was pretty bad news. They're painful, they're—"

"Gallstones?"

"Now, what on earth did you think?" Young Doctor Fleming and young Eggers, the assistant manager—both of them, when they wanted to be friendly and reassuring, restored to particularly irritating tone, a teasing fatherly tone. "I bet I know. Right away, you thought a malignancy. That's the way with you people. You enjoy scaring yourselves. If you just look here, at this, you can see for yourself."

He did not look. The pain was stabbing his side. Pain and relief blurred the desk and the callow young face.

"Gallstones. Nothing but gallstones. See?"

He was annoyed that he should nod like an obedient child. Someday at the office, green sick like this, with the strength for protest washed away, he would nod at some form letter, some poster, some radio blurb held out in Eggers' insistent hand. And chance would be on Eggers' side; chance was always with the young against the old. Whatever piece of junk he would let pass in his misery, that piece would turn out to be the success of the year. "Who did that?" the President of the Board would say. And a chorus would answer, "Who do you think? Your lucky find, Mr. President, your white-haired boy. Isn't it wonderful? Much better than anything the old dodo ever turned out."

"OF COURSE," SAID Doctor Fleming, "gallstones are nothing to joke about. They'll have to be taken care of, you know."

"Yes." He was willing to agree to that, for the moment at least. In this surge of nausea, he would never be able to tell a good promotion piece from a bad one. "And just how does one take care of—"

"Very neatly. We remove the gallbladder. Now, don't alarm yourself. It's not the operation it used to be. The gallbladder comes out, and the whole business is over—a little care about your diet, a few weeks' rest, and no more pain."

If he could carry this agony inside him through the summer campaign, through the autumn tea and dinner parties, through the first concert. . . . He drew his hand across his sweating forehead.

"It's two weeks in the hospital, Mr. Beatty."

"I think I could manage two weeks next fall."

"Next fall? Good Lord, man, there's no question of next fall. Next week, ten days from now. These things can get to be really pretty nasty, you know."

In spite of the ache in his side, he drew himself up and answered all young men who can dispense with their elders lightly; this doctor, and that other idiot who would consider himself capable, in a pinch, of carrying off singlehanded a very fetching summer campaign. "That," he said, "is out of the question. Some people can leave their positions at a minute's notice. I can't."

"Oh, now, somebody'll hold the fort."

Somebody'll hold the fort. Somebody'll storm the buttresses, scale the walls, get inside, bar the door. "I can't take leave of absence until next fall."

"My dear man, you'll be taking leave of absence whether you want to or not. One of these days you'll pass out cold, maybe at a concert, maybe in your office, and you'll wake up and find yourself in any hospital bed I can wangle for you."

In the office. He saw himself lying yellow faced and senseless on the floor. He saw them all: Eggers sprinkling water on his face in a perky and capable manner, the Chairman of the Board producing the required amount of distress, Max Hauser saying, "Poor soul! Poor soul!," and meanwhile coming to the conclusion that the most dignified people always look the most

ridiculous in a situation like this. As for Tibby—Tibby refused
to become part of the picture. He recalled with some pain that
she had never touched him, not once in all these five year. He
was probably downright repulsive to her. If he fell on his face
in front of her desk, she might simply wait, leaving him to the
tender mercies of the damned, jiggling fool.

"A very good room at St. Alban's," Doctor Fleming was
saying. "Let's get it over, before the summer heat sets in. I'll
make the arrangements, and you drop in on me here Monday,
just to make sure the whole business is in shape."

The interview was over.

Very briefly, knowing that the people in the waiting room
were his companions in fear and mortality, he forced himself
to show them an encouraging smile. Then he moved in the
direction of the elevator—erect, grave, and dignified, every step
distinguished.

FOR TWO OR three minutes, standing in the May sun and looking
for a taxi, he thought of going to his hotel. There was no way
of easing these attacks, but there were methods of putting up
with them: he could lie on his back with his knees drawn up,
so that nothing, not even the sheet, could touch his tender
spot; he could comfort himself with long swallows of hot,
unsweetened tea. Still, to go to his room was to surrender too
early. His desk was littered with radio scripts, speeches, posters,
form letters. In the ten-day interval that lay between this hour
and the hour when he must relinquish consciousness he must
put his incredible mark on the summer campaign. Hauser must
see him busy at his desk. The Board of Trustees must note his
signature at the bottom of the most important mailing pieces.
His own measured voice, his own precise choice of words, his
whole dignified style must be established at the beginning of the
business. Then maybe at the end somebody would remember,

somebody would say, "But the old dodo started it, you know. Eggers didn't run the campaign all by himself."

He gave the office address to the cabby and sat back, shivering, against the cold leather. Yet he was glad for more reasons than one that he was heading downtown. Tibby would be in the office, possibly alone. The jiggling fool had a date to meet a new woman cellist for the afternoon tea. And in that still, empty place, having Tibby to himself for an hour, he might wander to her desk and mention causally that he'd been to see his doctor. He might even go so far as to announce the measures that were to be taken ten days hence—oh, very off-handedly, of course, in a manner that would preclude any notion that he was asking for sympathy. But he saw, in spite of himself, fright and pity in her childlike, secretless eyes.

Even before he opened the door into the square, bright room the three shared, he knew by the sound of Eggers' voice that the tea party with the cellist had fallen through. Eggers was beating a quick retreat from Tibby's desk. And Tibby was smelling her faded lilacs with the tense self-consciousness of an actress who has been left alone on stage and must fill a charged and empty moment, to cover up for a fellow actor who has missed his cue.

MR. BEATTY WALKED past her, holding himself erect despite the pain. He sat down at his desk and watched her poking at the flowers. And he continued to watch until a flush spread over her cheeks. The stillness was uneasy, conspiratorial. He coughed, and she looked up.

"Did you have a nice time, Mr. Beatty?" she said.

"Lovely. Perfectly lovely." He wished there had been less irony in his voice. That silly question was her attempt to be pleasant. She could not know he had been sitting solitary among twos in Doctor Fleming's waiting room. She could not know he was sick, and afraid of the anesthetic and of the pain that must come with returning consciousness. It was not her fault that he was growing old and that another man—that fool, standing behind him at the window—meant to edge him out of his place.

"Well, that's nice." Her voice quavered. She was as incapable of hiding her feelings as a ten-year-old.

"And you, did you have a nice lunch?" he said.

"We didn't go out. We ate sandwiches here. That cellist called up and said she couldn't make it. So we decided to go to work and clean up everything. Odds and ends, you know."

How cozy, how very cozy, he thought. Just the two of you, eating sandwiches—isn't that cozy and sweet? In these free and easy moments they might have been talking about him. Tearing him to pieces. And odds and ends—what kind of odds and ends? That one, standing behind me, what was he about? Did he kiss your white neck? Or was he busy with a more significant matter? Was he writing one of his masterpieces, an awfully clever little form letter, just the thing to give a good, brisk start to the summer campaign?

She looked straight at him across the lilacs. He answer could not have been more to the point if he had uttered every furious word that burned in his head. "I finished typing your letters. Jim made about twenty telephone calls—the ones to last year's donors who haven't paid their final installment. After that, there wasn't much time left," she said.

"Sixteen donors said they'd pay." It was Eggers' voice, with the tired slur he resorted to when he was ill at ease. "One says he can't. He's broke, I guess. The other three are out of town."

He realized then that he had not so much as said "Good-afternoon" to Eggers. That was an unforgivable breach; since the beginning, he had hidden his dislike under a cool, continuous flow of amenities. Now, to make up for his surliness, he turned elaborately—a movement that did violence to his side. "Thanks very much, Mr. Eggers," he said.

"You're very welcome, Mr. Beatty. I should have got around to it a week ago."

Always, when he looked at Eggers after a spell of brooding about him, the young man seemed curiously inoffensive. He was slender and brown-haired and not a great deal taller than Tibby. His blue eyes were tired. Really, thought Mr. Beatty, I've blown him up again to an unconscionable size. Then he nodded and turned back to his desk, to the letters waiting for his signature and to the speech that must be cut down to fifteen minutes given to the Symphony by the radio station WLDJ.

He worked for a long time, his teeth clenched, forcing himself to think of the business before him, arching his thoughts like a precarious bridge over the greenish bog of pain. When the speech was reduced to the required size, when the light on the paper was no longer yellow with sunlight, but a melancholy blue, he realized that he need not tense his body any more—the pain was gone.

HE SAT BACK in his chair, wiped his palms and forehead with his handkerchief, sighed, and looked about him. The customary miracle was taking place: the room was being transmuted and beautified by his relief. The white plaster walls were touched by bluish shadows. The last of the sunset was reflected in the glass and polished wood. The lilacs were now purplish plumes, and, beyond the lilacs, pale and remote, was Tibby's childlike face. Her could not look at her for long. The sight of her, in his present tremulous state, was enough to bring on tears. He looked at the other one, hunched at his desk near the window. Plainly, the other one was working at some project, some clever idea that he would present at the right moment, when Hauser or the Chairman of the Board happened to be on hand. A form letter to donors, no doubt. None of your high-minded, distinguished stuff—nothing of the sort the old dodo had been slinging at the donors these past sixteen years. Something lively and chatty, something personal and warmhearted, something that would make every last one of them feel that it was their Symphony. . . . But now that the pain no longer goaded him, he could not feel the usual rage; he could manage nothing but a deprecating smile. Once this boy found himself alone with the summer campaign, he'd see how far from simple it was; he'd see.

It seemed to him then that he ought, for charity's sake, to warn the jiggling fool of the confusion in store for him. He ought to say, "Ten days from now, my dear fellow, I will be flat on my back, and everything—the whole exhausting, thankless business—will be on your head." Perhaps because he was freed of malice by the absence of pain, perhaps because Tibby, seeing him smile, smiled back, he felt that the situation was not so bad as he thought. Maybe young Eggers would not exult over his going down; maybe Eggers would look scared and say, "Good Lord!" and ask him for advice.

Young Eggers had risen and was coming toward him with a paper in his hand, his eyes bright with shy eagerness. "Mr. Beatty, if you have a couple of minutes, there's something I'd like to—"

The sentence did not trail off into a modest, self-deprecating pause. It broke or rather was shattered against something. Tibby? He wheeled and caught her signaling to her cavalier. She was plainly warning him off, her forefinger against her lips, her eyes alarmed.

For a long moment the three remained static in their humiliating positions. He was the one who should take the situation in hand, but what could he do? To turn to the pink and rigid Eggers and say, "Well, what would you like to—" was impossible, might make a scene, and was certainly beneath his dignity. He could tell them how foolish it was for them to conspire against him now, because in a few days they would have the place to themselves. But he rejected such behavior as melodrama. He shrugged and turned his back on Eggers. He bent his head so that he need not see the flushed, wounding face behind the lilacs. He took a piece of paper—a sheet from a yellow scratch pad, because he was not one to waste good bond on foolishness—and drew three snails sticking their heads out of coiled shells.

That his secretary and his assistant should conspire against him—he thought was as annihilating as a gallbladder attack. He drew a curlicue of seaweed under the largest snail, looked briefly across the room, and saw only her bent head. She was not in the least concerned about him; it made no difference to her that he was sick, defeated, frightened; she had no thought to spare for anybody but Eggers.

He drew a leaping dolphin on the crest of a wave and reconstructed the incident. The jiggling fool had come up behind him, all eagerness, wanting to show him a little masterpiece, hoping to get at least one of his creations edged into the summer campaign. And wasn't he clever? Hadn't he picked just the right moment? Wasn't it late, and wasn't the old dodo tired and bleary-eyed enough to let anything slip through? Oh, but she was by far the wiser of the two. Hadn't she seen the green cast of sickness on his face? Her lifted finger could mean only: "Wait just a little longer, dear. Soon you can show everything you write directly to the Board."

HE CRUMPLED THE paper, tossed it to the floor, tore off another sheet. At the top of the fresh page he wrote, "Dear Mr. Charlesworth." He would explain his absence and his sickness in the most impersonal and dignified manner; he would address a letter requesting a leave of absence to the Chairman of the Board. These two, sitting silent with him in the darkening room, would learn about his departure late; the news would seep down to them in conjecture and rumor; they would scarcely know he was going before he was gone.

"My dear Mr. Charlesworth: Inasmuch as my physician has just informed me that it will be necessary for me to absent myself—" By the shadow falling across the paper, by the rustle, by the smell of lavender soap, he knew that Tibby had crossed the room to him. He did not look up. "What can I do for you?" he said.

"Nothing. I wanted to know if there wasn't something that I could do for you. I—"

But what could you do for me? he thought. If I loved you, I could lean against your fresh pink blouse and breathe the scent of your lavender soap; but I do not love you—there was always another not-quite-wanted guise, I was never much of a lover, and now I'm old. If you loved me, you could listen while I told you how I am afraid to be alone up in the hotel tonight, afraid of giving up consciousness, afraid as a child is afraid to take a step into the dark. But as you do not love me, Tibby, as you have such bad taste as to love the jiggling fool—"Nothing," he said, "nothing at all."

"But isn't that something you could dictate to me?" Her voice sounded shrill, almost hysterical. "Do you have to write it yourself?"

He was sorry for her then. She is a child, he told himself, a naughty child, caught by her old uncle in a conspiracy with her lover, and properly ashamed of herself.

"Won't you let me do it, Mr. Beatty?"

"It's a personal matter."

"I'm sorry. I bet your pardon." And she and the smell of lavender soap and the chance to look at her were gone.

It was five fifteen, and Eggers put on his jacket and left the office. She stayed, probably to indicate her penitence and to make it plain that she was not going to dinner—not, at least, tonight—with the jiggling fool. She had a waiting air, sitting with her hands folded on her desk; but if she was waiting for him to stop and talk to her, she was very much misled. Erect and solemn, with distinguished steps he passed her desk. He did not pause there even long enough to catch a glimpse of her blond hair. He turned at the door and bade her a grave and dignified good-night.

MAYBE IT WAS over, and maybe it wasn't. Maybe, if this business of struggling up through warm white steam could be considered coming out of it, he was coming out of it too soon. The painful spot in his side—the one red, semisolid reality in the lambent mist—was something no human being should be allowed to experience. It was awful, but he would not permit himself to make any undignified noise. That round object, that sphere of congealed mist—that was Doctor Fleming's head. Any minute now, Doctor Fleming would say, "He'll need more anesthesia." But Doctor Fleming said nothing of the kind. His voice, muffled and blurred, went on for time immeasurable with a sort of lilting lullaby: "You're all right. It's all over. You're perfectly all right, you know. Just take it easy, take it easy."

Oh, but it wasn't as easy as all that. He let himself slip back into something that should have been unconsciousness and turned out to be a very bad dream. The dream corridor through which he walked was narrow, with translucent glass walls. To left and right there were rooms; but none opened on the hall, he could not find a single door. He could only peer through the glass, flattening himself against the undulating surface. "Don't stretch like that—it'll hurt your side." But he had to do it, because there beyond the ripples was Tibby, typing form letters and speeches and clever little ideas Eggers had written for the summer campaign, and there was Eggers, leaning over her chair and kissing her neck—which was very strange, because Eggers was also in the next room, talking in a shy and winsome manner to Mr. Charlesworth, the Chairman of the Board. "It's all right, you know, it's perfectly all right." And he supposed it was, for hadn't Max Hauser said that young Eggers could always be found wherever you wanted him, sometimes in two or three places at the same time?

And now that young Eggers had left Mr. Charlesworth, the Chairman of the Board began to read aloud from a long scroll decorated with snails in curly shells. "My dear Mr. Charlesworth: Inasmuch as my physician has just informed me that it will be necessary for me to absent myself, I must request a leave of absence whose duration I cannot quite determine, but which will last at least for the next five weeks, thereby making it impossible for me to take any part in the summer campaign." Mr. Charlesworth dropped the scroll from pink, pudgy hands shaking with delight. "Max," he squealed, "Max! The old dodo—he's down on his back, he won't be around for the summer campaign!"

And suddenly all of them were there—Hauser and Eggers and Tibby and Charlesworth—all skipping and tossing their heads and giving each other congratulatory kisses. Then they were singing a paean of sheer happiness at their release: "He's gone, he's gone, he's down on his back, maybe he's down for good. Maybe he'll die, maybe he'll die, maybe he'll die."

"Not don't talk any of that rot about dying. You're perfectly all right. And please relax, Mr. Beatty. If you want to moan, go ahead and moan."

He moaned and regretted it immediately, because there was Max Hauser, leaning against the translucent wall. "What a distinguished man!" Max Hauser said. "Such distinguished moans! Every moan distinguished!"

HE REJECTED THE dream. It was less bearable than the reality. He opened his eyes and saw Doctor Fleming's head, quite solid and completely recognizable now. Doctor Fleming's face showed signs of exhaustion, and the cheerful bedside mask had given way to real concern.

"Got yourself oriented? Know where you are, Mr. Beatty?" he said.

"Yes."

He was in a hospital room, whose window opened on a faded spring sky. There was a visitor's chair, but nobody was sitting in it. The top of the dresser looked empty—no flowers, not a single bunch of flowers.

"Feeling better now?"

He did not trouble to answer. Surely the doctor knew something about the nausea and the burning pain. It would be better to say nothing, to ask nothing, and yet he could not help himself. "Did anybody telephone?" he said.

"Not since I've been here. Just a minute, and I'll ask the floor superintendent."

They must have thought he could not hear their whispered conversation outside. When Doctor Fleming returned and started to explain that the floor superintendent was out of her office for the moment, Mr. Beatty waved the subject away, and saw the room grow steamy again with nausea and shame.

"It's pretty bad, isn't it?" Doctor Fleming said.

"Bad enough."

"Let me give you a shot."

He held his arm still under the needle and turned his face toward the wall to wait for another bad dream. The world changed, disintegrated, slipped like music moving through strange modulations into a remote key. "This is peculiar. Maybe I'll die," he thought, and did not greatly care. He wished only that his hand, loose and incapable of motion on the sheet, might feel the pressure of Tibby's hand, anybody's hand.

As SOON AS he opened his eyes, he knew it was evening. Dusk lay purplish across the sheet; the sounds of traffic were muted and desultory; a single rosy beam of sun struck the metal bar at the foot of the bed. Maybe he was dying. Maybe that was why the pain was less. A flake of ice lay between his lips. Yes, he was certainly dying, otherwise the person—whoever it was out there beyond the edge of the mattress—would not have bothered, or would not have dared, to press and stroke his hand.

Then the cool fingers withdrew, so abruptly, so definitely that he marshaled his wandering senses and decided he would not consider any of that dying business any more. The visitor's chair was not where it had been. Somebody had pushed it close to his bed. And in it, solemn and self-conscious, with the muted beam of sunlight crossing her silky hair, sat Tibby. Somebody has been holding his hand, and there was no alternate somebody in the room—there was only Tibby. The worst of the pain was over now, and he was coming up out of the healthful sleep into a world where Tibby—even though she was scared and ashamed to have been caught in the act—could touch his hand with something close to tenderness.

He could not talk at once. He had to wait while the sliver of ice melted. In the interim, he stared at Tibby, who kept her hands deep in the pockets of her blue summer dress and had a distinctly hangdog air.

"Is it all right?" she asked at last. "The ice, I mean."

"It's delicious."

"I'm glad, because I put it there. The nurse told me I could. Your lips looked terribly dry. I hope it didn't wake you up. I hope—"

"It's delicious. Anyway, I wanted to wake up," he said. He would have liked to tell her that no sleep, no healing could have compensated for the moment when, awakening, he felt her stroking hand. And if he suppressed his desire to tell her so, it was not for the sake of his pride, it was only because she looked painfully shy of him.

"I'm awfully glad you're doing so well, Mr. Beatty. When I was in this afternoon, they told me you were doing fine, and I—"

"Were you here this afternoon?" Did you give me part of that first conspirator's day, when you and young Eggers had the place to yourselves? Did you excuse yourself from typing his first clever letters, in order to come to see whether the old dodo was alive or dead? Well, then, you're kind, kinder than I thought. "What were you doing here this afternoon?" he said.

"Sitting out in the hall."

"For how long?"

"Oh, I don't know, and hour or so, I guess."

"Why didn't you come in?"

"I didn't dare, Mr. Beatty. The nurse told me I could, but I said you wouldn't want to see me."

"Why on earth wouldn't I want to see you?"

"Because—don't you remember?—you were awfully annoyed at me," she answered.

He did remember, of course. Ten days had passed since that afternoon when he had seen her with a warning finger at her lips, and in that ten days he had not permitted himself one moment of relenting. The office, as Max Hauser had remarked, had been as cheerful and informal as a funeral home. The jiggling fool had ceased to jiggle, had given up paper dolls, had stacked his clever ideas in his desk for future reference. As for her, she had plainly taken a vow not to speak unless she was spoken to. Even last night, when he had left the office—it was last night, he assured himself, though it seemed weeks ago—she had wished him no godspeed, had simply stared at him with big, blank eyes.

WELL, HE COULD not be expected to explain. He could not be expected to admit, aloud, the extent of his jealously and bitterness. "I wasn't exactly annoyed," he said.

She took her hands out of her pockets and looked him straight in the face. "Don't you say you weren't!" Her voice was quavering and high. "You were so angry you didn't bother to tell us you were going to the hospital. For all we knew, we might never have seen you again. You might have died. That was a rotten thing for you to do to us. That was a rotten thing for you to do to me. What did I do to make you do a thing like that? All I did was tell him not to go pestering you with his stuff when you looked so sick. I honestly thought you were going to die." She bent double, her fists in her eyes and her forehead on the sheet. She jarred the bed and gave him a disintegrating stab of pain. But pain was nothing. Her version of that charged incident had upon it the unmistakable stamp of authenticity. His version was the unreal, the unthinkable one. She had warded off her lover, not in her lover's interest, but to save an old man with a gray face from being plagued in the midst of his pain. She sobbed, and he raised his hand and let it come down on her hair.

"Don't do that," she said, weeping. "Don't do that now. It's too late."

Exactly what she meant by that, he didn't know. Perhaps she was merely trying to tell him that she was hurt beyond the possibility of amends. Perhaps she did not want an affectionate gesture of his to remember, a tender touch to give her an uneasy conscience while she and young Eggers were carrying on the summer campaign. He withdrew his fingers. There was a sound of footsteps in the hall, and Tibby straightened and dried her eyes just as a nurse, carrying two vases of flowers, edged expertly through the doorway.

"Oh, my, we are feeling better, aren't we?" the nurse said. "The roses are from Mr. and Mrs. Charlesworth, and the mixed spring bouquet is from Mr. Max Hauser."

"They're very nice," he said.

"Yes, they certainly are. My, you do look better. Really, you look very 'handsome' is the word, I guess." She turned briskly and walked out of the room.

"Distinguished," he said to Tibby. "The word is 'distinguished.'"

And Tibby was off again, quavering and high, her cheeks damp and pink, her eyes bright. "You think I don't know what you're thinking about, but I know perfectly well," she said.

"You're thinking about that every-step-distinguished thing Doctor Hauser said to Jim Eggers, and let me tell you, Doctor Hauser didn't mean any harm by that, and if he did mean any harm, it's no wonder, when he knows perfectly well you were sorry to see him take Doctor Fraser's place. Doctor Hauser didn't know you were too sick to want to go to any of his parties."

What she said was true: that and much more. He remembered another offense against Max Hauser; his cheeks burned at the remembrance. One afternoon, only two or three days before the every-step-distinguished incident, Max Hauser had sat beside him in a sorrowful and meditative state of mind. It was Max Hauser's mother's birthday, and her bones lay God knew where in Austria, in a mass grave, with no tombstone, no flowers. Then the telephone had cut through the moment of closeness, and a long business conversation had followed, and he had become and embarrassed and annoyed by the tragic eyes staring into his. He should have said, "Please go on, won't you?" as soon as the receiver was back on its hook. Instead, he had said, "I wired that cellist in Chicago. She'll be down for an audition next Tuesday afternoon." He had not seen the big, tired eyes go blank. He had—he knew it now—a cold, mean way of avoiding people's eyes and staring at their brows.

"I WAS SICK," he said. "I guess I was pretty nasty, but it was because I was sick."

"I know, Mr. Beatty," Tibby said. "All of us know."

If all of them knew, they would edge him out of his place, not with such devilish merriment as he had heard in his dream, but with pity and regret. "You'll never realize how much you've been missed," they would say to him when he returned to an empty desk, with the summer campaign successfully over. "Mr. Eggers is getting up a little something for the women's clubs. Won't you let him have your invaluable advice?" And try as he would to strangle it, the old anger raged in him again, dried his lips, dried his tongue, made him acutely aware of the pain in his side. No, there was nothing sweet in it, this business of being shoved aside, and it could not be sweetened for him, not even by their charity. He moved his dry tongue over his dry lips.

"Would you like another piece of ice?" Tibby asked.

Her charity was more easily tolerated than theirs. He nodded, and watched her deal nervously with the bowl and spoon and ice; he had never seen her capable fingers unsteady before. Then he knew she was afraid of touching the ice, afraid she might contaminate it.

"I don't consider you exactly poisonous, you know," he said.

She started, and the spoon dipped, and the ice went sliding down the sheet. "Don't you?" she asked. "I always thought you did." Her voice was sharp and high again. She struck the errant sliver of ice an angry blow and sent it skidding across the floor. "You always acted as if you might get leprosy if I handed you a pencil. You always had such a no-nonsense-in-the-office-please look on your face. You always seemed so put out when people acted as if they were flesh and blood." She stopped, dried her hands on the skirt of her blue summer dress, took another piece of ice between thumb and forefinger, and lifted it to his lips.

So she had been aware that he resented her subtle little skirmishes with the jiggling fool. He felt an unreasonable compulsion to tell her the truth, and yet the truth was unutterable, to speak the truth was beneath his dignity. Still, he wanted her to understand that it was not an old man's prudishness that had made him frown when their young hands crept together. "You and Mr. Eggers—" was all he managed to say before she dropped the cool, wet ice on his tongue.

"Yes, Jim Eggers and I—" She went to the darkening window. She stood with her back toward him, her palms and forehead pressed against the pane. He saw her shoulders, only dimly visible in the growing darkness, straighten and sag in a sigh. "I've been wanting to tell you about Jim Eggers, Mr.

Beatty. He's in love with me, and I guess I'm in love with him, if resigning yourself and taking not what you asked for but what the good Lord intended to give you can be called being in love. And it's all right, I'm very happy, it's much better than I ever imagined it was going to be. It's not like being a kind of moth and throwing yourself against an electric globe until you're dead tired, dead tired."

What was she talking about? What luminary had she assaulted with futile and pathetic flights? Charlesworth? Fraser? The concertmaster? "Tibby, who on earth—"

"Who?" She wheeled around. Her eyes shone for a second in the shadow. Then she covered them with her fists and wept. "Why do you want to make me say it? Why should you want to make me say right out that for five years I was miserably, perfectly miserably, in love with you? Oh, you knew it, you always knew it."

"Tibby, my dear child, I never knew it, so help me God."

SHE WENT TO the bed and sat down in the visitor's chair, resting her head close to his hand. He could not tell whether she had come to comfort him or to be comforted, but he allowed himself a luxury he had denied himself for years—he stroked her hair.

"I don't expect you to believe me, Tibby, but I loved you, too. In my own rather unsatisfactory manner, I loved you."

"You're lying, Mr. Beatty. You're lying to save my face."

"No, Tibby, I loved you. Really, Tibby, I—"

She lifted her head and looked at him. Even in the dark, he could sense the complete candor of her eyes. "Maybe you did, Mr. Beatty. Maybe you played around with the idea of liking me, to make the days at the office more interesting. But that was all. You never really loved me."

And that unwavering look forced him to arraign and judge himself. What she had said was true, though he would never tell her so. He had ornamented the day with the thought of her, but beyond the alert morning look and the dear, weary afternoon smile there was another guise. He had seen in her, and rejected, a vital woman, too fresh and ardent to inhabit without destruction the closed and dusty chambers of his heart.

"All right, dear. Have it your way. I loved you and I knew you weren't for me," he said, lifting her hand and kissing it gallantly.

It was fortunate that the lights in the corridor were snapped on at that moment. It was fortunate that the nurse came in to take his temperature and to imply tactfully that the first visitor oughtn't to stay too long. There was no time for formal leave-takings. Then, sinking back on newly puffed pillows, he listened to the nurse's lecture on not exhausting oneself. Later, when he would go back to an empty desk, Charlesworth and Hauser would talk to him in just that parental, well-intentioned, condescending way: "Let Eggers do it. Take it easy. You're not too strong." Everything was for Eggers, the campaigns and the blond-haired woman, the laurels and the roses, the glory and the love. . . . Well, he would not think of that; he would think about the soft hair under his fingertips. But before he could think of anything, he was asleep.

IT SEEMED THAT his encounter with Tibby had resulted in ominous behavior on the part of the thermometer. The nurse was unusually attentive that night; and the following morning, when Doctor Fleming gave the door a brisk inward swing, a "No Visitors" sign swished into view.

In a way, he was glad. If nobody came to visit him, he could tell himself the sign had kept half a dozen people out—the sign was a talisman against the indifference of the world. But the world was not indifferent, or at any rate did not mean to appear so. A new batch of flowers came—long-stemmed roses and Japanese iris and several other varieties—bearing cards from assorted donors and almost every member of the Board of Trustees. Tibby, with more thoughtfulness than he deserved and more of her salary than she could afford to spend, had bought him a pair of Moroccan slippers in a leather bag. And the following morning, there were more flowers, with cards from "The Office" and from Mr. Snyder, the manager of his hotel. He thought a little mournfully of having to go back to that hotel for his convalescence, of being helped across the lobby, of eating a soft diet alone in his stuffy room. The thought brought on a heavy mood, and he would probably have spent the rest of the day in fretfulness if it had not been for the package that arrived with the afternoon mail.

It was a small, home-wrapped package. On the brown paper, the return address was written in ornate German script: "Antoinette Hauser, 205 Cypress Street, City." He turned it over several times, thinking of Antoinette Hauser. She was a faded woman, blond and aging, who made one sad by being a walking reminder of departed good looks. She had embarrassed him by weeping unashamedly during a parlor performance of the Smetana quartet, *Aus Meinen Leben*. He wondered what she had sent him and was afraid to find out. She owned a little collection of original music manuscripts, which she had brought from Austria; they were distressingly dear to her, valuable in themselves, and doubly valuable because they had been washed over with the golden recollections of her happier youth. And when he had taken off the brown wrapping and the corrugated paper, he found that he had not been mistaken: here was her original phrase from Mozart's *Magic Flute*, exquisitely framed under glass. She had not been niggardly, she had sent her best; and in his weakened state, he would certainly have wept if it had not been for the realization that this was a sort of consolation prize: the goodhearted can bring themselves to offer nothing but their dearest to those who have suffered a great defeat.

What were they all doing at the office now? No doubt the

first mailing piece, the opening trumpet call of the summer campaign, had gone out the first day of his absence. That, at least, was signed with his name.

But something was the matter, something had gone out of joint, as he learned from Mrs. Henry Hammer, who stared down the "No Visitors" sign and sat beside his bed late that afternoon. Mrs. Henry Hammer had a long, loose, equine face constructed for complaining. He listened to her complaints without hearing them until she said that the first mailing piece had not gone out. She had not received it; other notable donors had not received it; and she had every reason to believe nobody had received it.

He was surprised that he experienced no malicious delight at this first hitch in the summer campaign. Some buried loyalty to his employees cracked his jealousy. He informed Mrs. Hammer, and rather huffily, that if there had been any delay in the mailing, there must also have been a sufficient cause. She took umbrage; and, annoyed by his intractability and the odor of iodoform, she presented him with two magazines and left. He felt the good leather of his slippers and brooded over Antoinette Hauser's little gold frame, instead.

HE HAD FOOD for dinner—soft food, but food. Later, when the nurse carried away his tray and the door swung behind her, he noticed the "No Visitors" sign had been removed. He settled down to endure an evening of isolation. They had sent flowers and presents, they had done their duty; but they would certainly not rush to see him, now that he was out of danger, now that recovery had transformed him from a cause for sore conscience into a tiresome liability.

Yet it was a pleasant evening, the sort that, in the days of one's youth, had been tremulous with the promise of miracles. On the breeze, he caught a scent of grass mown for the first time, of flower beds dug up, of blossoming boughs. He also indulged in a bit of self-congratulation: the acute pain was almost gone. He yawned and stretched without meditation that was almost as delicious as sleep.

And in that meditation he heard many feet and many voices. Fellowship, tender concern, rejoicing over an averted tragedy—these existed for other patients, even though they were not for him. Then a familiar voice, feminine and husky, said with a German accent the number of his room, and other voices, male and female assented, and before he could smooth his hair, his room was crowded—Antoinette and Max Hauser, Mr. Charlesworth, dear Tibby, in her blue summer dress, yes, and young Eggers, too, standing on the threshold, shyly.

"Well!" said Mr. Charlesworth, pink and pleased. "You're looking wonderful! You'll never know what it does to me to see you looking so well."

Max Hauser walked swiftly, ardently around the bed and clasped and would not release his hand.

Tibby, blushed at the sight of the slipper bag on the night table, and waved to him above Antoinette Hauser's head.

As for Antoinette Hauser, she came forward with tears in her pale eyes. "Kenneth—dear Kenneth," she said; and he realized that this was the first time any one of these, his closest associates, had dared to call him by his Christian name.

Mr. Charlesworth dragged Jim Eggers into the room. There was talk—so much talk that the nurse had to request a little more quiet, please. Tibby sat on the edge of the bed, and in the vivacity of the chatter forgot herself so far as to let her hand rest on his knee. And in the general conviviality, Kenneth Beatty found that he had unsuspected qualities to draw upon: he was able to make precisely the right remark about the slippers, and he voiced his appreciation of the phrase from the *Magic Flute* with a warmth and delicacy that brought fresh access of tears to Antoinette Hauser's eyes.

•

"I TOOK IT upon myself to phone your doctor today, Kenneth,"
Mr. Charlesworth said. "He assures me that you'll be out of
here in five days at the most, and I was wondering when you
thought you'd be—"

He wanted to spare them the necessity of pretending he was
indispensible. He shrugged and turned to Tibby. "You'd better
phone Mr. Snyder at the hotel and let him know when I'll be
back," he said to her.

Whereupon Max Hauser lifted his big, sad eyes to heaven,
flung up his hands, and said he had never heard of such a
thing—a sick man trying to regain his health in a hotel! Here
was a chance for them to make sure of the ten-room house they
had been forced to rent. And he could assure Kenneth that his
wife was an excellent cook.

As for Mrs. Hauser, she said with an urgency that would
have made refusal a cruelty, "Kenneth, we beg you to come!"

That matter settled, the Hausers excused themselves. They
had a previous engagement, which they would certainly never
have made if they had known he would be allowed to entertain
visitors so soon. Never since his childhood had be been given
such a sure conviction of being wanted. He turned his attention
back to the remaining three, thinking a little wistfully that it
was strange how a man could still be valued merely as a man,
even after he had outlived his usefulness as the manager of a
symphony orchestra.

He realized then that he had had no direct conversation
as yet with Jim Eggers. That cavalier had shared in the general
gabble, but he looked separate and lonely. His carefulness to
keep at a distance from Tibby had been almost ostentatious.
Now he did not permit his eyes to rest on Tibby's hand, and
Mr. Beatty knew that the sight of that hand lying lightly on
his knee would be certain to give young Eggers pain. It broke
upon him, too, with the suddenness of revelation, that young
Eggers knew himself to be a second choice, that Tibby, with

her usual candor, had certainly told young Eggers all about the futile gyrations of the moth.

"Well, Eggers," said Mr. Beatty, "how's it going?" And on receiving no answer other than a twitching of the face, he added that old Horseface Hammer had been in this afternoon, griping about the fact that the first mailing piece was late.

"I hope she doesn't hold her breath until she gets it," Eggers said.

Mr. Charlesworth rocked back and forth in the visitor's chair, lobster-red with malicious delight. "I hope she does. I certainly hope she does. My, my, my, won't she turn purple?" he said.

"Well, when is it going to turn out?" he asked, with the mild curiosity of one who is not in the struggle anymore.

"Well, isn't that for your doctor to say, Kenneth?" asked Mr. Charlesworth, patting his hand. "And we're not rushing him, you know, we're not rushing him at all."

A possibility—a wild, crazy possibility—struck him with such force that he started up from the pillows and felt a sharp but wholesome pain in his side. "What are you people talking about?" he demanded.

Tibby leaped from the side of the bed and stood in the middle of the room. Amazement, sudden comprehension, anger, wounded self-respect, loyalty to the new beloved and pity for the old one—all these raced across her secretless eyes. "You thought—you thought—Jim, do you know what he thought?" she said. "He thought we were going ahead and doing it without him—the summer campaign!"

He had been so convinced of it that he could not put on a show of denial, even though it was plain that what had been a bitter actuality to him was to them a sick man's fancy.

"But I never thought any such thing," said Jim Eggers, walking to the foot of the bed.

"But Kenneth, where on earth would you get such a notion?

I took it for granted you knew we'd put the whole business in the icebox until you came back," said Mr. Charlesworth.

"Really, Mr. Beatty, there are times when you act as if you were just plain crazy," Tibby said.

He was sitting bolt upright now, his glance darting from one of them to the other. But he did not really see them. He saw the glass walls of his dream shattered, and knew that there was no longer a hard, distorting barrier between him and his world. And when the wonder of it had abated, he mustered up his courage and looked Jim Eggers straight in the face.

That young man, who had rarely said more than two sentences in sequence in his presence, was going on at some length. "Even if the Board had ever dreamed of such a thing, I would have refused to cooperate," he was saying. "Not only out of loyalty and respect for you—because, whether you know it or not, I have a tremendous respect for you—but out of a very healthy sense of my own limitations. Try to imagine me running that campaign singlehanded! Can't you just see me stumbling fumbling around in front of the women's clubs? Wouldn't I be poised and graceful in front of a meeting of the Board of Trustees? After all, this thing has to be dignified—distinguished."

For a second the familiar word stung him so that he flushed. But the young man's unfaltering look proved that it had been said in complete candor and earnestness. Oh, well, he told himself, maybe it wasn't so bad, that business about every step being distinguished. Eggers once called Mrs. Hauser "The Weeping Willow"; yet I've a hunch that he likes her; maybe he even likes her because of her weeping-willowness.

Young Eggers was winding up his speech. "I'm in your office as an apprentice," he said, "and if you don't like having me there, I'm sorry. It's my fault too, I guess. Tibby told me I pestered you too much with my fool suggestions."

He answered, with honest conviction, "No, Jim, they're not fool suggestions, really they're not. Why don't you take a crack at sketching out the second form letter while I'm gone?"

He was worn out with the violence of discovery, and relieved when the nurse came in and looked at her wrist watch. In the fifteen minutes she allotted them, they talked shop: what things Jim and Tibby could do without him, what papers and letters had better be brought here for him to see.

When the warning bell sounded, Jim Eggers said to Tibby, "Why don't you do what you want to? Go ahead and kiss him good-night."

She did kiss him lightly on the left temple; and that, added to the rest, was more than enough. When they were gone, he took the slipper bag from the night table and put it on the bed, close to his hand. Then, remembering the lavender scent of her, he listened to the voices of departing visitors. Before the last of them had trailed off into silence, he was asleep.

On the Other Side of the Road

DURING HER FIRST days in this place—it was early June then, and she was fresh from high-school graduation, still dazed by the fervid oratory of the valedictorian and the aromatic smell of warm roses—during her first days in the house of her Uncle John and her Aunt Rachel, she thought of the boulevard that ran in front of their property only as a road traveled by those who were older and therefore naturally more fortunate than she. Just outside the house and half-covered with the leaves of an unpruned mulberry tree, like a Roman standard set on one of the highways of the Empire, the road sign stood: a pole bearing two white disks, one marked with a "30" and the other with a "22." Two great streams of converged traffic flowed past the house together; and in the cars that sang over the oiled black asphalt all through the summer nights were those who went eastward to the theatres and publishing houses and glittering shops or westward to the steaming city anatomized in Carl Sandburg's poetry. All night long they went and went, as the young can never go, to inherit and embrace the world.

But early in July, when she no longer thought of going, when there was no longer anything for it but a fretful, baffled staying, the road ceased to be an artery of traffic and became a barrier instead. It was a black space, sixty feet wide and yet immeasurable, between the drab, shingled house of her Aunt Rachel and her Uncle John and that pillared, ivy-softened brick edifice, too vast and fine to be called a house, that rambled for half a block on the other side of it. It was the black stretch of futility, the ineradicable dividing line between the actuality and the dream.

If she sat on the porch and looked across the tops of the flying cars, she could put behind her, she could almost blot out, the reality, the shabbiness. Certain shreds and patches of it, harsh and indomitable, would still assert themselves: Her uncle, in the sitting room behind her, would usually be listening to Bach on the phonograph. He liked to listen to Bach while he compiled the statistics for the doctor's degree he was going to take in sociology: "A Mighty Fortress Is Our God," "I Call Upon Thee Jesus," "Christ Lay in Death's Dark Prison"—chorus, tenor, solo, shivering declamation from the organ—poured into the heat of the July afternoons hour upon hour. *They* can hear it over there, she would tell herself, and it's always religious, and they probably know we're Quakers, and they very likely think we never do anything but sit around and meditate about God. Or her Aunt Rachel would carry on, loud above the music, one of her overaffable conversations with the maid. "Gooseberries?" she would shout in her strangely husky voice that sounded like a boy's. "They're beautiful to look at, Mattie, and they're very good as a stiffener in jelly, but they're not to eat." And what, she would ask herself, must they be thinking over there about people who keep a maid who doesn't know that gooseberries aren't to be eaten? She would console herself then with the knowledge that at least they couldn't *see* what was going on inside. Her Uncle John, narrow and seedy and ridiculous in his undershirt and his horn-rimmed glasses, bending over his statistics, looking up now and again, watery-eyed, when some voice rose out of the chorus in a shrill assertion of the glory of God; her Aunt

Rachel, thin and tan as a board, and dressed in a denim skirt with spots of starch on it, her blond hair dry and unruly and tied in a knot on top of her head with a threadbare ribbon or a string or anything—these they could not make out from their pillared veranda and their smooth green lawn. These—so she had assured herself one afternoon, walking on the other side of the boulevard and peering covertly over her shoulder—were blotted out completely in interior darkness. Nothing could be seen but the rusty trellis and the ill-kept clematis vine and the oblong of the front window, dark, blessedly dark.

She admitted to herself with a bad conscience—perhaps it was the bad conscience that gave these summer afternoons their strange quality of heaviness and disquietude, as though a storm that never materialized were always leadening the horizon, where she could not see it, beyond the rim of trees—she admitted to herself that her Uncle John and her Aunt Rachel had not always seemed as objectionable to her as they had seemed in the last few weeks. In fact when her grandmother had suggested that she might wish to stretch a summer vacation with them into a longer stay, might find herself inclined to live there indefinitely, there had been no automatic protest from her, only enough experience with moving from place to place to make for a guarded, "Well, we'll see." Her father was a surgeon, long attached to the Army. She had no brothers or sisters, and her mother was ten years dead. Though she had never "stayed a spell" with these particular relatives, she had felt a certain affinity with them when she encountered them at Christmas parties or marriages or funerals in whichever house she happened to be. If their conversation with her had been a little grave, a little rigid, it had never been couched in baby talk. If every stitch they had on their backs had plainly been washed too often and worn too long, whatever they wore was distinguished by what she took to be a Quakerish quaintness and simplicity. Their gifts, and they never forgot to bring her a gift, had always proved both surprising at the moment of opening and capable of yielding lasting pleasure: a folder of reproductions of Holbein's paintings; a box of water-color pencils; an ancient music manuscript from a shop in Boston, the parchment cracked and precious, the square notes done in black, the words in scarlet, the clefs in gold.

KIND PEOPLE. YET from the beginning she had been relieved of the burden of gratefulness. Her grandmother—a just woman, the fit begetter of a college professor with Quaker persuasions and an Army surgeon who, having seen the worst of Guadalcanal, had volunteered for Korea nevertheless—her grandmother had made it plain that her uncle and aunt would have their due rewards: The allowance sent home by her father would ease their straitened financial situation; and they were childless and had always wanted a child. She wondered how they had managed before the allowance. Even with it, they could not afford to trim the trees or paint the streaked shingles or send the sagging cretonne chairs to the upholsterer's. As for their entertainment bill, it couldn't have amounted to more than five dollars a week. On Saturday evenings a crowd of some twelve others singularly like them came to sit on the collapsed springs and chat above "I Have Greatly Suffered" and "Sleepers, Awake." The women brought knitting or embroidery; the men divided themselves into two groups, those who listened to Bach and those who played chess; and the refreshments consisted of small sandwiches—cream cheese and olive, sliced cucumber, leftover chicken, and the ground-up end of Wednesday's ham—together with three pitchers of iced tea.

Life was not here; nor was it, as she had once thought, in the turbulent cities pointed at by "30" and "22." Life had established itself in the brick citadel on the other side of the boulevard: the life par excellence, the only worthy life, the life that was one long, cool carnival. At eleven in the morning the mistress of that house, a peerless mother, issued onto the veranda in pastel linen, her ringlets prematurely gray around her pink, unwrinkled face. A maid, a real maid with a ruffled cap and a ruffled apron, came after her with a silver coffee service on a silver tray, a flowery cushion, and a book. At one, or at two for that matter, on days when the second-floor drapes were drawn to keep late sleepers safe from all but the squeezed-out honey of the sun, the luncheon guests crossed the blemishless lawn to the veranda. If it was the older crowd, they floated, the kingly gentlemen ambling along beside their queenly women, and these moving in clouds of airy cloth—raw silk, Shantung, organza, organdy. If it was the younger crowd, they flashed in, the daughter of the house running down the steps, to give them welcome in a snow-white skirt and a snow-white halter, her shoulders as smooth and polished as if they had been carved out of blond wood, her pale, baby-soft hair blowing across her sunburned cheek, veiling her pink mouth and her sea-colored eyes.

And the evenings, the evenings. . . . Sometimes the yearning and the bafflement had been so unbearable that she had taken herself away, into the brashly lighted parlor, where it was impossible to see the Japanese lanterns strung between the magnificent elms, or hear the music for the dancing on the veranda or the short, nervous laughter that could only come out of the throats of those in dark places making love. To be invited to one such festival—but no, that was to ask too much. It was even too much to expect the gray ringlets to nod at her across the boulevard some morning or the sea-colored eyes to flash her a look of recognition through the blown, fine hair. She had waited weeks now, and it was plainly not to be. But a person should be permitted at least to talk about her obsessions, and a kind of righteous stillness, a stiffening of backs and a pursing of lips, came on at the very mention of the ones on the other side. "Their honeysuckle is in bloom," "They have a gardener in pruning their locust trees," "They had a caterer for their party last night"—such leading comments led to nothing but more Bach, more embroidery patterns, more gooseberries. But one morning, at a dull and sodden breakfast, it came upon her all of a sudden that she could tackle the problem head-on, could pose a question that would demand an answer. "Why is it," she said, "that we don't speak to them? Our neighbors over in the brick house, I mean."

"Because," said her Uncle John, "they don't want to be spoken to. They made that pretty plain three years ago."

OBVIOUSLY HER UNCLE had been harried all night by his statistics. He had a yellow sheet covered with columns of figures beside his bowl of shredded wheat, and he kept peering at it wearily through his thick glasses. Suddenly she found herself staring at her Aunt Rachel and wondering how it would be to lie in a double bed beside a man harassed by statistics. Sordid, disgusting—but then her Aunt Rachel was no beauty either, with her freckled cheeks and her straw-colored hair. Some people have to take whatever they can get, she thought, exulting in the cruelty of her realism. Some people are banished from the beginning, by the very shabbiness of their natures, from the world of the exalted ones.

"They certainly did," her Aunt Rachel was saying. "Five years ago, when we moved in, we tried nodding. But they looked straight through us, didn't they, dear?"

"Maybe you only *thought* they did." It took daring to say so. For the first time since her arrival, she sensed anger in the room—insistent, almost audible, like the buzz of a mosquito; but her urgency was such that she could not let the moment pass. "It's hard to see through the clematis vine."

Her uncle abandoned the statistics and sighed. "Their gardener speaks to us," he said, slowly, so that there would be plenty of time for the implications to come through. "They sent him over to ask if we weren't going to have the field landscaped one of these days. They had definite ideas about what we ought to do. A nice, smooth lawn, they thought, maybe with a border of boxwood and a couple of pines."

"To do a job like that," said her aunt, "would cost two thousand dollars. That's about one third of your uncle's yearly salary at the university."

SHE BLUSHED FOR the field. Henceforth she would never be able to look their gardener in the face. She hadn't known that the field belonged to her uncle and aunt, that she must count herself responsible for that wilderness of sweet clover and timothy, milkweed and thistle, inhabited by wrens and squirrels and divided from the rest of the decent world by rotting posts and loops of rusted wire. But before she could bring herself to say that such a field might well be an eyesore to people who cut their lawns and clipped their hedges once a week, before she could call attention to the hazards of crab grass and thistledown and milkweed seed, her Aunt Rachel was saying, less to her than to the hand-embroidered mat in the middle of the table, that those people over there had never even missed the presence of old Cousin Theodore, had not so much as sent a card with their condolences the time when old Cousin Theodore died.

She stared unhappily at her blackberries. The field and old Cousin Theodore were both subjects better left alone. Concerning both of them, there was too much to be said that might accrue to the honor of this side of the boulevard. She had spoken in praise of the field one evening when she and her Uncle John, in a rare moment of warm communication, had looked at it from the porch at twilight and had seen the froth of the Queen Anne's lace and timothy skimmed by a twinkling multitude of fireflies. *Our* field—there was something of that in her uncle's pained and rigid face. *Our* Cousin Theodore— there was something of that in the shy, hazel look advanced and immediately withdrawn by her aunt. And though Cousin

Theodore had not really belonged to her Aunt Rachel—he had actually been some remote connection of her Uncle John's—the very fact of his detachment was all to that lady's credit; at least there had been occasions back home when she and every member of the family had found it so. She remembered a particular Christmas—Cousin Theodore's last Christmas in the world—when Aunt Rachel had run around the house in a sweat, trying to save the family festival from being turned into a tragi-comedy by the bizarre sallies of the old man's senility. He had taken a three-pound box of chocolates into the attic and eaten every piece, with dire alimentary results; he had caused a short circuit in the wiring of the Christmas tree; he had wandered away and got himself drenched to the bone. In spite of herself, she saw a sharp image of Aunt Rachel on her knees, pulling off the sodden socks and chafing the veined feet and saying that nobody ought to scold him and spoil his Christmas—how was *he* to know that a nice fresh snow like that was going to turn to rain?

Her Uncle John took off his glasses and polished them with his paper napkin. "Oh, well, forget it," he said. "He wasn't *their* Cousin Theodore."

You're right about that, he wasn't, she kept telling herself all day long; and the quarrel that was going on within her projected itself upon the world around her, made her refuse to tuck her legs under her when the maid was sweeping the porch, made her downright short and sullen when she was asked to go two blocks to the grocery to get five more pounds of sugar for the forthcoming and too-much-rejoiced-over batch of currant-and-red-raspberry jelly. It was sordid the way her uncle and aunt had to watch their money. Because there was going to be jelly for the winter, there could be nothing but cheap little chocolate cookies in a cellophane package for dessert tonight. The house was uninhabitable, filled as it now was with discredited loyalties and wounded sensibilities. They were too easily hurt, she told herself. Very probably their sensitivity had done much to build up the intolerable barrier between the two sides of the boulevard. Undoubtedly, once the gardener had made his unfortunate visit, they had walked about with their noses in the air, refusing to see a tentative nod, drowning out a possible "Good morning" with "Out of the Depths I Cry to Thee." As for the episode of Cousin Theodore—the people in the brick edifice had probably never been conscious of his existence and had therefore felt no emptiness when he had ceased to be. How could a person expect them, considering all that went on over at their place, to take account of a wizened old man eternally rocking in a rocking chair, scarcely visible through the tendrils of an overgrown vine?

IF THE DAY had been trying, the evening was wretched. The Bach in the parlor was louder than usual, turned up in order to drown out the shrill and asinine conversation the maid and Aunt Rachel were carrying on over the dripping jelly bag—her aunt was undoubtedly convinced that the only way to repay the maid for staying late to help with the jelly was by shouting inanities. Every now and then, over the ecstatic piping of some boy soprano, the husky contralto in the kitchen would assert that there were fewer flies around the garbage can this year; that DDT was very effective; that herb tea was *not* a cure for lumbago; that Dr. Lawson, a friend of hers, was glad to see patients of any race, creed, or color, and charged very reasonable fees.

And she, sitting on the swing with her back to the field—she could not look at the Queen Anne's lace, she could not look at the gathering convocations of fireflies—she set herself to thinking about her twenty-eight dollars and the dress that she was going to buy with it: a mental maneuver that always yielded her some illusion of communication with the opposite side of the boulevard when nothing was going on over there, when the lawn was barren of striding young men and leaping hounds, when the recesses of the shadowy veranda were sorrowful with

247

emptiness. Nothing was going on over there this evening. The windows turned into luminous squares a little after sunset, but no exalted shape made itself manifest in the stone archway of the front door. From one of the first-floor windows, somebody, probably one of the servants, called the dog, whose name was Junior. But Junior did not come, and nobody ran out to seek him, and the reddish clouds, small and widely spaced above the marvelous intricacy of the tall chimneys and elaborate cupolas, gave an impression of utter remoteness and emptyheartedness.

The dress, she thought. What kind of dress? Her Aunt Rachel had forestalled an immediate shopping trip by reminding her that there would be sales in the middle of July; she could have, if she cared to wait a week or so, two dresses for the price of one. Not that she meant to buy two dresses; she would buy for herself, instead, one piece of fabulous splendor worth two times twenty-eight dollars—a dress whose nature changed with her mood and the state of her concept of herself and the coloration of her tentative and elusive relationship with those on the other side of the black, oiled span of road where the cars kept humming east and west. Sometimes, when it was raining, the dress was gray, or hyacinth, or a somber violet; and somebody—sometimes the mother, sometimes the daughter, sometimes one of the peerless youths with the golf clubs— sighted it across the sixty-foot barrier, saw and hailed behind the rusty trellis an unexpected loveliness. Or, on very hot days, the dress was white, glaring white; and like a blade, like a flash of lightening, like a snow-capped mountain, she stood silent at the break in their boxwood hedge, demanding and receiving the tribute of their staring eyes. Or, on baffled, melancholy evenings like this, the dress was a sad color, ashy rose, a solemn blue. She walked in it across the road, drawn on by the music and the whispering and the Japanese lanterns; she went with a fixed gaze through the streaming traffic, heard the brakes shriek, felt the impact and the pain, and was gathered up and borne across the lawn—dying, perhaps, but in the arms of one of the exalted ones, nevertheless.

THE BRAKES *WERE* shrieking. She brought the swing to a shuddering stop with the toe of her shoe and knew the silence had been shattered by a terrible yelping and a grinding of brakes. She started up and saw that the smooth flow of traffic had halted and that something low and furry was going at a fearful, marred pace between the cars, making for the field, dragging itself into the timothy and Queen Anne's lace. "Uncle John!" she shouted into the window, above the organ blast of Bach. He was there, standing against the sill; and she knew of a sudden—because his face was white and his glasses were flashing in the headlights of the passing cars—that she had dreamed though the twilight and started up into the dark.

"What's the matter, Baby?"

"Listen!" But he had heard the howls, the grieving barks; she could tell it by the sudden stiffening of his shoulders.

"A dog," she said. "A poor dog. He's over in our field. He got hit on the boulevard."

He reached behind him and switched off the music, which ended in a shaking roar. What in another man's mouth would have been a piece of casual blasphemy came out of him in the shape of a prayer. Above the sickening yelping, he uttered the name of the Lord.

The animal cries—what part of the field they were issuing from it was impossible to tell; the poor beast was doubtless loping crazily through the tall weeds, trying dumbly to escape from his pain—the animal cries were so shattering to her that she moved very close to her uncle, in spite of his drenched jersey and the smell of his sweat. But he had turned into the direction of the kitchen. "Rachel!" he shouted; and she thought without humor and without malice that, having evoked his primary source of succor, he was now addressing himself to his secondary source, his helpmeet in a sorry world. "Rachel, they've hit a dog out there. I think he's badly hurt. He's in the field, poor thing."

Rachel came and stood beside her husband at the window. Her apron, spattered crimson with the juice of currants, somehow begot a vision of a furry creature horribly mangled and crawling through the stalks, drenching the stalks with blood.

She was sick—so sick that she had to reach over the sill for her Aunt Rachel's bony hand. "I can't stand it. Let's go and look for him," she said.

UNCLE JOHN FOUND two flashlights, one of them small, the other big enough but with an old and feeble battery. There was no word concerning the precious currant jelly; it was consigned automatically to the maid's inexpert watching. The howls could be heard in the kitchen, were lost in the closed dining room and picked up again—terrible, disintegrating—in the living room, where she bruised her knee against a misplaced chair. Then the three of them were on the sidewalk caught in the passing lights and visible to any eyes that might be watching them from the yellow, ivy-softened squares of the windows across the road, Uncle John in his jersey, and Aunt Rachel in what must seem like a butcher's apron, and she between them—shamefully and undeniably a connection of theirs, branded forever with their sordidness.

"There's no use in the three of us staying together," Aunt Rachel said.

Are human beings like moths and grasshoppers? she asked herself. Do they have invisible organs of perception, spiritual antennae, that carry on their subtle functions in the dark? Do the two of them know that I am bitterly ashamed of them, so ashamed that I would rather come upon the horror alone?

"Here, you take this one," her uncle said, pressing the

smaller and brighter of the flashlights into her hands. "We'll cover the far end. There's no telling where he may have taken himself." For the disintegrating sound had suddenly given way to an even more disintegrating stillness; there was not a whine, not a rustle in the weeds—very likely the dog was dead.

And it was sane and necessary, it was certainly sane and necessary, she told herself, for them to go their separate ways. The field covered an acre at least, and the growth was very thick, and high enough to snap and sting against her knees. Yet she was no efficient searcher. She started at every solid thing—stumps, clusters of thistle, clusters of milkweed pods; she had never seen anything, not even a dog, stark and austere in death. She had begun to wonder if she was actually trying *not* to find him when behind her a cool voice said, "Excuse me," and a great swath of brightness swept before her, picking out the feathery heads of the timothy and lessening the light of the fireflies. It was the daughter of the house; the passing headlights kept moving across her baby-blond hair. "Did I hear somebody say something about a dog?" she said. "Our dog Junior's been missing since this afternoon."

"A dog was hit out there." I—she could not bring herself to say the incriminating "we"—"I saw him go into the field, but I can't find a trace of him now."

"It *would* be difficult, in this mess of weeds." That came in another's voice, probably the mother's. She also carried a powerful light and cast it pitilessly across the foamy surface of the field until it caught and showed them both—the jersey and the bloody apron in the disgraceful tangle of timothy and milkweed and Queen Anne's lace.

"Well, what are we waiting for?" It was the girl again. "We'd better start looking. Did you see which way he ran?"

"No, I didn't quite see; I wasn't looking." It was strange, it was stupefying, it made her far more stupid than she was to talk to these much-loved and too-long-brooded-upon shapes in the blackness, without seeing their eyes. And since there was nothing else to talk about, they moved a little apart, though it could not be said that exchange was broken off, that the stumbling search through the weeds was without certain indications of humanity and neighborliness. The daughter warned her against a patch of thistle; the mother observed that there was no purpose in their beating around at the other end of the field, since "Our neighbors are covering that part of the territory very efficiently indeed." She was grateful for their flashlights too: The great white fingers of light were turned steadily upon everything, down to the roots, and relieved her of the responsibility of turning her shaking beam in any perilous direction.

"Junior," they said in the darkness behind her. "Here, Junior, come, Junior, poor Junior, poor old boy." And their voices, their darkling presences, invoked the magic or a recollection of the magic. I have never touched them; I will never have a chance to touch them again, she thought, and allowed herself to stumble toward them, to move between them, to own for this one time the transitory blessedness of contact with the exalted ones.

THEN THERE WAS some change, some shift in the scene—a static moment, an assertive stillness. She looked out over the black road and saw that the cars had stopped to make way for a frilled white apron and a frilled white cap, which moved with hasteless dignity across the boulevard, over the pavement, up to the twisted loops of wire. "Madam," said the wearer of the frills in a voice raised only enough to enforce itself over the renewed humming of the tires. "Are you there, Madam?"

"Yes. What is it?"

"Junior came home. It wasn't Junior. He walked in through the back door a couple of minutes ago."

"It wasn't Junior?" Their lights, deserting the field and the animal loneliness of the dead or the dying, leaving the field to the two weak beams, swept the sky in triumph over Junior's safe return. "Oh, good! Oh, wonderful! Junior's home; it wasn't

Junior," they said, and turned their backs, and crouched under the wire, and went their way, leaving the blackness eloquent with the hammering of her stricken heart. Not *their* dog, not *their* Cousin Theodore.

Her aunt and her uncle were coming toward her from the opposite end of the field. She could not look at them at first; she knew their approach only by the sound of it, the swish of weeds and their breathing, coming out of them slow and laborious, like sighs. When they were very close to her, she forced herself to raise her flashlight and saw their faces, shining with sweat. Her Aunt Rachel must have collided with a dry twig or a piece of the wire—there was a bloody scratch across her brow.

"They went," she told them, doing what she could to steady her shaking light. "Their Junior came home, and they weren't interested any more." She felt a desperate need to state it harshly, nakedly. "It wasn't *their* dog, so they took their flashlights and went home."

"Maybe we'd better go home ourselves, Baby." Her Uncle John's eyes short-sighted and watery behind his glasses, mercifully avoided her eyes. "We'll never find him, not in the dark. Come on, you're awfully hot and white; your aunt'll make you a pitcher of iced tea."

HE DIDN'T MEAN of word of it, of course. It was not that their Quakerish charity went out any less to the beast; it was only that the two of them had silently agreed upon the priority of her human wretchedness, had pitied her shattered dream and were respecting the enormity of her loss. But she could not take such an indulgence; such an indulgence would be an everlasting shame, not only to her but to them and to every member of her line. Nothing in her life had ever seemed so forlorn and pitiable as the deserted field. Looking across the almost invisible, uneven top of it, thinking of the dog alone among the weeds, she felt very close to her father; she understood why he had gone to Korea, even though he had been discharged with honor after Gaudalcanal; she sent a kiss to him across half the curve of the world; she placed a kiss in the middle of his wrinkled, hard, inelegant brow. "No," she said at the top of her voice. "Who would think of it? Who would leave a hurt dog out here alone?"

They looked for him together then. For an immeasurable amount of time they strode through the tangled stalks and the snapping twigs; and now she searched in bitter earnest, unafraid. Over and over again she called to him: "Here dog, here cur, here mongrel," she said—loudly, because her father was in Korea and her uncle worked day and night to set down for unborn scholars the findings of the sociologists and her aunt looked after the senile and the dying—and it did not behoove the inheritor of such a bounty to whisper and creep about. And sometimes, when she had detached herself from the others, she found herself making strange speeches, saying things a person would say only in a dream. "Dog," she said, "nobody's dog, anybody's dog, God's dog, suffering hound without pedigrees, come to us; don't be afraid to put yourself into our hands. If you can be saved, we will save you; and if you have to die, come and die in our kitchen. We take care of the dying—anybody's cousin, anybody's dog; whatever is sent to us, we take for our own."

It was close to midnight when her Aunt Rachel stumbled against him and dragged him up out of a pile of last year's leaves—and he like the leaves, the same dun color, the same moldiness: God's dog indeed, since only an innocent and blessed fool among men would claim such a rag, such a piece of misery, for his own. That he had a home now was established before the length of him, flea-bitten and clumped with burs, was lugged across the field and into the house. That he would live to enjoy security and tranquility was also plain. One forepaw was broken—it hung limp and wet with warm blood—but the rest of him was intact, the shaggy head unhurt, the nose moist and feverless, the ribs unshattered under the loose hide.

•

ONE PROBLEM, ONLY one, remained to be solved. Uncle John gave them to understand that, with the best will in the world, he could not splint a broken paw and no veterinary would do it for less than five dollars; but after all the purses had been turned upside down and all pockets had been turned inside out, the total yield was eighty-four cents. They could borrow from Mattie, the maid, of course; and Mattie, having let the jelly boil over in a moment of reverie, was eager to offer a loan, though she would have to have it back tomorrow to pay for her sister's ticket to Baltimore.

"Oh, no, don't do that, that won't be necessary, I have twenty-eight dollars," she said. And since they were humble people and did not dare to snatch at good gifts, but waited in patience until things were laid securely in their hands, she went on to explain to them that whatever she owned was theirs, that she didn't need a dress, that the things she had were quite fine enough for the sort of life they lived together here, that she must remember to write to her grandmother one of these days and ask to have her fall clothes sent down together with her books and the few little things she had dragged from house to house since she was a child. And when the moment grew too charged, too intense to be accepted, she turned to her Uncle John and asked him didn't he want to finish playing his Bach. Play it loud, she thought. Play it loud enough to sound above the hum of the cars and storm the frozen bastion on the other side of the road. It's your solace, it's your comfort; and a man has a right to his comfort when he lives with decency and humanity in a harsh world.

255

The Day Before the Wedding

IT NEVER ONCE occurred to him that there was nothing extraordinary about his case, that he was like other husbands. He would not have believed that, out of twenty husbands chosen at random, as many as twelve might be urged into confessing they had wakened on the day before their wedding totally devoid of the traditional bliss. It was he and he only (so he told himself) who had gotten out of bed stiff in the bones and sour in the mouth and in the soul. Nobody else could have sat wan at a breakfast table in wan October sun, curtly rejecting a second hot cake with a shake of the head, stubbornly reading an advertisement for free aviation goggles in order to avoid his mother's conscious bravery in the face of the oncoming loss. Nobody else had ever thought on such an occasion that life and the coffee were equally tasteless and tepid, or had related the unglamorous familiarity of a cracked fruit bowl seen on a depressing number of mornings or a lean and lazy she-cat desultorily licking herself to the questionable charms of the bride.

No, his case—or so he thought, forcing himself to drink his coffee to the syrupy brown dregs because his mother was looking and this was his last morning cup of home coffee—his case was singular. Other men, to be sure—his brothers, for instance—had married a sorry lot of women. A sorry lot of women were somehow always getting married in this world. But had any of those others ever dreamed his dreams?

Since this was the last morning, he indulged himself for a few minutes. He stared through the window above the piled-up sink: He was the only one on a melancholy holiday; all the others had gone about their usual business, leaving behind them plates smeared with egg yolk and saucers marked with brownish rings. He stared at the faded sky and the dried blossoms on the tops of the dahlia hedge that divided the yard from the bigger, finer yard belonging to the neighbors. He stared and permitted himself to conjure up one, only one, of all those dreams.

The best? The most ridiculous? A mature man, past his twenty-third birthday and on the eve of marriage, ought to laugh at it; and if his mother had not been hovering about between the stove and the sink, he would at least have smiled. He saw himself, sixteen and sullenly dark and skinny in a hideous red shirt and tight blue jeans, sitting on the floor of his aunt's living room, or hanging secretively around the newsstand in the drugstore, or standing at the call desk in the periodical room of the local library, but always paging feverishly through women's magazines. And why? To look for the blessedly recurring vision of a certain model, whose hair, if you were lucky enough to find it in color, was orange like a new penny, with the help of coconut oil, secret chemical processes, or pure lanolin. Her sorrowful, faintly drooping lips were desecrated according to the season with moss-rose pink, field-lily scarlet, tangerine-orange, and cranberry red. Her shoulders and her collarbones—strange, if he closed his eyes he could see them yet—emerged heartbreakingly delicate from the folds of genuine wool jersey, "available this year," according to the tastefully restrained caption, "in subtle tones of cattail brown, pond gray, and cloud blue."

"Are you going down to the apartment to meet Angie?" his mother said.

"Yes." It came out of him loud and snappish. His mother had an exasperating way of starting conversation when no conversation was necessary by asking questions whose answers she knew as well as she knew her own name. He had told her, only last night he had told her, that he and Angie would have to spend most of the day in that blasted hole in the wall. Furthermore, she set his nerves on edge by the tone in which she had been saying "Angie" lately. She had begun to put the same soft bloom on "Angie" that she put on the names of his brothers' wives: a since-you-love-her-I-am-bound-to-utter-her-name-with-tenderness sort of bloom. He was not clear in his mind why the slow, distinct rendering of the name made him want to jump of out his chair. Maybe because it implied an ardor that he could not possibly hope to produce, and maybe because, even if Angie did not have delicate collarbones, she deserved better than to be put into the same category as those others—that raw-boned Hilda, that insignificant Suzie, that asinine Annabelle.

"You'll feel better, darling." His mother had come up behind him and was running her fingers slowly and maddeningly through his hair. "You'll feel better when it's all over and the two of you are settled down and you're back at the office."

"What makes you think there's anything wrong with the way I feel?"

HIS QUESTION WAS so aggressive it had to be answered. "I don't know; I thought you were looking a little depressed or something—"

"Depressed? I'm not depressed. I'm only thinking. Every time I think, you ask me am I depressed. Is it necessary for a person to keep an imbecile smile on his face? Is it necessary to—"

He held his tongue, seeing that she was taking the unwanted

hot cake out of the frying pan and flopping it into the garbage pail. Last hot cake, last morning. He rose and looked at her for the first time since he had come into the kitchen and wasn't aware, in spite of his harassments, of the unusual brightness in her big faded-green eyes and of the iron-gray streaks in her coarse bobbed hair. Once, he thought, she lived through a morning like this, and so did my father, and his father, and *his* father—He stood by the table, crackling the waxed-paper lining inside the cereal box and considering the appropriateness of a kiss.

"I do hope the paint dried out lighter," she said.

Why was she always doing that? It was bad enough that twenty minutes from now he would have to look at that rotten paint. Did she have to make him suffer beforehand too? "It won't," he told her bitterly. "I know it won't; I told you so last night."

She pushed the lid of the garbage pail down with her hand and sighed.

"In fact, it'll dry out darker." The very notion that it *could* dry out darker, breaking upon him, goaded him on. "It'll be Oxford gray, it'll be gun-metal gray, it'll be darn near black—"

She gazed at him with insulting comprehension, infuriating indulgence.

"It'll look awful; it'll look worse than anything you ever laid eyes on. The blue sofa will look hideous against it, absolutely hideous! The gray chairs'll be freakish; they'll just melt into the wall. And the lamps, and the pictures, and the bookshelves, and the china dogs—"

Her eyes widened. It was as if she were staring into a growing fire. It was as if she knew exactly what he was doing: taking everything in his new house and throwing it onto his kindled anger, hurling every dear and frail and much-discussed object into the flames to be burned up in a sacrifice to some nameless and angry god.

"The linens too," he said—she had made the linens—"those pink linens will be impossible."

But she did not wince. Just when he mentioned the linens, quite unexplainably, she began to smile. The gradual, muted kind of smile that is usually a smile of remembering shaped her closed and faded lips.

"There's your jacket, on the chair." She nodded at it across the table. "You'd better wear it. It got cold last night. In fact the roofs were white when I got up; we had the first frost." Slowly, wiping her knuckles up and down on the sides of her apron, she came from the stove to the place where he stood and kissed him ceremonially. Not on the lips—she seemed to be implying that she had consigned his lips to Angie—but a little to the left of his chin. "I'll make dumplings for supper, and maybe they'll come out hard, and then if the paint dries dark you can complain about the dumplings. You used to do that when you were little—let me have it if you lost your allowance; tell your father off because your rabbit died."

"Did I? I guess I did." He touched the shoulder strap of her apron, touched it long and definitely enough to feel the sweater under the cotton and the shoulder under the wool.

But she had to do it again; she never knew when to say nothing. "Honest, you'll feel better. Even tomorrow you'll feel much better," she said.

ANGIE WAS STANDING on the front porch of the silly house that belonged to her silly family. She was standing far back from the crazy green wooden spindles, on the verge of the vestibule, as if she had been waiting a long time in the cold and was on the point of taking her legs, thinnish and bare between her rolled-up jeans and her ballet slippers, away from the pinch of frost. She looked pretty much the way Angie usually looked, except a little worse because her thin, triangular face was bluish in patches.

261

Her fair hair, doubtless done up in bobby pins in expectation of the great day, was completely covered by a red babushka. As he walked up the front steps he expected to see reproach—and saw only an incomprehensible flutter of something allied to fright—in her mild, brown eyes.

She should have stepped forward to meet him; but instead she stepped backward and encountered something and made a little rattle of wrapping paper with her foot. "It's a present," she explained defensively, reaching behind her to pick it up by its loop of twine. It was flat and big, ominously big; and nothing except the prospect of paint dried out Oxford gray could have been more depressing than the thought of a picture of that size chosen with execrable taste. "It's a special present from my family."

"What kind of picture?" He snatched it out of her hand by the loop and started with it down the steps and onto the street.

"A good picture. You expect it to be rotten, but you're mistaken; it isn't." Her voice was tremulous, perhaps with the recollections of her final cup of morning coffee, her final dish of cereal and milk eaten while her loud-mouthed mother stood behind her and her obscenely fat little brother hung onto her knees. "They saved it for a surprise, and they gave it to me this morning. And it isn't anything dreadful like 'Old Ironsides' or 'The Country Doctor,' no matter what you think. It's a Renoir—they heard you say you liked him, and they looked all over the place. Besides, it's a beautiful print, a perfectly beautiful print, and they had it framed in white, to go with the gray walls—"

SHE STOPPED. HE was a little ahead of her, carrying the picture, and he did not look back; but her knew that her face had gone blank, that her skinny little hand had gone up toward her half-open mouth at the remembrance of those walls. All last evening she has behaved exactly as if it had been she alone who had kept dribbling more black and purple into the gray;

and actually—he admitted it in sour justice—he had been just as eager to darken up the chalky tone as she. A fact that in no way whatsoever absolved her from the responsibility of having allowed her family to intrude a picture—a large, heavy, unhidable picture—into the privacy of their new living room. Maybe it was a Renoir, but there were Renoirs and Renoirs; certain of those fat, naked bathers by Renoir actually made him physically sick. Leave it to them to choose something fat and pink—they thought her little brother was pretty fetching that way. Leave it to them to choose something vulgar—they were vulgar themselves.

"*What* Renoir? *Which* Renoir?" he said.

"I don't know—some lady—"

"Oh, for heaven's sake!" A person would think she would have enough sense to look for the title. "Dressed or undressed?"

"I don't remember. I think sort of half-and-half—"

"A *bather?*"

"I don't *think* it was a bather. Why don't you wait and see?"

They had come to that shabby street whose name he would henceforth have to write on any blank that asked for his address. They were within sight of that fantastic white frame house, all Victorian towers and scalloped shingles, whose topmost floor, drafty in winter and stuffy in summer, would be his home. Yet even here—his throat tightened at the thought; he really had no grasp on himself—even here the yearning eye might come unexpectedly upon beauty of a kind. The atrocious towers glittered at the edges and gave the illusion of having been transported out of some fine old English etching, traced as they were in delicate lines of frost. The Norway maple was burnt-yellow against the peeling white paint; the barberry bushes that veiled the terrace had been kindled during the night to an orange-and-scarlet fire; and a remembrance could have walked there, its lips touched with holly-berry red, its fragile figure draped in folds of cattail brown or cloud blue.

"Maybe you'll actually like the picture," she said, but with just that undertone of dubiousness to make him expect the worst.

"I'll tell you this much: I'll be surprised if I do. I hope you remembered to bring the key." It wasn't fair, and he knew as much: She had never forgotten the key; the key had been forgotten only once, and the person who had left it at home in another pair of pants was undeniably himself.

SHE FITTED THE key into the lock. They went through the hall that smelled unpleasantly of carpet cleaner and up the stairs with only one incident: Mrs. Painter stuck her head out of one of her own bedrooms and gave them that waiting-for-the-wedding-bells look. Angie took the stairs two at a time, as if she had a pressing engagement, and then stopped dead still on the little landing in front of their door.

Possibly it was some connection between Mrs. Painter and his mother—both had iron-gray streaks in their hair—that had made him wonder for an instant as he stood there behind Angie what kind of rooms his parents had come to, the lively woman and the dark, sober man with the neatly trimmed moustache, who had been a bride and a bridegroom before they had taken upon themselves the workaday role of his progenitors. There was a photograph of them someplace at home: The bride, he recollected, looking at Angie's narrow back in the leather jacket, had been beautiful and misty in a foam of white lace. But on the day before their wedding—what had she looked like then? Had she come up to the second or third floor of somebody else's house in a tailored blouse and one of those inanely tight skirts they had worn right after the first World War? Had the thick bangs, curling so naturally under the lace bonnet and the orange blossoms, been plastered down in preparation for the transitory hour of glory that was yet to come?

"What do you have a babushka on for?" he said.

"To keep my head warm—what do you think? It's cold; it's below thirty-two."

"Oh. I thought maybe you had your hair put up in bobby pins."

"You know I wouldn't. You know I know you hate it. You know I wouldn't dare, even if I have to look a fright tomorrow," she said, and squared her thin little shoulders, and took a deep breath like a solider who is about to lunge into cross fire, and took hold of the knob, and opened the door.

Oxford gray, mouse gray, rat gray. The filthy paint had dried out—and he had never actually faced the possibility—at least two shades darker than it had been before. The chairs simply disappeared into it. The peacock-blue sofa—and it had been so beautiful in the store on a day when they had been reasonably happy that it was wounding to remember it—the blue sofa was a hideous discord. The pictures standing on the floor against the wall—the delicate drawings by Watteau and the exquisite pastel-colored Degas ballerinas—it would be a sacrilege to hang them; he would never hand them now! That other picture, that veiled monstrosity whose loop of twine was cutting into his hand—he set it down with a bang, not caring in the least that he might shatter the glass. In fact in his mind's eye he saw a sliver of glass cutting into the fleshy, roseate shoulder of an overblown bather, and the emotion he experienced at the vision was a keen, shrill variety of delight.

Angie had languidly dropped her leather jacket into the coffee table and was languidly walking over to the window. "It's too dark, but it doesn't have to stay that way," she said, not to him but to the uppermost yellow burning of the maple boughs. "We can paint it over; we could come back from Ligonier a day early and paint it all over before you go back to work."

"And live in that smell, and try to sleep in that smell—" But his voice was less cutting than he had thought it would be, partly because he knew how she had planned every hour, every meal, of that trip to Ligonier and partly because she had pulled off her babushka and revealed the silky, childish insufficiency of her fair hair.

"It goes away fast. We did it all yesterday and you can hardly notice it now. It'd only be for one night."

"*I* notice it. Plenty." He took a deep breath.

ANGIE TURNED AROUND, away from the fire-yellow leaves and frosty angles of the roof, and faced him; and there was in her face that subtle, complicated look of love and resignation and self-distrust that had become, of late, her most characteristic expression. He knew she was thinking, I should have said it wasn't very dark; I should have said to let it alone and it would look all right. Her shoulders under the silly bare white blouse— trust Angie to wear a summer blouse on the morning of the first frost—her neck, rising like the stem of a weak flower, the sideward drooping of her head, all gave voiceless utterance to her profound conviction of defeat.

And he was sorry, very sorry, but not so sorry as to be entirely unaware that the kind of regret she begot in him at times like this was a maddening regret. Why did she always make him feel as if he had kicked a puppy? Or broken somebody's old family heirloom, a dish that was all the more pathetic lying in pieces because it had never been any good in the first place? "Well," he said, trying, disciplining his mouth into a stiff semblance of a smile, "there's no use standing around moaning. Let's do something. What'll we do?"

"Hang the pictures?"

That was stupid, even if they *had* mentioned last night that they'd hang the pictures first thing. What was the good of hanging pictures if you were going to repaint? Undoubtedly it was the slovenly leaven of her family working in her; undoubtedly she was thinking how she and he would enjoy themselves and stay that final day in Ligonier and come home and get used to it all and live with it forever, the way her people lived with the dead sticks of ancient lilac bushes in their back yard and the brown, hexagonal holes left by missing tiles in their bathroom floor. "Scarcely," he said.

"No, of course not." She raised her thin hand to her mouth and shook her head at her own inanity. "We wouldn't hang pictures, not when we've got another coat to put on. But look—" Was she trying a diversionary movement, or had some actuality kindled a bona-fide light in her weary and dubious face? "Oh, look, look over there on the chair by the other window! They must have put it in early this morning or late last night! We've got it—we've got our telephone!"

Why, he did not know, but he had to admit that the black little object sitting in the middle of the gray cushion was singularly gratifying, its dial clean and shining, its wires passing over the plump arm of the chair and going into the plug above the newly varnished baseboard. He went with her to pay respects to it; he even put his arm around her waist while she lifted the receiver from its cradle and held it against her ear. "It hums; just listen to it hum," she said. "Now people'll call us and we'll call people." She *was* a puppy; she rubbed her face against the black rounds; it was a wonder she didn't jump on the thing, didn't lick the thing. And all at once, as he looked at her, small and ridiculous in the frivolous bare blouse, without so much as trying to do it, he smiled.

But she presumed upon that smile. She closed her twiggy fingers on his wrists, she turned him around, she made him face the forgotten monstrosity in its ill-tied twine and its brown-paper shroud. "We forgot out present," she said, and there was in her reedy voice that mournful quality that suggested remorse over unfaithfulness—last cup of home coffee, dear clutter of an abandoned kitchen, smell of cabbage and soap powder and babies and stew, forever forfeited, forever lost. "Can't we look at it? Please, let's look at it. Maybe you'll even like it. Couldn't you just see?"

•

THE TIME FOR that sort of thing would certainly have been later, much later, after they had cheered themselves by putting the new dishes in the china closet, after they had spread the sheets and put on the pillowcases and sat for a little, head against head, on the side of their new bed. Still, it was the way she wanted it, let her have it. Let her have it and take the consequences thereof. Let her see exactly how he felt. He flew to the kitchen and grabbed up a paring knife and went murderously at the twine. Let her make no mistake about his state of mind. He ripped the wrapping paper off in shreds, and it was as if he were flaying whichever one of her idiots it was who had put that paper on. Pink, green, flesh, rose, drapery, white—they showed ominously between the shreds. A pink toe emerged to him, a coy eye smirked up at him through glass. A bather, the worst of all bathers, as fat as *her* little brother, as obscene as *their* notions about beauty, a horrid bather, looking smug and drying herself.

He waited until the last crackle of the paper had died down before he spoke, and then he spoke low, as if in wonderment that anything so objectionable could exist. "It's atrocious," he said. "Of all the awful bathers, this is the worst."

"It isn't as bad as you're trying to make out." He could not see her, because she stood behind the spot where he crouched on his knees over the sickening print in its expensive and taste-lessly ornate white frame. He could not see her, but there was a sturdy timbre in her voice, and he knew how she must be standing: like a person waiting imperviously to take a beating, her hands behind her back, her chin thrust out, insolence at last glinting in her eyes.

"It's as big as an elephant and uglier than anything I ever saw."

"You don't think so. You only say so to hurt my feelings, to make my wedding miserable for me. You only say so because you want to think they're too ignorant and vulgar to buy us a decent present. You only—"

He interrupted her with another soft sound of unbelief, half whistle, half sigh. "Look at it. Just look at it, if you please. How could a person hang a thing like that, I'd like to know?"

"YOU'LL HANG IT." The voice behind him was almost as quiet as his own, toned down to a shaking determination. "You'll hang that picture and in a decent place or I'll never walk into this apartment again, never eat at this table, never get into that bed." She too—he saw it with surprise—could kindle a fire as violent and consuming as his, could hurl their dishes onto it, could give to its lapping flames their pillows, their blanket, their candlewick bedspread. "You'll hang it—*that's* sure. I'm going to have one thing out of this wretched marriage, and that picture happens to be the thing."

"Don't tell me you really *want* a mess like that. I know better. It's only because you're afraid their feelings might be hurt. Heaven knows, you've got enough good taste to see what a monstrosity it is yourself."

"No," she said, "I haven't any taste. I hate everything we bought. I hate those ridiculous dancers in their rose-colored panties, I hate the iron candlestick, I hate the metal fruit plate—it looks like the lid of an old garbage can. Those pink linens—just because your mother made them doesn't mean they don't look silly and arty and affected. That's the way everything is, silly and arty and affected, everything in your hateful old house—"

"Shut up," he said, stung by the mention of the linens, all the more vulnerable on the question of the linens because, not an hour ago, he had hurled them onto his private conflagration. "Shut up and I'll hang your disgusting picture. What do I care what happens to the place? It isn't ours, it's your peoples'; it has to be decorated for them to visit, not for me to live in—"

He rushed past her into the disorderly kitchen, where a red

stepladder, incongruously gay, stood among boxes of packed pans and dishes. He laid hold of the stepladder with one hand and jerked it into the living room while she stood in front of the gray chair, her back to the telephone, her hands hanging stiff at her sides. Her mouth was open, and he knew with triumph that she was frightened by his speed, frightened by his panting and by his contorted face.

"Don't hang it now," she told him feebly. "What do you want to hang it now for? You said—you said—"

He grasped the ponderous picture and hauled it up to the top of the ladder, where his head was close to the ceiling and the air was thick with turpentine. A bit of twine still lodged in the carved molding of the frame, and a streamer of wrapping paper still hung from the glass. He had chosen in the blind instinct of his fury precisely the spot where it would look most objectionable—over the mantelpiece, where the orange-and-yellow bittersweet in the peacock-blue vases would jar most violently with its loathsome pinks and greens. "It'll look exquisite here," he shouted, knowing that Mrs. Painter would be getting a nourishing earful through the loose boards of the ancient floor. "Get me a nail! What's the matter with you? I need a nail, and I'm not going to drag this piece of trash up and down the ladder twenty times before I hang it. Find me a nail, and I'll get it over with once and for all!"

THE HABIT OF meekness—possibly the chief inheritance of daughters of large families—was asserting itself over her rage and her pain. She went to the kitchen and came back with the wrong kind of nail—a veritable spike that was bound to stick a good inch out of the plaster—but nothing made any difference to him now.

"Don't hang it," she said, holding up the nail to him as if to indicate that she meant to plead, not to disobey. "Don't, please; don't you remember we said we were going to paint the walls?"

"Paint the walls! I'll never paint the walls!" He bent down so violently that the ladder shook beneath him and snatched the spike from between her fingers. "They can stay rat gray forever for all I care! Once this piece of junk is up, everything else is spoiled for me. Where's the hammer? Hand me the hammer. What's the matter? Are you blind? You're looking at it; it's right in front of you on the cane-seat chair."

She brought it and held it up. And it was good, good to have the spike wedged against the wall and an implement of force to beat it with. Once, twice, three times he attacked the spike and knew that it resisted him. Every blow called up a loud ringing sound as of metal or brick hidden somewhere inside.

"You can't drive it in, not there," she said. "You're hitting the bricks in the chimney or something. You'll just knock a big chunk out of the wall."

"What's the difference?" He hammered again and again and again. "A hole as big as a crater wouldn't mean a thing to me. This room couldn't look worse if it was blown to bits by a hurricane, not if it was struck by a bomb, not if it—"

And suddenly, horribly, he had nothing in his hand to strike with. Suddenly, horribly, he knew that the hammer had leaped out of his grasp, that it had fallen, that she was below him, and that the weight of iron and fury had come down upon her innocence. Her head? he asked himself. Iron, bitter iron, on her fair, childish head? His eyes were so beclouded with a stinging surge of tears that he could scarcely make her out, sitting on the floor at the foot of the ladder with her head between her knees.

"Oh, Angie, oh, my God!" he said, and there could not have been more love in his voice had he said, "My bride, my beautiful one, my dove." He thought of her face and her hands and the touch of her hands, known through five winters and summers, known and dear. He thought of their pillows, lying on the bed in the next room, still undented by their heads. He thought of the quaint and exquisite and lively imaginings that glinted like hummingbirds through the mysterious temple closed within her

271

little skull. And if he had cracked that skull—he was afraid of that; he had always been afraid of that sort of thing since the day the boy in grade school died because he had been hit by a flying baseball bat—if the temple was shattered and the bright birds all had gone, what was there left for him in the world?

"You didn't hit me on the head," she said, raising her head slowly. She said it because she knew he was afraid of that sort of thing; and to reassure him, she did her best to smile. "You hit me of the shoulder." He was coming down the ladder now, carrying the picture in his arms as if it had been her body. He came very slowly, because his knees were shaking, and she lifted up to him a steadying hand. "Right here on the shoulder." He knelt beside her and watched her pull down the blouse to show him the place, not to exhibit her suffering, only to prove to him that what she suffered was a minor thing.

Red-and-purple bruise on a shoulder as delicate as any ever shadowed forth on glossy paper, and flawed enough to be most preciously human—there was a mole and a branching vein, and he covered them with kisses, accepted them and their mortality into his life through his seeking lips. He kissed her forehead and her eyelids and her fingernails, which smelled like bananas because she had given herself a manicure for the great day; and he thought, with a fervor that outdistanced Mrs. Painter's and his mother's, of the blessed closeness of that great day. He kissed her ears and the place on top of her head where he had thought the hammer had fallen, and he might have sat for half an hour, cradling that head against his chest and saying crazy, unrepeatable phrases about how much he loved it, if a little, unsteady, bell-like sound had not broken hesitantly in upon them and then been transformed into a long, assertive ring.

"Listen," she said, putting her fingers up to her lips. "Our telephone rang. That's our telephone."

•

As HE WENT to answer, it came into his head how many times the telephone would ring in the future, sometimes sweetly, when they sat in this room with their after-dinner coffee in their laps; sometimes exasperatingly, to interrupt a kiss; sometimes fearfully, in the middle of an anxious night. It would ring to tell them of friends on the way to their house; to say that somebody had returned safe from a long journey, that the crisis of an illness was over, that a child had been born, that a parent had died. Looking out at other roofs and windows through the window, he fancied too that the ring was not for him alone but for all mortal men, that the pulsing signal of life and love and death was vibrating round the vast, curved reaches of the whole world.

But this time it was only his mother, saying that she hadn't known whether or not they were connected but thought there was no harm in trying. She'd had an idea—he needn't blow his top; he could take it or leave it once he'd heard what it was—but first she wanted to know how the parlor paint had dried. A little darker? Well, she'd been afraid of that, and she'd taken the liberty to call up his sisters-in-law, and luckily they were all at home with not a thing to do—all three of them, Hilda and Suzie and Annabelle. And they'd said they'd be delighted to lend a hand, if he and Angie wanted them to. Five people putting on one coat of paint in a room as small as that could finish within three or four hours.

The gratefulness in his answering voice was not there because the paint would be the right color after all: The paint and the shabby address and the fat pink bather seemed small matters to him now. If he sent to her across the wires such a conviction of joy as he had never given her face-to-face in the twenty-odd years he had lived under her roof, it was because she was granting him a last, inestimably valuable chance to be grateful, to cancel out all uneaten hot cakes, to assert that something was perfect, something could give him an instant of unstinted happiness.

He planned his replies in such a way as to give Angie a complete knowledge of what was going on. This was a new technique, a husbandly art, and it livened his spirits to such a degree that, before he hung up, he was saying that Angie's family had given them a surprise this morning, a very fine print of a Renoir bather (it *was* a fine print, though the bather was something of a mess), framed most expensively (and *that* was no lie, either; they must have spent at least thirty dollars on the frame). And when the receiver was laid back in its cradle, he turned and saw that Angie was putting the pink linens into a tissue-paper-lined box. "We've got to take care of these. It would be dreadful if we got any paint on beautiful things like these," she said.

The Uninvited

S HE RESTED HER back against the wall, and looked into the
telephone booth in which Mary Catharine had so pointedly
closed herself, and wondered why all high-school basements,
though nobody had ever hung a wash in them, should smell
like soap powder and damp sheets and old stationary tubs that
never got quite dry. She wondered also how Mary Catharine was
doing in there, discharging the "delicate errand" for which Miss
Withers had chosen her; and seeing the brown bangs still slanted
at the same angle, the dime still held meditatively between the
full pale-pink lips, she decided that Mary Catharine, in spite
of the well-advertised "poise and charm and self-possession,"
hadn't as yet summoned up the nerve.

Not that she herself would have done any better. If Miss
Withers had been waiting up in 303 to hear how *she* had got on
with a business like that, Miss Withers could have gone on waiting, among her Osage oranges and glass-covered autographs
and elongated calla lilies, all night. But she, at least, had found
the telephone number—Mary Catharine could never have done
that, since she had a terrible astigmatism and was much too vain
to be seen in her glasses at school. It was *she* who had peered

through thick lenses; it was *her* finger tip that had traced the fabled name up and down the fine, pale columns, and actually had found it there—Norma Klaus, *Klaus Norma,* turned backward just like anybody else's name.

Yet not quite like anybody else's, either. For one instant the first name had fallen away and let the last one stand alone, so that greatness burst from it with the clang of a cymbal in the dingy basement hall. Klaus—Thackeray, Dickens, Hawthorne, Eliot—Klaus. Voice of Charlotte Bronte, available with an electric hum, over a mile of telephone wire . . .

Mary Catharine, feeling herself stared at, dropped the dime into the slot and got the little ching. Her pearl-tinted fingernail, innocent of dirt and cuticle, dialed the never-to-be-forgotten number: Plymouth 1-7083. "Hello," she said, with poise and grace. "Is this the residence of Miss Norma Klaus?"

Residence! The woman lived in a house, like anybody else. "Is Miss Norma Klaus home this afternoon?"

She said "at home" so that it sounded as if it had been printed on an invitation: *At home, three to five. Afternoon tea.*

Miss Norma Klaus was plainly at home in her residence. The brown bang was crushed against the call box; the enviably round bosom adjusted itself upward in a general mustering of charm. "Miss Norma Klaus? My name is Mary Catharine Simmonds. I know how occupied you are, and much as I hate to intrude upon your busy life . . ."

And on, and on, and on. Cliché after cliché after cliché. With poise, with self-possession, with grace. For a few wild minutes, watching the pretty mouth chewing on the candy of the words, she, Susan Herrick, thought how *she* would have said it, if Miss Withers had found her worthy—which Miss Withers never did. "Look, I'm Susan Herrick, and I'm a miserable high-school student, but I've read every word you ever wrote, and I try, idiot that I am, to set down my own ridiculous agonies and my own unfounded blisses in those high words that came to us from our hallowed and eloquent dead. My school journal wants me to write an interview with a writer—but that is only my wretched excuse. I would give ten years of my life to walk into your house and sit in your chair and hold your holy pen. Let me hear your voice, let me see your face."

"How very kind of you," said Mary Catharine, "how very gracious! Wednesday? At four? At four on Wednesday, then. Thank you very much." She turned and hung up the receiver. She was rosy and triumphant. "Believe it or not, she said okay."

She had never said okay, not Norma Klaus. And whatever she *had* said would be lost forever now in the pink mediocrity of that amiable brain. The glass door of the booth, opening outward, yielded to the watcher a darkened image of herself—skinny, pale, swathed in dull calico which, at the moment of purchase, had seemed the color of April fog but had since been reduced by wear and familiarity to dishwater gray. Her hair, of an indefinite brown that looked dingy even when it was newly washed, was swept severely to one side of her low and unimpressive brow. The long oval below it was dominated by a totally unacceptable nose, thin and sharp and surmounted by glasses. The eyes, behind the glasses, looked scornfully at their wan reflections in that door of the booth, and turned aside and fixed themselves on Mary Catharine's exultant face.

"She said okay, at four, next Wednesday."

"Yes, I know. I heard every word of it, even though you were so careful about closing the door."

"Now, Susie, don't take on again like that over absolutely nothing. I closed the door because I was nervous."

"Do *I* make you nervous?" It was without belligerence, it was almost pleading. If the answer was affirmative, then it would be necessary to quarrel here in the smelly basement, to part from Mary Catharine in anger, to walk home with no companion but envy in the mean, thin April rain.

"No, of course not."

"Then . . ."

"Then what, Susie, for heaven's sake?"

"Then take me with you!" It was abject, it was passionate; a boy in shorts and a jersey was summoned out of a locker room by the mournful echo in the empty basement, and looked and shrugged his shoulders; but she could not stop herself. "Next Wednesday, when you go to see her. What harm could it possibly do if I went with you? Why shouldn't you do me this one little favor?" She felt herself turning red and patchy—she had never begged Mary Catharine before. "I want so much—you can't possibly know how much I want—" And she stopped in hopeless silence, mocked by more echoes, clutching the metal buckle of her belt until the edge seemed to be cutting into the palms of her hands.

"But, Susie," said Mary Catharine, arranging herself in that gentle and graceful attitude—hands clasped, head inclined a little—that she always assumed in the presence or at the thought of authority, "Miss Withers said that *I* was to go and see Miss Klaus—"

"Don't call her Miss Klaus. It makes her sound silly. It puts her in the same class with old Withers. She didn't say—and don't tell me different because I heard her—she didn't say you were supposed to go alone."

"Well, no, she didn't but she implied it."

"Implied it? You're a fine one to know what she implied. How could you see what she implied without your glasses on?"

"Oh, Susie, you're so difficult!"

The naked bricks on the wall, the cracked cement on the floor, the metal of the empty lockers repeated the accusation, and she was forced to ponder it, staring at the clean black toes of the slippers on Mary Catharine's decorous and always-softly treading feet. She thinks, she told herself, that I will make a mess out of her delicate errand. She sees me falling over my own feet on the way into Norma Klaus's residence. She knows I will intrude most ungraciously upon the gracious lady's busy life, and say something ugly, something terrible and true, something that will fall like the blow of a hammer to smash the tinkling frailty of her own clichés.

"Difficult as I am, I've read her books. I'm the only one in the class who read anything more than the flaps on the jackets. At least I'd be able to talk to her about her books."

"Susie, I know." The dry, pliant hand took hold of her fingers and detached them from the wounding buckle. "I know all that, everybody knows you deserve to go to see her far more than I do. Only Miss Withers said—"

"Who cares what Miss Withers said?"

But it was no use going on with that sort of thing. Mary Catharine was good, had probably never spit out her pablum or broken a dish or been guilty of insolence from the day she was born. Mary Catharine, having goodness and Miss Withers on the brain, could be appealed to only on the humiliating grounds of charity and love. Slowly, with intense concentration, she summoned up for Mary Catharine's benefit one sparse and burning tear, made it gather in the corner of her eye, expelled it, stared out at nothing while it rolled down her cheek and slide off the side of her chin. The flesh was servant to the spirit: for months she had been able to double the speed of her pulse by singing the "Love Death" from *Tristan* to herself, and only a couple of weeks ago she had learned that nothing was more effective for the conjuring up of tears than Mercutio's last speech in *Romeo and Juliet*.

"Oh, all right, all *right*," said Mary Catharine, gulled but compassionate. "Only you mustn't say a word to Miss Withers, no matter what, and you must really try not to—" She did not finish, perhaps considering it better not even to conceive of the sort of thing that might be perpetrated at Miss Norma Klaus's residence next Wednesday afternoon.

"I'll be grateful to the end of my life." It was not an exclamation. It was a bald statement of fact, and she rendered it in the same tone in which her father always said, "I'll be paying off the mortgage for the rest of my days."

"I'd better go up now and tell Miss Withers." But the bloom of joy had been rubbed off the fruit of her enterprise. She was a good, honorable young lady, and whatever she said up in 303 was bound, now that she had made an unauthorized commitment, to be partially a lie.

"Go ahead. Who's keeping you?"

"You'll wait, won't you?"

She wanted somebody with her on the way home through the rain, somebody to down out the chirp of her tender conscience with loud and colorful inanities.

"Yes, I'll wait. Why shouldn't I? But hurry. I feel conspicuous, standing around down here alone."

And she was conspicuous: the janitor glanced at her, the boy came out of the locker room and gave her a cold and disparaging stare. He looks at me as I look at that piece of rubbish, she thought, watching the discarded wrappings of somebody's lunch blow crazily around on the floor. And maybe that's what I am—a piece of rubbish, but at least I'm not sodden—at least I'm picked up by the great winds and blown about. I will be borne next Wednesday to a room in which the voice of Norma Klaus, the authentic voice of greatness, will bless and trouble the afternoon air, will move outward in widening circles, the last of which will enter the caverns of my ears and be preserved forever in the dark inward vault of memory. A piece of rubbish, but blown about, she told herself again as she walked the hall. Blown about by the mighty tempests that issue out of the mouths of gods.

That was on a Friday, and from Friday to Wednesday is five days, and five days is long enough for building the future, for making of the future such a house as one's spirit can occupy with equanimity. Norma Klaus—so she told herself, helping her mother clean the refrigerator, helping her father find the radio selection in the Sunday paper, helping her little sister locate Afghanistan—Norma Klaus was a plain woman. The photograph of the dust-jacket of her latest book proved it. She had been made up for the occasion, yes; but the jutting nose, the hollow cheek, the furrow in the brow and the strain in the dark eyes showed through. The books themselves, skimmed wildly at trolley stops and among tossed blankets, yielded up some other encouraging signs. This woman evoked such scenes and such sufferings as she herself was familiar with: kitchen table covered with worn oilcloth; yearning exile walking alone in an unfamiliar neighborhood and guessing what fullness of life must lie on the other side of a curtained windowpane. Susan and Norma Klaus—not that she could mention the fact to Mary Catharine—would be bound to greet each other like sisters. Like sisters they would meet in a barren room, a room scornful of foibles, a kind of shrine in which a single object of unquestionable beauty—a bough of a blossoming cherry, a Chinese figurine, a faded wooden medieval saint—would crown and explain the general austerity.

What she would say to Norma Klaus, what Norma Klaus would say to her, she did not dare to think. Unintelligible speech, uttered sometimes in stern whispers and sometimes in reverberating oratory, troubled her dreams. Three times she wakened in a sweat, knowing that a few words had made themselves plain, only to realize that what she had salvaged was inane or cheap: "an umber, opulent canticle overdone in the oven now" or "a pediment purpled with hyacinths and blood." Nor were her walking hours less ridden than her sleeping ones. She forgot to study for a Spanish test, she lost her locker key, she made herself despicable to her fellow students, distressing Miss Withers and a cross to Mary Catharine. In fact, on Tuesday, when she had been seized with an incongruous fit of excitement at the very mention of Shelley and had gone on for five minutes of good class time answering a question that could have been settled with a "yes" or a "no," she glimpsed at the icy possibility that Mary Catharine could withdraw her commitment, could say: "After *that*, I think you'll realize we had better cancel our engagement for tomorrow afternoon." But Mary Catharine said nothing. She was totally ignorant of the magical process of tear-conjuring by means of literature; and to break a promise watered into green growth by a tear was at least as unthinkable as betraying a teacher's trust.

She even postponed all tidying up for the occasion until they were sitting side by side on the trolley that was carrying them, the one to her destination and the other to her destiny. The trolley lights were brash and revealing, and begot a number of suggestions: "There's a teenie-weenie spot of tomato soup on your blouse, and I think you could rub it out." "Haven't you got a *clean* handkerchief? Well, here's some Kleenex." "*Please* use one of them on your glasses. They're so smudged I don't know how you can *see*." Through the mist on her glasses Susie saw that the trolley was moving into such a neighborhood as the great Klaus could not possibly have settled in; surely some other district, lying beyond this one, would be her dwelling place; only among crotchety streets, only among earth-colored stoops, never here among these ivied Gothic arcs of gray stone . . .

No, she could not accept the facts as they were, even when the motorman had shouted the expected stop and brought the trolley to a halt in front of a wide expanse of lawn screened off from the pavement by a row of peeled and ancient sycamores. She sat mutely, stupidly on the leather seat, picking at her dress, staring at her hands. Not here—she would not admit it until Mary Catharine had beckoned to her, blushing that such absent-mindedness should be witnessed by the other passengers. "Good heavens, Susie, what a daze you're in," she said, paying the fare. "Wake up, your country needs you."

Look, she said to herself, dawdling up the driveway behind Mary Catharine, you never believed she would live in a dingy house, not even on Sunday evening when you imagined her coming home from vespers in a little side-street chapel and kicking off her overshoes and setting them beside and old clothes rack in a barren hall. She has done these things, perhaps, but now her life is otherwise, and justly. Whoever soars high is weary and needs a softer nest. How can you take exception to a Tudor house of time-darkened brick, with a sloping roof and a pigeon-haunted chimney and a line of windows all crisscrossed with bars of lead? Ivy stuck crisply out around the great glass door at which they stood; and reason controlled hate for the moment at least; she did not do what she wanted to do—did not rip a tender leaf from its stalk and tear it into bits.

WHAT CAUSED THE outburst, why she should have blown up like a rocket in Norma Klaus's august presence and elaborate living, she was never able to tell. It had not happened because of the room, she told herself a hundred times, re-enacting the incident in her thoughts in other rooms and other cities, returning to it while she waited to sign a contract for a book in a publisher's office or when she walked with one of her students through an April afternoon. The house had surely prepared her for the room, and even though within those four walls she glimpsed a life so rich as to be almost repellent in its elaborateness and complexity, it was not the damask and the velvet that undid her there, not the pink and the bronze and the olive-green, not the sconces and the figurines and the candlesticks, nor the moss-green carpet so deep that it stood a good half inch around the muddy soles of her shoes.

Nor was it the mistress of this golden clutter who was responsible for her crises, either. In all justice, she was forced to admit, even at the moment, that if greatness must sink from the clouds and be congealed and shrunken into a human shape, this shape might serve—might even come, with resignation, to seem like the proper thing. The presence that settled itself—brown hair, white face, draped gray woolen, and aging, delicate, almost motionless hands—on the flowery sofa and close beside her was no more aggressive or offensive than a gray heron settling on a bank at dusk; and the voice, grave and controlled, was not altogether disappointing, even when it was contrasted with unheard melodies vibrating along telephone wires.

Nor could the blame be laid entirely at the door of Mary Catharine, though she was exasperating enough. She abhorred silence as nature abhors a vacuum; she poured a constant stream of blasphemous gibble-gabble into the holy vessel of the allotted half-hour; she made all participation impossible by the sheer volume of her output, and dashed the soaring spirit at the outset with a shameful explanation: "And this is my classmate, Susan Herrick, who *insisted* on coming along, and I couldn't refuse her because she *adores* you, simply *worships* the ground you walk on. Believe it or not, Miss Klaus, she's read every single word you've ever written." They had not been settled for five minutes before she produced a notebook in which she had written a series of infernal questions, got up between her and old Withers for the express purpose of confounding the artist and degrading the art. They sprang out of her in groups of twos and threes: "Do you know everything that's going to happen in a story before you begin it? Do you write with pencil? With pen? On the typewriter? Why, imagine that! Do you ever put friends or members of your family, just as they are, drawn from life so to speak, in any of your books?"

Oh, stupid, stupid, stupid! And the one time the spare hand alighted on *her* knee, she started away from the touch, wanting no condescending kindness given in exchange for cheap and foolish adoration: the desk in the corner of the room was heaped with correspondence—the great Klaus was worshipped by thousands, and hundreds had been idiotic enough to tuck into envelopes the ridiculous things they carried in their hearts. The one time the grave voice addressed her, saying, "Why don't *you* ask me a question?" she turned with a wild look in her face and only unutterable things in her head. Oh, she thought, if I were the questioner, you could not listen. You would run upstairs and throw yourself on a ruffled coverlet and pull a lace pillow over your head. I would ask you, Have you ever burned a poem you wrote to a friend and felt the fire consuming your heart? Have you ever been crazily in love and wished yourself a cat or a dog, so that you could follow the one you loved, without offense, into his house, up and down the street? Have you ever asked yourself whether your soul has not been ruined with correspondence and damask and candlesticks, whether—weighted down with all these things—it can ever look again in a February dusk toward the pure, stern face of the moon?

She was doing what her little sister so hatefully called "spilling over." Her spirit was spilling over into her body, her shame and her disgust were spilling over into her eyes. She caught sight of the tight and desperate lines around Mary Catharine's rosebud mouth, and told herself: Watch out, watch out. Never mind the asininity of the questions and the shallow promptness of the answers; do not ache because the birdlike presence, giving off a faint, dry sweetness, dips forward and looks across you, looks around you as if you were a pillar; say lines from Shelley, count the beams in the ceiling. But Mary Catharine was saying, "Which do you rely on most for inspiration, imagination or reality?" and the controlled voice was answering, "Reality, always reality," with such offhandedness that it was a downright betrayal of imagination, of Keats's Greece and Shakespeare's fairyland. Suddenly, without quite believing she was doing it—it was some other brash and ugly girl who was shattering the elegance with a harsh voice—suddenly she was saying as hatefully as possible that reality was despicable, that the world was a dull and rotten place, that a person couldn't live in it, couldn't put up with it unless he covered it up with dreams.

"Susie!" said Mary Catharine, darting a significant and astigmatic glance at the Famous Personality in the other corner of the sofa, to indicate that such scenes—deplorable enough among contemporaries at soda counters and in locker rooms—were simply unthinkable here and in such company as this. The little fool actually assumed a proprietary attitude, was protecting the Lady of the Hour from uncouthness and unnecessary exasperation, and no answer was possible except a furious "Don't Susie me!"

And strangely enough, the Lady of the Hour did not interfere, did not say, like a schoolteacher, "Let's settle down, girls," did not say, like a sophisticate, "If I were you, darlings, I wouldn't let it spoil my beautiful friendship," did not utter even an "Oh, come now" or a "My, my, my." Without even looking, she knew that the Famous Personality had pulled her spare person as far back as possible into the damask corner; and she saw, among other visions—torn ivy leaves, smashed figurines, correspondence scattered about and trampled on—a gray heron ruffling its feathers in fright and dipping its head under its wing.

She might have fallen silent, too, in pity and in amazement that such a one could beget pity, if Mary Catharine had not been fit to improve the shining hour with a bit a salutary advice. Miss Klaus's valuable time was limited, she said. It wasn't mannerly or fair to interrupt, to inject—she said "inject" in such a way as to call up an image of a jabbing needle—one's own opinions and problems into the interview. Now if Miss Klaus would be good enough to answer just a few more questions—

"What's the use of putting down all that stuff?"

"*Susie!* Whatever stuff are you talking about?"

"Her answers, all her answers. She doesn't mean a one of them. Not one of them is the truth."

There was a flutter beside her—a thin body getting up, folds of gray woolen agitated, sharply drawn breath. Anger? Maybe she wanted anger; maybe she wanted the authentic voice of greatness to call her something, even if it was only an impertinent fool; maybe she wanted another touch from that hand, even if it was only a slap in the face. But the small brown eyes into which she looked for a still and obliterating instant were not furious, were only startled. Flight was a possibility: she knew with a gaping conviction of emptiness that this one might simply flee, might disappear forever through the door.

"Really, Susie, *really*—"

"Wait just a minute, Miss Simmonds. Miss Herrick is furious with me, and I don't want to leave it like that. Miss Herrick thinks I was telling a lie, or at least something less than the truth—"

She was forced to keep on staring, and knew at the core of her being that for the rest of her days she would see the great Klaus standing and looking down at her like this. The beauty of the face—she realized it now, with a miserable sinking sensation in her vitals—the beauty of the face was nothing but a frail overlayer of gentleness and intelligence: the eyes were small, the nose was sharp and birdlike, even the lips were fine only because the line where they lay against each other was a line of tenderness. As for the figure—it, too, was wounding in its vulnerability. It was so spare as to be pathetic; it held itself with dignity; but the shoulders were forcibly straightened and the neck was forcibly erect, and one guessed at what a bitter cost.

"A person could never tell all of the truth and get through an interview," she said, asking for indulgence, producing a slow and uncertain smile. "Let's take the question about imagination and reality—it was the answer to that which offended you—"

Her throat was too tight, she could not say that she was sorry, sorry, sorry—

"When I said I depended mostly on reality, I wasn't lying. My books, my stories, even the poems I used to write when I was young—they came not out of my head but out of the world. Maybe it's a miserable world, maybe it isn't worth what we have to suffer in it, but we have no other. To spit on it, to hurl it away, to muffle it up in rose-colored dreams—that seems a little impious. And I am pious, and you are pious, too, I see—" she looked at the silver cross dangling against Susan's blouse—"and since the Creator made the world according to His taste, I can't reject it, I don't dare to think anything I could piece together could rival it, coming to us as it does out of God's hands. I know I should have answered Miss Simmonds' question more accurately, more fully, and honestly, I think I would have given it more thought and time if I hadn't somehow felt that you hated this room and wanted to be out of it as fast as you could. What I mean to say was something like this: When I write the way I want to write, it's as if I were seeking rather than making, as if I were groping through darkness for infinitely subtle, infinitely destructible things, as if I were feeling out the shapes of secret truths with my nerves and mind and blood. Whatever I can't find, I have to guess at, and whenever I guess—you're perfectly right, Miss Herrick—I'm using my imagination. But that's a kind of failure, that's second best. You do know—don't you—what I mean?"

Mary Catharine was scribbling, wildly scribbling in her notebook, not that she understood a single word the great Klaus had said. For as long as the slow count of ten, there was silence in the room and no motion anywhere. Then, having borne Susan Herrick—who understood what it was to seek piously with nerves and mind and blood—upward, cloudward, moonward on the meager strength of her wings, the gray heron came down again, settled on the dusky bank, sank back into the corner among the damask roses, and laid a thin hand—very shy, very tentative—on the unresisting wrist of her neophyte.

"And if," she said, quietly and intimately, as if Mary Catharine's struggle with her notes had actually carried that conscientious recorder beyond the range of sound, "if you find this room cluttered up or overdone, I can't blame you, Miss Herrick, you may be perfectly right, you know. I never had a house before this house. I did a dull, hard, stupid job and lived in broken-down old houses until I got rich quite unexpectedly on one of my books. Maybe there *are* too many cupids and candlesticks, but some of them were gifts, and some of them were odds and ends from my old life, and some of them I had to buy and use simply because I liked them so much."

The puzzled astigmatic eyes looked up and the pencil went into another fit of scribbles. The unbearable tactlessness of it made her furious, but she tuned her voice down to that other voice, even though the words were a little wild. "For heaven's sake, Mary Catharine, don't write *that* down. Don't you know the difference between something for publication and a private communication?"

THE REMAINDER OF the interview was conducted so discreetly that it was almost impossible to believe that violence had ripped across the middle of it. The last three questions—more intelligent, surprisingly, than the ones that had preceded them—were asked and answered in some detail. A picture was requested, to be reproduced in the magazine at the head of the article, and the two of them followed Miss Klaus deviously among precious things to the desk in which she stored her photographs and another heap of correspondence. Fan mail, no doubt—on many of the letters she had written the word "Replied."

The photos were all of a kind: six-by-four glossies, showing a remote and wanly smiling lady seated in a somber chair, with her hands in her lap and a silver chain trying in vain to drag down her neck and shoulders. There were many, many copies, and Mary Catharine was carried away and asked for an additional one for herself—with an autograph, if Miss Klaus would be so good; the last name was spelled with an "i" and a double "m," and there were two "a's" in Catharine.

"And you—do you want one?" said the great Klaus.

"Yes, I guess I do." She stared at the hundreds of letters and could not look at the brown eyes.

"You spell your last name with a double 'r,' of course, like the poet Herrick." She closed the big, rather public drawer from which she had taken the glossies, and opened a smaller, more private drawer, cluttered with old pens and dog-eared letters and empty match covers—such mementos as ought to be thrown away, if only a person could find the heart. She sighed, and reached into that clutter, groping after something. "Maybe you're a distant relative of his—Herrick's, I mean. If not in the flesh, then maybe in the spirit. He was a favorite of mine—just wait a minute, I'm trying to find him." Pleasure broke in the faint wrinkles on her face, and she dragged out a homemade paperweight, a big oblong glass slab, with a sketch of a bewigged and hook-nosed gentleman staring mournfully through the glass. "There, that's Herrick. When I was your age, I used to put myself to sleep almost every night by saying three or four of his poems to myself. My sister made me this paperweight when I was seventeen."

"My, but he's so impressive-looking," said Mary Catharine.

"Do you think so, Miss Herrick?" The brown eyes requested the truth.

"No, I don't think he's impressive-looking at all. Fact is, he's plain ugly. He must have known it, too, because he was shy with people, and kept pretty much to himself. He raised pigs in Devonshire, and was a poor country parson and everybody thought he was a little queer—

"And he was, he was. Ugly and queer. Or distinguished and unusual. Or strangely handsome and the possessor of a rare talent. You can say it any way you like, and what he said of himself, how he felt to himself, making his poems in his little sitting room in Devonshire, we'll never know. But it isn't so bad to be peculiar and ugly. It isn't so bad to be poor. It isn't even so bad to be alone. Plainness and poverty and loneliness make the nerves sensitive for groping and seeking and finding. If he had been as beautiful as Adonis or as rich as Croesus, maybe we—and he—would never have had his poetry."

She put the paperweight back into the dusty darkness and felt about in there for something else. "I want to give you a different picture, Susan," she said, slipping something old deftly into an envelope that had once held a birthday card. "It's a private communication—not for publication." She laid it in Susan's palm, and added a lingering touch to it, and turned and shepherded them across the hall and through the door.

"What did she give you?" asked Mary Catharine when they were in the world again.

"I don't know. I'll look at it later." But she knew perfectly well what it was: a picture of the great Klaus in those days when she had been a skinny fledgling in ill-fitting feathers, beating her untried wings and falling back to earth, far, far beneath the arc of an unattainable heaven. And she could wait, could wait honorably until the price of the relic had been paid, until the world in the shape of Mary Catharine had given her the deserved and acceptable scolding. "Go ahead. Tell me what you think of me. Tell me how I acted, how I spoiled everything. Tell me what you're going to tell old Withers," she said.

"Miss Withers? If you don't mind my saying so, you have the unfortunate habit of making things worse than they are. I haven't the slightest intention of saying anything about you to Miss Withers."

"Well, let me have it then for upsetting Miss Klaus and taking up her valuable time with nonsense and a lot of rot."

"No. Miss Klaus is yours. What you said to her or she said to you is none of my affair."

"What do you mean—she's mine?"

"You know perfectly well what I mean. She touched you, she gave you a special thing, she bothered over you like a hen bothers over her chickens. She just put up with me—not that I have any grievances, she was perfectly polite and gracious and altogether very nice. But anybody but a blind man could have seen it five miles away—you were the one she loved."

The Man Who Found Himself

H E GOT UP into the coolness that hangs over Manhattan like a false promise of love on early mornings in warm weather. He got out of his bed quietly, so as not to wake his wife, and went to the window. The roofs, the tiers of sun-whitened windows, the green of penthouse terraces and the whiteness of water towers had not yet wholly emerged from the seven o'clock mist; and all that he saw from the window took on the softness and the sadness that had haunted his sleep.

Several roofs away, in a patch of green garden, somebody had left a scarf or a stole, bright orange, over the back of a blue chair. It was a good color scheme—tangerine and leaf green and the palest blue. As soon as he got to the store he would make a water-color sketch of it and take it in to Miss Anders, his employer, as a suggestion for the living room in the Hoffman place.

She would not like it, of course; but some sort of color chart would have to be crumpled up and thrown into the wastebasket in the course of the day, and this one would serve as well as any. He would label the colors to save himself the necessity of hearing her ask: "What am I supposed to make out of *that?*"

or, "Now what on earth did you intend to do with *this*?" Green for the rugs, he thought, orange for the detail, pale blue for the walls. And a touch of white somewhere, maybe in a hassock—yes, a white-wool hassock set splash in the middle of everything; nubby like a sheep . . .

But as soon as he felt himself becoming excited about the Hoffman job, as soon as he began to envision the room as he would like to do it, he stopped himself. There was no point even in thinking about it. He forced himself to see instead Miss Anders' impervious profile, and imagine her cold disdain if he should mention his thoughts on the matter.

A friend of his, a dabbler in psychiatry, had said the other evening that since love and hate were intertwined at the roots, maybe he'd better ask himself if he mightn't be in love with this woman, seeing that he hated her so much. He had smiled at such a thought—to him, love and hate were utterly divided. Hate was the woman who sat behind an Empire desk at Hearth and Home, Incorporated; love was the woman who lay asleep in the bed beside him.

He turned from the window and stood by her bed, looking down at her. He wanted very much to wake her, to talk to her, to hold her close, but he did not.

She stirred, feeling herself gazed upon, and then surrendered herself to sleep again, turning her head sideways so that her breath moved a few strands of her short, light-brown hair. Her arm lay over the sheet; it was thin and white and traced with branching veins. There was no sunburn yet, like last year—you didn't expose a woman three weeks out of the hospital to the chilly wind on the beach . . .

He sighed and went into the kitchen to put on the coffee, and then into the bathroom to make himself impeccable for the omniscient gray eyes of Miss Anders. Then he went into the living room to set two places on the bamboo mats and to drop flakes of food into the tank of tropical fish.

He bent over the big oblong aquarium and peered in curi-

ously. The suddenly he straightened and shouted, "Trudy!" at
the top of his voice. A change had come in the course of the
night: A black viviparous female with the silvery fin tips had
clouded the water in the left-hand corner with a pearly, multitudinous birth—so exquisite, so shimmering in their minute
and continual motion that he almost called into the bedroom:
"The fish had babies!" Then painfully, he remembered that her
answering thought could be only: Maybe the fish did, but we
didn't. Ours was stillborn.

Hearing no rustle of taffeta housecoat, no pad of ballet
slippers, he went back to the kitchen and found a cup and an
old glass fruit dish. That would serve to isolate the male fish,
to keep the black-and-silver streak of child-devouring destruction imprisoned at least for the day. He was bending over the
tank, pursuing the male fish with a teacup through green and
slimy strands of vegetation, when Trudy appeared at the door,
barefoot and in her nightgown. "What are you doing?" she said.

"Catching the male." He caught the fish and poured it, with
a cupful of water, into the fruit dish.

"Oh," she said, coming up behind him, "just look—the fish
had babies!" And she did not seem to be making any connection
between this triumph and their own failure; she stared into the
living, shimmering cloud with nothing but delight.

In fact, he thought, for a woman who had lost her first
much-yearned-for child in the eighth month, she was in a puz-
zlingly lively state. Darting into the kitchen and back to the
aquarium again, she said that she was perfectly capable now of
making their breakfast and that she wished he wouldn't turn
off the alarm the instant it began to tinkle, wouldn't leave her
sleeping an unwholesome and needless sleep until close to
noon. She came away from the shining plenty in the water and
twined her long, slight arms around his neck; her lips, dry and
delicate without lipstick, rest against his, and for an instant he
was like a man offered a warm loaf after long fast.

•

WHAT IF HE stayed home with her a while this morning, so they could have a long, leisurely breakfast together? Suppose he walked into Hearth and Home, Incorporated an hour late? What could Miss Anders do about it? Weren't there worse fates in the world than being fired?

Then, in his mind's eye, he saw again the crumpled charts and sketches going one by one into the wastebasket. He wondered whether anything he ever produced would be any good. The housekeeper who had sternly supervised him as a child, after his mother's death, had swept up his crayon drawings and thrown them away with just such cool disdain. At the Arts Academy, too, his efforts had been nervous and tentative. One "C" in Design had been enough to prove to him that he had valued himself too high, that he had better pack up his canvas and his kit of paints and depart. Was whatever issued out of him destined for defeat—including the little creature coming into the air and light—for what? For death.

"It's getting late," he said, and sat down and drank his coffee, tepid with sitting too long—tepid and sickening, like his unsuccess.

The feeling of unsuccess was upon her also, in the stoop of her shoulders as she bent to spoon her cereal, in the faint line—precursor of her first wrinkle—across the white dome of her brow. The silence between them was made obvious by the increased volume of sound coming up to them from Second Avenue: horns blew, tires hummed, engines thrummed away, other people's children uttered shrill hilarities on their way to school. It would be hot—the day's discouraging heat was prefigured for him in the droop of the roses set in the middle of their glass-topped table. It would be hot, and the frozen gray eyes of Miss Anders would follow him around the store all day, watching for him to loosen his tie.

It was Trudy who started the conversation. During these last three weeks, she had been the one to try to dispel their silences, and there was something infinitely pathetic and childish about her efforts: she always seemed to him like a little girl sitting in confusion amid strewn building blocks, trying to begin all over again after her tower, laboriously built, had been smashed by a careless passer-by. "Did you think up a color scheme for the Hoffman living room?" she said.

"Yes," he said. "Green and orange and pale blue—" He was staring at the aquarium, and suddenly he smiled. Fish—that was it! "There ought to be a big glass tank of fish beneath the wide, curving shadow of the room," he said, "under the flower boxes, under the philodendron and the amaryllis—" The idea came to him complete, as strong as his desire to create that room, to do the job himself in his own way.

The Hoffman apartment was up—twenty stories up—an ultimate home for two aged people who were sitting down at last after violent storms and long wanderings. They were past seventy; they would not be going about much any more; so everything—all of the basic stuff of life—should be there in that one room, he thought, for them to see and know.

"All the basic elements," he said aloud, "everything gathered in one place—fire on the hearth and water in the aquarium and earth in the flower boxes, and air—there's plenty of air up there. I saw it—a beautiful blue, nothing but blue on the other side of the window—" He stopped, feeling slightly ridiculous, but he was encouraged by a look in her eyes. "That old doctor and his wife"—he went on—"they'd like it; they'd know what I mean. They wouldn't say, 'Elements? What elements? What are you talking about?' They'd get it right away."

For a long moment she smiled at him. Then she reached across the table and touched his hand. "Why are you afraid of her?" she said.

He looked at her in amazement—he had thought the reason was obvious, but Trudy apparently did not know. Well, then, he would never tell her, never tell her that Miss Anders' icy gray eyes under their heavy lids saw more clearly than his own wife's eyes, that they sent a pitiless X ray into the very core of him, and detected there something insufficient, despisable, incurably wrong. It was some shameless flaw, but so hopelessly damning that it tainted everything he did.

"Why is it you hate her?"

"Why shouldn't I? She has such power—"

"The power of what? To hire and fire? Who cares?" There was desperation in her quieted voice. "I often wish she'd let you go," she said.

"If she fired me—" He could finish it only in his mind. It was unthinkable to tell her how, if he went from that place without justifying himself, he would go with a mortal sore in his life, would move from failure to failure, each one more shameful than the last.

"If she fired you, you'd have a better job in a week," Trudy said. "Anybody else would see what you're worth."

It was useless to answer, useless to talk about it at all. He shrugged and kissed her on the forehead and went out, leaving her sitting beside the wilting flowers . . .

There was a bowl of roses, too, on the Empire desk in Miss Anders' air-conditioned cubicle at the end of the store; but these were fresh and fine—yellow tea roses that seemed to have taken on some of Miss Anders' own perfection and imperviousness. Even though it was close to two o'clock now, they showed no sign of wilting; a person would have to smell or touch them to be certain they were real.

And she, sitting in the flowing sand-colored silk with lace at her throat and at her plump white wrists, she with her hair wound in taffy-colored coils as unchangeable as loops of spun sugar, she with no flaw or mole or freckle on her dull white cheeks and nose and brow—was *she* real? Somehow, he doubted it. If only his little hole of an office did not face directly onto hers! The thirty feet of space between them, crammed with swathed drapery materials and little tables and samples of carpeting, was not enough—only a fifty-mile stretch of the Gobi desert would have sufficed.

Try as he would, he had not been able to keep his eyes or his mind on the color chart for the Hoffman living room. Again and again he had looked up, always encountering her vigilant eyes. And now the orange looked dull and the green was dim and the blue seemed insipid. Nothing in the streaks of color on the paper before him even vaguely suggested the vibrancy of that blowing scarf he had seen this morning, or the living green of the penthouse plants, or the cool luminousness of a seven o'clock sky.

So far, it had been a bad day—one of the worst. He had, first of all, been late this morning. But when he came in, Miss Anders had merely lifted back the lace frill at her wrist and glanced meaningfully at her little Swiss watch, as if he were beneath her admonitions, too hopeless to be worthy of her reprimand. When she called him to her desk, it was only to inform him that there wasn't much point in his continuing with the Hoffman assignment, since she and Miss Cairnes had worked up some clever ideas of their own; still he could play around with a color chart if he chose.

HAVING FINISHED WITH him—after all, he was easy prey—she had taken on a worthier opponent. Janie MacIntyre, twenty-four and pretty—and courageous from the knowledge that marriage would liberate her from all this in a couple of months—had, in a fit of sheer high spirits, put her arm around the waist of the aged elevator operator and waltzed him down the corridor. The lace frill had flipped back again from the round white wrist; a delicate finger with coral-lacquered nail had crooked in an ominous summons.

What had followed had been audible not only to him but to everybody in the back of the store: Janie had been accused in a cool but strangely piercing voice of giving a questionable tone to the place. Janie had offered no defense. She had said only: "All right, Miss Anders, all right!" and had walked away.

But at lunchtime, in the hot little hole-in-the-wall where Janie and he often ate to save money, Janie had gone on for half an hour about what her silence had cost her, what she could have done, what she could have said. "You know," she had told him between bites of a rye-bread sandwich, "I had a tough time keeping away from that vase of roses. I wanted to bump into it and knock it over her lap. I wanted to see her look upset and messy just once, like anybody else."

To see Miss Anders upset and messy, reduced to the stature of the rest of humankind—all through lunch and for a long time thereafter he had tried to imagine it. But he simply could not make himself see a spot on the perfection of her sand-colored skirt or a look of consternation on her immobile face.

After lunch there had been another scene. Two prospective customers, a middle-aged mustached man and his plump, rather flamboyant wife had been ushered into her office; and she, who had lunched on lobster bisque and iced coffee at her favorite French restaurant, had confused and belittled and shamed the couple for the better part of an hour. They were not—so she would tell the members of the staff later on in the afternoon—the sort of customers whose business was appreciated at Hearth and Home. Slowly, enjoying every minute of it, she priced them out of the store, showing them a few fabulous imported coffee tables within reach of nobody but a millionaire, eliciting their admiration of hand-blocked silk and informing them casually that it could be had at the relatively reasonable price of eighteen dollars a yard.

AFTER THE COUPLE had left, probably despising themselves for having dared come in at all, he saw that Miss Anders was, for the moment, unoccupied. She was gazing in his direction with a faraway but thoughtful look in her gray eyes. He realized he was to be the next victim: nothing more interesting had offered itself. "Mr. Corbett," she said then in her piercing voice, "could you bring me what you've got?"

"Yes, Miss Anders." He was too beaten down with dullness and heat to sense the impending crisis. He detached the drab color chart from his drawing board and carried it across the thirty feet of carpet between them as if it were the fallen standard of a defeated army. Standing in front of her desk, he looked at the coils of her taffy-colored hair and at the little lace collar that stood almost as high as her chin; but he could not bring himself to look at her eyes.

And suddenly it seemed to him that he was standing in the kitchen of his childhood—a dreary, buff-colored room he had not remembered for twenty years, except, perhaps, in evil dreams. He was standing there, small and trembling, his forehead pressed against the edge of the table; and he was mourning in loud and terrible sobs over a sin that the housekeeper insisted he had committed: with his paints he had spoiled a white scarf that belonged to her. He had not meant to spoil it, only to make it doubly beautiful; he had decorated it all over with wonderful orange butterflies.

Even now he remembered seeing his brushes scattered on the floor, feeling her hard hand slapping at his back and face. "Devil! Now you've done it! I can't put up with you any longer. I'll tell your father I'm leaving this very night." As much as he hated her, he had realized he needed her, and he had been relieved when she had failed to make good her threat.

"Is this what you've done since nine fifteen this morning?" Miss Anders was saying.

"He shook himself out of his memory and said, "I beg your pardon?"

"I said: Is this what you've been at since nine fifteen?"

He stared at the yellow roses on her desk. "That's right," he said. "This is the assignment you—"

"Well, if you had any initiative of your own—" She stopped and coughed slightly, looking at the chart he had given her. "Orange, green, pale blue—" She could find no fault with it; in fact, from the meditative tone of her voice he could tell that she rather fancied it and would be forced to look hard to discover a flaw. "What was your idea?" she said.

"I'm not sure what you mean."

"Your basic idea, your underlying thought—"

Damned if he was going to let her poke and maul his concept of the elements, he thought. "I don't know, I can't remember," he said. "Just that the Hoffmans are old, and we ought to give them something vital and yet restful, I guess."

"I hope you weren't tactless enough to mention their age to them. People don't usually like to be reminded—"

"I didn't mention anything. All I ever said to them was good morning." His gall was surging up in him. He could have said: I never had a chance. You thrust yourself into it—

"And how did you intend to use these colors?"

"Blue on the walls, green for the rug, the orange mostly in accents—cushions, pottery, flowers." He saw a cold interest growing in her eyes, and he knew he should proceed with caution: she had a cavalier way of taking other people's ideas and claiming them as her own. "White too," he said. "There ought to be something white. I thought of a hassock, off-white and woolly—"

"And what," she asked, with the air of one who is about to pose a profound philosophical question to a ten-year-old, "what do you mean to do about that big curved window at the end of the room?"

"Plants at the window—masses of plants—philodendron and amaryllis. Under them, right up to the windowsill, a glass tank of tropical fish. They'd enjoy sitting and watching the fish—"

"Fish," she said, obviously stirred, clasping her white-and-coral hands under her chin and looking him straight in the face. For an instant he had the vain hope that, after two years of trying and failing, he had at last captured her grudging admiration. But of course it turned out immediately to be otherwise. She was interested in the fish, she explained, because somebody had given her just such a tank as a gift, equipped with a hose and a pump and filled for the time being with nothing but aquatic plants and shells. She had been meaning to get some fish for it, but she knew nothing about the slimy creatures.

"A fish," he told her, feeling somehow that he was defending himself and Trudy and their mutual enthusiasm and their home, "is not slimy, Miss Anders. If you put your hand down in the water and let one of them brush against it, fish are smooth and clean as wet silk."

"Really?" she sad. She straightened and brushed his color chart aside. "Where do you get your silky fish, Mr. Corbett?"

"At Marmorra's, down here at the corner."

"I'll tell you what," she said, and laying a sheet of carbon paper, carbon side down, on top of his morning's work, she opened the middle drawer of her desk and pulled out a small, sand-colored calfskin purse. "Since there's no point in your doing anything more about *that*, suppose you run down to Marmorra's and get me what you would consider a decent collection of fish. They put them in containers or something, don't they? It's not even four o' clock, and you might as well use your time for something."

IN THE HALF hour of the working day that remained after he had come back with the fish, he examined his motives. He knew perfectly well why he had done what he had, and he felt a dry humorless joy that he had dared for once to vent his hate. In his fury at having been used as an errand boy, in his humiliation at having taken money out of her hand like a child sent off to the grocery store, he had spent an hour in Marmorra's, peering into the glass tanks in search of the ugliest, most frightening, most vicious-looking fish he could find. "I'll take that horrible one with the hanging jowls," he would say, and, "Given me that hideous fellow with the popping eyes."

He'd brought back ten fish—she had not looked at them as yet—which were now swimming about in a Manila-container with a wire handle, set on the corner of her desk beside the roses. And when she opened the container—if only she would do it here in the store!—she would be stupefied. He had created for her a masterpiece of loathing, a peerless collection of nightmares.

He had only one regret: there was a certain fellow in the carton that he hated to render up to Miss Anders' cool dislike. It was a fat black fish, and he would have liked to give it to Trudy—who would have been able to see its sloppy, droll, good-humored ugliness. His foolish urge to rescue that fish from Miss Anders had driven everything else into the background of his mind. He was not even stirred out of his daydream by a piece of news passed on to him by Janie MacIntyre: it seemed that old Dr. Hoffman had just wandered in to see how the living room was progressing and Miss Anders, being caught short with nothing else to show the customer, had been forced to produce Mr. Corbett's color chart. Furthermore, the doctor had been impressed and had carried it off to show to his wife.

"Mr. Corbett!" He had a distinct conviction that she had said it two or three times before he actually heard it. "Is it safe?" she was calling out to him. "Taking fish home in a paper carton?"

There was an uneasiness in her tone that roused him, brought him across to her office, without a summons. She's afraid of those fish, he thought, and smiled, for he had never seen her afraid.

"You'd think they'd give you better containers than this—something that couldn't possibly break."

"I've carried fish in those any number of times. I never have had one break."

"Still—" She ran a tentative finger along the edge of the

carton. "Maybe I ought to leave them here tonight," she said. "Maybe I could bring something more suitable from home tomorrow night."

"They'd die." His voice was strong with protest against such unthinkable cruelty. "They've scarcely got room to move in there. Leave them here tonight, and tomorrow morning you'll find every one of them dead."

"Oh," she said. He could see her considering possible ways out. Would she fill the washbowl in the rest room and leave them there? He knew suddenly, and with wonder, that she wasn't at all clever; she'd never be resourceful enough to think of such a solution. Would she order him to take them back to Marmorra's? No, she wouldn't do that—not now. Since he had raised his voice she was looking at him with a new uncertainty, and for the first time he found that he could sustain, without flinching, the steady gaze of her cold gray eyes. Would she offer them to him as a gift? For an instant he half thought she would. And he knew that, even if it meant acquiring the good-humored black monster, he would certainly refuse.

"You know, Mr. Corbett," she said, "this wire holder isn't awfully secure, is it?"

It won't be, he thought, if you keep pulling at it like that.

"It might come off."

"Lift it and see."

She lifted it, holding it gingerly over the desk at a safe distance. The waxed Manila carton was not quite opaque, and he could see the shadowy shapes inside. Then, suddenly, one of the creatures leaped in fright, and the delicate fingers flew open, and the carton went down, broke on the desk, spattered the rose-scented air with water and fish, and splashed the inviolable coronet of her taffy-colored hair.

ONE FISH SLID along her arm before it landed among its leaping, struggling fellows on top of the carton paper. She screamed at that, so loudly that Janie MacIntyre and the elevator operator and the stockboy came up behind him to see. He stood with his hands in his pockets, smiling. Like the woman who had abused his childhood, she was nothing to be afraid of—and he knew it at last. She was not perfection, she was not omniscience, and the power she had was an illegitimate and meretricious power. She was as weak as she was cold, afraid of fish and cruel enough to let ten of them writhe under her nose without lifting a finger to save them.

"They're horrible!" she cried. "Mr. Corbett, do something! For Heaven's sake, get them out of my sight!"

He waited, his hands still in his pockets, knowing that a fish can live out of water for a surprising length of time.

"Please, Mr. Corbett," she said, and for the first time in two bitter years he saw that she was actually seeking his help, as an associate and as a man. In answer, he turned and asked Janie MacIntyre, very calmly and deliberately, if she'd be good enough to fill the washbowl in the rest room. Then he took her precious roses out of the vase and threw them on the floor. "This'll do to transport them in," he said, and rescued the poor wretches, one by one.

IT WAS LATE, almost half past six, when he opened the door of his apartment. There was the smell of an over-cooked dinner coming from the kitchen, but he did not care; he had been obliged to stay at the store long enough to make sure that none of the fish in the washbasin was shocked or weak enough to fall prey to the others. After all, he owed them a debt of gratitude; they had proved to him once and for all that he could rise to a situation and master it—even with Miss Anders looking on.

It was amazing, he thought, but he no longer wanted to depart from Hearth and Home, Incorporated, as he had departed from the Arts Academy. He had triumphed at last and he would stay, coolly laying claim to his proper share of the work, stepping in to shield Janie and the others from Miss Anders' petty rages, salvaging the self-respect and good will of scorned customers by showing them fine materials within their means.

And Miss Anders, he knew, had recognized all of that: she knew exactly how it was going to be. She had even remarked how lucky it was that his color chart had been carried off by old Dr. Hoffman before the accident. She had even said—spreading her spotted skirt to dry—that Dr. Hoffman had been downright impressed. And under the circumstances, Trudy's withered meat loaf seemed a small loss.

Besides, he had a present with which to appease Trudy. He came into the kitchen with a tumbler in his hand. "Look," he said, "I bought you something. Isn't he a wonderful monster? I snitched him from you-know-who."

"You snitched him from Miss Anders?"

"Yes," he said, and laughing a little he told her about the ten ugly fish wriggling and leaping about on Miss Anders' desk and on Miss Anders. "I finally rescued her," he said, "but I took my own good time about it."

Trudy dropped the pot holder and gave him a wild look.

"I'm doing the Hoffman living room," he said matter-of-factly. "They're coming in day after tomorrow, and I'm going to tell them about the four elements—"

"Of course you are!"

"What do we do to celebrate?"

"Couldn't we go to the beach?" she said. "It's so hot, and there's nothing the matter with me—I'm perfectly all right."

He smiled and nodded and held out his hand to her. "How are the babies?" he said. "Let's put the monster in with the other male and go and have a look at the babies."

And so they did. For another ten minutes, while the meal turned cold on the table, they stared at the shimmering cloud of life spread wide now on the water, and they held each other's hands and knew the soundness of their hearts.

Prometheus

THOSE WERE THE days when the world was new, and the great winds had never yet been heard by human ears, and the forests and stony peaks and surging many-colored waters had not yet been seen by human eyes. The Monsters had been driven into caves to die by the mighty Titans, a race of giants who stood as straight and high as the strongest trees. The Titans roamed the earth, rolling stones down slopes and bathing in waterfalls. And high above the earth the gods sat on the golden peak of Mount Olympus, where there was whiteness and glitter and soft air and light everlasting. There they filled a life that could never end with such pleasures as lovemaking and music and eating ambrosia and drinking sweet wine.

Zeus was the first of the gods, the hurler of thunderbolts. As lord of the world, he could say how everything was to go in the lands below. But the life of ease was pleasant to him, and he lightly passed his duties on to two brothers, sons of a powerful Titan—brothers named Epimetheus and Prometheus.

To Epimetheus, whose name means "afterthought," he gave the right to distribute all the gifts of heaven to the creatures of the earth—all gifts except immortality, which belongs only to the gods. To Prometheus he assigned the task of helping his brother in the labors of creation.

Now, Epimetheus was, like most of the Titans, strong and generous and free of hand and high of heart. Whatever he thought of doing, he did at once, and was highly pleased with it. He took great joy in creating all sorts of creatures: fish to swim in the waters, goats and deer and lions to climb mountains and graze on level stretches, birds to soar over the peaks and skim the waves. Whatever he made, he gave a gift—strength to one and bright fins and scales to another, and power to ride the air to yet another, so that every creature he made was happy and blessed.

Meanwhile his brother Prometheus, whose name means "forethought," sat on the clay bank of a river and pondered what *he* might make. And, as he kneaded the raw clay in his great careful hand, it came into his thoughts to make the creature called man. Slowly and gently he made this one creature. And, because he had made only man, he felt a great fondness for him and pity for his helplessness.

"Look what I have made," he said to his brother Epimetheus. "This is my creature, and I have called him man. Leave off for a little your giving out of swiftness and strength and fur and feathers, and hand me one gift that I can give the creature I have made."

Epimetheus came and looked, and found his brother's creature a very poor creature indeed. It was frail and had no fur. It went on all fours, but had no great strength nor any extraordinary power. And, to make matters worse, Epimetheus in his generosity had given out all the good gifts to his own creatures, so there was nothing good left to draw upon.

"Very well, then," said Prometheus. "I will think of something to do for my creature." And, since the clay had not yet dried and man could still be changed, he raised him upright so that he could walk on two feet, and he put love into his heart and reason behind his brow. Quickly—for the clay was drying fast—he made the hands more shapely and useful, and the body and face more beautiful. As he worked he thought of the glory of those on Mount Olympus, and he gave the poor creature man something of the splendor and radiance of the gods.

Epimetheus saw what his brother had made, and, being generous, admitted that it was a good enough creature now, even though it had received no gifts from anybody but Prometheus. "Who knows?" he said, casting a dolphin into the ocean and setting a doe on a mountain. "This man-thing, now that it stands upright and looks a little like a god, may some day become the ruler of the earth."

BUT THAT DAY was a long time coming. Though man used Prometheus' gifts, and woman came down from Olympus to help him, and children were born, it was a wonder any of them could survive in that hard early world. Whatever he ate he had to kill or wrest from the stony earth with his own hands. He had only such weapons as he could make from stones or wood to defend him against the wild beasts. He was terrified by the howl of winds and roaring of the sea.

The days were hard enough, but the nights were unbearable. In the blackness he could not see his hand in front of his face or tell whether the monster that rushed upon him was truly a monster or only a dream. His body, without the gift of fur or scales or feathers, turned blue with cold. Waking in pain and fear between one evil dream and another, he sighed and wept aloud. Of all the gods on Olympus and all the Titans that still lived on earth, only one heard him: his maker Prometheus.

Sitting near the peak of the mountain of the gods, hearing their music and their laughter, Prometheus would see, night after night, the black veil of darkness drawn over the earth; and he would pity man, lost and naked in the night. He had begged Zeus that one more gift should be added to the many that Epimetheus had given. But Zeus had no great fondness for the two-legged creature who looked too much like the immortals and troubled the peace of Olympus with his groans and sighs.

"Then, since he will give nothing, I will steal what he should give," thought Prometheus. And he rose from the ledge of stone where he had been brooding over the sorrows of man. He plucked a stalk of fennel, hollow and strong, and hid it in his breast. Swiftly and of his own will he propelled himself up and up, past the gates of horn and ivory in front of the palace of the gods, through the clouds into the purer air, upward toward the molten glow of the sun.

As he approached the sun, the air grew hot and dry. He was in a dangerous and forbidden place, where no Titan had ever dared to go before. The sun grew vast as he drew near it—a sheet of brazen fire. There, in the intolerable heat, he drew out the stalk of fennel and kindled it at the sun's holy flame. "What is it to me," he said in his heart, "that my beard is singed and my skin in blackened and I have stolen from Zeus, the most powerful and vengeful of the gods? Let him do what he will, for here in the hollow of this stalk is fire, the protector and nourisher—the greatest of all gifts for my creature man."

FROM THAT DAY on, man and his fire and Prometheus were galling wounds in the side of the greatest of the immortals. Zeus no longer heard sighs and groans coming up through the dark. Instead, through the veil of night, he saw bright bonfires and hearth fires and lamps, and heard earthly music—less beautiful than the hymns of Olympus, but music nevertheless. Once, when he sat at his marble table and feasted on ambrosia and wine, he smelled the delicious savor of roast oxen floating up from the earth, and he summoned the disobedient Titan and said that both the beast and the fire belonged to the immortals, and that henceforth he would have the best share of whatever the puny creatures of the world feasted upon.

"Surely, Lord Zeus," said Prometheus. "The fire is yours,

and I stole it. The beasts were made at your command by my brother Epimetheus, and they, too, are your own. But you can see for yourself that tonight's earthly feast is almost over. Man has eaten all the better parts. Tomorrow, just at twilight, come down from Olympus when the feast begins, and you shall have—tomorrow night and forever—whatever part you think in your infinite wisdom is best."

Zeus agreed, and Prometheus hurried back to the world, knowing how much his creatures needed the meat, determined to save the best of it for man.

By morning he had placed on a high altar on a holy mountain two heaps of cooked meat: one, the best of the flesh covered with stones and twigs and whatever other unseemly things he could lay hands on; the other nine big, bare bones covered over with a layer of gleaming fat cooked to a turn.

Twilight came, and with it the greatest of the immortals, with the thunderbolt and the jagged lightening in his hands.

"Here, choose," said Prometheus. "Take what you please, and my creature man will live as well as he can off the rest. Only swear that what you take will be yours forever and the rest you will never touch."

Zeus looked at the great bone-heap, rich with the fat and sweet with the smell of singed crust. "So I swear, and this I take," he said.

When he saw how he had been cheated, he shook the world with thunder and tore the trees with lightening in his fury. But he could not take back his oath, for the oath of Zeus is as everlasting as his life. So from that time forth man was well nourished. The best of the meat went into his frail body, and only the fat and the bones were burned on the altar of Zeus in sacrifice.

THEN ZEUS, UNABLE to vent his rage on the creature man, loosed it upon the rebel Titan, Prometheus. Zeus sent his ser-

313

vants Force and Violence to carry Prometheus to the wildest and dreariest place on earth, the cold black mountains of the Caucasus. There the two servants of the greatest of the gods bound Prometheus with iron chains to a flinty, wind-lashed peak where he hung—his naked body as helpless now as man's—exposed to icy blasts and bitter snow.

"How long am I doomed to suffer here?" he asked.

And the servants of Zeus, Force and Violence, said their master had decreed that Prometheus should hang there forever—or as good as forever, since he could be released only on an impossible condition: that some being who carried in his veins the holy fluid of immortality should give up his right to life everlasting and go down into the land of the dead for Prometheus' sake.

Left alone on the sharp rock, he was without hope. For what immortal being would offer so great a gift out of pity for a chained and forsaken Titan? His torments were increased, for Zeus sent a great eagle down from Olympus every day to attack him in his defenselessness. It plucked open his side; it tore at his liver; it made him lament his own immortality and yearn for the peace and painlessness of death.

There, according to all the ancient tales, he hung for ages in lament, and the black ridges of the Caucasus shook with his writhings and rang with his cries. Man did as well as possible without him, making use of the gift of fire and the gift of meat, building cities and temples, growing stronger and wiser, able now to distinguish between real dangers and frightening dreams.

We do not know how or when the eagle was driven off and the iron chains broken. We know only that, ages afterward, a helper came to help the helper, a savior to save the one who saved the wretched creature, man. Some say it was a wise centaur, half horse and half god, who pitied Prometheus and gave him his life in order to release him. Some say it was the hero Hercules, who had carried his immortality in his veins, since he was the son of a mortal woman by Zeus.

One way or another, this much is certain: a day came after hundreds of years when Prometheus was set free and healed and permitted to walk again on the world. There he took on again his old duties, caring for the being he had made out of clay. And whenever a good thing came to the mortals, they said among themselves that it was still another gift from Prometheus.

The Marianna Brown Dietrich Notable Books Series

The Collected Stories of Gladys Schmitt edited by Lois Josephs Fowler and Cynthia Lamb is the inaugural title in Carnegie Mellon University Press's Marianna Brown Dietrich Notable Books Series. On September 7, 2011, William S. Dietrich II, a member of the Carnegie Mellon Board of Trustees and former Director of Dietrich Industries, Inc., pledged the largest gift in the university's history. In response to this gift, and to honor Dietrich's mother, the university renamed its College of Humanities and Social Sciences as the Marianna Brown Dietrich College of Humanities and Social Sciences. Subsequently, the dean of Dietrich College, John P. Lehoczky, made funds available to the Press so as to publish, from time to time, books of merit. Gladys Schmitt, the author of this first title in the series, founded the Creative Writing Program at Carnegie Mellon in 1968. Schmitt, who achieved acclaim as a novelist during her lifetime, also wrote and published short stories in popular and literary magazines. Carnegie Mellon University Press is privileged to publish her collected stories in a single volume which is appearing forty-two years after her death.